dangerous secrets

Also by **Lisa Marie Rice**

Fiction
Dangerous Lover

dangerous secrets

LISA MARIE RICE

red

AVON

An Imprint of HarperCollinsPublishers

HarperCollins books may be purchased for educational, business, or sales promotional use. For information please write: Special Markets Department, HarperCollins Publishers, 10 East 53rd Street, New York, NY 10022.

FIRST EDITION

Designed by Diahann Sturge

Library of Congress Cataloging-in-Publication Data

Rice, Lisa Marie.
  Dangerous secrets / Lisa Marie Rice. — 1st ed.
    p. cm.
  ISBN 978-0-06-120860-7
  I. Title.
  PS3618.I2998D37   2008
813'.6—dc22   2007047966

08 09 10 11 12 OV/RRD   10 9 8 7 6 5 4 3 2 1

A very grateful nod to my editor, May Chen,
and my agent, Ethan Ellenberg

Prologue

Iceman's mission was over. So why was he still here, on a frozen hilltop, watching a burial in the valley below?

It was cold, even for November. The undertakers' assistants found it hard to break the frozen ground for the large mahogany and brass coffin lying on the grass a few feet away. The sound of their shovels rang like steel and carried easily in the bright, cold air. A few people stamped their feet on the snowy ground, trying to warm up, then looked around uneasily. It wasn't done to look uncomfortable at a burial, so they surreptitiously rubbed their arms and huddled miserably in their winter coats, hoping it would be over soon.

Iceman was in his hiding place two hundred feet up the wooded hillside, watching through the Steiner 8 x 30 tactical binoculars he'd kept from his Delta days.

He didn't stamp his feet and he didn't huddle. The cold didn't bother him. Heat didn't bother him. And he didn't care about what the onlookers felt.

He was there for the widow.

She stood apart, pale and stiff, bareheaded, dressed in black. She didn't seem to notice the cold. She didn't fidget, she didn't move. She just stood, small and straight, watching dry-eyed as the assistants laboriously dug. It seemed to take forever.

The undertakers' breath rose in white plumes of vapor and their breathing grew harsh, like workhorses pulling a heavy load. Finally it was over, and there was a coffin-shaped hole in the ground.

As if by an unspoken signal, the onlookers gathered around the widow. An elderly gentleman dressed in a black cashmere overcoat briefly cupped her elbow and bent down to her. She shook her head and he stepped back.

The pastor, a young, pasty-faced man, opened his heavy Bible and read from a page that had been marked beforehand with a long white silk bookmark. He read slowly and solemnly while his nose turned bright red.

At last he came to the end of the passage, closed the Bible, and bowed his head. Everyone else bowed their head, too, except the widow, who continued to stare stiffly ahead. The elderly elegantly dressed lady with the elderly gentleman tried to walk toward the widow, but stopped when her companion laid a hand on her arm. He looked at her and shook his head. She looked confused, then stepped back.

The assistants had placed inch-thick ropes under the coffin which had been maneuvered over the gaping hole, and were slowly, laboriously easing it down. The coffin was huge, heavy. The assistants grunted with the strain, the sound carrying up the hillside. Finally, the coffin reached the bottom and the assistants stepped back respectfully.

The preacher spoke to the widow and she moved for the first time, bending gracefully to grab a handful of earth. She walked to the rim of the hole in the ground, threw a handful of earth onto the coffin, then looked blindly up.

Iceman stepped back sharply. It wasn't that he was frightened of being seen. He was a master of camouflage and had chosen his lookout wisely and well. There wasn't a chance in hell he'd be spotted. What hit him like a punch to the stomach was the raw, naked pain on the widow's face.

A lovely face. A face he'd kissed more times than he could count.

Stop that, Iceman told himself. *Think of the mission.*

He lifted the powerful binoculars again and the graveside scene sprang back into focus.

The quiet ceremony was over. The onlookers were slowly moving away, grateful to get back to warmth and life and away from the cold hand of death hovering over the scene. The widow was the last to leave, on the arm of the elderly gentleman.

Suddenly the widow stiffened and stopped. She whirled around and ran back to the grave, where the grave diggers were already shoveling dirt over the coffin. The widow stopped just at the edge of the hole and the tears that were coming freely now streamed silver over her face. She knelt in the dirt and slipped her wedding ring off. She brought it to her lips, kissed it, and reached down to place it gently on the coffin lid, her hand lingering for a long moment, as if she couldn't bear to break this last contact.

The elderly gentleman walked slowly back to her. When she showed no sign of standing, he cupped her shoulders, urging her to her feet. She stood and allowed herself to be led away, stopping just once to turn and gently blow a last kiss behind her.

It was a heartbreaking scene and Iceman felt his heart grow heavy with sorrow, then he shook himself.

Foolishness, he told himself impatiently as he started taking precautions to erase all traces of his presence from the underbrush.

He had to leave, right *now*. He had no business being here at all. The mission was over, for him at least.

Still, it wasn't every day a man got to watch his own funeral.

One

At first light, as agreed, the pilot was waiting, alone, at the bottom of the rolling stairs. It was an undeclared flight with a plane that didn't officially exist and no copilot would be welcome. The fewer people involved, the better.

They were on a runway on the far side of the military airport, which had been decommissioned when the Soviets lost power. A pilot and a nuclear engineer.

They had only been told first names, Lyosha and Edik. Both names were false, but it didn't matter.

The nuclear engineer, whose real name was Arkady Sergeyevitch Andreyev, knew the only thing about the pilot that was necessary—that he was a *zek*, a former guest of the Russian Gulag. They were members of that very exclusive club—men who didn't die in the Russian Bear's cruel embrace.

The two men didn't shake hands. But when the pilot stretched out his hand to help Arkady maneuver the hand truck to shift the heavy container from the van to a loading pallet, Arkady saw what he expected to see—a barbed-wire tattoo around the pilot's wrist.

Former prisoners had their experience in hell etched into their skins, not just their souls. Arkady was covered in tattoos, from the stars on his knees that meant he bowed to no man, to the crosses that were a symbol of the years in the Gulag. He wore them proudly.

The only part of his skin that was clear was a large, shiny scarred patch over his heart where once had been the tattoo of the distinctive, goateed Tatar features of Lenin. Soviet prison guards were a superstitious lot and would never shoot the holy image of Lenin.

The day the camp fell, he'd stolen a soldering iron from the deserted guards' barracks and burned the head of Lenin off himself. He hadn't even felt the pain, he had been so happy to rid his body of that monstrous image.

The two men, Arkady and the pilot, silently noted each other's tattoos. Nothing more had to be said. They were members of the Bratva, the Brotherhood. That was all they had to know.

The heavy lead container was lifted into the cargo bay of the Tupolev Tu-154 aircraft, where the pilot carefully strapped it to the bulkhead. Inside the lead container was a large lead-lined canister filled with cesium 137, enough for a very powerful dirty bomb. Enough material to close down the city center of London, or New York, or Paris, or Rome, or Berlin, or Washington, D.C. Wipe it off the face of the earth as a viable city, turn it into deserted concrete canyons forbidden to humans or any other life-form for ten thousand years.

The pilot closed the cargo bay door and entered the small cabin where Arkady had observed the stowage of the container.

"Is everything all right?" the pilot asked quietly.

Arkady knew exactly what he meant. He wasn't offended. This was a dangerous business.

Though he was a superbly well-trained and careful nuclear engineer, and had taken all the necessary precautions, the pilot couldn't know that.

Instead of answering, Arkady opened his briefcase and extracted a small Geiger counter. He switched it on, walked to the cargo bay, and waved it over the container. They both listened to the welcome sound of soft, gentle ticking. The Geiger counter was picking up on the ambient radiation, higher than normal in the area surrounding a nuclear power plant, but nothing more than that.

The pilot nodded, satisfied, and without a word made his way to the cockpit. Arkady walked down the steps onto the tarmac. There was one thing more to take care of before takeoff.

Telling the Vor that the first stage was successful.

If this trip proved successful, there were many more such trips in the future. His Vor, an already powerful and rich man, would become one of the most powerful men in the history of the world.

Arkady opened the green cell phone. He had three of them, one for each stage of his long journey. Three brand-new cell phones, onetime use only. He dialed a long number, connecting to a remote mansion in the northern state of Vermont, in the United States.

The cell phone was unencrypted. If there was one thing guaranteed to catch the attention of America's frighteningly powerful electronic surveillance agency, the NSA, it was an encrypted cell phone message to the United States. So there was no encryption and no nonsense about packages on their way or delivery times.

The NSA's endless banks of supercomputers, trolling daily and tirelessly through a terabyte of data spanning the globe, was trip wired with a number of key words, *package* and *delivery* being two of them, that would have immediately picked up on those words.

The Vor's money had bought the services of one of the junior NSA officers and the Vor had the list of words. The Vor thought of everything.

No packages, no deliveries. Their code was the weather.

The cell phone at the other end was picked up immediately. It, too, was a one-off, to be destroyed after the message. Arkady had memorized each of the Vor's one-off cell phone numbers, though they were twelve digits each.

A laughable exercise. Child's play. In Kolyma, numbers had kept him sane. He'd memorized pi to the thirteenth decimal, prime numbers up to the first five hundred, and had perfected in his head a risk calculation method the Vor used to this day.

The Vor himself, a literary genius, had memorized every word of Pushkin's *Queen of Spades*. Vassily Worontzoff, the greatest man in the world. The man who'd saved his life and, perhaps more important, his sanity in Kolyma. His Vor.

"Slushayu." I'm listening. The Vor's deep voice, with its cultivated Muscovite accent, reassured Arkady at the deepest possible level that all was right in his world.

"Greetings," he replied, looking up at the black clouds roiling in the sky. A fierce Siberian wind was blowing, and the temperature was well below freezing. He huddled more deeply into the sheepskin jacket the Vor had bought him. "I just thought you might like to know that the weather here is perfect. Sunny skies. Very warm weather."

"Excellent," the Vor replied. "Stay safe, my friend."

Content that this enormously important project was off to a good start, Arkady removed the cell phone's SIM card, threw it into the woods, where it disappeared into the dense undergrowth with a whisper of rustling leaves, and crushed the plastic casing of the phone beneath his heavy boot.

Arkady trotted back up the steps, sat down in the leather seat, buckled up, and made himself comfortable. This was the first stage of what was going to be a long journey.

The cabin was quiet and comfortable. The pilot had chosen well. The Tu-154 could take off from the gravel runway of the abandoned military airfield and could fly above the rest of Russian air traffic.

They were in the lower reaches of Siberia, the largest uninhabited land mass in the world. They would reach their destination—a remote airfield near Odessa—in about twelve hours, stopping only once to refuel. Then, to Budva, in Montenegro, by bus. From there, a ship would be waiting to take him and his cargo to Canada. The final leg would be a truck crossing into the United States, into Vermont.

The pilot quietly announced that they would be taking off in one minute. Exactly sixty seconds later, the sleek plane taxied, then lifted, heading west.

Parker's Ridge, Vermont
November 18

The man with the shattered hands and the shattered soul used his stylus to punch the Off button on his cell phone. He still had the use of his index finger and thumb, but only as a pincer. The zealous prison guards who had taken a hammer to his hands had been thorough. He could use the stylus to tap out letters on a keyboard or a number pad. He could feed himself. He could pick up a glass of vodka.

It was enough.

Vassily Worontzoff glanced outside the big picture window of his study, noting the wind whipping the big leafless oak tree's branches into a frenzy. Though it was only early afternoon, the sky was almost black. The forecast was for snow during the night and for the temperatures to dip well below zero. The forecaster had stated all of this in the somber tones of a man announcing certain disaster.

Vassily would have laughed if he had still been capable of laughter. How weak the Americans were! How easily they despaired! He was a survivor of Kolyma, the Soviet Union's cruelest prison camp, where the prisoners had to work the gold mines in temperatures as low as minus ninety degrees Fahrenheit.

It had been so cold that tears froze on the cheeks. They fell with a merry tinkle to the hard frozen earth in crystals which belied the hell the prisoners lived in. The zeks called this "the whisper of the stars."

How many tears he'd shed when he'd lost his beloved Katya. How the stars had whispered.

He'd written a poem about it, in ink made from burnt shoe leather on a piece of intact shirt, donated by a zek who, improbably, was being released. It had been published back in Moscow. When word filtered back from five thousand miles away that the zek Vassily Worontzoff had written a poem about Kolyma, the guards had gone into a frenzy of cruelty. They'd shattered his hands, thinking a writer without hands couldn't write.

Foolish, foolish men.

So much had changed since then.

If the guards who'd tormented him weren't dead of vodka poisoning, they were living on the equivalent of fifty dollars a month in some rathole back in Russia. And he—he was already rich beyond their comprehension and about to become one of the most powerful men on earth, able to switch great cities off like a light.

Able to be with his beloved Katya.

He'd lost her in Kolyma but he'd found her again in this small, pretty American backwater, with its birch trees and larches, so like the woods around the dacha they'd had outside Moscow.

Charity, she was called now. Charity Prewitt. Absurd Yankee name. He hated calling her Charity. She was Katya. His Katya, though she didn't realize it yet.

But soon this charade would be over and she would be with him again.

He was the Vor. Immensely powerful.

So powerful he could bring Katya back from the dead.

Parker's Ridge

"Read any good books lately?"

The pretty young woman stacking books and sorting papers in the Parker's Ridge County Library turned around in surprise. It was closing time and the library wasn't overwhelmed with people at the best of times. By closing time it was always deserted. Nick Ireland should know. He'd been staking it out for a week.

"Oh! Hello, Mr. Ames." Her cheeks pinked with pleasure at seeing him. "Did you need something else?" She checked the big old-fashioned clock on the wall. "We're closing up, but I can stay on for another quarter of an hour if you need anything."

He'd been in that morning and she'd been charmingly helpful to him. Or, rather, to Nicholas Ames, stockbroker, retired from the Wall Street rat race after several years of very lucky investments paid off big, now looking to start his own investment firm. Son of Keith and Amanda Ames, investment banker and family lawyer, respectively, both tragically dead at a young age. Nicholas Ames was thirty-four years old, a Capricorn, divorced after a short-lived starter marriage in his twenties, collector of vintage wines, affable, harmless, all-round good guy.

Not a word of that was true. Not one word.

They were alone in the library, which pleased him and annoyed him at the same time. It pleased him because he'd have Charity Prewitt's undivided attention. It annoyed him because . . . because.

Because through the huge library windows she looked like a lovely little lamb staked out for the predators. It had been dark for an hour up here in this frozen northern state. In the well-lit library, Charity Prewitt had been showcased against the darkness of the evening. One very pretty young woman all alone in an enclosed space. It screamed out to any passing scumbag—*come and get me!*

Nothing scumbags liked better than to eat up lovely young

women. If there was one thing Nick knew with every fiber of his being, it was that the world was full of scumbags. He'd been fighting them all his life.

She was smiling up at him, much, *much* prettier than the photographs in the file he'd studied.

"No, thank you, Miss Prewitt," he answered, keeping his deep, naturally rough voice gentle. "I don't need to do any more research. You were very helpful this morning."

Her head tilted, the soft dark-blond hair brushing her right shoulder. "Did you have a good day, then?"

"Yes, I did, a very good day. Thank you for asking. I saw three factories, a promising new Web design start-up, and an old-economy sawmill that has some very innovative ideas about using recycled wood chips. All in all, very satisfactory."

Actually, it had been a shitty day, just one of many shitty days on this mission. A total waste of time spent in the surveillance van with two smelly men and jack shit to show for it except for one cryptic call to Worontzoff about a friend staying safe.

Nick smiled the satisfaction he didn't feel. "So. It's closing time now, isn't it?"

She smiled back. "Why, yes. We close at six. But as I said, if you need something—"

"Well, to tell you the truth . . ." Nick looked down at his shoes shyly, as if working up the courage to ask. Man, he loved looking down at those shoes. They were three-hundred-dollar Italian imports, worlds away from his usual comfortable but battered combat boots that dated back to his army days.

Being Nicholas Ames, very successful businessman, was great because he got to dress the part and Uncle Sam had to foot the bill. He had an entire wardrobe to fit those magnificent shoes. Who knew if he'd get to keep any of it? Maybe the two Armanis that had been specially tailored for his broad shoulders.

And even better was dealing with this librarian, Charity Prewitt, one of the prettiest women he'd ever seen. Small, curvy, classy with large eyes the color of the sea at dawn.

Nick looked up from contemplating his black shiny wingtips and smiled into her beautiful gray eyes. "Actually, I was hoping that I could invite you out to dinner to thank you for your help. If I hadn't done this preliminary research here, with your able help, my day wouldn't have been half as productive. Asking you out to dinner is the least I can do to show you my appreciation."

She blinked. "Well . . . ," she began.

"You have nothing to fear from me," he said hastily. "I'm a solid citizen—just ask my accountant and my physician. And I'm perfectly harmless."

He wasn't, of course, he was dangerous as hell. Ten years a Delta operator before joining the Unit. He'd spent the past decade in black ops, perfecting the art of killing people.

He was sure harmless to *her*, though.

Charity Prewitt had the most delicious skin he'd ever seen on a woman—pale ivory with a touch of rose underneath—so delicate it looked like it would bruise if he so much as breathed on it. That was skin meant for touching and stroking, not hurting.

"Ms. Prewitt?" She hadn't answered his question about going out. She simply stood there, head tilted to one side, watching him as if he were some kind of problem to be sorted out, but she needed more information before she could solve it.

In a way, he liked that. She didn't jump at the invitation, which was a welcome relief from his last date—well, last fuck. Five minutes after "hello" in a bar, she'd had his dick in her hand. At least she hadn't been into pain like Consuelo. God.

Charity Prewitt was assessing him quietly and he let her do it, understanding that smooth words weren't going to do the trick. Stillness would, so he stood still. Special Forces soldiers have the gift of stillness. The ones who don't, die young and badly.

Nick was engaging in a little assessment himself. This morning he'd been bowled over by little Miss Charity Prewitt. Christ, with a name like that, with her job as chief librarian of the library of a one-traffic-light town, single at twenty-eight, he'd been expecting a dried-up prune.

The photographs of her in his file had been fuzzy, taken with a telescopic lens, and just showed the generics—hair and skin color, general size and shape. A perfectly normal woman. A little on the small side, but other than that, ordinary.

But up close and personal, Jesus, she'd turned out to be a knockout. A quiet knockout. You had to look twice for the full impact of large light-gray eyes, porcelain skin, shiny dark-blond hair and a curvy slender figure to make itself felt. Coupled with a natural elegance and a soft, attractive voice—well.

Nick was used to being undercover, but most of his jobs involved scumbags, not beautiful young women.

Actually, this one did, too—a major scumbag called Vassily Worontzoff everyone on earth but the operatives in the Unit revered for being a great writer. Even nominated for the friggin' Nobel, though, as the Unit knew well but couldn't yet prove, the sick fuck was the head of a huge international OC syndicate. Nick was intent on bringing him down.

So on this op he was dealing with scumbags, yeah, but the mission also involved romancing this pretty woman—and on Uncle Sam's dime, to boot.

Didn't get much better than that.

"All right," Charity said suddenly. Whatever her doubts had been, apparently they were now cleared up. "What time do you want to pick me up?"

Yes! Nick felt a surge of energy that had nothing to do with the mission and everything to do with the woman in front of him.

"Well . . ." Nick smiled, all affable, utterly safe, utterly reliable businessman, "I was wondering whether you wouldn't mind going now. I found this fabulous Italian place near Rockville. It has a really nice bar area and I thought we might talk over a drink while waiting for our dinner."

"Da Emilio's," Charity said. "It's a very nice place and the food is excellent." She looked down at herself, frowning. "But I'm not dressed for a dinner out. I should go home and change."

She was wearing a light blue-gray sweater that exactly matched the color of her eyes and hugged round breasts and a narrow waist, a slim black skirt, shiny black stockings, and pretty ankle boots. Pearl necklace and pearl earrings. She was the classiest-looking dame he'd seen in a long while, even in her work clothes.

"You look—" *Perfect. Sexy as hell.* He bit his jaws closed on the words. Ireland, roughneck soldier that he was, could say something like that, but Ames, sophisticated businessman, sure as hell couldn't. Even if it was God's own truth.

"Fine. You look just fine. You could go to dinner at the White House dressed like that."

It made her smile, which was what he wanted. Her smile was like a secret weapon. She sighed. "Okay. I'll just need to lock up here."

Locking up entailed pulling the library door closed and turning a key once in the lock.

Nick waited. Charity looked up at him, a tiny frown between her brows when she saw his scowl. "Is something wrong?"

"That's it? That's locking up? Turning the key once in the lock?"

She smiled gently. "This isn't the big bad city, Mr. Ames."

"My friends call me Nick."

"Okay, Nick. I don't know if you've had a chance to walk around town. This isn't New York or even Burlington. The library, in case you haven't noticed, is full of books and not much else besides some scuffed tables. What would there be to steal? And anyway, I don't remember the last time a crime was committed in Parker's Ridge."

The elation Nick felt at the thought of an evening with Charity Prewitt dissipated.

Parker's Ridge housed one of the world's most dangerous criminals. An evil man. A man directly responsible for hundreds of lives lost, for untold misery and suffering.

And he was Charity Prewitt's best friend.

Two

A *date*. She, Charity Prewitt, was actually going out on a *date*! Charity hadn't been out on a date in . . . God, she couldn't even remember the last date she'd been on.

There were ten bachelors in Parker's Ridge, not counting Vassily, of course, who was fifty-four years old and horribly scarred from his time in a Soviet prison camp. Each and every bachelor within a radius of forty miles had asked her out, repeatedly. Each and every bachelor was lacking in something important—teeth, a faculty, a job. Certainly all of them were lacking in a sense of humor.

And the surrounding towns weren't too much better. Most of the bachelors there were bachelors for a good reason. And one date was more or less enough to figure out what that something was.

Charity might even have gone further afield, but ever since Mary Conway had gone on maternity leave and then quit when her child was a preemie with problems, Charity had been more or less on her own in the library. The retired chief librarian, old Mrs. Lambert, would come in for an emergency, but she was seventy-four and almost deaf. And the town council kept putting off budgeting for another librarian. So Charity was more or less *it*.

Plus, of course, Uncle Franklin and her ailing aunt Vera required her constant presence and help. Charity had a range of about forty miles and desirable bachelors—even only bachelors that weren't repugnant—were not exactly thick on the ground in that radius.

So being asked out by Mr. Nicholas call-me-Nick Ames, who was the most handsome man she'd ever seen—and who clearly had all his own teeth, all his own limbs, and seemed to be independently wealthy—well, it was like Christmas a month early.

He'd come in that morning to do some research on the area, saying he was thinking of making some investments. Charity had been impressed by how much he knew about the area already, but she supposed that businessmen had to be well informed. He'd let discreetly slip that he'd retired early after some very good years with a brokerage firm and was looking to open an investment firm of his own.

He was so outrageously handsome. Charity kept sneaking glances at him while he wasn't looking. Tall, with midnight black hair, deep-blue eyes surrounded by ridiculously long lashes, a straight narrow nose, and a firm mouth.

Hard body.

Wow.

In Charity's experience, businessmen were soft and pale. All that time spent behind a desk, making money. Or losing it, depending. Nick Ames didn't look like he had wasted much time losing money.

He had all the visible accoutrements of prosperous

businessman-dom. The elegant blue suit—Armani was her guess—the glossy shoes, the expensive leather briefcase, the manicured nails, the flat, expensive watch.

But that was where the resemblance to a typical business-man stopped. Underneath the elegant suit was clearly a very strong, very fit body, with amazingly broad shoulders. So at odds with the amount of time he must spend analyzing data, clipping articles, and peering into his crystal ball—or what-ever it was stockbrokers did.

It was a lovely evening. Very cold—but that was a given for November in Vermont. The snowstorm all the weather forecasters had been talking about was still holding off and the night sky was bright with brilliant cold stars. Charity loved these clear frozen nights, and it was a good thing, too, she often thought, since moving somewhere warm was out of the question. Even a long weekend in Aruba was out of the question. Certainly as long as Aunt Vera was so sick.

To her surprise, Mr. Ames—Nick—took her elbow, as if she could have problems navigating the broad, even sidewalk stretching out before her or needed guidance in the small town she'd grown up in. Still, it was really nice. Men rarely took one's elbow anymore.

Uncle Franklin often took her arm when she accompanied him somewhere, but it was for balance. Nick Ames certainly didn't need to hold her arm for balance.

Up close, he seemed even taller. The top of her head barely reached his shoulder, even with heels. He seemed broader, too, the shoulders incredibly wide beneath the rich dark-blue overcoat with the hand stitches. Cashmere. Uncle Franklin had one just like it.

For a fraction of a second, Charity wondered what she was doing—going out for dinner with a man she didn't know.

She'd surprised herself. He'd asked and she knew she should say no to dinner, perhaps yes to a drink in town, and then . . . her mouth opened and *yes* simply plopped out.

Of course, that he was handsome as sin and had a killer smile might have something to do with it.

Manners, too. He'd positioned himself on the outside, next to the curb. It had been years since she'd seen a man deliberately place himself between a woman and the street. The last man besides Uncle Franklin that she'd seen doing that had been her father, always instinctively courteous with her mother. That had been over fifteen years ago, when they were still alive.

She and Nick walked down the block and he turned her right, onto Sparrow Road, with a gentle nudge of his hand. Halfway down the block, he stopped right outside a big black luxurious car. A Lexus, she thought, though she wasn't sure. The only thing she was sure of was that it probably cost the equivalent of a year's salary of a librarian.

He walked her around to the passenger door, unlocking it electronically with the key fob, and helped her into the passenger seat as if she were the queen of Parker's Ridge.

A second later he was in the driver's seat and helping her pull the seat belt over and down. To her astonishment, once the latch clicked, he didn't pull back but leaned forward and planted a soft kiss on her mouth.

Charity stared at him. "What—"

He'd already put the big car in gear. He looked over at her and grinned, teeth white in the darkness of the car, as he slowly pulled out of the parking space. "I figure we're going to spend the entire evening wondering whether we'll have a good-night kiss, so I thought I'd just cut right through that. We've already kissed, so we're not going to obsess about it. It's already done."

She folded her hands in her lap. "I wasn't going to obsess about a kiss."

That was a lie. She'd been obsessing about it since she'd accepted the dinner invitation. If she was perfectly honest with herself, which she usually was, she'd been obsessing about kissing him since she'd laid eyes on him this morning.

He was right, though.

It had only been a chaste little kiss—a buss, it would have been called a century ago. But it had definitely broken the tension. They'd kissed. They could now have an easygoing dinner together.

Smart man, she thought. *No wonder he'd become rich.*

He drove sedately out of town. Too sedately, actually. To her surprise, he kept to the speed limit even outside the city limits. For some reason, some feather-brained bureaucrat somewhere had declared a speed limit of thirty-five miles an hour within a ten-mile radius of town. No one in town was crazy enough to respect the speed limit, except Mr. Nick Ames. He was driving the powerful car as if he were carrying a carload of eggs over bumpy terrain.

He braked to a complete stop at the intersection between Somerset and Fifth, where on a clear day you could see into Canada. *No one* stopped at that intersection unless a car was coming, which you could see from miles out in every direction. Parker's Ridgers simply slowed down a tad, but they never stopped.

Nick Ames stopped while the light was yellow and waited patiently for it to cycle through yellow, red, then green.

It was nice being in a car with a careful driver, but Charity found herself pressing her right foot to the floor, wishing he'd do it, too, silently urging him to go just a little bit faster. There was a thin line between safe driving and poky driving and he crossed it several times. Poky driving in Parker's Ridge, where you had to work really hard to get into a fender bender, was overkill.

Getting to Da Emilio's wasn't easy. There were several turnoffs and very little signage. The locals got there easily enough, but it was hard for out-of-towners. Nick Ames didn't seem to have any problems, though. He drove straight there.

The parking space outside the restaurant was nearly empty. It would fill up later, but for now the only patrons were those here for a pre-dinner drink. He drove into the first empty slot and killed the engine.

She smiled at him as he turned into the parking lot. "You have either a good sense of direction, an excellent memory, or both."

He turned to her, big hand draped over the steering wheel. "Both, actually. I think they're the same part of the brain. I also have a really good memory for faces. I don't often get lost." He looked down at her bare hands. "You might want to put your gloves back on, it's really cold outside."

"Yes, Mom," Charity said with a roll of her eyes, but it was wasted. He'd already rounded the car and was opening her door, helping her out.

The little kiss had somehow changed the chemistry of the evening. From being a nice thank-you gesture, the invitation to dinner had turned into a real date. Sex was in the air—pleasantly so. Nothing overdone, just little sparks flying about in the crystal-clear air.

Charity drew in a long, delighted breath. The air was pristine, smelling of a hundred miles of pine trees and the delights wafting from the air vents of Emilio's kitchen. The smell of a wonderful evening.

Her life lately had been a little gray. Not gray, really, just a little . . . unchanging. Routine. She didn't like to admit to herself just how much of her time and energy was taken up with Aunt Vera and Uncle Franklin. By the time Friday rolled around, after she'd put in five full days' work at the library, checking in on her aunt and uncle two, three times a week, doing whatever was necessary for their comfort and safety, she only had enough energy to do household chores over the weekend.

Slowly, without noticing it, she started going out less and less, going to fewer movies and concerts. The one thing she made an exception for was Vassily. When he called, she always had the time and the energy.

Nick opened the door for her and ushered her in with a hand to her back. A woman could get used to those old-fashioned manners.

Da Emilio's was, as always, warm and welcoming, with a huge roaring fire in each room. A cozy bar area beckoned off to the right and Nick steered her toward it. The portly maître d' came up to them. Nick stopped and murmured, "Reservation in the name of Ames," to him, but the maître d' didn't pay any attention to Nick at all. He just barreled on toward her.

Charity sighed and braced herself.

"Signorina Chaaariteee!" She was enveloped in an embrace of big hard arms and a big hard belly. A hug fragrant with Versace and garlic.

"Sergio." Charity smiled at him when he finally released her. Emilio's brother-in-law was a much more outgoing personality than Emilio himself. He made a very good maître d'.

"Welcome, my dear. Where have you been? Why have

you not been eating here?" He held her at arm's length and looked her up and down critically. "You're looking *magra*. Too thin. Have you been eating enough?" He frowned and shook his head. "What am I saying? Of course not. Emilio!" he called while taking her coat and—clearly as an after-thought—Nick's. "*Vieni qui subito!*"

Some customers walked into the door but Sergio ignored them. "Emilio!" he bellowed.

Charity winced, glancing up at Nick. He looked amused, totally relaxed.

"Emilio's going to be delighted to see you, Miss Charity. Why, just the other day he mentioned you. Anna came home for the weekend and—"

"Charity!" Emilio came out from the kitchen, a tall, lean, handsome man. His food was so good, Charity couldn't understand how on earth he managed to keep so trim. Probably because he worked so hard. He'd landed outside Parker's Ridge over twenty years ago, a good-looking young Italian student from Bologna, hitchhiking his way through the States after college, eventually bringing his fiancée and his sister and her husband over from Bologna.

God knew why he'd elected northern Vermont to settle down in, but Parson's Ridgers were grateful he had. It was the most successful—and best—restaurant in this part of the state.

Emilio folded her in his embrace, then held her at arm's length, looking at her critically, just as Sergio had done. "You haven't been—"

"Eating enough," Charity said on a sigh. "I know, Sergio already told me. But I am, you know. We're not all fortunate enough to have Silvia's figure."

At the mention of his beloved wife, who handled the accounts and ran their family ruthlessly and well, leaving him time to create, Emilio smiled. Silvia weighed thirty pounds more than Charity did and every ounce was composed of drop-dead curves that were magnets for male eyes.

"This is true," he said proudly. "Still, you should be eating more."

Charity refrained from rolling her eyes. It was time to change the subject. Emilio was perfectly capable of keeping this up forever if she let him.

"But enough!" Emilio held up an imperious hand and the waiter Charity would swear had been across the room materialized in a second by his side. Without turning around, Emilio said, "Dario, two glasses of our finest Prosecco and some hot antipasti." In the blink of an eye, the waiter disappeared again.

"Come, sit down." Emilio led them to the nicest part of the bar area—comfy armchairs upholstered in brilliant red brocade ranged around an antique door that served as a coffee table, just to the side of the huge roaring fire.

Emilio sat with them, as if he had all the time in the world, though it was coming up to dinnertime and the restaurant was starting to fill up.

"How's—" Charity began, but Emilio ignored her. He swiveled and stared at Nick, a frown between his heavy black eyebrows.

"So," he said, showing acres of white teeth in what was not quite a smile. "You're dining with Miss Charity. Are you a colleague?"

Nick was sitting back, relaxed. "No, not at all. An acquaintance. Charity did me a favor and I asked her out to dinner to thank her."

"Have you known each other long?"

Nick didn't even blink at the personal nature of the question. "No. We just met today."

Emilio narrowed his eyes. "So, do you live in this area or are you just passing through?"

Charity gasped. Emilio was *grilling* Nick, exactly as if she were his daughter and Nick an unwanted suitor. She opened her mouth to protest when she caught Nick's smiling gaze. He winked, subtly, and shook his head. The message was clear. *Don't interfere. It's okay.*

"Actually, I live in Manhattan, but I'm thinking of relocating and have been scouting out areas. I'm also looking to make some investments. I retired a couple of months ago from my job in a big brokerage firm and cashed in on the bull market before it turned south. I'd like to set up my own little boutique brokerage firm, but I haven't decided where yet. All I know is that I wouldn't mind eventually getting out of Manhattan. So my life is pretty much up in the air at the moment."

How clever of him, Charity thought. He managed to convey very neatly that he was single, well off, unencumbered, and willing to settle down here in a few short sentences. She had no idea if what Nick said was true or not, but it definitely got Emilio off his back.

Emilio's face relaxed. "Well, enjoy your evening. It was nice meeting you, Mr. . . . ," he paused delicately.

"Ames. Nicholas Ames. And the pleasure is mine."

Emilio stood as the waiter arrived with a bottle of Prosecco, two tall crystal flutes, and a platter full of delicacies with mouthwatering scents that he placed on the coffee table.

Looked like Nick had passed some kind of test. And not just with Emilio.

Charity popped a hot *oliva ascolana*, a stuffed, breaded, and lightly fried olive, in her mouth and barely kept from moaning. "Try one of these," she urged. "They're—"

"Olive ascolane," Nick said and she looked at him, surprised. He smiled. "I've got my own Emilio, back in Manhattan. Off Bleecker. Only his name is Mario and he comes from Ancona. Makes fabulous olive ascolane, and the best Bolognese sauce in the world." He chewed thoughtfully. "These olives beat Mario's, though. Hands down. That's got to be our secret." He winked again. "I don't dare tell Mario. He'd ban me forever."

A log in the huge hearth broke apart, falling into fiery pieces in a shower of sparks. Heat blossomed in the room, painting her skin with its glow.

It wasn't just the fire warming her up. The fire was a convenient excuse for the heat, which had surged up inside her at Nick's wink. Incandescent, almost shocking in its power.

She could feel the heat from his body, more intense even than the heat from the fire. Or at least it felt that way.

She wasn't naive. Nick was flirting with her. It was mild, but unmistakable—the old man-woman game she'd once played so well and so lightly and had almost forgotten. How long had it been since she'd gone out to dinner with someone attractive and flirted? Way too long, to judge by her intense reaction.

Had he noticed? Those deep blue eyes seemed so observant. It was very likely she'd flushed. Her skin was like a beacon advertising every emotion flitting through her.

This wouldn't do. Charity forced herself to sit back, still her nerves, and smile blandly into Nick's eyes, when—shockingly—what she really wanted to do was climb into his lap, nuzzle her face up against that square jaw, find out with her hands whether he was as hard underneath that elegant suit as she suspected. Place her lips precisely against his throat, where she could see the fine line where his whiskers stopped. Feel his heartbeat against her mouth. Lick that smooth, tan skin.

Whoa. Think of something else.

By the time they'd made their happy way through the fried mozzarella balls, tiny calamari, and huge fried Pantelleria capers, their table was ready.

Dario appeared as if by magic and escorted them to their table with a maximum of fuss. It was the best table in the restaurant and it took him a full ten minutes to get them settled. He seated Charity like an empress, whisked away a water glass with a spot on it as if it had been full of cockroaches, and guided them through their orders. He suggested that they let him take care of the wine. "Something special for you, Miss Charity."

He came back with a bottle of Barolo from their special reserve, uncorked it deftly, and poured a finger into Nick's glass. But even though Nick nodded his pleasure, it wasn't until Charity had sipped and smiled that Dario relaxed.

He needn't have worried. It was like drinking bottled sunshine.

"Wonderful," Charity murmured. Dario beamed and disappeared into the kitchen.

"Well." Nick sat back in his chair. He hadn't taken his eyes from her face through the entire wine pouring. "I didn't realize I'd invited royalty out to dinner. Why didn't you tell me you were the queen of Parker's Ridge?"

She smiled. "It *was* a little over the top, wasn't it?"

"Absolutely." He looked over his shoulder at Emilio chatting with some guests, then back at her. "Are you guys secretly related?"

"No, of course not." Though at times, belonging to the big, boisterous Luraghi family sounded wonderful. She was an only child and her parents were dead. Her only family was her frail and ailing aunt and uncle. "I, um, helped Emilio's daughter last year when she came to the library to do some research."

"From what I've seen, they're grateful for something a little more serious than explaining the Dewey decimal system to a student."

She sipped some more of that wonderful wine. "We use the Library of Congress classification system."

"Charity . . ."

She sighed and told a prettier version of the truth. "Emilio's family is great. It's a big one and they are all very close. Sometimes, though, that closeness can get a little . . . intense. His youngest daughter, Anna, felt hemmed in and used to come in a lot to the library for research projects. We became friends. She'd been having problems in school, but after a while she got back on track."

It had been much more serious than that. Anna Luraghi had been cutting classes, dabbling in drugs, and moving arrow-straight toward the hard stuff. She'd fancied herself in love with a nasty little weasel Charity suspected of being a pusher.

Anna had been on the road to self-destruction, so desperately unhappy that Charity's heart had gone out to her. She'd spent hours and hours talking with Anna, who clearly needed an adult she could respect outside the family to talk to. Emilio was a wonderful father, caring and involved, but his idea of dealing with a problem was to yell at it until it went away.

Anna was now at MIT, doing fabulously well, dating the cutest computer nerd on the Eastern Seaboard. Ever since, Emilio and his family treated Charity like she could walk on water.

Nick had listened to her with a slight smile on his lips, eyes narrowed, intent. His eyes were just magnificent. Dark, cobalt blue framed by black lush eyelashes any woman would kill for. They were beautiful, yet somehow managed to fit his purely male face.

"There's more to it than that, but you're clearly not talking, so we'll skip over to another topic of conversation. What should it be? The weather? Books? Movies? I'd like to rule out politics and religion on principle. Other than that, I'm fine with anything you choose."

This was startling. Charity wasn't used to men who actually paid attention to what she said. Who let the woman get the conversational ball rolling.

Most dates listened with half an ear until the conversation bumped around to their main topic of interest—themselves. They'd make exceptions for their jobs, cars, and, lately, plasma TVs, but that was about it.

So Nick Ames was not only the sexiest man she'd ever met, he was also highly intelligent and perceptive. It meant that the gentle irony she sometimes used, and that always zinged right over her date's head, had to be curbed.

She smiled. "Well, books are always good."

"I should imagine so, seeing as how you're a librarian."

"No Marian the Librarian cracks," Charity warned, alarmed. She'd heard them all.

His eyes were so very blue. He held up a large hand, index and middle fingers raised. His mouth tightly repressed a smile. "Not a one, Scout's honor."

"Were you a Boy Scout?"

"Made Eagle. Yes, ma'am. Racked up the highest number of points in my troop. So—getting back to you, how did you end up being a librarian in Parker's Ridge?"

Make a long story short, Charity thought. "Well, I love books and tend to have a reasonably organized mind, so library science seemed like a good choice for undergraduate studies."

Before taking off for Paris, her lifelong dream. And she'd almost managed it, too, with a grant to study French literature in Paris and a one-way economy-class ticket. She'd put her few belongings in storage and had one foot out the door when Uncle Franklin had called to say that Aunt Vera suddenly couldn't remember the names of the days of the week.

There had been no question of what she had to do. The next day she was back in Parker's Ridge, plane ticket refunded, applying for old Mrs. Lambert's job.

"And why are you here?" He was listening so intently, you'd think she was telling some thrilling tale. "Why settle in Parker's Ridge? It's pretty, but it's small."

Charity repressed a sigh. Yes, it was small. And remote. *Definitely* not Paris.

She was here because this is where her duty lay. But that was too depressing to say, certainly in those terms. Charity had learned that the word *duty* should be used very sparingly in the modern-day world. She sidestepped. "My family's been in Parker's Ridge for over two hundred years." No matter that she'd longed to escape the ties, the ties had brought her back.

He filled their glasses and lifted his. "Well, if it can keep the Prewitt family happy for two hundred years, Parker's Ridge must have a lot of hidden virtues. I propose a toast, then, to Parker's Ridge."

She lifted her own glass and he touched his to hers. The clear ring of pure crystal sounded and he smiled at her over the glasses filled with bright, ruby red wine.

His smile went through her like lightning, an electric current that jolted her, inside and out. Suddenly, everything took on a heightened tone. The fire in the room burned brighter, the luscious smells from the surrounding tables were more potent, the silverware gleamed more brilliantly. She was aware of everything around her and especially of the big man sitting across the table from her, watching her closely.

There was no mistaking the masculine interest. She'd seen it enough in men, though not very often lately, to tell the truth. It seemed that lately she'd been living in a totally sex-free zone. But right now, in Emilio's restaurant, sex was in the air and . . . she was up for it.

Charity's heart skipped a beat at the thought. Wow. She was up for sex with this man. Right *now*. She'd never done anything like this in her life. Never even wanted to.

It took her a while before she felt ready to go to bed with a man. Weeks, sometimes.

But with a clarity that astounded her, she knew that she was going to sleep with this man. Soon. Maybe even *tonight*. Oh yeah. Instead of going to bed with a hot water bottle and the latest Michael Connelly, she might be going to bed with this sexy, totally hot man she'd met just this morning.

Her thigh muscles clenched at the thought. It was scary and exhilarating at the same time.

Her head instantly went into caution mode, listing all the reasons she shouldn't do this. She didn't know him. He could have a disease—though, frankly, the way he looked, not even her anxious subconscious took that one seriously. He radiated health and strength. Or . . . he could be a serial killer. They could find her dead body in a lake of blood and no clues. They'd interview Emilio and he'd say *he looked fine to me. We had no idea he was a monster.*

Or—or he could be into something really kinky, something she'd hate, like handcuffs or spanking. *Ew.*

Luckily, her body wasn't paying her anxious, neurotic mind any attention at all. It didn't really have to because any possible danger was all in her head. Her body wasn't picking up on any vibes of serial killerness or kinkiness. All it perceived was a gorgeous, healthy male with a healthy interest in her, which she was feeling right back.

Oh yeah.

She held her glass up and saw that her hand was trembling. The liquid rippled against the sides of the glinting crystal glass. He was watching. He saw. Those deep blue eyes were perceptive. He was looking at her as if he could walk around inside her mind. So he could see her hand trembling and would notice the flush she could feel rising from her breasts. She had to work to bring her breathing pattern back down to normal.

This was a little scary. Charity was a reader, and like most readers, she lived mainly inside her own head. She was most comfortable on the sidelines of life, observing. Consequently, she was used to studying people without being studied back. It was disconcerting to think that he was reading her desire. That he could read *her.*

Put it back on a light, impersonal footing.

"Well then, I propose a toast of my own." Again, their glasses clinked, with a clear ring of crystal. "To . . . to Nick Ames."

And may he stay awhile in Parker's Ridge.

Three

John Di Stefano held up a bottle of Coke and wished with all his heart that it was a beer. But this was a job, and alcohol and work didn't mix, to his regret. A beer sounded great right now, to wash the taste of frustration out of his mouth.

To an impossible job. He held the Coke bottle up long enough to make the silent toast, then chugged its contents down.

He'd been holed up with Nick Ireland, aka Iceman, and Alexei Nestrenko in a surveillance van for the past week now and the inside of the van looked it and smelled it. Stale pizza lay in boxes piled on top of takeout cartons and ramen noodle containers, and the stench of unwashed male permeated the closed space. It was goddamned cold, too, since turning on the engine for heat too often would leave a telltale plume of exhaust.

The surveillance van was painted a mottled green that blended well with the pine trees surrounding them. They were a mile from Vassily Worontzoff's mansion, high up in the hills, with a direct line of sight that allowed the laser-microwave beam to pick up vibrations off the French windows of Worontzoff's study and digitally transform them into sound.

There were taps on the phones, but Worontzoff used the landline sparingly. Iceman had wanted ten dishes in an array around the mansion. He'd pounded desks, which usually worked—a Delta operator was like a lion in the geeky Tech section of the Unit—but this time the brass stood firm. One listening device. One. Larry down in Tech said it was the best way to keep surveillance from a distance.

Anything Worontzoff said in his study could be heard. They heard all conversations Worontzoff had in his study and landline conversations. Nothing specific had been said yet, but according to Alexei, something was brewing.

There had been chatter, a lot of chatter in the past months. The NSA had intercepted a message between two tangos in Islamabad about "the Russian in Vermont." A mole in a Mafiya network in Bulgaria operated by Worontzoff's organization had said that something big was in the pipeline. But it was all bits and pieces with no smoking gun.

Alexei was their smartest analyst and could speak Russian, Georgian, Bulgarian, Polish, and Ukrainian. He'd been sitting with heavy earphones on for over a week, listening to Worontzoff and his staff basically pick the lint out of their bellybuttons. And listening to music.

There were probably three thousand people of Russian extraction in Vermont, but only one *Russian*. The big man himself. Vassily Worontzoff wasn't the grand old man of literature everyone thought he was, but rather the head of the Russian Mafiya in America, come to straighten out the assorted and disorganized scumbags in Brighton Beach, making mere millions off gas tax fraud and girls when there were billions to be made off counterfeit medicines and organ transplants and arms, the bigger the better.

Di Stefano almost choked on the mouthful of stale nachos as sounds came from his partner's headset. Something going down! At last!

"What? What did he say?" Di Stefano rounded on Alexei and fought the urge to grab the smaller man's grubby sweatshirt and shake the words out of him.

Slowly, deliberately, Alexei lifted one earphone away from his ear. The other he kept covered with the foam rubber earpiece. Alexei had been offered earbuds and even a sleek, pricey Bang & Olufsen headset that conducted sound through the ear bone, but he'd refused them all. He wanted to hear everything, he said, and for that he needed the big old-fashioned foam rubber pads that covered his ears.

They couldn't operate the laser beam at night. The light beam became visible in the dark. But from first light to last, Alexei was on duty, eating and drinking and pissing and crapping with at least one ear covered at all times, listening.

This was what the Unit was all about—a secret government agency tasked with studying the growing contacts between terrorism and international organized crime, bringing together military operatives and law enforcement officers to combat this unholy alliance.

Alexei blinked as if coming out of a trance. "Not much. He picked up the phone and said hello, listened, then said *excel-*

lent, then listened some more, then said *have a safe journey, my friend*. That's all I heard him say."

John's mind raced. "Okay, okay. He's happy about something. He's happy about something that's moving. Or rather someone that's moving." Di Stefano closed his eyes at the thought of all the bad people who could be moving around. "So now all we have to do is find out what it is that he's so happy about, if it's coming here and when."

Alexei, who was a 36-level Doom player, grinned and lifted his can of diet Coke. "Piece a cake."

Four

To Nick Ames.

Nick lifted his glass and drank to himself. Or rather to Nicholas Ames, jolly retired stockbroker, nonexistent though he might be.

Ames had a pretty good deal, sitting here in this elegant restaurant across the table from one of the prettiest women he'd ever seen in his life.

It sure as hell beat his last undercover job, as Seamus Haley, former PIRA fighter who was hiring himself out to the highest bidder as an enforcer after peace broke out in Belfast. Nick did a very credible Northern Irish accent—it was probably in his DNA—even if Guillermo Gonzalez couldn't tell the difference between an Irishman and a Frenchman. As far as Gonzalez was concerned, Nick was one more corrupt gringo he paid to break legs and deliver packages.

Nick had spent twelve very long months rising through the ranks in Gonzalez's organization, step by step. Living and breathing and acting the part of a scumbag.

He'd even had to fuck Consuelo, Gonzalez's sister. Christ, that had been hard. Not because she was ugly—no, Consuelo was a looker. Worked at it, too. She spent more than the education budget of some third world countries on clothes, jewelry, and cosmetic surgery.

The instant she'd laid eyes on him, she'd staked her claim. Guillermo found it funny. He'd once walked in on Consuelo giving head and had stayed to watch, critiquing her style.

Nick had had more sex in that twelve-month period than a teen pop star and every second of it had been sheer, unadulterated vomit-inducing hell. Consuelo was heavily into pain—her pain, not his, thank God. He drew the line at that.

Still, *her* pain had been bad enough. She was into bondage and whips, with a hellish range of sex toys and sex paraphernalia she kept in a big red chest. She liked her sex so rough he sometimes spent the rest of the night driving the porcelain bus when he finally crawled back into his small, spare bedroom.

Nick never got used to it, never found it got easier. When he fucked her hard, knowing he was hurting her, her face got red, her eyes glassy, grunting then screaming while she came, urging him to hurt her even more.

It had been the hardest thing he'd ever done in a hard lifetime.

He'd seen quite enough pain during his childhood. Stopping people from hurting others was what he was all about. Being forced to hurt a woman made his gut clench, turned him inside out.

He was seriously contemplating quitting when all of a sudden, in a flurry of activity, Gonzalez put together a guns-for-cocaine deal that was the biggest Nick had ever seen. Two tons of cocaine for enough firepower to keep an African civil war going for years, which had been the point.

They had a system in place for Nick to get the word out and Gonzalez had gone down in the raid, caught in a cross-fire so vicious the only thing left of him on the warehouse floor had been human hamburger.

The cocaine had gone into a warehouse instead of up yuppie noses, the arsenal had been destroyed, and fifty-seven people slapped in jail. Enough work to keep an army of DAs busy for the next ten years. Not bad for his first mission in the Unit in terms of results. It had been hell, though. The mission had lasted a year, but it had felt like a century.

This was a better mission. Way better.

The waiter rolled a cart to their table and started plating the food. It smelled otherworldly. Nick took in a deep sniff and Charity smiled at him. "You're in for a treat."

"Smells like it."

He waited until she picked up her fork, then dug into what looked like a plump ravioli that the menu called a fagottino. When he brought the fork to his mouth, he nearly moaned. Cream, mushrooms, and truffle shavings in featherlight pasta. God.

Charity had her eyes closed, too, chewing delicately. She'd chosen a mushroom risotto.

Charity had the daintiest manners he'd ever seen. She enjoyed her food and didn't treat it as if it were radioactive like other women did. But though her pleasure was visible, every movement was delicate.

Nick watched her smooth, slim white throat work as she swallowed and swallowed heavily himself. He caught himself watching her next bite avidly. His eyes were riveted on her fork as the tines speared the morsel of mushroom and followed it every inch of the way into her mouth. That lovely, delectable, soft pink mouth.

He flashed suddenly on a vision of Charity opening that pretty mouth over his cock. It was a disturbingly intense vision and very, very detailed. He could see it, as clearly as if it were happening right now. Right in front of his eyes.

They were naked, stretched out on a carpet in front of a fire, exactly like the one in the big dining room. Nick was stretched out on his back and Charity was bent over him, the smooth shiny bell of her hair tickling his thighs, watching him out of her witchy, upturned light cat's eyes. That soft mouth opened. He could feel the heat of her breath against the sensitized skin of his cock. She licked him once and . . .

Goddamn! What the hell am I doing?

Nick shook himself out of his fantasy—a fantasy so lush and enticing his cock had twitched in his pants, hard. Jesus. Of all the places and times . . . getting a woody in a fancy restaurant while dining with a woman he needed to pump for information.

And *fuck*. The instant his mind thought the word *pump*, his head was filled with another vision. This time it was a picture of Charity stretched out under him while he pumped in and out of her.

It was like he was on the ceiling, looking down. He saw everything. Her slim thighs twined around his hips, slender arms around his neck, his butt working as he moved in and out of her. . . .

He swelled fully erect.

Right there, in Emilio's elegant dining room, in the middle of at least fifty other patrons happily eating and drinking, unknowing that there was a woody in the room. How fucking lame was that? Luckily his lap was covered by the peach linen tablecloth, but he didn't dare move.

If he'd had on his stiff jeans, maybe he could have hidden it, but he had on very expensive lightweight pure virgin wool pants that outlined him completely.

If someone yelled *fire!* he was a dead man.

This was unheard of. His cock obeyed him at all times. When he said *go*, it went. When he said *stop*, it stopped. When he said *down*, it went down and stayed down.

And Christ, he wasn't hurting for sex. True, he hadn't had a woman for a couple of weeks, except for one girl who'd picked him up in a bar the night after the takedown, when he was still pumped full of adrenaline. Four whiskeys and he was more than ready for the brunette who'd sidled up to him and told him exactly what she wanted. Waking up next to her had been depressing, though, particularly since he couldn't remember her name.

All the sex he'd had in the past year had been depressing, come to think of it.

Sex with Consuelo had been creepier'n hell and with what's-her-name had been completely unsatisfactory, like being given wax food when you're hungry.

Sex with Consuelo had felt like one of those sexual perversions in psychiatric manuals, like fucking dead people or something. It took a lot to put Nick off sex, but Consuelo had done it. The memory of sex with her made him nauseous.

The thought of sex with Charity Prewitt, now that was something else entirely. Another activity altogether.

Everything about Charity was delightful—her skin, her voice, her manner, her smell. Feminine and elegant. Totally enticing.

No wonder his dick was standing to attention, like a divining rod that had finally found a cool, fresh spring after panning over mud flats for a year.

"You're staring," Charity said dryly. He met those amazing eyes—like looking directly into a pale summer sky at noon.

"Yes, I am," he confessed. "But then that's what men do—stare at pretty women. It's what makes us different from, say, trees."

She smiled. Charity didn't seem to have the coy gene most beautiful women were born with. She didn't simper, she didn't flutter her eyelashes—though they were so long she could probably blow candles out at twenty paces just by batting her eyes—she didn't breathe deeply to showcase her breasts. Nick had been on the receiving end of every single one of those ploys and could write the script.

Charity simply kept on eating serenely.

Nick had to get his head out of his ass and start pumping—no, *don't think of that word!*—for intel. There was a reason he was here, and it wasn't to stare into Charity Prewitt's beautiful eyes and fantasize about being inside her. And he sure as hell wasn't here to eat Emilio's delicious fagottini, though that was a lucky fringe benefit, too.

By all rights, Nick should be with his partners in a freezing cold surveillance van, washing his socks and briefs out in a bucket of cold water, pissing in a jar, shitting in the woods, just like the bears. The reason he wasn't was because he was acknowledged as being good with the ladies.

And, of course, because he was a really, really good liar.

Tough job, but someone's got to do it.

However, having all the blood rush down from his head straight into his blue steeler was not good news. He needed that blood above his neck so he could pry information out of her. Hard to do that with a hard-on that hurt.

Think Worontzoff, he told himself. *Think what a scumbag the man is.*

Vassily Worontzoff. Man of letters, novelist, the last of the Russian intellectuals sent to the Gulag. The Soviet Union was dying, but like a scorpion that still has a sting in its dying tail, it lashed, sweeping Worontzoff away.

It wasn't supposed to be like that. The air had been full of perestroika and glasnost. Newspapers blossomed, the Berlin Wall came down. Intellectuals were the flavor of the month.

But something went wrong somewhere and Worontzoff and his lover Katya were sent to the place humanity forgot—Kolyma. The most notorious of Stalin's camps, where the prisoners were used as slave labor in the gold mines. Where so many died that the road to Kolyma was called the Road of Bones. Where it was said every ounce of gold mined cost a human life. It certainly cost Katya's.

Nick could almost feel sorry for the poor fuck, except for the fact that in the prison camp he joined the *vory v zukone,* the thieves-in-law. A criminal underclass sworn to revenge against society. The vory rejected everything about society—its mores, its laws, its affections.

After the fall of the Soviet Union, the vory roared to power, an engine that had been idling, waiting for the brakes to come off. Post–Soviet Russia was a giant that had been felled, its prone body ripe for gutting. And gut it they did.

The Russian Mafiya exploded. In a little over a decade and

a half, it had become more powerful than the state. It owned factories and railroads and telcos and oil wells. It held the power of life and death over something like two hundred million citizens. It signed contracts and treaties, with almost the dignity of a separate country.

Powerful Vors—Mafia dons—arose from the ashes of the Soviet Union, the stuff of legend. The thieves-in-law weren't talking, but Chechens and Azeris weren't sworn to secrecy, and slowly intel leaked out. The greatest Vor of all was a *kulturny chelovek*—a man of culture. He'd been a zek, had survived the Gulag. His hands were useless, scarred beyond repair.

There was only one possible man who fit that description, Vassily Worontzoff, a man revered inside Russia, a legend throughout the world. The writer whose *Dry Your Tears in Moscow* was considered one of the classic novels of the twentieth century. After the Gulag, he never wrote another word for public consumption. Many speculated why this was so, but Nick knew why. The thieves-in-law swore they would never again toil at legal work. So Worontzoff's legend grew while he pulled the strings of an increasingly powerful Mafiya network.

As his power and reach expanded, so did the legend. His name was spoken only in whispers on street corners. He was insulated by layers and layers of lawyers and flunkies. Few knew his real identity.

One of them had been a Russian former Special Forces operator Nick had worked with trying to run down Khan's nuclear network in Uzbekistan, Sergei Petrov. Brother-in-arms. Straight-up guy who was handy with his GSh-18, was a good man to have at your back and who liked his vodka just a little too much.

They'd been on a mission in Waziristan, tracking down possible al Qaeda nests when Sergei stumbled onto a drug operation his contact in Peshawar said was run by the Russian Mafiya. Sergei had sniffed around a little, was given Worontzoff's name, which he passed on to Nick. One more sniff, and it turned lethal. Forty minutes after giving Nick the name over a cell phone, his throat had been slashed so deeply the knife nicked Sergei's spinal column. His penis had been sliced off and stuffed in his mouth—the universal symbol for keeping your mouth shut.

The memory of kneeling in Sergei's blood helped get Nick's dick down.

There are two ways to be a bad guy and Worontzoff covered both. You could do bad things to things or to people. Nick didn't really give a shit about crime against property, though Worontzoff was in the hit list of top ten men doing damage to the world economy. Thanks to him, the Russian economy was starved of cash, several banks had crashed, and a couple of third world economies had gone bankrupt while their presidents for life played with their dicks and their money in Geneva.

Bootleg gas scams, laundering billions, reselling stolen Mercedes—it was all bad stuff, sure, but Nick could live with it. What he couldn't live with—what he'd dedicated his life to fighting—was people being hurt.

As far as Nick could tell from the file, Worontzoff had gone into prison camp a writer and had come out a monster. Over the past fifteen years, he'd been personally responsible for death and misery on an unimaginable scale.

Twelve-year-old Moldavian girls kidnapped and sold into the sex trade, used brutally on an industrial basis and dead by twenty. Mountains of AK-47s put into the hands of Sierra

Leonean child soldiers barely big enough to carry them. Cut heroin guaranteed to kill the poor sick fucks shooting up on the streets of a hundred cities.

Nick was going to take him down. Oh yes. It was what he did. What he lived for. He'd dedicated his life to taking down the bad guys and Vassily Worontzoff was as bad as they come.

Pity the road leading to the destruction of Worontzoff ran right through this beautiful woman sitting across the table, smiling at him.

"So." He put his fork down and leaned forward slightly. He could feel the heat of the candle flame against his face. "What do pretty girls do in Parker's Ridge? What are the local attractions?"

Charity shook her head. It was physically impossible, but it felt as if her scent covered him when she moved, as if it were a fine, pearly powder.

Head. Out. Of. Ass. *Now!*

"Parker's Ridge isn't Manhattan, Nick," she said, with a gentle smile. "The pleasures here are more provincial than you are perhaps used to. Still, we do have some attractions. And there's always Vassily Worontzoff's musical soirées. He manages to attract world-class musicians to our little corner of the world."

Not by a flicker of his eyelashes did Nick betray any emotion. He furrowed his brow, clueless businessman trying to place a name he knew he should know, but didn't. "Worontzoff," he said, frowning. "Isn't he that Russian . . . Russian what? Musician? Dancer?"

"Writer." Charity laughed. "Russian writer. A very great writer, the author of *Dry Your Tears in Moscow*, one of the great masterpieces of twentieth-century literature. Each year he is nominated for the Nobel Prize for Literature. And he would undoubtedly have won if he had continued writing, but he never did. He was one of the last of the dissidents sent to a Soviet prison camp. After he was released, he never wrote another word."

Her face and voice had turned serious. She looked down at the tablecloth, tracing a pattern with a pink-tipped fingernail. She looked up at him, gemlike eyes gleaming with emotion.

"And he won't talk about it, either. He's a wonderful man and we've become friends since he's moved here. As a matter of fact, he's having a musical soirée this Thursday evening."

Oh God. Nick felt his heart nearly stop. Friends. What the hell did that mean? Was she *fucking* him? It was bad enough that she'd spend next Thursday in Scumbag Central, without him having the image of Charity spending time under Worontzoff, those slender legs wrapped around the fuckhead's hips. . .

This was bad shit. He didn't even want to think about it. This was worse than Consuelo's chest of toys, way worse.

Nick looked at her carefully. She met his eyes, her gaze calm and serene. He relaxed. If she'd been Worontzoff's lover, she'd have shown some sign. A little blush, evading his gaze, a slight smile. Something. But there was nothing.

So, she wasn't fucking the bastard. Good.

Not that he cared.

Much.

Jesus. Oh, shit.

The short hairs on the back of Nick's neck stood up. He'd just been handed an opening—an honest to God opening wide enough to drive a Humvee through—to insinuate himself into Worontzoff's house, as Charity's guest. It was a goddamn huge window of opportunity, it was why he was here and not in the smelly surveillance van and the first thing that flashed through his mind wasn't *How do I wangle an invitation into Worontzoff's house* but *Is Charity fucking the guy?*

He'd been completely sidetracked from the mission. *Pow!* It had been punched right out of his head. Being sidetracked went against every single ounce of training he'd ever had, not to mention it being an excellent way to get killed.

Undercover work is like proctology. You poke and prod around assholes, looking for something bad, and then you zap the bad things you find. His line of work required utter concentration, day and night.

If Nicholas Ames made a big mistake, he lost money. Nick Ireland paid for his mistakes in blood.

Time to get back on track, fast.

"I haven't read anything by him, sorry. How long has this guy—what's his name? Worontzoff?"

Charity nodded.

"How long has this guy Worontzoff lived here in Parker's Ridge? It seems a strange place for a Russian exile to settle down in."

"Well, maybe not so strange. I'm told upstate Vermont is much like the area around Moscow, only our beech trees have larger leaves. And Vassily isn't a Russian exile. He got out of prison camp more or less in the same period the Soviet Union fell. In Moscow, he was greeted like a king when he was released. I remember it still. I'd just read *Dry Your Tears in Moscow* and I followed what happened to him in the newspapers."

Nick did some fast calculating. "Good God, you must have been—"

"Twelve." She shrugged, more of that fairy dust coming his way. "A very precocious twelve. And . . . that summer I had . . . a lot of time to read."

Damn straight. In the summer of 1993, when Worontzoff was released to return like a conquering hero to Moscow, Charity Prewitt had been in the hospital. Her father had thrown her out of a third-story hotel bedroom window in a desperate attempt to save her life during a hotel fire. The two Prewitts, man and wife, perished, and Charity suffered a T12 fracture. She'd had three operations and spent that summer and most of the winter in a full body cast.

Nick waited for her to tell her story, but she didn't.

Interesting.

In Nick's experience, people who have been through trauma are almost always eager to talk about it. It was like a badge of honor—*look what I went through, look at what I survived.*

Charity's story was particularly dramatic. Fire started by a disgruntled employee breaking out on the fifth floor of the five-star hotel in Boston where she was staying with her parents. Her father wrapping her in blankets and throwing her off the balcony in a desperate attempt to save her, then rushing back into the room to try to save his wife. It took two days for the room to cool down enough to collect the charred bones for a funeral. Charity never got to attend the funeral. By that time, she'd already had two operations and was sedated.

Why wasn't she telling him all about it?

But she wasn't, and she wasn't uncomfortable with silence, either, like most women were. She sipped her wine and watched him calmly.

Nick finally broke the silence.

"So he leaves Russia and moves to the States? Why? I mean the Soviet system fell, after all. Why didn't he just stay? Particularly since apparently he was a big shot there."

This was bullshit. Nick knew exactly why Worontzoff was here and he was looking at it right now. Charity Prewitt. A dead ringer for a woman long dead, Worontzoff's lover, Katya Amartova, who had perished in the labor camp.

Nick had seen the photos of Amartova, and the resemblance to Charity was uncanny. A normal man wouldn't ever expect that a woman who merely looked like the woman he'd once loved could be her, but Worontzoff had gone well beyond normal years ago.

She was silent another moment, then rested her chin on her fist. "I don't really know why Vassily moved here. He's never actually talked about it. I just assumed he wanted a clean slate and immigrated here to wipe out the past."

Well, to set up a criminal empire here, too. There *was* that.

"We don't really talk about these things," she continued in her soft voice. "Mainly we talk about books. Vassily has a great mind. It's a privilege to spend time in his presence."

Fuckhead, Nick thought sourly, then caught himself again, appalled. The secret to undercover work is to stay in character, even inside your own head. *Especially* inside your own head. He'd been carrying on an internal monologue all this time and if he'd been chatting with someone a little less harmless than Charity Prewitt—with, say, Guillermo Gonzalez, who'd shoot a hole in anyone's head at the least suspicion that someone was double-crossing him, blow your kneecap out for the hell of it and your elbow off for target practice—then he'd have been a goner.

This *never* happened. Ever. Nick was as focused as the laser beam that every morning was aimed at the window of Worontzoff's study. Always. As a soldier and now as a member of the Unit.

He had to get his head out of his ass and pretend he was dead from the belt buckle down from now on.

Charity turned her head to the big picture windows. Snow had started gently falling, dusting the big spotlit evergreens in the sloping lawn outside the restaurant, a scene straight out of a Christmas card. She sighed and pushed away her half-eaten tiramisú. She dabbed her mouth with the big linen napkin and placed it on the table.

She needn't have bothered wiping her mouth. Nick couldn't even imagine her being sloppy with her food. Her moves were all so graceful, just watching her was a pleasure.

Head. Out. Of. Ass. If he kept repeating it enough to himself often enough, it might just happen.

"Nick."

His head snapped up. She'd pushed back from the table, body language clear. Oh God, he hadn't pumped her at all for enough intel on Worontzoff. Again, at the word *pump*, his cock leaped in his pants.

Jesus.

He let his left hand drop to his lap, wondering whether he should surreptitiously pinch himself. Maybe if he hurt himself enough, it'd go down.

"Yeah?"

She smiled at him. "It's starting to snow. I don't have snow tires, so I should get to my car before the streets become too slick."

A drop of sweat ran down his back. He didn't want this evening to end. Of course, he hadn't gotten as much info as he wanted, but he also . . . didn't want the evening to end. This was the nicest evening he'd spent in . . . shit. Since before the Gonzalez job, which had lasted a year. And before that had been Afghanistan. We were talking years, here.

He relaxed his face. "I'll drive you home, don't worry. And I have snow tires and they're brand-new. We can still have coffee. Or would you like a brandy?"

Her eyes were so clear, it was like looking into limpid pools of water. That pale pink mouth tilted up. "That's very nice of you to offer, but I'll need my car tomorrow. So if you'll just drive me back to the library, that'll be fine."

With bad tires? Nick balked. No way.

But that pretty, pointed little chin looked just a little stubborn so he couldn't just say, *Hell no, I'm not letting you drive home in lousy weather with the wrong tires.* Much as he'd like to.

He glanced out the window himself. The snow was falling more thickly now. He turned back to her.

"Tell you what. I really like my java after a meal. Offer me a cup of coffee at your house and I'll not only drive you home, but I'll stop by in the morning, pick you up, and drive you back to the library."

She blinked. A moment of uncertainty.

Nick was really good at finding even small chinks to make people do what he wanted. It was a gift and he'd had it forever. He leaned forward.

"Please," he said softly. "I really can't stand the thought of you driving home alone in the dark in bad weather with the wrong tires. My mom drummed that sort of thing into my head and she'd turn over in her grave if I let you do it. And I'd just drive right behind you to make sure you got home safely, anyway, so you'd be doing me a big favor if you'd let me drive you home."

Charity gave a half laugh. "Well, if you put it that way. . . ."

"I do. And you just tell me when you want me to pick you up and drive you to the library to get your car tomorrow, and I'll be there."

She shook her head, the soft dark-blond bell of her hair swinging and sending some shampoo scent full of phero-mones his way. "Don't you have things to do tomorrow?"

He looked her straight in the eyes. "Not important things," he said softly. "Not as important as this."

It was his first overt move. His meaning couldn't have been clearer if he'd written it in Day-Glo letters on the wall. *I'm putting the move on you.*

To her credit, Charity didn't simper or blush or look away. She watched his eyes for a long moment, then finally spoke in a soft voice.

"Okay."

Fucking A!

Five

I'm going to sleep with this man, Charity thought in bemusement. This New York businessman, this Nicholas Ames, whom she'd met for the first time today—she was going to go to bed with him.

And not just in some vague moment in the future, after thinking about it endlessly, turning various scenarios over in her mind, they way she usually did, but *tonight*. Maybe. Probably.

Not only had she never done anything like this in her life, she'd never even thought herself capable of it. Her roommate in college said she was incredibly picky, and she was. It sometimes took her weeks to decide whether she wanted to go to bed with someone, and if the man lost interest beforehand, too bad.

Her last affair had been in college, after two months of dating, and it hadn't been anything memorable. In fact, she couldn't remember his face or even his name. Mickey. Mickey . . . something.

It had been just before she was supposed to leave for Paris. A few days later, a distraught Uncle Franklin had called to say that Aunt Vera was ill, Charity'd rushed back to Parker's Ridge, and that had been that. The new boyfriend—Mickey Whosit—had vanished into the ether, along with her trip to Paris.

Her job, her aunt and uncle . . . since then, there hadn't been time or energy for much more than that. Certainly not for love affairs.

Slowly, so slowly she hadn't noticed it happening, the world had closed in on her. The dull, gray world.

It wasn't dull and gray now. She felt as if she'd been shocked by a jolt of electricity that had awakened all her senses. Her skin was so sensitized that she could feel the movements in the air when Nick moved his hands, when the waiter walked by. She was aware of every item of clothing she had on. She was aware of her lace panties biting slightly into her hips, the feel of her thigh-highs, her bra rubbing against her sensitized nipples.

When he looked at her, it was as if he touched her with his hands. Those big, rough, well-manicured hands so at odds with his profession.

The world was saturated with color. The flames from the huge fire in the dining room painted the left side of Nick's face a dusky rose. His black hair gleamed a shiny ebony, his eyes were such a searing blue. He had the most beautiful male mouth she'd ever seen. Firm, mobile, a rich red. Redder, after he started flirting with her. It had been fascinating, watching him watching her.

There was no doubt that she turned him on. The blue fire in his eyes as he looked at her was like a punch to the stomach.

What had been amazing was that she felt the desire right *back*. It was then that Charity realized that she'd been living in a little glass bell of sadness, in a world leached of color and desire.

They were at the door. Somehow, between getting her coat for her and helping her into it, he must have paid the check, because they just walked right out of Da Emilio's.

Nick stopped just under the eaves and looked down at her, frowning. "They wouldn't let me pay for dinner," he said, in an annoyed tone.

She sighed. "I thought that might happen. They never let me pay, either. And so of course I try not to come too often. Pity, because the food is so very good."

He reached out a big hand and stroked her cheek with the back of his forefinger. "I think you bewitched them," he said, that deep rough voice suddenly soft. "I understand completely."

"No." Charity fought against the urge to rub her cheek against his hand, much as Aunt Vera's cat Folly did when someone scratched her head. "I think it's more a question of adoption than enchantment."

An errant snowflake fell on her cheek and she looked up. Big fat lazy flakes were drifting out of the inky night sky, seeming to come from nowhere. She lifted her face into the night and breathed deeply, completely content.

Nick seemed to shake himself. He looked up at the sky and back at her and tugged his scarf off. "Here." Before she could protest, he'd wrapped it around her neck twice. "It's turning chilly. And as pretty as that coat is, it doesn't look quite warm enough."

The scarf was a deep midnight blue, very soft. Cashmere, triple ply. It still carried his body heat and the scent of him—a primal scent, male musk and pine, with a faint overlay of citrus.

"There." He knotted it tightly, patted it, and stepped back, pleased. "That's better."

Actually, it was. She'd felt the chill and hadn't been dressed warmly enough. "Thank you, but now you're going to be cold," she protested.

He just looked at her. But it was a look that spoke volumes. It was the kind of look men didn't give women anymore. She recognized it as the look her father had given her mother when she tried to lift something heavy and he rushed to take it out of her hands.

It was the look only a certain kind of man could give to a woman and she hadn't seen it in a long, long time. A totally politically incorrect look, sexy as hell.

Nick had almost ridiculously old-fashioned manners. He walked her to the passenger door, handed her in as if she were indeed the queen of Parker's Ridge—maybe she should just buy herself a tiara and be done with it—buckled her belt for her, then got in himself.

She gave him quiet directions and they pulled out, that outrageously beautiful and powerful car doing something like thirty miles an hour.

Though Charity's heart drummed, her hands were steady, folded in her lap. Anticipation zinged through her system, though. She couldn't remember feeling so alive. Or so incredibly female.

Nick had barely touched her, and yet, it was as if they'd already had foreplay. Her breasts were so sensitized, she could feel the lace cups of her bra every time she breathed. When the car took corners, she could feel the pressure between her legs. It was entirely possible that she was already wet.

If the evening ended up with sex, she'd be thrilled. If not, she was still thrilled. It had been so long since she'd felt *any-thing* like this. Soft, female. So utterly alive.

They were gliding slowly through a heavily wooded area on their way back to town, the light snowflakes drifting down gently, two horizontal columns of gentle snowfall lit by the powerful headlights. The landscape looked enchanted, time-less. They could have been a prince and a princess in a horse-drawn carriage a hundred years ago.

Charity smiled at the thoughts in her head, so unlike the background hum of worry and duty that was its usual fare.

She turned her head to look at Nick, at his clean, strong profile outlined in the dim lights of the dashboard. What-ever happened between them, she owed him thanks for the gift of this evening.

At his glance, she smiled at him.

He didn't say anything. The silence inside the car was unbroken. She liked it that he didn't feel the need to chat. There was something magic in the air and words, the wrong words, could kill the magic.

Nick reached out and took her hand, bringing it to his mouth and pressing a kiss in the palm. She was so excited, she'd forgotten to put on her gloves. His breath was hot, like steam, and she felt that little kiss down to her bones. He re-turned her hand to her lap. She curled her hand around the kiss and waited, heart pounding, for what life would throw her way next.

It was like being encased in a magic bubble. Something big, something wonderful was about to happen and this was the moment just before. The very air was charged with anticipa-tion. Even the weather cooperated, knowing it was a very special night.

Charity hated bad weather but this wasn't bad—it was enchanted. Big fat flakes drifting out of the sky, gently settling on the ground, forming a thin blanket. Visibility wasn't good, but it didn't seem to matter as the big car purred slowly down the street. It was like being in a snow globe, cut off from the rest of the world.

Without Charity having to give any further directions, Nick somehow made his way unerringly to her door. The car glided up her driveway and Nick killed the engine.

The street lamp ten feet away gave just enough light for her to make out his expression as he turned to her, one big arm draped over the steering wheel. He wasn't smiling, trying to charm his way into her pants. His face was drawn, the skin tight over his cheekbones, eyes intense even in the darkness of the car.

"So," he said, his voice low. "About that cup of coffee you promised me."

She waited a beat because her heart was pounding and her throat felt tight. She opened her mouth, but found that no words came out. Nothing at all. Even if she had words, she couldn't find the breath to say them. Excitement had lit a ball of fire in her chest, making it impossible for her to speak.

So she nodded.

In a second, it seemed, he was at the passenger door, lifting her out with a strong hand. They stood for a moment outside the car. Nick must have pushed the key fob because behind her, all the doors of the Lexus locked with a quiet, expensive-sounding *whump*. So unlike the tinny sound her own car made.

He was standing so close to her, she had to tilt her head back to watch his eyes watching hers. Big puffy snowflakes touched her skin like cold little kisses, but she was so hot they melted immediately.

There was an unnatural hush, as if the entire world were waiting for them to take a leap into the unknown. She lived on a quiet street, it was true, but there were no noises whatsoever. They could have been the last man and woman on earth.

He bent down, slowly. So slowly she could have protested or turned her head if she wanted. The idea never even crossed her mind. If anything, Charity lifted herself a little on the balls of her feet, to meet him halfway.

Nick kept his hands by his side, so she did, too, though she had to curl her fingers into her palms to keep from reaching out for him. It seemed as if she'd wanted to touch him all evening, touch that un-businessman-like body hidden underneath the staid business suit.

Their lips met, clung. Charity opened her mouth to him, not thinking about it. Her mouth just opened as her eyes drifted shut. She didn't want anything to distract herself from the feel of his mouth on hers, hot and soft at the same time. When his tongue touched hers—just a quick stroke— she felt it down to her toes.

She especially felt it between her legs.

Oh my God. A gentle kiss, they weren't touching anywhere except their mouths, and Charity was as turned on as she'd ever been in her life.

Nick turned his head to get a bigger draft of her. She was on tiptoe now and she stumbled. Or would have if he hadn't immediately put his arms around her, pulling her hard up against him, upsetting her balance. But she didn't fall. Before she even had time to realize it, her world tilted and he was carrying her.

"Don't want those pretty boots to get ruined," he whispered against her mouth, and started walking.

The romance of it touched her heart. She didn't protest, she didn't wriggle or squeal. It was too luscious, this airborne feeling. She'd read too many books, and probably way too many romances, she knew that. So it wasn't surprising that in her head, this nice New York businessman and a staid librarian from a small town in Vermont morphed into a knight carrying his lady to their bower.

He carried her easily, as if she weighed nothing, which told her he was as strong as he seemed. He didn't look down, though the ground was slippery and icy. He didn't even look forward, up the path to her front door. His eyes were locked with hers, gaze so intent it was as if he were pulling where he needed to go from inside her head.

It was all so magical, so bright and fresh.

Magic didn't exist in this world, Charity knew that. She knew perfectly well what she was getting into. This was probably a one-night stand. A two-night stand, maybe, if she got lucky. It was the beginning of the weekend, after all. But when the weekend was over, Nick Ames would get into his brand-new shiny black Lexus and head on out to greener pastures, meaning more or less anywhere other than Parker's Ridge, which didn't have much to recommend it to a sophisticated New Yorker.

So Charity was determined to wrest every ounce of magical pleasure from the night. She concentrated on all her senses, on this particular moment, which might never come again.

The feel of him, the heat of him, the smell of him. It was all so incredibly enticing, his arms more comfortable than the softest bed. Without thinking about it, she lay her head on his shoulder and closed her eyes for a moment to concentrate on her feelings. Her cheek lay against the softness of his cashmere overcoat. When she opened her eyes, she could see where his beard started. The line of his jaw was so severe it was almost at right angles and his cheekbones were sharp. As a matter of fact, the only soft thing about him was his overcoat. She rubbed her cheek against it, feeling rock-hard muscle right underneath the material. Rock hard muscle underneath her hands, too, bunching and releasing as he carried her up her icy walkway, as casually as if strolling under the warm summer sun.

No change in his breathing, though he was carrying an adult woman, as easily as if she were a child. He looked down at her. She'd been studying him and she didn't hide it. When he glanced down, she smiled.

"Do you have your key handy?" he asked quietly.

She did. In a special pocket in her purse. He took it, then walked up the four steps onto her porch. Bending with her still in his arms, he opened the front door and carried her over the threshold.

It might be the only time in her life a man carried her over the threshold and Charity wanted to commit it to memory. Everything about it. She greedily soaked up every single sensation, all her senses alive and firing, drinking in every detail of the moment.

The feel of him beneath her hands, strong and hard, covered with the soft trappings of a businessman. The wonderful smell of him, stronger now that she was so close. It was a huge temptation not to lick him, to see what he tasted like.

The open door behind her, visible over Nick's broad shoulder. It was like an old-fashioned painting, the yellow streetlight perfectly centered in the open doorway, the door framing a snowy scene straight out of Currier & Ives. Snowflakes falling like featherlight stars out of the black night sky.

Nick kicked the door closed behind him and slid her down his body. There was no way on earth she could miss his erection, even through his pants and overcoat. As she felt that hard, steely column, her stomach muscles contracted and she shivered.

A second later, his scarf and her coat lay on her hardwood floor and he cupped her head as he kissed her. Deeper kisses these, harder, longer. Luscious, never ending, electrifying.

Charity was standing slightly on tiptoe, holding his thick wrists when he lifted his head, those mesmerizing cobalt blue eyes locked on to hers. His thin nostrils were slightly flared, his cheekbones were flushed red underneath his heavy tan. His beautiful mouth was flushed and wet. Still, though he was definitely aroused—the erection pressed against her belly was vivid proof of that—he looked utterly in control of himself.

Unlike her. Charity felt as if she were melting. Inside she was buzzing, dizzy with desire, hardly able to catch her breath against the tight band around her chest. The only thing holding her upright was her hands around his wrists. Otherwise she'd collapse in a puddle at his feet.

Somewhere far away something was ringing, some kind of bell. Well, that fit. A celebratory bell was a perfect soundtrack for what was going on inside her. It took her bedazzled brain almost a minute to realize that it was the telephone ringing. Her answering machine in the living room picked it up and she could hear her own voice asking whoever called to leave a message. Whoever it was, it couldn't have been anything important, because there was a click as they hung up.

Thank God it wasn't Uncle Franklin calling about yet another problem with Aunt Vera. Charity liked to think that she would, *could* break the spell of this moment if her aunt and uncle needed her, but she was glad she wasn't being put to this test.

Nick behaved as if the phone hadn't rung at all. He was watching her intently, gaze focused on her face, searching for something. Whatever it was he wanted, it was his.

"Charity," he said, his deep voice low, then stopped. There really wasn't anything else he had to say. What he wanted was clear. Every line of his big body was drawn in desire.

There was only one possible answer.

"Yes," she whispered.

Vassily Worontzoff's mansion

Vassily used his stylus to punch in Charity's number and listened, with growing apprehension, to the empty line and the far-off ringing, then her lovely voice asking him to leave a message. He didn't want to leave a message, he wanted to talk to her.

She wasn't home. Why wasn't she home? Where was she?

Charity seldom went out. She might be with her aunt and uncle, but she'd spent the evening before with them. And they were so elderly they ate at six and were in bed by nine. It was now almost ten.

Vassily put down the phone with a frown, clawed hand hovering over the receiver. He daren't call again. He had to ration his calls to Katya—*Charity!*

He limited himself to no more than two calls a week and rationed their occasions out together. Two, three times a month. He didn't dare go beyond that. Not yet.

But soon.

They'd already met for tea this month and he'd casually dropped by the library to bring her a package of piroshki he'd had specially ordered and airlifted from Moscow, just for her. She wouldn't know that, of course. He'd said a friend had brought by several boxes and too many sweets weren't good for his health.

And then of course there was the soirée he was organizing on Thursday. His soirées were for her, only her. He loved music, but he had a very extensive CD collection and he could have himself driven down to New York or to Boston any time he wanted when he desired live music. New York in particular had proved very satisfactory that way. He kept an apartment on Park Avenue, owned by a corporation with ten shells around it. No one would ever know it belonged to him.

The apartment had been decorated in the pastel colors Charity loved, filled with her favorite music CDs, stocked with her favorite teas. He'd bought an entire wardrobe of designer clothes in her size, just waiting for her to step into them. Everything was ready. His new life was there, shimmering just beyond his reach. With each passing day, its outlines grew more and more solid, more substantial.

Soon now. *Soon.*

Soon, she'd see, and understand. Soon, she would be his.

He'd been waiting for this, working for this, since he'd

moved here five months ago. Charity was meant to be his, his Katya come back to life. This is what he'd been working for, without realizing it, since December 12, 1989, when the KGB had come for them. It was a date carved into his heart with acid, never to be forgotten. The day he'd ceased being human.

They'd just finished making love, he and Katya. Once was never enough with her, he'd found, so as he lay next to her, his cock had been still half erect, still slick from her. The room smelled of her perfume and their sex.

He wanted her, endlessly. They'd been lovers for a year, and he knew he could have her as much as he wanted, but the wanting was always there. The first, frantic desire, where he'd bedded her as often as he could, for hours a day, had subsided a bit. Not because he desired her less, but because he knew she was his. All he had to do was reach out a hand, and she was there.

Katya, his beautiful Katya, had been lying on her stomach, sated, rosy, smiling. He lay next to her on his side. One hand propped up his head, the other lay in the small of her back. He was composing a poem in his head, an ode to woman, for it seemed to him in that moment that Katya embodied every beautiful, desirable woman who had ever walked this earth.

The smell of woman was in the air, and he knew generations of men had lived and died for that smell, the smell of slick, hot love.

Idly, he began to compose an "Ode to Woman," a poem that had simply welled up inside him. The first poem in his life that had come to him perfect and complete and whole in one simple rush.

He had been touched by the gods that afternoon.

The words had come, powerful and golden, in perfect cadences. He didn't need to write them down; the words were etched in his heart as they came to him. He beat out the rhythm of the poem with his forefinger, against the swell of Katya's perfect white buttock, like the beat of a song, the music of poetry against the skin of his woman.

She'd known what he was doing. Of course. Katya knew him, knew him down to his soul. He wouldn't have been surprised if she'd been able to pluck the words from his head.

His finger tapping the cadences of the words on her soft skin, he'd just ended the poem, the best thing he'd ever written, when the harsh knock sounded at the door.

He hadn't even been given the time to get up, put his clothes back on, armor himself with dignity. The KGB goons kicked his door down and, weapons drawn, dragged him away from a screaming Katya.

This is impossible, he thought frantically. *No! Russia has changed! The world has changed! The Berlin Wall has just come down!* he screamed, before a rifle butt in the head felled him.

He shook his head, stunned. This wasn't happening, couldn't be happening. Gorbachev had introduced glasnost, perestroika. Russia was, finally, opening. The long Stalinist nightmare was over.

And anyway, Vassily was no dissident. He was apolitical. A writer. A writer of the New Russia, with no agenda other than creating great literature. He was lionized amongst the intelligentsia, a New Russian, a man freed from the shackles of the past.

But the men who broke down his door were throwbacks–

brutal brutish men, coming out of the murky hallway like orcs out of a dark cave, out of a darkness before time.

This was a mistake. He was Vassily Worontzoff. *Dry Your Tears in Moscow* was a best seller. One of his short stories had been made into a film that had won a Leone d'Oro in Venice. He'd been interviewed on TV, on a number of the brand-new channels that were opening Soviet society up. He hobnobbed with the new businessmen, with the media darlings.

They'd named him a Chevalier de la République in France.

He had to contact someone, get this cleared up, he thought, as the goons tossed him his pants, then dragged him, bare chested, into the hallway.

And then his heart stopped, simply stopped, when the third officer went back into the house and dragged a screaming Katya out into the hallway.

His gaze locked with hers.

The great Soviet scorpion was dying but its poison-tipped tail still had the power to sweep lives away. He would be accused of anti-Soviet propaganda—such a huge joke when the Soviet Union was falling apart. Daily, pieces of it were breaking off, like floes off a huge iceberg, floating away on the tides of history.

He would be accused and sentenced to a prison camp, a certain death sentence. A long, lingering death sentence. There would be no getting out alive.

And now they had Katya. This was beyond his worst nightmare.

He thought being taken away by the KGB would be the worst thing that could happen to him. But he'd been wrong.

Screaming, raging, fighting every step of the way, desperate to shield Katya, he was dragged out of the building on Arbat Street and into a waiting Zil.

The twelfth of December, 1989.

The day Vassily Worontzoff died.

Six

Yes!

Nick had known that the answer to his unasked question would be yes. Letting him come in for coffee was girl code for *Do you want to have sex?* And the answer was yes. *Hell, yes!*

Nick thought of nothing else as he drove them back to her house. She'd murmured directions, but he didn't need them. He'd driven so often to her house on his stakeouts, he could find the way blindfolded.

And now that he'd spent an evening with Charity, he could probably find *her* blindfolded, by smell alone. She had the most enchanting scent. The whole car was filled with it. Some fresh springlike perfume mixed with shampoo and soap and warm woman. Unique, heady.

In the car, her scent alone had been enough to make his cock sit up and take notice, not that it needed any stimulation. Good thing he had on his expensive cashmere overcoat.

Nick was a good strategist. He set goals and figured out how to meet them with the tools at hand. This was the staging phase, the one right before battle. This was when his body started readying itself for combat. His senses heightened, his heart rate slowed, he saw and heard with unusual clarity.

The next stage was crucial. He had to convince her to trust him. Taking a woman to bed was the best way to do that, he knew from long experience. So he should be moving things slowly around to getting into her pants.

Nick knew exactly how that was supposed to work. Walk her to her door, a light kiss before she opens it, just to break the ice, another kiss after she'd poured their nightcaps. Sitting on the couch, listening to the music she'd put on, idly chatting. Another light kiss, then another, less light this time, with a little tongue. . . .

Everything slowly, with style, giving her time to get used to him.

He could do it. He'd done it before, countless times. He always kept his cool during sex. Hell, with Consuelo, he could have recited from memory whole chunks of the Army Field Manual while fucking, trying not to wince while Consuelo's razor-sharp claws dug into his back. Keeping his cool before, during, and in the aftermath of sex was easy, he'd done it all his life.

No matter how heated the fucking, a part of him remained detached and was sometimes even able to comment on the proceedings, as if he were at a show.

He needed that cool right now. This was a job. A pleasurable job, okay, and man, did he deserve it after the shit details he'd been on in Afghanistan and after a year in the employ of the Drug Lord from Hell and his sister, Cruella De Vil. He had the moves, all shiny and polished from lots of use. He had the moves, the words, he had it all in his ar-mamentarium. This should be a snap.

Have sex, make sure she was pleasured, gain her confi-dence, seduce some intel on Worontzoff out of her, gain an invite to the musical evening Fuckhead was organizing . . . that was the mission. He'd done harder things in his life, he could do this. Easy.

So why was he finding it so hard to focus on the job while she was in his arms?

He stopped just inside the door, back against it, just for a second. His knees had turned weak when her tongue met his. It was crazy. Maybe it was the bottle of wine he'd pol-ished off over dinner, though he was known for being able to hold his liquor. He was Irish, after all.

So maybe it wasn't the wine, but her mouth. The taste of her, spicy, sexy, with an overlay of the chocolate and cream desert.

He lifted his mouth for a moment and looked down at her. Her hair spilled over the collar of his overcoat, light against the dark color. Her lips were red, slightly swollen, pale gem-like eyes wide, the pupils dilated. A vein beat against her neck and he wanted, violently, to feel that beat against her breast.

She was watching him, taking cues from him, though the only kind of cue she could get right now was *How fast can I get you into bed?* Should he be slowing this down? Her eyes fluttered shut and she lifted her mouth to his in a kiss that was all too short.

Maybe he didn't have to slow this down. Which, all in all, was a good thing, because he didn't know if he could.

"Do you want coffee?" she whispered finally, pulling back and searching his eyes. Did he want coffee? Shit no, he didn't need coffee, he didn't need any stimulants. The way he was feeling right now, he needed someone to hose him down.

"No," he whispered back.

Christ, she was pretty. No, she wasn't just pretty. She was beautiful. Not many women were beautiful, magazine articles to the contrary. They gussied themselves up, and a lot of them that were secretly dogs wore so much makeup you really couldn't tell what they looked like in there, under all the glop. And then of course there was the knife and the needle, giving half the women in America the same thin, upturned nose and big pillowy lips.

Charity had a natural beauty that didn't scream *look at me!* in any way, and yet once you did, once you really *looked*, it was almost impossible to tear your gaze away.

Her makeup had almost gone, but she didn't need it. That clear, porcelain poreless skin that looked softer than anything human could possibly be, the big, tilted light-colored cat's eyes, the delicate shape of her cheekbones and jaw—they were a magnet for the eyes.

"You're so fucking beautiful," he whispered, then winced. "*Whoa*. Sorry."

"Thanks," she whispered and laughed softly. "Why are we whispering?"

They were whispering because it was a whispering moment. Actually, it was a magical moment. She felt so good in his arms. Everything about this felt good. The night, the woman . . .

It was utterly silent, as if they were the only people left in a white world of snow and silence. She was smiling dreamily up at him, beautiful and welcoming.

This was the best place he'd been in since—shit, since he didn't remember when.

Nick leaned against the door with her in his arms. He leaned against it because it was there and because, crazily, his knees were buckling.

It wasn't Charity's weight. She was slender, even slight. He'd bet the farm she didn't weigh more than one twenty, tops. He'd climbed a mountain in the Kush carting a rucksack weighing more than eighty pounds, sixteen liters of water, and his XM8 with nine magazines, which weighed over twenty pounds. He hadn't done it laughing and he hadn't leaped like a mountain goat, but he'd done it.

Holding Charity was a snap in comparison. So why were his legs having problems holding him up?

Their eyes met and they moved as one. He bent down to her again just as she lifted her face to his. The kiss was long and deep, his cock rising painfully every time his tongue touched hers. He lifted his head again and smiled down into her eyes. Might as well just ask it.

"So—we headed for the bedroom?" Please God, let the answer be yes. If it wasn't, he was going to howl. Tonight his fist simply wouldn't be enough for the blue steeler in his pants.

She nodded. *Yes!*

Another kiss that had his thigh muscles clenching. He was about ready to carry her off to the bedroom when the three molecules of brain matter he had left rang a warning bell.

The house was large, particularly for a single woman. It had been her family's home. It was large enough to have to ask where her bedroom was.

He knew perfectly well where her bedroom was. He'd been in her house twice—he'd picked her locks while she was in the library, combing the house for clues to who she was.

Initially, it had been to find weaknesses, things he could leverage for intel. Drugs would have been good. Lots of alcohol would be good, too. Maybe a stash of heavily used vibrators and sex toys, though he'd sincerely hoped not at the time.

Addictions were like a door with a WALK THROUGH ME sign on it. Weaknesses, champagne tastes on a beer budget, sexual deviancy—they were all chinks in the armor, chinks he wouldn't hesitate to use.

Thank God there'd been nothing. Consuelo had put him right off that stuff. If he never saw a fur-lined handcuff, if he never fucked a woman who was high in his life, he'd be delirious.

As it happened, there was nothing in Charity's house but beautiful furniture, books, and paintings. Charity's life was as easy to read as a book, appropriately enough, because her house was full of them. Full of CDs, too. The bought kind, which he thought was overkill in the upstanding citizen department. He was a law enforcement officer and he hadn't bought music since 2001. Charity did, which spoke volumes.

There were watercolors everywhere, signed Clarissa Prewitt. Her mother.

The house, he realized now, was a reflection of her. Elegant, classy, feminine.

Another kiss that had his thigh muscles clenching. "Which way to your bedroom?" he asked against her mouth. He knew the answer. Corridor to the left. First door to the right.

"Corridor to the left," she said. "First door to the right." He started moving as soon as the words were out of her mouth. She looked up at him, wide-eyed. "You're going to carry me to the bedroom?"

"Oh yeah." It was the fastest way to get there. He needed fast because he was burning up. He needed fast before his knees gave out and he tumbled with her to the floor.

If they fell on the floor, he'd fuck her there, which was not good. Not romantic. This had to be romantic. He could do romantic. Couldn't he? Since when wasn't he in control?

Since about five minutes ago, apparently. He was kissing her and panting and sweating by the time he made it into her bedroom and gently put her on her feet. It would be easier to get her clothes off if he could just stop kissing her, but that seemed beyond his ability. He had one hand around the back of her head and he was fumbling with her clothes with the other.

Damn! Why didn't he have *three* hands so he could undress himself at the same time?

He worked fast. Sweater, bra, skirt, stockings—thigh highs! *Yes!*—panties, shoes. *Ding!* Charity done. He lifted her again and placed her on the bed. An uncharitable observer would have said he threw her on the bed, so hard she bounced.

Now him.

God, he broke the land-speed record for undressing. Overcoat, shirt, undershirt, pants, briefs, shoes, socks.

Put on a rubber in record time.

Thank *God* he wasn't on a mission because then it would have taken him minutes to get out of his shoulder rig, get rid of the ankle holster, unhook the spare magazines and flashbangs, lose the combat knife and sheath. . .

No wonder soldiers didn't fuck in the field. It took them an hour to get undressed.

Finally, finally, he was naked and looking down at an equally naked Charity, spread out on the bed, a luscious little soft pale morsel, arranged solely for his delight.

As stoked as he was, as horny as he was, as much as he wanted to jump her bones, he paused for just a moment to look at her, the pale perfection of her. Besides that delicate, slender body, all female grace, the expression in her beautiful eyes was enough to stop him dead. Softness, humor, affection . . .

It wasn't what he was used to seeing in his sex partners. He was used to seeing lust and desire, and no emotions at all.

He frowned. Was she turned on? Or was she all wrapped up in this romantic fantasy she'd created in her head?

Only one way to find out.

Nick leaned down and clasped his hand around her ankle, pulling her leg out a little, anchoring it to the mattress. He was sidetracked for a second by the sight of her foot emerging from his dark fist.

God, even her *feet* were lovely. High-arched, narrow pink-tipped toes. Good enough to eat. If he were to start at her toes, though, it would take him all night.

Some other time.

His eyes tracked from her pretty feet, up over the narrow ankles, up the long length of her legs and . . . ah. There it was, the source of all delight.

Here, too, she was perfection itself. A little cloud of pale brown pubic hair surrounding puffy pink tissues that, yes, thank you, God, glistened. It was official. She was turned on. He could get going.

Well, one last thing.

Nick let go of her ankle and ran his fingertips up her leg, enjoying every inch of the trip. She was smooth and warm and entrancing. He slowed his hand down to savor the sensations, watching her eyelids droop a little.

Oh yeah. Her cheeks were tinted pink now, as were her nipples. He could see her heartbeat in her left breast, rocking the soft tissues. She was getting turned on by his finger on her leg.

Oh, and maybe what she could read in his eyes.

"Nick," she whispered.

"We're getting there," he answered. Oh God, this was just such a delight.

Finally, his hand arrived where it wanted to be, against her soft little cunt. She was wet and getting wetter by the second. His finger was enough to call up moisture out of her body, which he spread against the lips of her sex. He dipped his finger into her, just a little, and felt her jolt and sigh. He pressed his free hand against her knee, pressing it closer to the bed, opening her more for his touch.

The instant she understood what he wanted, she spread her legs for him. Nick could barely tear his eyes away from her—pink and puffy and soft.

Her eyes were closed now and he knew she must be concentrating on the sensation of his hand on her, at times in her. She sighed.

He could keep this up forever, just touching her lightly in the silence of the night, but when he glanced down at himself, he realized he'd better do this the old-fashioned way before he blew all over her belly and embarrassed himself and her.

He was enormous, red and swollen and hard as a club. His hand was having a good time and his head was, too, but his cock was protesting.

Do it right or I'm out of here.

Okay, he told his dick. It always had been a hard-ass.

Keeping his right hand cupping her cunt, he leaned his left hand on the mattress, right next to her sharp little hip bone and mounted her.

Now the sensations changed. He no longer felt a dreamy sort of pleasure, as if in a daze. Now the feelings were sharper, harsher, keener. Acute and hard-edged.

No more slow, dreamy motions, no more enjoying her with all his senses. Now he had only one sense and that was concentrated between his legs.

Using two fingers, he opened her up, fitted himself to her and thrust, harder than he intended. He gritted his teeth against the pleasure, holding his shaking torso up on one arm so he wouldn't crush her, breathing hard through his nose.

Jesus, she was tight. Incredibly tight. A little blood drifted back up into his head. He frowned. *Too* tight.

He looked down at her. She looked uncomfortable, almost in pain. Goddammit.

"Charity," he croaked. "Please tell me you're not a virgin."

She looked up at him, appalled. "Oh my God," she whispered. "It doesn't grow *back*, does it?"

A laugh exploded out of his chest and somehow exited his cock and he collapsed on to her, laughing and coming in equally excited bursts.

Seven

Vassily stared into the fire, listening to the silence of the house. Normally, he listened to music at night. Some nights it relaxed him enough to sleep. Most nights, though, he sat in his armchair, hoping to keep the memories at bay.

He didn't want music or vodka or even the company of one of his men.

He needed *her*, needed to talk to her. Oh how he longed for that connection with Katya—with Charity. That soft female energy wrapped in such a beautiful package, truly a gift of the gods. Katya had been his soul mate; she'd kept him going when he sank into his depressions.

He felt completely bereft, half a creature. He'd thought his heart and soul had died with Katya, but this new Katya revived them. He was whole again. Once Katya was completely his once more, he would turn back the clock. He had the power to do what only the gods could do, bring back his Katya.

Charity.

He cursed. Lately he'd caught himself several times calling Charity Katya. He stopped at the first syllable and Charity though he was calling her a cat.

He covered up by saying she reminded him of a cat. Elegant, self-contained, graceful, with brilliant clear eyes. She smiled every time.

And yet—and yet she *was* Katya. Nothing would convince Vassily that Charity wasn't the reincarnation of his very heart.

He hadn't been able to save Katya. She'd been tossed into a pitch-black hole with ravening sharp-toothed monsters at the bottom.

The scene came to him nightly, with a drumbeat of slick sweat and panic. The scene was always the same. The frozen tundra stretching for eternity, gray and featureless, the strongest fence imaginable—ten thousand miles of frozen nothingness. No one had ever escaped alive across that endless, frozen fence.

The prisoners—most sick, dehydrated, half starved, and without enough clothes for the subzero temperatures—had been herded out from the train wagons like cattle. Blinking dazedly in the meager winter sunlight, the first sunlight they'd seen in ten days, they'd tumbled out of the freight wagon on unsteady limbs, half dead already merely from the journey.

Vassily had tried to shield Katya as best he could through the endless journey. He'd given her his coat and had maneuvered her against a wall with his back to the pack to give her a modicum of privacy.

He had no food or water to give her, nor comfort. They both knew what was coming. They'd heard the stories.

Vassily had once interviewed a zek from Stalin's camps for a newspaper article.

They knew.

Katya knew.

They spoke little through the endless journey. There was little to say.

Vassily had done his best to hide Katya from the guards when they stumbled down the ramp, but it didn't work—couldn't work. Katya moved like a beautiful woman.

He'd put his coat over her head and ordered her to walk hunched over, like an old lady. But Katya's beautiful ankles had been visible. And snatches of her glorious pale gold hair slid out from the tight bun to curl around her shoulders.

Vassily's heart sank when he heard the first guard cry out, a wolf scenting fresh meat. In a second, the whole pack had descended, ripping her out of his arms, carrying her away, meat for the night.

Vassily could still hear her screams, see her slender white arm outstretched, drowning in a sea of louts. He'd fought, as hard as an intellectual could. But these were brutal men, one step up from the prisoners they guarded, and used to violence. One blow from a guard's rifle butt and he went down like a felled bull.

He gained consciousness to the sounds of Katya's screams. They lasted all day and all night. Through a small window in the freezing hut where the new zeks had been herded, Vassily could see the guards lined up, most with their pants open, rigid cocks out. Waiting for their turn to fuck the beautiful Moscow intellectual. Laughing and smoking. Going right back to the end of the line once they'd had their turn.

Some hadn't seen a woman in decades.

By the second day, the screams stopped.

Vassily had been utterly helpless to save Katya. A zek in a prison camp was nothing, not even worth the air it breathed. Less than the dirty snow on the bottom of a prison guard's boot. Less than the shit in the latrines.

He'd lost Katya, but now he'd found her again. Katya had come back to him. And he wasn't a helpless zek now, oh no. He was rich and powerful beyond measure. He commanded billions of dollars, thousands of men and women. He bought the governments of countries and bent them to his will.

He was the Vor.

And soon he would have the power to destroy cities, sweep everything before him in his revenge against the world.

Everything was possible with Katya by his side.

Parker's Ridge
November 19

Nick woke up in heaven, or at least that's what it sounded like. Soft harp music played somewhere, as gentle and harmonious as he'd imagined music in heaven would be, not that he'd ever imagined actually making it up to the Big Op in the Sky.

It felt like heaven, too, with a soft down comforter with big cabbage roses resting lightly over his naked body, his head cushioned on an even softer down pillow.

God, it even *smelled* like heaven. Roses and lavender. The scent of clean sheets and furniture polish, freshly baked cinnamon buns, and something light and flowery, utterly feminine. And over it all, the smell of sex. Oh yeah. If there was a heaven, there'd definitely be sex, just like he'd had all night. Exactly like that.

Nick smiled, swept his hand over the mattress, and opened his eyes when his hand encountered nothing but smooth sheet. Well, almost heaven. Something was missing. Someone.

He threw back the lavender-scented comforter and sat up, looking around him. Last night he'd been too blasted by lust to notice, but how had he missed the beauty of the bedroom when he'd come in on his recon prowl through the house?

It looked like something out of a magazine, only a place where people lived, not an empty stage. Polished hardwood floor. Big high bed with an antique carved wooden headboard, antique chest of drawers polished to a high gloss, two tea-rose-colored small armchairs with a pie crust table between them. Pretty, feminine knickknacks, small rosebuds in a blue vase, some fabulous landscape watercolors, a bookshelf full of books, all neatly arranged.

Still Life of Lady's Bedroom.

He glanced outside the window. It had snowed all night and there was at least a foot of snow. A big maple tree outside in her garden looked like a big fluffy cloud. Well, of course.

Heaven.

Nick rolled out of bed, lifted up on the balls of his feet and stretched, feeling refreshed, revved even. It wasn't just the fabulous sex, though there was nothing guaranteed to fire the system like it. Unlike the horrifying sex he'd had with Consuelo, which left him feeling drained and depleted. Sex with Charity was like being inside a rocket, going off.

Plus, he'd slept. *Really* slept, for the first time in what felt like forever. A deep sleep that wiped out all traces of the grainy fatigue that had been gumming up his head for the past year.

He'd never slept the entire night through in his time un-dercover with the Gonzalez clan. Each second that passed could bring something that would blow Nick's cover, something completely out of his control. If Gonzalez decided to come after him, he'd do it at night.

Nick forced himself to nap instead of sleep, and to wake up at regular intervals, scan his surroundings for danger signals, then allow himself to fall back into a sleep so shallow he could become combat ready in a second.

It was the way soldiers slept in the field, under fire. In combat, shallow sleep could save your life. In danger, you're operational in a matter of seconds. As a way of life, though, it pumped the body full of cortisol, the by-product of stress, sure to waste the kidneys if it went on too long. In Nick's case it had been going on for a long time—in Afghanistan and the year with Gonzalez. His kidneys were probably shot.

He was going to die young, anyway. It was something he knew deep down, in his bones and blood. He'd always known it. It was what had made him so fearless as a soldier. Might as well go down fighting.

So the sleep he'd had had been like a little gift of life. He knew why he'd slept so deeply and so well, besides the delightful sex. Deep down in his blood and his bones, the part of him that told him to duck a millisecond before the bullet whistled by, that whispered to him to recheck his weapon for the tenth time and to recheck his parachute, told him there was no danger in Charity's home to him. None at all.

Nothing here to harm him, so unlike the Land of Bad Things where he'd spent most of his life.

At ease, soldier, he told himself. Though it wasn't necessary to think the words. His body had told him already. He knew from the lack of muscle tension that he was in a safe environment. Safe and beautiful and welcoming.

No one knew where he was. He hadn't been tailed, he'd made sure of it. And while Di Stefano and Alexei might suspect he'd seduced the pretty librarian, they couldn't be certain. So no one knew where he was, and there was no danger to him in this house.

No danger at all. Not even sharp edges. Only soft furniture in pastel colors, pretty music, nice smells, and one hell of a pretty woman. Speaking of which . . .

Nick eyed his clothes on the floor. He had zero desire to put on his formal clothes. Suit pants, dress shirt, jacket, *ack.* He had jeans and a sweater in a bag in the trunk of the car; he'd wear those today. But right now, he wanted Charity.

A little clatter of noise from the kitchen told him where she was. He padded naked across the living room and stopped at the kitchen door, watching her. She kept her back to him, humming softly.

Nick had been trained in hard places to move silently. Charity had no clue that he was there, so he was able to look his fill.

The CD had changed to a medley of Celtic music. Nick recognized the song that was playing, though he didn't know the title. Something about green fields and coming home, which was more or less like every Irish song he'd ever heard. The Irish weren't big on love songs. The music celebrated survival and comradeship, the basic elements of Nick's life so far.

Charity knew the words and was singing softly under her breath. She had on a pink track suit that hugged her slender curves, her dark-blond hair shifting on her shoulders as she waggled her head to the music. That pretty ass swayed, too, as she fussed in her kitchen.

The kitchen was as pretty as she was. Cream and peach tiles, a line of thriving herbs in cream-colored pots along the windowsill, light-colored curtains at the window. Big ceramic canisters along the counter against the backsplash.

And the smells—almost better than the smells in the bedroom. The surprisingly rich smell of tea threaded in among the smells of something with cinnamon baking in the oven. A small pinewood table was set for two, with slices of bread, butter, an array of jams and jellies, and slices of apple. Nick could see a fantastic breakfast in his immediate future.

He watched her swaying gently to the beat of the music, listened to her singing. Though her voice was soft, it was surprisingly true.

Everything about the scene was delightful.

Beautiful woman. Beautiful music. Beautiful room. Sheer delight.

Nick felt something odd move inside him, something he didn't recognize. It rolled right through him, and whatever it was, it left peace and contentment in its wake.

He stood there, mulling that over. Peace and contentment. They weren't things he'd felt often in his life. He'd never sought them, never even wanted them. His life was one long mission and he did what it took to get the mission accomplished. Peace and contentment simply didn't factor in.

His mission in the orphanage and then in sometimes brutal foster homes had been survival, for him and Jake. Then as a Delta operator, accomplishing the op, whatever it was. Usually the op meant danger in hellholes. And now, since he'd joined the Unit, the mission was putting away bad guys.

So what was this? Leaning against a doorframe, watching a woman fiddle at the stove? What was it? The mission? An op?

It felt like more. No, it felt like something else entirely. Nick wasn't completely comfortable with all these . . . things going on inside himself. He was comfortable in his skin. He knew what he wanted in life and he usually went after it like a bullet to the bull's eye. This felt . . . different.

And good. Definitely good. In fact, he felt better than he could ever remember feeling.

Unexpectedly, Charity turned around, as if she'd suddenly sensed his presence, and smiled at him.

In an instant, that supernatural feeling of well-being disappeared, as if it had never been. *Whoosh*, gone. In its place came a burning, itching feeling, a drive to touch her, touch that smooth, creamy skin he knew was underneath the soft pink cotton of the track suit. Put his hands on her and never let go.

"Hi, so you're up . . ." Her voice trailed off as her gaze dropped and her face went from the slight flush of someone cooking to stoplight red. Charity's soft pink mouth made an O.

Oh yeah, he was up. Massively. It was as if his cock were trying to stretch its way across the room to her.

It couldn't, of course, but he could. It took him a second or two to firm up his knees and then he was crossing over to her, eyes never leaving hers. She looked down at him again and heat washed over him, as if he'd walked in front of an open oven door. The heat even pulsed in his veins.

He was clenching his jaws so hard his teeth hurt.

This was sex but it was more than sex. He wasn't hurting for sex and they'd been at it practically all night. By rights, he should be all fucked out.

Right now, instead, it was as if he'd never fucked before, never even touched a woman in his entire life. This felt urgent, with all the adrenaline of combat in the field, the moves as necessary as ducking under fire or scrambling out of the way of flames or bullets.

This was a place he'd never been in before, a foreign country. Nick didn't do urgent, pressing desire. He was the Iceman.

Whenever he fucked, a part of him—a big part—remained detached, observing. Sex made men drop their defenses. A lot of guys got offed while boffing. Not Nick. There was no way anyone could get the drop on him during sex because he was always aware of what was going on, always cool. Iceman.

Oh Jesus, he wasn't Iceman now. He was burning up, breathing hard, focused like a laser beam on Charity.

He wasn't even thinking about what he was doing. His body had taken over completely.

Moving fast, Nick hooked a chair with his foot and plonked down while reaching out to Charity. Hands a blur, he had her sweats and panties down in a second, positioned her over him, opened her with his fingers and thrust. Straight up into her soft little cunt.

Ahhh! Christ!

Sweat beaded on his face, a drop trickling down the side of his face and dropping onto her shoulder. He was holding her so tightly she was probably having trouble breathing but he couldn't seem to let her go, or even relax his death grip. He was holding on to her like you held on to a lifeline, not to a beautiful woman.

He leaned his forehead against hers, eyes closed tight. "Sorry," he whispered roughly.

Fuck. She was dry, not ready for penetration, wriggling a little to find a comfortable position, to adjust herself to him. Her toes barely reached the ground, so almost the full weight of her body anchored her to him. Shit, he hoped he wasn't hurting her, but he wouldn't take bets on it.

"No you're not," she whispered back. "You're not sorry at all."

His eyes opened. He'd kept his eyes screwed shut because what was happening inside him was overwhelming, but also because what he had left of his brains told him she'd be furious. You don't jump a woman, strip her, and shove your cock in without even a second's foreplay. He was half expecting her to tell him to fuck off.

But no—wow—against all the odds, she wasn't angry. How did that happen? When his eyes opened, they were an inch from hers. He stared into those eyes, mesmerized. That clear, crystal gray, like an early morning sky. There were slight crinkles around her eyes as if she were smiling. Yes, thank you, God. Nick's gaze dropped to her mouth, slightly uptilted. That was definitely a smile. Oh yeah.

He kissed her, a long, deep plunge into that smile. When his tongue stroked hers, she clenched around him, gasping into his mouth.

She wasn't furious at being manhandled, at the suddenness with which he'd grabbed her, at being held ferociously tight.

"No, you're right, I'm not," he croaked back when he came up for air. Hell no, he wasn't sorry. He'd kill to remain right where he was, naked on a wooden chair with his cock buried in the most delightful woman he'd ever met.

Nick smiled back. Or tried to. His mouth couldn't make the right moves. How could he smile when every atom in his body was concentrated on her, the feel of her against him and above all, the tight, warm feel of her cunt around his cock?

There was something about that thought that rang a warning bell somewhere far away in his head. Something about the feel of her . . . tight and just a little wetter now and warm . . .

Something about that didn't feel right. Or rather, felt all too good. Better than anything had ever felt before . . .

Fuck.

He wasn't wearing a rubber.

His head nearly exploded.

This was impossible. Nick never fucked without a rubber, never. Never ever, *ever.* He knew exactly what was out there and though he expected to die young, he wanted to go out like a man from a bullet or a knife to the heart and not hooked up to machines in a hospital. *Gah.* Better a bullet than disease. No question.

Suiting up was second nature, simply part of the sexual act. As natural as brushing his teeth. He never went anywhere without rubbers and had even brought them with him to Afghanistan, not that there'd been any chance of using them in that hellhole. They'd expired in his pocket and were probably dust now in his flak jacket in the basement of his condo.

But right now, in his pants pocket on the floor of her bedroom were several packets of brand-new top-of-the-line rubbers, just waiting for him.

They might as well have been on Mars for all the good they were doing him there. The normal way to go get them would be to withdraw from Charity, get up and walk over there, but every cell in his body rejected the notion. He couldn't pull out of her if they put a gun to his head.

Not to mention the biggie—he was on a hair trigger here. Yep. Nick Ireland, Mr. Cool, Iceman himself, who had fucked Consuelo for hours while calculating probabilities that her dick-wad brother was changing lieutenants, was about ready to blow.

He could feel it, a volcanic pressure rising from his loins, the little electric tingle along his spine, all telltales he was familiar with. Just Charity breathing caused a little rustle in his system, bringing him that much closer to shooting his wad. Any movement, any at all, would just push him over the edge.

Pulling out would mean friction, sliding out of those smooth, soft, warm walls . . .

Oh God. He had to tighten his groin to keep from coming at the thought. If he pulled out he'd embarrass himself by spurting into the air. Or worse—into her.

He stared into her eyes, shaking slightly from the effort of not coming.

"I'm not wearing a ru—a condom." His voice was hoarse, as if he'd spent hours screaming. His throat was tight. Huge steel bands were gripping his chest. "I'm really sorry about that."

If she wanted to haul off and hit him, she'd have every right. He couldn't even flinch because any movement was a no-no. All he could do was stare in the eyes and take it like a man.

Charity was silent.

"Sorry," he said again. It came out a wheeze. With every second that passed everything in him wound tighter. His cock in her lengthened, thickened, and then—*whoa*—she clenched around him. His cock responded immediately with a strong ripple. He bit his back teeth together so hard it was a surprise he didn't crack a tooth.

His head was going to explode. And right after that, his cock.

He was shaking, trying to rein himself in. *"God, Charity, I'm going to—"*

"It's all right." Charity's face was an inch from his. She was somber but her body was trembling. All on its own, her little cunt clenched again and they both moaned. "It's not the right time of the month, so there shouldn't be any prob—"

Whatever else she was going to say was lost in his mouth. He closed the little distance between them, holding on to her tightly, ravishing her mouth, thrusting hard up inside her while coming in long, almost violent spurts that shook him from his toes to his head. He ate at her mouth, as if his life depended on it. Maybe it did. He felt one long hot liquid pull through his body, from his mouth to his cock, drowning inside her.

He shook and groaned throughout the climax, grinding himself into her, totally out of control. He left her mouth because he was afraid he'd bite her in his excitement, and buried his face in her hair, hanging on to her as if he was drowning and she was his lifeline to shore.

His skin prickled, his chest felt tight, he was burning up. He felt especially hot in his groin, right where he was joined to her. Hot and wet. He'd spurted so much come into her, they were wet to their thighs. It should have been a turnoff, but actually it was a huge turn-on. Huge. Knowing his seed was inside her. And in particular, knowing she was now wet.

Not wet because he'd managed to get in a little foreplay, no, not that kind of wet. But still. Wet is wet. Wet meant he could move in her without hurting her.

First, though, some amends. "Sorry about that," he whispered. His breath moved a lock of her shiny dark-blond hair. *Sorry*. Nick didn't believe in a God, but if he did, he deserved to be struck down by lightning immediately because he wasn't sorry. Not sorry at all.

Not only was he not sorry in any way that he was buried to the hilt in the warmest, tightest little cunt he could ever remember being in, but he was not sorry for anything about the situation. Her soft breasts were plastered against his chest, rubbing against him with every breath she took, his arms tight around her narrow rib cage.

"That's okay." Was that a wheeze he heard in her voice? Though it cost him, Nick gentled his hold slightly. She had to breathe.

Since his mouth was right there, he blew another perfumed lock of hair away from her neck and began kissing her, running his lips along the soft skin of her neck, kissing the even softer skin behind her ear. Her hair tumbled over his face and it was like being in a soft, perfumed dark-blond cloud.

His lips picked up the beat of her heart, fast and light. He could feel that beat against her left breast, too. Was it excitement?

Only one way to find out.

He eased back a little, wondering which hand to use. They were both extremely happy exactly where they were. If there were any justice in this world, he'd sprout a third hand so he could touch her where they were joined without letting go, but he'd learned long ago that there wasn't.

So which hand to use? The one that was cupping the back

of her head or the one wrapped around her back, fitting precisely into the sharp indent of her waist? God, what a choice.

Finally, reluctantly, his right hand left her waist, trailed around her back, over the top of her thigh and rested on her mound.

Charity wiggled a little on him and he surged and lengthened inside her. She caught a little breath, the sound loud in the silence of the kitchen.

"You're still, um—" she wiggled on him some more, the movements so exciting his stomach muscles jumped. "Still . . . hard," she finished breathlessly.

Hard? Oh yeah.

He brought his mouth around to hers and kissed her deeply, like plunging into a sea of warm, scented flowers. He opened his mouth more widely, taking in a sharper taste of her.

Her arms curled around his neck, one hand toying with the hair at the nape of his neck.

Nick fisted his hand in her hair and pulled gently. Her head fell back and he admired the long line of her white throat. Wow, maybe vampires weren't so dumb after all because right now, he felt like growing canines and feasting. Failing that, he nipped her, right where her neck met the smooth line of her shoulder.

Charity jolted. Inside and out. A sharp clenching of her cunt and he swelled inside her. She gasped and twined her legs around the legs of the chair, impaling herself more heavily on him.

It was all he needed. Wrapping his arms around that narrow back, Nick began moving inside her, sharp short thrusts, made easier by the gallons of come he'd flooded inside her.

It was as intense as hell and couldn't possibly last. When

she gave a sharp cry and started climaxing, he shouted and thrust up into her in one last, hard jolt and exploded.

He had no idea how he had all that come in him, seeing as how he'd just climaxed. Maybe his spine melted and drained straight into his dick. Maybe he was using up all the liquid in his body and would dry up and blow away into dust.

Whatever.

"Wow," Charity whispered. She lay with her cheek against his shoulder, arms looped around his neck, body completely relaxed against his.

Their groins were wet, stuck together by his juices and hers. He was still just hard enough to stay inside her. If she moved, he'd slip out but for now she wasn't moving and he loved being inside her still.

It was . . . pleasant. More than pleasant. She was the softest thing he'd ever felt beneath his hands, soft and warm and fragrant. Nick felt like he could stay like this forever.

She flattened her palm against his back in a small caress, then stopped, puzzled. A swift pass over the spot as she rubbed her cheek against his shoulder.

He knew exactly what she was feeling. A circular puckered scar on the front with a matching circular scar on his back.

"That's my most embarrassing scar," he said easily, running his hand up and down her back. "I never tell anyone the story, but I'll tell you, if you promise to feed me whatever it is you cooked in the oven."

"Cinnamon buns. Deal." He could feel her lips move as she smiled against his shoulder. "Unless they're burnt. And if they are, it's entirely your fault."

"Fair enough." He kissed her hair. "So this is the story. When I was eighteen, my aunt Milly moved in next door. She only stayed a year but in that year, she elected me her own personal slave. I helped the moving guys bring her furniture in. She loaded me down with too much stuff, mostly for the upstairs bathroom. One of the moving guys had dropped a soap dish on the stairs. I tripped and fell. Straight onto a brand-new steel curtain rod. Skewered me but good."

She shuddered. "*Ouch*. Talk about no good deed going unpunished." Charity fingered the scar on his back, then bent to kiss the scar on his shoulder. "That must have hurt."

Like a bitch.

And it hadn't been a curtain rod; it had been a 9 mm round. The round that had nicked his lung and finished his army career.

He pulled back and smiled into her eyes. "Now how about those buns?"

Eight

Nick followed Charity back to her house, staring at the back of her car as if he could will her to stop, get out, and let him get behind the goddamned wheel.

He hated this. Why couldn't she have just left the car where it was? He'd dropped hints aplenty, had even contemplated an order, but though she stated her wishes in the softest voice possible, Charity was like a rock. She just lifted that pointed little chin of hers and that was that. She wanted her car and she was going with him or without him to get it. In this weather, without him wasn't an option, so with gritted teeth he'd driven her to her car near the library and was following her home.

That the weather had worsened—the roads were slick with ice and sleet—was a condition that Charity had totally ignored. Nick had to clutch the steering wheel hard to keep from shooting out in front of Charity and forcing her to slow down.

Unexpectedly, his classy little librarian liked speed. That was fine, but not on a day like this and not when he suspected she couldn't quite handle her car. It slid when she braked and took corners. His jaws clenched each time.

He longingly eyed the cell phone on the passenger seat. He could call her and tell her to slow down. Make it seem like he couldn't keep up, which was ridiculous for anyone who knew him. There wasn't a vehicle in the world he couldn't drive, as fast as he wanted, in any kind of weather. He was a qualified combat driver instructor and was one of the best.

His cell phone buzzed. Not Charity. Nick smiled when he saw the display. Jacob Weiss, his best friend. He switched his cell phone to speakerphone mode.

"Hey, Jake. Howzit hangin'?" It was their usual greeting and was usually answered in unprintable ways.

"Hey big guy, guess what? I did it!" Jake was too excited to engage in their usual banter. Nick could hear it in his voice. "*Yee-hah!* Or *hoo-ah!* Or whatever it is you military types say. I did it!"

Nick rolled his eyes. At any given moment, Jake was accomplishing a bazillion different things, not least accumulating more money than a third world country. "It" could have been buying Microsoft, doubling the income of a Saudi prince or single-handedly raising the world price of gold. Jake was one of the prime financial geniuses of the world. That wasn't Nick's opinion, it was Bloomberg's.

Whatever "it" was, though, it had Jake in a state.

"Great. Glad to hear it." Jake couldn't see Nick's shrug but he could probably hear it in his voice. Nick just wasn't that into money, to Jake's everlasting sorrow. "What did you do? Buy Corsica?"

"No, though I *did* purchase a resort . . . never mind. Listen, you remember those Russian bonds I told you about?" Jake waited while Nick processed. Should he lie and say of course he remembered? Jake was smart as a whip. He knew when Nick was lying. No, wait . . . Nick remembered something. Vaguely.

Jake didn't let the thought gel. "If you had a decent cell phone instead of that crap POS you use, you'd see me rolling my eyes. I talked to you about investing in Russian bonds six months ago. I talked to you for *two hours*, Nick. Your head's hard but it can't be that hard."

Oh yeah. Nick had taken an afternoon off from being a scumbag gopher for the Gonzalez clan and had gone to see Jake and his family. Being with Jake and Marja was like breathing in cool, clean air, except when Jake talked money, which is when Nick zoned out.

"I sort of remember. You thought it would be a good deal, right?"

"It turned out to be an excellent deal, thank you. Paid off four to one. I wasn't expecting that until next spring, but by God, I'm looking at the e-mail right now."

Nick, instead, was watching Charity's back fender. Was that a *wobble*? Goddamn it, if she was having trouble holding the road, he was going to signal her to stop and have her come back to his car. They could leave hers there and he'd pick it up as soon as the weather cleared. He watched carefully as she rounded a corner, finally letting out a pent-up breath. Okay. She'd taken that one smoothly. But damn, her tires weren't suited to this weather. He'd taken a good look before she got into her car and had to bite his lips not to say anything.

"What? What was that?" Jake had said something, something he was excited about. Nick gave him half his attention, the other half focused like a laser beam on Charity in front of him.

Bonds were infinitely less important to him than making sure Charity didn't crash.

"If you'd been *listening*," Jake said, in an exaggeratedly patient tone, "you'd have heard me the first time. But I'll repeat. Do you remember when I told you I'd make you a millionaire? And you gave me all your money?"

Nick smiled. Good old Jake. "Yeah."

Him, a millionaire? He could sooner sprout wings and fly. He never worried about money management. He spent very little and the rest just sat in a bank, gathering dust.

In exasperation, Jake made him take everything out and give it to him. It wasn't peanuts, not for Nick, anyway. Nick had banked his entire salary while in Afghanistan, where he whooped it up on stale water and field MREs, there being absolutely no place to spend it. And again, his salary had accumulated while he was with the Gonzalez clan, and he'd handed that over to Jake, too.

Yeah, Nick remembered. A hundred fifty thou. More or less everything he had in the world and probably what Jake made in a minute. "You lose that for me?"

"No, I just told you! Weren't you listening? I put your money in Russian bonds and Hong Kong gold futures. The Russian bonds just quadrupled and Hong Kong gold went through the roof. You were highly leveraged there for a while, I'm not afraid to say. . . ." Nick frowned. Charity was driving way too fast again. He zoned back in to what Jake was saying. ". . . and I got you in and out of an Indian IPO fast, you came out smelling like a rose. In fact, as of right now . . ." Nick could hear a computer keyboard clacking, "your net worth is $1,003,000. Congratulations, Nick. You are now a millionaire. I just more than quintupled your investment, my man. Jesus, I'm good. I'm a god. Wait a second, while I do a little victory dance."

Nick heard tapping sounds and smiled. Jake had undergone the last of eleven operations over the past ten years to straighten out his spine and being able to walk without pain and move quickly were both huge victories.

Wait a minute.

"Whoa." Nick finally focused on what Jake was saying. "Hit rewind, would you? What was that again? I thought I heard you say that—"

"That you're a millionaire. Rich, big guy, you're *rich*. Absolutely. Welcome to the club." Jake laughed. Actually, Jake was a billionaire, many times over, but Nick appreciated the thought. The Millionaires' Club.

"Jesus." Nick took a deep breath, then another. "Jesus, I'm rich." His mind whirled. "I'm rich." He gave a breathless laugh.

"Yep. Don't spend it all in one place. Tell me I'm good."

"You're a genius," Nick said, meaning every word.

"Damn straight." Jake laughed again.

Nick swallowed. He flashed on the first time he'd seen Jake.

He'd been eleven and looked sixteen and Jake had been nine and looked five. Jake had suddenly appeared in the orphanage, a shell-shocked, whey-faced odd-looking little boy with a crooked back and toothpick legs. His family had emigrated from Israel the year before and his parents had just died in a freak accident. There were no other family members the state knew of, and they couldn't immediately find a family willing to take on a cripple, so he'd been dumped in the orphanage, where he was immediate prey.

He barely spoke English, was badly underdeveloped, and scoliosis had turned his back into a huge crooked S. The death of his parents had traumatized him so much he couldn't talk.

It had been like dumping a crippled guppy with a BEAT ME UP sign pinned to its fin into a tank of piranhas. Five minutes after arriving, Jake was bleeding.

Nick had been outside shooting hoops when he saw the biggest bullies in the orphanage kicking something small and white on the ground. A minute later, he was pulling the fuckers off, breaking an arm and a nose and was carrying an unconscious Jake to the dispensary. He'd weighed nothing.

The dispensary, necessary by law, was staffed by an indifferent nurse Nick suspected was dealing pain-killers. She had no desire to look Jake over and did so only when Nick got right up into her face.

She patched Jake up and Nick made sure he was around Jake most of the time and that everyone knew messing with Jake meant messing with *him*. Jake was prey but Nick wasn't. Nobody fucked with him or with those he protected.

For the next few years, Nick had a pale, silent shadow. Jake never spoke, hardly ate, and could sleep only if Nick was in the same room.

They bounced from foster home to foster home. The first time Nick was dumped in a foster home, the social worker refused to place Jake in the same home. The social worker, an obese lady with a honeyed southern accent and mean eyes, raked in 10 percent of the take from the foster homes she placed kids in.

She wanted to split them up. Jake was to go to a home that specialized in mentally and physically handicapped children. There was a 50 percent bonus for those kids. Nick had heard tales about that home that made his skin prickle. Two kids had died there over the past couple of years.

Nick pushed the social worker against a wall with a knife to her side and told her he'd cut out her kidney if Jake didn't go with him. They were never separated after that.

When Nick was seventeen and Jake fifteen, some sociology students came to the foster home they were in at the time. The students were conducting a survey of children in foster homes who had spent time in an orphanage. The survey consisted of an IQ test, a Rorschach, and interviews. Jake refused to answer the questions and was silent when administered the Rorschach.

The IQ test was another story.

The survey team refused to believe the initial results and had Jake take the test again. And again. And again.

Each time, the survey group grew, until finally, a professor from MIT came and took Jake away.

Jake's results were off the charts, particularly in math. Genius didn't begin to describe it. From then on, foundations vied for the privilege of educating him. He had a masters in economics and in math by the time he was eighteen; a PhD in economics by twenty-one. By that time, too, he knew what he wanted. Money, and lots of it.

He had it, too, Nick thought in satisfaction. Piles of it. Tons. Boatloads of the stuff. Good for him. He'd earned every penny.

"You're rich, now, buddy," Jake said quietly. "So what are you going to do about it? No sense dying young when you're rich, is there? Rich guys die of old age. In their beds. With a couple of hotties."

Nick winced. Once, between missions, he'd gotten shit faced with Jake. Four men under his command had died and he saw their faces nightly in his dreams. Nightmares.

Jake had sat and listened quietly to him, nursing one drink to Nick's ten until Nick had been rendered down to rock bottom. There had been nothing left in him, an exhausted, heartbroken mess of a man. And that was when he confessed to Jake that he was convinced he would die young.

After that, Jake refused to let it go, like a dog with a bone. He said he would make it his life's work to get Nick out of the military. When Nick was wounded and resigned his commission, Jake bought a whole vineyard in Champagne to celebrate . . . and then got angry as hell when Nick joined the Unit and went undercover.

Suddenly, Jake's voice roughened. "I'm not going to let you die young, Nick. I simply won't allow it. You're going die in your bed a rich old man and that's that. Get used to it."

He hung up.

Nick drove, concentrated on watching Charity in front of him and on what Jake had said.

Not dying young. Wow. Now there was a thought. Though come to think of it, he was thirty-two. Maybe he was too old to die young.

For the very first time in his life, Nick thought of the future. Not the immediate future, like making Delta or joining the Unit. No, the long term. Being forty and fifty and sixty. Christ, maybe seventy and eighty. The thought that he was going to die young was so ingrained in him that he had never given a thought to becoming middle-aged and then old. Wasn't going to happen.

But—just suppose it did? Just suppose he lived. And he had money, to boot. Well, that changed things.

Suppose, like Jake insisted, he quit doing dangerous jobs and got married and settled down with a family?

Of course, it was easy for Jake to talk. He had the most beautiful wife in the world and three great kids. Marja was a stunning beauty. A platinum blonde, a head taller than Jake, a great mother, and a fantastic wife. Everyone assumed that with his billions, Jake had bought himself a trophy wife, but the truth was he had met Marja, a Swedish exchange student, while still studying and trying to survive on a grant at MIT. He and Marja were a love match.

It never even occurred to Nick that he could have that. Good thing, too, because he'd never met anyone he could feel about the way Jake felt about Marja.

But just suppose . . . he eyed the car in front of him, which Charity was driving just a little too fast for her ability and her tires. It was just like her—flares of unexpected fire under a soft, unassuming exterior.

Suppose he settled down? And just suppose he settled down with Charity? Living with that beautiful woman in that beautiful house in a pretty, peaceful town.

Nick waited for the feeling of constriction, of claustrophobia that always took him when he thought of settling down. It wasn't coming.

Charity zipped down her street and pulled too fast into her driveway. Nick gritted his teeth and parked right on her back fender. If she wanted to get out again, she was going to have to ask him. And as far as he was concerned, she wasn't getting her hands on another steering wheel until the weather cleared.

He was at her door before she could get out, hand out-stretched. "You drive way too fast," he complained. Damn, that sounded like a whine in his voice.

She laughed up in his face and poked him in the ribs. "And you drive way too slow. Boring. You might as well be driving a Fairlane instead of that beautiful car."

Nick had worked as a development test driver for a car manufacturer one summer. Once he'd gotten a racing car up to 175 miles an hour on the straightaway.

He smiled down at her. "I guess I'll just have to work on my driving skills."

Nine

"More?" Nick whispered into Charity's ear Sunday night. From behind her, he shifted a damp lock of her hair to one side and licked the skin just behind her ear. She shivered.

More? Good God, he was buried so deeply inside her it almost—but not quite—hurt. How on earth could she want more? More of anything he could give her?

She was already completely his, completely in his grip. He was arched around her back, one muscled thigh between hers, opening her up. One hand held her breast, the other was holding her labia open around his penis.

"This feels so good, I don't even want to move," he murmured, his lips so close to her ear she could both hear his voice and feel the vibrations in his chest against her back. "But maybe—" the hand at her groin moved, opened her even farther, "maybe you want more."

His hips tightened against hers and, impossibly, he slid in a little farther, to a place deep inside herself she had no idea existed.

Heat blazed from her groin and she could feel herself getting wetter by the second, just from having him there, inside her, hot and heavy and unmoving. So still she could have sworn he wasn't even breathing.

Everything about this was a delight. His big, strong hands, powerful yet delicate. Capable of touching her just so. His chest hairs tickling her back, the rough hairs at his groin scratchy against her bottom. The strong, hair-roughened legs against hers. And of course, the biggie. Literally. His penis buried in her to the hilt.

She closed her eyes as her body spasmed helplessly around him. He reacted instantly, growing even longer and thicker inside her in the space of a heartbeat.

More. He'd asked her if she wanted more and was giving it to her. She hadn't answered him, but her body had. And his had responded.

He withdrew, just a little, the friction against the walls of her sheath like painless fire, then moved back in. Oh God, she was starting that delicious slide into orgasm already. How did he do it?

She'd always been so slow to climax. A lover or two had even complained about it. She wasn't slow now. All Nick had to do was touch her, enter her, and she was primed to go off.

Nick started slow, languid pulls and thrusts, lazy and leisurely, his chin nestling against her shoulder. Breathing relaxed and deep. Heart thumping hard and slow against her back. Muscles hard but not tense.

Experience told her that he was settling in for the long haul and could keep this up for hours. Recent experience. A lot of it.

She couldn't keep it up for hours, though. No, in an instant her heart started racing, heat prickled in her veins, everywhere he touched her, inside her vagina, against her back. The musky smell of sex clouded the air. She was starting the slide. . .

The phone rang.

Nick stopped for a moment on the outstroke and Charity wanted to scream. So close, she was so close! She needed him back inside her, now. A whimper escaped her. Her thighs shook. She tightened around him and felt an answering surge.

The phone rang again. Nick was still, unmoving. What was he waiting for? His penis was barely in her, at her entrance and her sheath contracted sharply, anxious for him to fill her again.

The phone rang again.

It was just far enough away so that she couldn't stretch out and turn the handset off. If she reached for it, she would pull away from Nick's penis. Unthinkable.

The phone rang again.

Her heart pounded, her lungs felt tight. She was shaking all over now. So close. She was so damned close—

Her eye happened to fall on the big clock on her dresser drawer. Twelve fifteen. Past midnight. Who on earth—

Suddenly, reality crashed in on Charity, chilling her.

The only person who would call her at that hour was Uncle Franklin. And there could only be one reason to call. He needed her.

Charity moved, pulling away entirely from Nick's penis, worry rising in her like a dark tide, so overwhelming she didn't even have time to mourn leaving his embrace.

"Sorry," she gasped and lunged for the cordless handset. "I have to get this." How long had it been ringing? Was she too late?

"Hello?" Her voice sounded breathless to her own ears.

"Charity?" Uncle Franklin's soft, quavering voice sounded dim, as if he were speaking from the bottom of a well. Her anxiety ratcheted up a notch.

"Uncle Franklin? What's wrong?"

Holding the handset between her ear and her shoulder, Charity scrambled to get dressed. Whatever had happened was bad. She needed her clothes for this. Panties—where Nick had thrown them in a corner. Pants—over a chair. Sweater—at the foot of the bed.

"Your aunt, honey. She's gone. I don't . . ." Uncle Franklin's shaking voice drifted off, the last word said away from the phone.

"Uncle Franklin!" Charity's voice was sharp with worry. "Where? Where has Aunt Vera gone?"

Silence.

Desperately hopping on one leg to pull on her pants, Charity spared a second to look out the bedroom window at the heavy sheets of snow falling from the sky. A delight while in bed with your secret lover. A nightmare for an elderly and confused woman.

Uncle Franklin's voice came back, a little stronger. "I'm sorry, honey. I thought I saw her out the window, but I was mistaken."

"How long has she been gone?" Boots. Charity looked around frantically for boots. She dived for the closet and pulled out a pair of waterproof boots, shaking with urgency.

"I-I d-don't know." Uncle Franklin's voice shook so badly she could barely understand him. "I woke up and wanted a drink of water. But I'd forgotten to put my usual water bottle on my bedside table because we had a leak in the downstairs bathroom and I had to call in a plumber, and by the time he left, it was time for dinner and I just completely forgot."

He could keep this up forever. For an instant, Charity mourned the Uncle Franklin she'd known all her life. Judge Franklin Prewitt, sharp-minded, sharp-tongued. Steely intelligence wrapped up in a take-no-nonsense demeanor; a rapier wit, which he often flashed in court. Woe betide the defense attorney who hadn't done his homework. He'd leave the courtroom with his hide in strips.

She saw that man less and less.

And Aunt Vera—elegant, ironic, well-read. Devotee of chamber music and the theater. Who read Rimbaud in French and Isabel Allende in Spanish. That Aunt Vera was gone forever.

"I'll g-go outside and l-look for her—"

"No!" Charity said sharply. God, the last thing she needed was for Uncle Franklin to get lost in the snow, too. "You stay put, now. I'm coming right over."

She clicked off so he wouldn't have time to protest. It was entirely possible that Aunt Vera was in the basement or had wandered into the cellar. It wouldn't be the first time.

Charity yanked out her down parka from the closet, rattling the hanger, and turned around with a heavy heart.

Through the haze of anxiety, she could still feel Nick inside her, that warm column of hard flesh making her glow with heat, his large hands gripping her, the feel of him hard against her back. The signs of sex were still in her body—her panties were damp, her supersensitized nipples grazed the sweater she'd pulled on—yet her body already felt bereft, lost and cold without him.

This might actually be the breaking point. When Nick decided she was more trouble than she was worth. There was no time to explain that she had to rush off, that it was her duty. He'd have every right to be annoyed. Bed partners aren't supposed to disappear in the middle of the night. Certainly not in the middle of making love.

He was too good to be true, anyway. Maybe the sooner he left, the better, before she started hoping—

Zipping up the parka, she turned her head toward him as she rushed to the door. "Nick, I'm sorry, I really am, but I have to—"

But he wasn't on the bed. He wasn't anywhere in the room. Oh, heavens—had he somehow *left* while she'd been fumbling in the dark? Wouldn't he have at least said good-bye?

She switched on the overhead light and there he was, fully dressed, waiting by the front door. Oh God, he *was* going.

"Nick, I'm really sorry, but my aunt Vera is missing and I have to leave. Believe me I wouldn't go unless I had to." She swallowed heavily. "But, wouldn't you like to stay the night? I might not be too long."

Just the thought of coming back to an empty house made her heart clench.

He didn't answer, just opened the door. "Let's go, Charity." He had a grim expression which she couldn't decipher. She was in a hurry, but she stopped when she saw his face. Was that anger? No, not anger. But what was it?

"Go?"

Snow was already accumulating in the foyer through the

open door. "I'm not letting you drive in this weather. You can tell me all about this in the car. Now *move*."

Charity started at his tone. "But—" She was talking to the empty air. He'd disappeared into a white swirl.

Charity locked up and followed Nick as fast as she could over the slick ice-covered path down to the street where Nick's car was parked. What a nightmare of a night.

Her heart squeezed and she prayed to the god of good, elderly women that Aunt Vera had simply wandered into the basement or the garage.

It felt like forever but was probably only a minute before the shiny black fender of the Lexus appeared between sheets of snow.

It looked like they were taking Nick's car. This was good news and bad news. His car was undoubtedly better equipped to deal with bad weather than hers. It was powerful and would hold the road much better than hers. That was the good news. The bad news was that Nick was a poky driver, overly cautious. Charity wanted to get to her uncle's house as fast as possible and Nick was guaranteed to take forever getting there.

In good weather it was a twenty-minute drive. In bad weather forty minutes. Nick, slow, careful driver that he was, could take almost an hour. In that hour, Aunt Vera could die.

Nick was behind the wheel, the engine running, windshield wipers clacking back and forth, passenger door open. Charity poked her head down.

"Nick, um, do you want me to drive? I know the way and—"

"No," he answered curtly, jaws clenched.

"But—"

"Get in. Fast." There was real command in his voice, flat and imperative. "Now, Charity." He glanced at her briefly. One look was enough.

Charity instinctively obeyed, scrambling into the passenger seat as fast as she could. The powerful engine idled, the vibrations a low hum of power under her. It was like sitting on a tiger in the instant before it leaped.

"Buckle up." Charity turned her head. Nick's face was completely impassive, devoid of all expression. She was so disoriented and frightened she'd forgotten to buckle her seat belt. Driving in a snowstorm without a seat belt was just asking for trouble.

"Tell me where we're going." Nick's tone was flat, remote.

"Ferrington. It's a small town about fifteen miles—"

"I know where Ferrington is. Hold on."

Hold on? Charity reached for the pull-down handle over the door, wondering why she had to hold on, when the car suddenly shot forward violently, pressing her against the seat back like an astronaut during liftoff. In a second, it seemed, they were at the end of her street, still—amazingly—alive. A miracle considering she'd never dared to drive this fast on a sunny, dry day, and she was a woman who liked her speed.

On icy roads and in the middle of a snowstorm, this speed was suicidal.

A scream vibrated in her throat and she clamped her lips shut. A scream might distract Nick and that could prove fatal at this speed, in this weather. One wrong move and they'd die.

Nick continued gunning the big, heavy car, somehow knowing the next corner was near, though it was almost impossible to see past the white flurries. You could only see the road ahead in fleeting moments when the curtain of snow parted for only the briefest of instants. The Lexus was shooting ahead at an impossible speed, rounding the corner onto Wingate inside a couple of seconds. She clamped her lips shut against a scream. They were sliding wildly out of control. . . .

No.

Not sliding out of control. The car straightened and remained steady on the road, traveling much too fast, but in a straight line.

Braced to die, Charity finally pulled in a deep breath, her first in what felt like forever. Nick was driving so fast it terrified her, but he seemed to be in total control. Just when she thought they'd crash into a van parked on the street or would climb onto the sidewalk and hit a tree, Nick somehow righted the car without braking. He seemed to have a sixth sense for what the car could do on the icy roads and pushed it to those limits and never an inch further.

"What's in Ferrington and why are we going there?" Nick's voice was utterly calm as he corrected for a skid the instant the wheels slid under them. Thank God there were no other lunatics on the road other than them, or they'd already be dead. Charity braced herself as they whizzed around another corner and Nick took what she recognized as a smart short-cut to Ferrington.

She had to remember to breathe, transfixed by the bright columns of the headlights creating two yellow tunnels in the white nightmare.

He'd asked something. . . .

Charity had been staring at the road ahead, ready to shout useless instructions to Nick. At the sound of his calm voice, she turned and watched him for a second—steady, in complete control—and relaxed a tiny bit, just enough to gather her thoughts.

"My aunt and uncle live in Ferrington, or rather in the country outside town. They're elderly. My uncle called to say that my aunt is missing. He can't find her anywhere."

"How elderly?"

"Uncle Franklin is eighty-seven and Aunt Vera is eighty-four."

A muscle jumped in his jaw. "So you're telling me that an eighty-four-year old woman might be out in this weather?"

Impossibly, the car picked up a little more speed while Charity's heart leaped into her throat.

"Yes," she whispered. "Aunt Vera gets a little, um, confused at times."

This was so hard. Uncle Franklin refused to accept even the idea that his beloved wife was deteriorating mentally. Each time something happened, he would put it down to her having the flu or to not having slept well or having accidentally forgotten something. He refused to acknowledge her failing mental health to the outside world, to her, and—perhaps most tragically—to himself.

It was why he called Charity instead of the police when his wife disappeared in a snowstorm. In this case, Charity understood. He was probably right. Ferrington's police force consisted of an overweight county sheriff who drank and lived twenty miles away. His clueless, borderline retarded deputy would be of even less help. Sheriff Hodgkins could never find Aunt Vera, not in a million years. He could barely find his way home after a night on the town.

And by the time Uncle Franklin got through to the Highway Patrol or some law enforcement authority that could actually be effective, hours would have passed and Aunt Vera could die.

"Confused, how?" Nick didn't look over at her but she could feel his attention on her like a hand touching her.

Confused, how? Very good question. Uncle Franklin would be devastated if she gave too much away. What was happening to his wife was eating him alive. He didn't want Aunt Vera exposed to criticism or ridicule. "She, um, sleepwalks. Sometimes."

"Sometimes? How often?"

More and more lately. "Some. I think that's what must have happened tonight. Uncle Franklin woke up and she wasn't there. I'm really hoping that she didn't go outside in this weather. Once we found her in the basement. Another time she'd, um, climbed up into the attic. He needs me to help look because his knees aren't very good and the stairs down to the basement and up to the attic are very steep."

He was frowning. "Doesn't she trip the alarm when she leaves the house?"

"Um." She took in a deep breath. "The house isn't alarmed."

"Jesus." The frown was deeper, deep grooves between his eyebrows. Heavens, even his eyebrows were gorgeous—thick, black, finely arched. God, how could he be so impossibly good-looking even while frowning and driving a billion miles an hour over ice? And how could she even notice it when she was terrified for Aunt Vera and, frankly, for herself, whizzing at insane speeds on icy roads?

That was when Charity realized how badly sex messed with her head. She was worried sick about Aunt Vera and terrified she was going to die in a car crash. And yet those thoughts faded for a second as she watched Nick's grim face in the space-age glow of the lights on the dashboard.

The dim glow highlighted his beautiful cheekbones, his strong jawline, the cords in his neck standing out from the tension of driving fast in impossible weather. He was so handsome her heart squeezed as she looked at him.

Even after rolling out of bed and into his clothes, he looked liked he could walk into a boardroom right now. Charity was sure she looked like she'd spent the night sleeping on the floor and that she had those fine worry lines only Uncle Franklin and Aunt Vera could call up.

"Two elderly people living alone in the middle of nowhere and they don't even have an alarm system?" Nick took his eyes off the road for a second to shoot her a glance. "That's not good, Charity."

No, it wasn't good. She'd asked Uncle Franklin a hundred times to put in burglar alarms, more for Aunt Vera than in anticipation of a nonexistent crime wave. Ferrington didn't run to burglars, but an alarm would act as a tripwire if Aunt Vera wandered.

Charity sighed. "Uncle Franklin keeps promising he'll put one in. But he doesn't get out much and he doesn't know much about alarm systems."

"I do." The muscles in Nick's jaw jumped again. "I— uh—invested in a security company and when I invest I do my homework, so I know a lot about them. Tomorrow a security system is going in. I'll order it and oversee the work myself."

Wow. "That—that's very kind of you." Charity blinked. This was entirely new territory not covered by any sex etiquette she knew of.

Casual lovers didn't take on this kind of responsibility. Certainly not for elderly relatives of a bedmate of three days' standing. It was incredibly generous of him. Not so much from the monetary point of view—he could clearly afford it—but from the perspective of time spent.

She had no idea how much wealthy businessmen earned by the hour but surely buying a security system, then overseeing its installation, would eat up thousands of dollars' worth of his time. If Uncle Franklin would accept, which he might not. "I'm not too sure, though, that Uncle Franklin would acce—turn left!" she said sharply.

Oh my God, she'd been so busy mooning over Nick and going over his offer she'd almost missed the turnoff. They would have lost precious time turning around.

Now that they were close to her aunt and uncle's house, Charity's heart started thumping. For the first time, she willed the car to go faster, even though it was impossible. Nick was making time as fast as any ambulance could. Faster.

She peered anxiously out the window. If anything, the snow had stepped up during the trip. Great white sheets fell out of the sky in increasingly fast waves. A sharp wind had risen, driving icy particles of sleet against the windshield.

Aunt Vera might well be somewhere in the huge house or outlying buildings. Or she might be out in this weather— alone and dazed.

Maybe dead.

Charity's throat swelled shut with unshed tears. She opened her mouth to say—*turn right*—but no words emerged. Her hand waved to the right and Nick understood. They took the corner into the driveway of Hedgewood, her aunt and uncle's home, Nick driving almost blind.

"Stop," she whispered. Though she could barely see the house as a dark shape in the swirling night, the sudden dip of the tires where the runoff from the gutters had etched a depression in the ground told her they'd reached the entrance. She swallowed heavily. "We're here."

Nick killed the engine instantly. "Stay put," he growled and before she could object, he'd opened his door and shot out. The door was only open a couple of seconds, but in that time, the warmth in the car dissipated in the icy wind. A second later, her door was opened and Nick was lifting her out bodily.

He had to because she froze the instant she was out of the car. It was instinctive—her body's unwillingness to face the extreme temperature. Ice particles bit into her cheeks and eyes. She lifted her arm to cover her face. Confused, she tried to figure out where the path to the front door was. It was impossible to make out any directions. The only possible bearings were up and down.

Something strong against her back propelled her forward, a force so impelling she couldn't resist. She was forced to scramble, her feet slipping on a patch of ice. Before she even had time to scream, she was picked up one-armed and rushed forward.

Nick practically carried her up the big marble steps to the entrance, her feet barely touching the steps.

Uncle Franklin must have been looking out for them because the big front door opened immediately.

"Charity! Oh my dear, you made it!" Uncle Franklin threw his arms around her, and she hugged him back, alarmed at how thin and fragile he felt. The fact that he wasn't impeccably and elegantly dressed scared her even more. Growing up, she'd never seen him en dishabille. He was such a natty dresser, always immaculately turned out, freshly shaved and barbered, smelling of a special eau de cologne he had made for him in England.

Now he was in his bathrobe, and white stubble marked his thin face. He smelled of fear and sour milk. As she hugged him, Charity could feel his thin limbs shaking.

She stepped back. "Uncle Franklin, this is a—a friend, Nick Ames. Nick, my uncle, Judge Franklin Prewitt." She needn't have bothered wondering how to explain showing up with a man after midnight. Uncle Franklin didn't even notice.

"Judge Franklin." Nick took his hand in a swift shake. "When did you last see your wife?"

Uncle Franklin blinked. For the first time in her life, Charity could see her uncle at a loss. He shook his head sharply, loose skin around his jowls flapping. Charity stepped in. "They usually go to bed around nine, nine thirty, don't you, Uncle Franklin?"

He nodded his head gratefully. "Yes." His voice was papery thin, shaky. "We went to bed a little after nine thirty. I woke up at eleven thirty. I was thirsty. I felt for Vera and she was—she was gone." He looked up at Nick, the strong young male in the room, as if at a savior. "Gone," he repeated.

"What was she wearing?"

The old man blinked at Nick's urgent tone. "Ah, a pink nightgown. Pink slippers."

"Okay." Nick nodded. "Did you check all the doors?"

Uncle Franklin looked blank. "No. No, I didn't think—"

Nick turned to her. "Charity," he ordered. "Show me all the doors leading to the outside. Fast. If she's gone out, she's in trouble. If she hasn't gone out, if she's still in the house, she'll be okay for a little while longer. So we have to eliminate the possibility that she's left the house."

Charity led him around the enormous house. He checked each door carefully, then they moved on. The French windows in Uncle Franklin's study were slightly open, the wind making the thick burgundy curtains sway gently.

Nick turned to her, face grim. "This is where she's gone out. Stay with your uncle. Make him drink some whiskey; he's in a state of mild shock."

Charity gasped with outrage. "I'm going with you! We have to search for her together. I know these grounds intimately and you don't. And anyway two people are better than one."

"No." Nick shook his head sharply. "In this case, two people are worse than one. You'll just slow me down. Trust me; I know what I'm doing. Your job is to look after your uncle. When I find your aunt, she'll be suffering from hypothermia. Whether mild or severe depends on how long she's been exposed. So I need you to make sure you have plenty of warm blankets on hand. Put a big pot of water on to boil. Make sure a cup of hot tea with sugar is ready."

She opened her mouth to argue and he clasped her shoulders hard in his big hands and shook her. "Blankets. Big pot of boiling water. Tea with sugar. And don't even think about coming with me. I don't want to have to end up chasing your pretty tail out there."

Before she could reply, he'd slipped out the door and was lost in the swirling storm.

Nick had learned to track from the best of the best. Colonel Lucius Merle had grown up in the Ozarks with a shotgun in his arms and five generations of Merle hunters behind him. Tracking was in his DNA. Oddly enough, the colonel had done most of his professional tracking in filthy urban streets and that was the lore he'd passed on to Nick, in Baghdad and in Basra, in Kabul and Kandahar, in Caracas and Cartagena.

Still, sign was sign.

Nick scanned the ground right outside the big French windows. They gave out onto a covered terrace, so the snow hadn't accumulated much. There were clear prints in snow half an inch lower than the surrounding grounds. Nick followed them as they angled sharply off to the left.

He wished he knew the terrain better. Damn! It hadn't occurred to him to scout out Charity's elderly relatives' home while he'd been studying her. He wished he had now. He wanted to find the old lady fast. Out of the house less than a minute, he was already cold and he was young, healthy, and conditioned. He didn't want to think of what was happening to a frail, elderly woman.

His heart had clenched watching Charity's uncle, shaking and defenseless, almost naked in his fear.

Got to him every time. Old people and kids. Adults can fend for themselves, life sucks, you embrace the suck and go on, but he had a real soft spot for geezers and ankle biters.

The wind bit at his heavy coat, icy fingers reaching inside. Jesus. It was fucking *freezing.*

For just an instant, Nick flashed back to the heat of being inside Charity. The soft, warm, wet feel of her. That warm back heating his entire front. And Jesus, his cock in her. Clamped tight, so hot it was like sticking his dick in a little oven. Just the memory sent a flash of heat over him and then it was gone.

Get your head out of your dick, Ireland, he told himself. *Now.*

The snow was easing up, thank God. Where before it had been almost a complete whiteout, now he could discern big dark shapes all around, punctuated by the feeble glow of lamps. At least the old geezer kept outdoor lights on. Local scumbags would simply assume that rich old folks would have an airtight security system to go with the security lights. Otherwise they would long since have broken in.

Nick didn't buy for a minute Charity's nonsense that this was a crime-free zone. There was no such thing as a crime-free zone. Where there were humans, there was robbery and murder and rape. That ancient couple living alone with no security was a burglary just waiting to happen. If not worse.

Nick had only spent a few minutes inside the house, talking to Charity and her uncle, but he could multitask and he was a good observer.

The Prewitts were loaded. Old money. With lots of expensive stuff, just begging to be carted away by dickwads who'd rather steal than work. Thick antique Persian carpets, real artwork on the walls, loads of antique silver. They were lucky to still be alive.

Nick followed the footsteps down from the terrace to the gardens below and for a second lost the trail. Fuck! She'd been out in this cold for at least an hour, probably more. With each passing minute her chances of surviving went way down.

Nick crouched, taking out the powerful Maglite he always kept in the car. It had a narrow intense beam, which he focused on the surface of the snow.

There! A slit in the snow, like a little valley. His jaws clenched. He knew what that long depression meant. It meant that a few steps outside the house, she was already shuffling. Probably already losing sensation in her feet.

This was not good.

Still crouching, holding the light at an oblique angle, he followed the depressions, the ground dipping beneath his feet. A big oak was ten feet to his right, a building that looked like a garage to his left. Another building was visible just beyond it.

For a horrifying moment, Nick lost her track, then noticed a pink puff of material hanging from a laurel shrub and next to it, another long depression. The tracks paralleled the thick shrubs that ended abruptly next to another large building. This one was made of glass, dimly lit from within. Nick could make out rows and rows of plants in terra-cotta vases.

A greenhouse. The orangery, Judge Prewitt's generation would have called it.

He followed the shallow depressions around the building, hoping they were going to lead to the greenhouse. Greenhouses were often heated. It was the one place an old lady could have a hope of surviving a snowstorm.

Nick opened the side door of the greenhouse, trying to make out shapes in the gloom. The temperature inside was at least thirty degrees warmer than the icy hell outside but it was still cold. He had to check this place out fast. If she wasn't here, her time would be running out.

Nick walked fast down the aisles, exactly as if clearing a room during combat, checking in a grid. Five minutes later, he was back at the door, teeth clenched. The old lady wasn't here. It was entirely possible she was already dead. Charity would be devastated.

He stood with his hand on the door, still and silent. He had to move fast but something stopped him. A hunch. He trusted his hunches. They'd saved his life more than once. *Something . . .*

He stopped breathing for almost a full minute. The sound of air in his lungs was distracting him.

There was something . . . again! A—a snuffling sound. At two o'clock.

Nick headed for the sound at a run, heavy boots pounding, the echoes loud in the large space. And there she was, curled up behind some gunnysacks. He saw one long, bony white foot attached to a pink slipper.

The animal in her had found the one place she could survive outside her home. In the northeastern corner was a pile of fertilizer sacks and empty gunnysacks. She'd nestled in them, and they had saved her life.

Nick lifted a sack. There she was, huddled in on herself, rail thin and bony. Once beautiful, now ravaged, shaking with cold, lost and forlorn. But for all that, alive.

She turned her head, pale blue eyes blank and rheumy.

"Frank-lin?" She blinked rapidly, mouth trembling. "Franklin, I want to go home. Take me home. I'm cold."

Nick crouched next to her. She reached out a hand and touched his face. Her hand was thin, long-fingered, the skin crepey and mottled. She was shaking as she laid the flat of her hand against his cheek.

"Franklin," she sighed, a tear falling down her wrinkled cheek. "Home."

Nick's chest felt tight. "Yes, Franklin," he said softly, sliding his arms out of his coat and wrapping it around her. "I've got you now." He lifted her as easily as if she were a child and strode to the door. "I've come to take you home."

Ten

Charity would never forget the sight till the end of her days. She'd pulled back the living room curtains and turned on the porch light before setting herself to reassuring Uncle Franklin.

He was aging so fast. His skin hung from his jaws with the weight he'd lost in the week since she'd last seen him and he was paper white. The bone structure beneath was easily visible. Any more weight loss and his head would resemble a skull. He ran a bony hand over his face and she could hear the rasp of his white beard stubble. "What's taking him so long?"

Charity took his hand and winced at the tremor. "It's only been about ten minutes since he's gone out, Uncle Franklin, even though it feels like more," she said gently. "Don't worry. Nick will find her."

At one level, the words were empty reassurance, but Charity was astounded to find that she meant it. How was that? How on earth could she be sure Nick knew what he was doing? She couldn't. And yet every instinct she had told her that she could trust him to find her aunt.

He was a businessman who led a soft life, making money in the city. There was nothing about him that suggested he'd grown up on a farm or hunted in some way. Most hunters, in her experience, tended toward the tedious about their guns. Nick had never once mentioned hunting or safaris or anything of the sort. What could an investment broker possibly know about tracking someone in the snow?

And yet, when he'd told her to stay put, she'd instinctively obeyed, instantly, though it went against common sense. She knew her aunt and the area around the big house, and he didn't. If she didn't have a bone-deep sense that if anyone could find Aunt Vera, it was him, she would never have stayed behind.

It had been an instant, a flash of something like steel. She'd met his serious, beautiful eyes, sensed the power he was keeping leashed while trying to convince her to stay put. And the moment she'd let him go out alone it was as if something had lit up inside him, as if she'd freed him somehow. Like a wild animal let out of a cage to do what it did best—hunt.

It was crazy, but it was true. There had been a blast of—something. Something almost frightening. Something potent. Primordial and utterly male. As if Nick had been infused with an otherworldly power and was only now letting it show.

She shook her head. Wow. Massive amounts of sex and lack of sleep were driving her crazy.

Still, she did what he said. A big pot of water was on the stove, almost at boiling point. Two mugs of tea with three teaspoons of sugar apiece were in the microwave, waiting to be nuked. A pile of blankets, a clean nightgown, and several towels were on a kitchen chair.

"Sit down, Uncle Franklin," Charity said gently. She guided her uncle to a chair, putting her hands lightly on his shoulders. He sat abruptly, as if she'd pushed. Or as if his legs wouldn't carry him any more.

Head bowed, he covered his eyes with his hand, weary and despairing. His voice was a whisper. "Look out the window, honey, and tell me if you see anything."

More to humor him than anything else, Charity walked to the kitchen window. All the outside lights were on, including the spotlight under the huge oak in the back garden. The snowstorm had left almost a foot of snow on the lawn. It had spent itself in the last hour and was now slowly abating. A few minutes ago she could barely see the oak she'd spent her childhood climbing. Now the stark, bare, black branches stood out in the field of white.

"Well? Can you see something?"

Charity turned to her uncle, pained at the dejection in his voice. *Be cheery*, she told herself. The last thing he needed was to hear her own desperation.

"No," she said, injecting false confidence in her voice. "But I'm sure—"

She broke off, peering out the window. Could it be—oh God, *yes!*

The lawn sloped sharply down on this side of the house, so she saw his head first as he approached.

It was a sight she'd never forget, till the end of her days.

A coatless Nick, walking up the slope, with Aunt Vera wrapped up in his coat and clasped in his arms. The snow and dim light blurred perspective, so it looked like he was rising up from the bowels of the earth instead of walking up toward her. The snow was halfway up his shins but he moved forward easily—a warrior coming home from battle, carrying a wounded comrade in his arms.

Wounded, please God. Not dead.

Nick shifted Aunt Vera in his arms and Charity clearly saw her aunt tighten her arms around his neck.

She was *alive*!

Charity's breath left her lungs in a *whoosh* and her legs trembled. She shot out a hand and gripped the counter, otherwise she'd have simply tumbled to the floor. For the first time, she admitted to herself how terrified she'd been that they would find a corpse in the snow. Her eyes burned and she blinked to keep the tears at bay.

"There they are—" The words came out a dry croak, inaudible. She cleared her throat and coughed to try to ease the tightness and speak, but then it wasn't necessary. A sharp intake of breath behind her told her Uncle Franklin could see them outside the kitchen window.

Charity lost the battle with her tears and could feel the wet cold on her cheeks as she threw open the door, just as Nick reached the steps up to the porch.

In a second they were inside and Nick was barking orders.

"Get those wet things off her and wrap her in as many blankets as you can. Charity, bring that pan of water over to the table with a big towel."

Charity and Uncle Franklin scrambled to strip her aunt. Somehow, Nick was there, helping, while making sure he couldn't see Aunt Vera's naked body.

It was at that moment that Charity fell in love with him. As charmed as she'd been by him up to now, she'd managed to keep a little something of herself apart.

It was so over the top, having an outrageously handsome, incredibly rich man sweep her off her feet, and ply her with out-of-this-world sex. Deep in her heart, Charity knew that Nick was too good to be true.

What could she possibly hope for? He was passing through Parker's Ridge on business, his mind probably already on the next thing. Charity would be insane to think that their time together was anything more than a brief affair.

She'd had quite enough pain for one lifetime, thank you. Losing her parents at the age of twelve. Almost a year in the hospital with a broken body and all of her teens spent doing rehabilitative physical therapy so she could walk again. Oh yeah, she'd had quite enough pain. She hadn't suffered in love, because she hadn't given herself in any significant way.

Sex hadn't meant all that much up until now. Pleasant, comforting at times, a little boring at times. She'd always gotten out of bed the same person who'd tumbled in.

Sex with Nick was an order of magnitude stronger than anything she'd ever had. Mind blowing, frighteningly intense. She'd had to work to keep herself together, to keep the whole thing as casual as possible. Physically exciting, yes, but that was it.

And now, watching her lover walk into the kitchen with Aunt Vera in his arms, helping to disrobe her gently and discreetly, Charity felt a huge hole open up inside and all the little defenses she'd put up simply crack wide open.

Inside a couple of minutes, her aunt was cocooned in a thick bundle of blankets, drinking hot tea while Nick held a finger to the pulse of her other hand.

He met Charity's eyes. "Pulse is almost normal. Temperature is a little low, though. We need to raise her core temperature."

"How?" What more could they possibly do?

Nick put the big pot of boiling water on the table and took a towel in his hand. Gently, he positioned Aunt Vera so that she was breathing in the steam, then put the towel over her head like a cowl, directing the steam toward her. "Breathe deeply, ma'am."

To Charity's relief, her aunt did just that. By some miracle, the clouds in Aunt Vera's head parted and some meaning shone through. It was erratic. You never knew when she'd understand you and if she did understand, whether she'd respond.

But perhaps something in Nick's tone penetrated what was dulling her mind because the deep breaths she was taking were audible under the towel.

"That's right, ma'am," Nick said reassuringly. "Just keep breathing."

In all of this, Uncle Franklin sat, spent and passive, head bowed. Exhausted and frail.

"Why does she need this?" Charity asked.

"Core rewarming by inhalation. Sends heat directly to the head, neck, and chest area, which is the body's critical core. It warms the lungs and the hypothalamus, which regulates the body's temperature. She'll need to do this for at least ten minutes."

Nick sat back down next to her aunt and kept a finger on her pulse. Charity walked to her uncle and put a reassuring hand on his shoulder. The bones beneath her hand felt fragile, like bird bones. She leaned down to whisper to him. "She'll be all right, Uncle Franklin."

He looked up and forced a smile. It occurred to Charity that now she had Uncle Franklin to worry about, not just Aunt Vera. He'd been such a rock for her, all her life, especially after her parents' death. He wasn't a rock now. Now he was a tired, anxious old man who was barely keeping it together.

Okay. Time for her to step up to bat. She shifted mental furniture and included caring almost full-time for elderly relatives into the parameters of her life.

It was daunting. She was only twenty-eight and had hardly begun to live. She hadn't traveled at all as much as she'd like to and now knew that she never would, as long as Aunt Vera and Uncle Franklin were alive.

If her love life had been difficult before, now it would be impossible, since her priorities would be wrapped up in caregiving. What man would put up with that? Once Nick left, she could kiss even a semblance of a love life good-bye.

She nearly sighed at the thought.

When she looked up, Nick caught her eye and winked.

Then again, for now she did have Nick. He'd leave, but he wasn't leaving right this minute, and so there might be a little more of that spectacular sex in her immediate future. Oh yeah.

Twenty kilometers south of Budva
Coastline of Montenegro
5 a.m. November 21

She was a rusty freighter flying the flag of the Union of Comoros, stinking of rotting fish and cabbage. The *North Star* was just one of the hundreds of thousands of vessels making a marginal living by trawling in overfished waters, destined to be decommissioned by her owners as soon as she cost more to run than she earned by her catch.

No one paid any attention to her at all, in a world of huge, sleek container vessels making 20 knots an hour.

She lay quietly at anchor in a deserted cove, rocking gently on the calm Adriatic. It was the darkest moment of night, just before dawn began. American satellites had excellent tracking abilities but night maneuvers eluded them. So the transfer from the truck to the boat was made in the dark. The crew seemed to have a supernatural ability to see in the dark, for they didn't need flashlights as they went their quiet, efficient way. There was a half moon and that seemed to be enough.

After twenty-four hours in the back of the truck over pitted back roads, Arkady was stiff and a little disoriented. He tripped twice, once emerging from the back of the truck and once on the gangway up onto the ship.

He felt a thousand years old, particularly in front of the crew, who were all young and strong. The four crewmen who preceded him made their way back onto the ship like agile monkeys.

Below, on the rocky shore, hired hands manipulated the canisters from the truck, ready for boarding on the rusty fishing boat.

No one would look twice at the *North Star*, which was a good thing. Because beneath the rotting boards of the deck lay a gleaming, stainless-steel heart driven by a Wärtsilä-Sulzer RTA96-C turbocharged two-stroke diesel engine and a new retrofitted hold designed for the transport of humans.

The human cargo wasn't meant to be transported in comfort but in safety, to be delivered alive at the port of destination. They were goods, after all, and worth money at the end of the journey. So there were toilets and spigots to hose them down at the end, before delivery.

The hold was designed to carry 150 passengers. Its last cargo had been 200 Senegalese who'd boarded north of Kayar and been locked in for two weeks. The man responsible for stocking food had run off with the money and the men had been on starvation rations for the trip. Two had boarded with tuberculosis. Only eighty survived.

The Vor's stipulations had been clear. The hold had been completely cleaned and disinfected. Arkady could smell disinfectant over the smells of the food on a small table.

A simple meal. Local sausage, goat's cheese, bread with a bottle of Vranac wine and *rakija*, the Montenegrin brandy. The Vor had thought of everything.

A space built to hold 150 people was more than roomy enough for one lone nuclear scientist.

Two seamen silently brought in the canister and started fixing it to special brackets in the wall. They spoke quietly to each other as they worked. Arkady recognized a few words from the many operas he'd listened to.

They were speaking Italian, though not the Italian of Verdi. It was a rough dialect of Italian, probably Pugliese, the language of the Sacra Corona Unita, the local mafia of the area right across the straits, Apulia.

The Vor had been making strategic alliances all over the world. Indeed, right now, he probably had diplomatic relations with every criminal group on earth—like a potentate—which was what he was—with embassies spanning the globe. Vassily was the new Tamburlaine. On his way to becoming the most powerful man on earth. It was Arkady's duty and pleasure to help the Vor to this position.

The two seamen departed and Arkady went back above deck. He walked to the railing and stood for a moment. The familiar scent of pine overrode the unfamiliar scent of the sea. He'd only seen the sea once before in his life, on a family trip to Crimea. That was before his father was taken away and destroyed in a Siberian camp. They never found out which one. Arkady had no idea where his father's remains lay.

Arkady was second-generation zek. There were some families who had lost a member every generation since the Revolution.

He pulled in a deep breath, savoring the night air, before closing himself again down below. He knew the trip would take around a week and this would be his last chance to see the stars and smell the sweetness of fresh air for a while.

He pulled out the blue cell phone, punched a number in, and waited. There was a delay as he imagined the signal bouncing off a satellite and down to a small town in Vermont.

"Hello." Arkady's heart leaped at the sound of Vassily's voice. It was as strong as ever, even though it was three o'clock in the morning, Vor time. His master was well, but not sleeping.

No zek ever slept easy. The memories came with sleep.

Though no one was listening, Arkady curled around the cell and lowered his voice. "It's me. So far so good. Things are going well. The sea is calm."

"Good. Very good." And Vassily cut the connection.

Arkady smiled and leaned over the railing. The moon left a bright path to the horizon. Just a few short miles away was Italy. He'd never been to Italy but he loved art and music and had always dreamed of seeing Florence and Venice.

There were still 100 canisters of cesium 137 left back in Krasnoyarsk and Vassily had plans for every single one. For a total of a billion dollars. But after they were all gone, Arkady would ask the Vor's permission to spend time in Italy. Perhaps be the Vor's ambassador to the various mafias in the country.

He looked down. The Adriatic was completely calm. He dangled his hand over the railing and let go of the cell phone. A second later it disappeared into the sea with a soft *plop*.

Arkady watched the rings of disturbed water flow outward and then waited until the water was calm again.

With one last look at the starry night sky, he made his way below deck, ready for the long journey.

Eleven

The snow plows had already cleared the roads, so driving back was a snap, certainly compared to the trip over. But even if they hadn't cleared the roads, Nick could handle it. There was very little he couldn't handle behind a wheel.

It wasn't a skill he had ever intended to show Charity, but he'd had to break cover on the way over. It had saved the little old lady's life, but he just hoped that Charity's worry allowed her to overlook the fact that it wasn't normal for a perfectly average, staid stockbroker to know how to drive a car at eighty miles an hour in a snowstorm.

So he made a point of driving back very slowly, even though every cell in his body wanted to get back to her house as fast as possible so that he could get back in her as fast as possible.

"Thanks so much, Nick," she said quietly. He kept his eyes

on the road ahead. Not because of the danger, but because if he looked her way, he'd just keep on looking.

Not even he could drive down icy roads with his head turned to stare at the most desirable woman he'd ever seen. It was bad enough driving with a huge boner so strong the muscles in his abdomen and the long muscles in his thighs were pulled tight. It seemed as if every muscle in his body was centered around his groin. All his blood, too.

They'd end up with the front fender wrapped around a tree, covered in shards of glass, if he stared the way he wanted to. Not how he wanted this evening to end up. *Well, not evening,* he thought after a lightning fast glance at the dashboard. It was three in the morning and the weekend was officially over.

"You're welcome." He kept his voice as quiet as hers.

"I'm so grateful to you. I don't know how I can ever repay you."

"Yeah?" Nick's hands tightened on the wheel. "That's nice to know. Really nice. So, since we're on that subject . . . how grateful?"

"I beg your pardon?" Nick could feel the air displacement as she swung her head around to look at him. He kept his eyes resolutely on the road but he had excellent peripheral vision. Her pretty pink mouth was pursed in an O of astonishment.

"You heard me. How grateful are you?"

"Oh. V-very."

"That's good. Because we were interrupted at a very important point when your uncle called. You remember what point we were at, don't you, Charity?"

He could almost feel the heat of her face, glowing in the darkness. "Oh yes," she said softly.

"That's good. What point were we at?"

The heat intensified. Great. He was burning up, himself. It's good that they were in this together.

"We were, um—"

"Yes?"

"We were—you know . . ."

Her whole body was glowing with heat now. It came off her in waves. Nick didn't know why he was pushing her. She was wildly uncomfortable with this conversation. Hot as she was in bed, she was also very ladylike. He'd never heard her swear, ever, let alone say *fuck*. So this wasn't easy for her.

Tough shit. It wasn't easy for him, either. Besides being hard as a pike, his skin felt way too tight for his body, his blood felt hot and thick in his veins. It was a pity he knew a lot about hypothermia, because every instinct he had was telling him to pull over, stop the car, pull Charity's pants down, drag her into the backseat and mount her.

Pick up where they left off.

Oh yeah. A second after entering her, he'd be fucking her like a wild man. Nick was really good at visualizing. All soldiers were. You went through the steps of a mission, one by one, visualizing success like crazy. It was the only way to deal with walking into danger. So he could see in his mind's eye exactly how it would be. Charity, lying in the backseat, long slender legs wrapped around him and him on top of her, fucking away so hard even the heavy Lexus would rock with his thrusts.

Unfortunately, he could also see how dangerous it would be. Once he was in her, he'd be oblivious to everything else. If another dense snow flurry came and buried the car, he might find it hard to get it going. If they were stuck, he'd have to turn the engine on to keep the heater going. He was a little low on gas and once the gas ran out, they could be stuck in a freezing car, waiting for a break in the storm.

Charity could die.

The thought kept him from pulling over, but it didn't cool his blood.

He'd been a good boy. He'd let her pull away while they were fucking, he'd come to the rescue and he'd saved the aunt.

It was payback time.

"We were what?" he prodded.

"We were in the middle of . . . making love." Her voice was small.

His knuckles tightened on the steering wheel. "That's right. We were right in the middle of making love. We were getting it on just fine, until we were interrupted. And that's about all I can think about right now. Picking up where we left off. I'd give my right nut to pull over and get back in you, but the weather's too severe for that. So I'll have to wait. But the instant we walk through your door, I'm going to be inside you one second later. And I want you ready."

A little indrawn breath. "Ready how?"

His jaws clenched. "I think you know. But if not, let me spell it out for you. I want you all wet for me. I want that luscious little cunt all soft and warm and wet for me." His voice was harsh, hoarse. The crude language came naturally, as a direct expression of his deepest desires. Something of his desire had communicated itself to her because he could hear her breathing speed up in the quiet darkness of the car. "I want all that before we arrive. Because I'm sure as hell not going to have time for foreplay once we get there."

"O-okay," she breathed.

Nick shifted in his seat, eyes resolutely ahead. On the way

over, he'd been in total control of himself and the car. Short of an RPG hitting the Lexus, they wouldn't have had an accident. Right now, he didn't feel in control of anything, least of all his cock. An accident was perfectly possible, except it really wasn't.

Even far gone in the throes of red-hot lust, he was master of the car. He was always master of the car. It was such a deeply inbred skill, it was as if it were in his bones, as if he'd been born with it. He'd once driven from Kandahar to Kabul after catching the tail end of an IED that had blown up the car in front of him. He'd been concussed, had lost his hearing in one ear, and was bleeding like a stuck pig over his left eye from a piece of shrapnel that had sliced across his forehead like a scalpel. The road was pockmarked with big holes left by previous IEDs, they came under fire twice, and through all that he'd driven his team to safety as if they'd been on the German Autobahn.

So, yes, he had a blue steeler and it almost fucking hurt when he moved to shift gears, most of his mind was taken up with the beautiful woman in the seat next to him, but it didn't make any difference. Even if he had only two neurons left in his head, they were enough to drive with. His muscles could manage alone, without guidance from his head.

"Take your pants off. And then your panties."

The swish of her hair on her shoulders as her head swivelled toward him was audible. "What?" she breathed.

"You heard me." Jesus, even his throat muscles were tight. He could barely get the words out. His voice came out harsh and guttural. "I want your pants and panties off. And while we're at it, take off your bra under your sweater. You can keep the sweater on." It was a tough concession, but having her pretty white breasts bared might just be too much for him. He had a lot of self-control, it was true. But shit, there was a limit to everything. "Pants, panties off. Bra. Off."

He reached down and turned her heater on high. He wanted her turned on, warm and receptive. He didn't want her blue with cold and goose bumps.

It was silent in the car for long moments. Nick flexed his fingers on the wheel and kept his gaze resolutely on the road.

"I—I'll need to take my seat belt off."

His jaws clenched as he slowed the car down to a crawl. "Do it."

She unbuckled the seat belt, holding it over her body, hesitating.

Finally, she moved and ah, yes. There were the lovely little sounds of a woman disrobing, so different from men. A woman taking her clothes off was a miracle of nature.

Nick remembered all too well what it was like living in barracks. He and his teammates would come in from a fifteen-mile run, sweaty and smelling like goats. They'd strip down, swearing a blue streak, weapons and flak jackets and combat boots clunking heavily to the floor. Followed by the sound of twelve hairy paws scratching twenty-two hairy balls.

How did women do it? How did they make such cute, soft sounds? Everything so delicate and tender.

Nick could follow what was going on by sound alone. The little rip of the pants zipper going down. The seat creaking slightly as she lifted to slide her pants down to her thighs. The silky sound of her pants sliding off. Neat as always, she folded her pants carefully along the seam and put them down in the footwell.

"Stockings." The word came out through what felt like a boulder in his throat. "Panties."

Oh yes. Even more delightful sounds. The small *thud* of her boots coming off. The whisper of nylon-clad legs rubbing against each other as she slipped her stockings off.

Almost there. He felt a drop of sweat fall down his temple and plop onto his sweater. It was hot in the car after he'd turned up the heat, but even if it had been freezing, he'd have sweated at the thought of Charity almost naked.

She lifted again and he saw a scrap of pale yellow silk flowing down her body. Oh yeah.

"Take your bra off under your sweater."

"Okay." He heard her swallow. She was trembling but she was also excited. He could smell it. Over the leather of the seats and Charity's perfume was the scent of her arousal. He'd recognize it anywhere. She was turned on.

Damned right. She had to be because he was going to start fucking her hard just as soon as they were in a place where he physically could without driving them both into a tree.

Charity reached up between her breasts under her sweater and in a few graceful moves had removed her bra, the same pale yellow silk as her panties. It joined the rest of her clothes in the footwell.

Nick would have given anything to make her take her sweater off. He loved her breasts, so pale and soft, with the pale pink nipples that turned cherry red when she was turned on. He'd take money on a bet that they were cherry red now. But he didn't want her to catch cold, and he didn't know if he could keep his eyes on the road with her bare breasts inches from him, so against his will, he let her keep the sweater on.

A second into her warm house it was coming off, though.

They were crawling slowly. Now that she'd taken most of her clothes off, they needed to make better time. "Put your seat belt back on." As soon as he heard the little click, he pressed the accelerator. They had another quarter of an hour before they got to Charity's house. He had fifteen minutes to get her ready. Or rather, she had fifteen minutes to get herself ready.

His jaw clenched, back teeth biting together. In his peripheral vision he could see the long elegant line of her legs gleaming palely against the black leather seat, a pale puff of hair between her thighs.

Charity naked was a wet dream. Fully clothed, she was the classiest lady he'd ever seen. With her clothes off, she became sex on a stick. Classy sex on a stick. The most erotic thing he'd ever seen.

"Tell me what you're feeling."

She let out a little breath. "All right." She shifted slightly, arousal and her perfume billowing out with each slight movement. Nick's hands tightened again on the wheel, slippery with sweat. "What I'm feeling. *Whew.* Well, um, the seat was shockingly cold at first but now it's warming up. I feel—I feel the heat from the vents on my bare skin. I've never felt that before in a car. I mean, against my—my intimate parts."

"Open your legs," he said harshly. "Position the vent so that you have warm air directly on your pussy."

Another little huff of breath, and hesitation. Not reluctance, he could feel it. Just surprise.

He was a little surprised himself, at how hard he was pushing her. It was like he had a fever, an itch he couldn't scratch, just under his skin.

It was post-op horniness, he suddenly realized.

Oh my God.

He always had a hard-on that wouldn't quit at the end of an op. All that adrenaline had to go somewhere and it always ended up in his dick. It was a kind of horniness that he could rarely fuck away, too, much as he tried. The women he found after an op, particularly if there had been a firefight, were used hard. He went at it for hours.

He hadn't been on an op but he'd definitely been on a mission. There hadn't been danger to him, but there had been to the old lady, like a wounded teammate who needed rescuing. He'd been super-charged while looking for her, he realized with hindsight. Every sense sharpened, heightened, totally focused like a laser beam on finding her and bringing her back to safety.

So he'd had an adrenalin dump and it was working its way out of his system through his dick. That explained the steel hard-on and his total inability to even contemplate foreplay or anything other than ripping Charity's clothes off and entering her just as soon as it was safe to do so.

What it *didn't* explain was that this time, it wasn't just any woman who'd do. Oh no.

Usually, all he needed was someone reasonably attractive with the correct human number of limbs and female plumbing. He usually kept his eyes closed during sex, anyway. As long as she was wet enough, he didn't care who it was.

This time, only Charity would do. No one else.

Fuck. For just a second, Nick tried to visualize getting rid of his hard-on with another woman and for the first time in his life, Generic Woman wasn't enough. He put a couple of women he'd fucked, and whose faces he could recall, in his imaginary bed and his hard-on actually went down a little.

Nope. Just any woman wouldn't do.

This was serious shit. He'd have to think about it. Later. When some blood had returned to his head.

Right now, he had to make sure that when he got Charity home, she'd be able to take him.

"Touch me," he ordered. "Put your hand on my cock. Feel what you do to me." Thank God he hated driving in a coat. There was only his jeans and briefs between her hand and his hard-on.

Charity reached out hesitatingly, then lay her hand on his crotch. His cock immediately lengthened as a surge of blood went through it at her touch. Her hand jerked in surprise. It must have felt as if he had a landed trout in his pants. They were on a broad avenue and he spared a second to look down at himself.

Her pale hand gleamed in the faint light coming from the digital readouts. After her initial surprise, she'd put her hand back on him, cupping her palm around him. He could feel the heat of her hand through the two layers of cloth. His cock and her hand started doing a little dance. She'd squeeze lightly, his cock would respond enthusiastically, which made her squeeze him again, while he surged against her.

It was torture. Why was he doing this to himself? Nick wasn't big on teasing self-denial, but if this was all he could get, well, he'd take it.

He had to concentrate fiercely on the road and worked to keep his breathing even. She was driving him crazy, yet he'd kill himself if she stopped touching him.

"Touch yourself." Her eyes turned big. "Touch yourself," he repeated grimly. "With your other hand. Open your legs and touch yourself." In his peripheral vision, he watched as her right hand hesitated over her thighs. Then, slowly, her thighs opened and she reached between them with her forefinger, running it along the slit.

God, he remembered doing that himself, sliding his finger along the silky opening, tender and fascinating, puffy and pale pink. Like a little flesh flower.

"Are you wet?" They were passing the McBain mansion, a huge, decaying Victorian monstrosity surrounded by woods that just cried out for a crazed writer with a pickax. It meant that they were just a few minutes from her house. "Please tell me that you're wet, because otherwise I'll shoot myself."

Charity gave a little snorting laugh. "No, you're okay. You'll live a little longer. I'm wet, though . . . ," she paused delicately, "not quite as wet as you make me." Her fingers tightened around his cock.

The muscles in his thighs pulled, hard, and a line of fire raced down his spine. For a shocked second, he thought he would come in her hand. He managed to pull back from the brink, shaking, jaws clenched.

Charity ran her hand up him once, then back down. "Wow." He could see her looking at him. "Something almost happened there."

Nick's jaws clenched. "Yeah." He chanced a glance at her. They were almost home. "You little witch."

He saw the beginning of her smile before concentrating again on the road. "That better have excited you."

"Oh, it did," she assured him softly. Her thighs opened wider and he could actually hear the wet sounds as she pushed her finger inside her, then pulled it slowly out. "I am very . . . ready."

Nick had one big punch to his system as he started the free fall to orgasm. No! Not here, not now. Again, he had to use all his self-control to pull himself back.

They were there. He drove up the driveway, killing the engine just as the front fender of the Lexus kissed the garage door. He turned to look at her, wincing. Every movement fucking hurt. "Pull on your pants and shoes. Leave your underwear here. Get your key ready, too."

She was fast, he had to give her that. By the time he made it to her door, she had her pants, shoes, and coat on. Panties, bra, and stockings were a pale, silky gleam on the floor of the footwell.

Charity lifted up her arms to him, in utter trust, a mysterious half smile on her face. "I'm looking forward to this," she whispered, once she was in his arms, where she belonged.

"Not as much as I am." Nick smiled down at her. His hard-on still hurt, but for just a second, he was able to forget it. She felt so light and soft and . . . and *right* in his arms. His cock was squeezed tight inside his jeans but something was squeezing him in the chest area, too.

His senses were heightened. The pine trees of the forest surrounding her house gave off a heady, resinlike scent that mixed with the steely smell of snow and whiff of gas coming off the hot hood. Above all those, her scent, Charity's scent, rose like a grace note.

He could see so clearly, it was as if he had on night vision goggles. The faint light given off by the streetlamp a hundred yards away and Charity's pitifully weak porch light were enough for him to take in everything. He could have taken a sniper shot.

And his skin—Jesus. His skin felt supercharged, one huge erogenous zone from the top of his head to his toes. Each stray snowflake felt like a little pebble pinging against him. All the textures of his clothes and hers, the light wind that felt like a gale—everything was heightened.

He made it up the walkway and the stairs as fast as he could without slipping on the ice and breaking both their necks. A second later they were inside the door and a second after that, he had her up against the door, both hands plunged into her hair, cradling her skull, kissing her wildly.

His hand went to his pants and he freed himself

She lifted herself up on tiptoe so she could cradle his hard-on and it brought about a second's relief. Not enough, but Christ, it was better rubbing himself against her softness than against his jeans.

He left her mouth for the second it took to whip her sweater up and off, missing her fiercely, moaning as he took her mouth again.

He had another second to get her naked and to get himself suited up. He couldn't do both in a second.

"Take your pants off," he whispered against her mouth, stepping back. "Fast."

He pulled a rubber out of his pocket and donned it, wincing at the feel of his hand smoothing the condom over himself. He felt ready to explode.

She held his eyes as she unzipped her pants. They slid to her ankles. She toed her boots off, tugged the pants past her feet and tossed them into the room somewhere.

Before they landed, Nick had pressed against her, lifting her and stepping between her legs. She opened for him, an instinctive gesture of welcome and his cock brushed against her soft pubic hair. He gritted his teeth.

He was completely dressed except for his dick hanging out and she was utterly naked. He didn't need arousing, it felt like steam was coming off him as it was, but the sight of her naked body against him shattered what little control he'd still had.

Nick's hands cupped her bottom, lifting her up, and he slammed into her, hard and fast. She took him. He shook, letting his forehead droop onto her shoulder. She could take him. Thank God. She'd done her own foreplay and this was going to work.

He was breathing hard, lungs bellowing, trembling, trying to hold on to his control. She clasped him like a warm, wet fist. He needed to wait just a second before fucking, make sure she was used to him.

Charity's head was tilted back against the door, long slender neck exposed. Again, Nick wished he were a vampire. He got vampires, totally. Understood precisely what made them tick. That neck was a bite magnet, positively *made* for biting.

He shifted his head, brought his lips to her throat, licked her, then bit her. A delicate but hard nip. Right over where her heartbeat pulsed.

Charity jolted, gasping. At the same time, her cunt clenched around him, from root to tip, tight and hot. His entire body clenched back and he lost control.

Keeping his mouth to her throat he started pounding in her, holding her up and keeping her legs spread with his hands, the entire world reduced to his mouth on her throat and his cock in her, completely open to him. Her back thumped against the wooden door. Too hard. He was being too hard on her but he couldn't stop himself, it felt like he'd been waiting for this forever, like a dam that had just burst.

He had no idea if he could stop if she asked him to, his body had taken over entirely, trying very hard to pump as deeply into her body as it was possible to go. As if he were trying to punch a hole to her heart with his dick.

It was too much, too intense. His heart raced, sweat poured down his back, he picked up the pace for a wild second, cock swelling inside her and then he erupted, coming wildly, in huge waves, shuddering and moaning.

Was she—yes!

With a wild cry, Charity started coming, the small contractions milking him tightly, drawing his climax out. Damn, he'd give anything not to have a rubber on. To spill into her warm, welcoming body instead of into latex, feel every inch of her, as he had yesterday.

One last, hard thrust and it was over. He leaned heavily against her, panting, knees so weak he had to stiffen them.

Slowly his senses returned. He could hear his own heavy breathing in the quiet of the room.

He winced. His fingers were clutching the soft cheeks of her ass so hard he was bound to leave bruises. He loosened his fingers, one by one. It was surprisingly hard to do.

He was leaning against her so hard, he was keeping her up against the wall by his weight alone. He stepped back a fraction and allowed her to slip down until her feet touched the ground.

He also allowed himself to slip out of her. He didn't want it, but it had to be done. She'd be sore, and the rubber would start leaking soon.

He also found when he lifted his head that he'd been sucking on her neck so hard while coming he'd left a hickey.

He should be ashamed. He should. But he wasn't. It looked just fine on her neck, like a little brand left by him. Like a little message to the world.

Mine.

Twelve

Late Monday morning, Nick rapped his knuckles on the steel
door of the van.

He was in a foul mood. He'd spent the past three hours
overseeing the company that put in a top-of-the-line security system at the Prewitt mansion. The company was a good
one, but the salesman had tried to snow the elderly, confused
judge with unnecessary bells and whistles.

It made him so goddamned *angry*. The instant a human becomes weak, the wolves come out to prey. He remembered
reading in a book a Roman saying—man is wolf to man. Well,
that just about summed up humankind.

It got to him, every fucking time, how the strong preyed
on the weak. Jake would have died in the orphanage,
either from the beatings or sheer neglect, if he hadn't been
there.

Nick made it his life work to stand between the weak, the young, and the old and that section of humankind that was born without a heart. That saw other humans the way the butcher sees the pig. Useful, but only when slaughtered.

He'd fought them in Iraq, in Afghanistan, in Indonesia. And now he was fighting them here at home. These aliens in human bodies.

But no matter how hard he fought, no matter how many he took down, there were always more and more and more of them. The supply never ended.

Nick was so familiar with the type he could smell it—the alien who would cut you up for parts as soon as look at you.

Nick could actually watch the thought processes of the slick company salesman who drove out with the workmen. Maybe he was from the area and knew the family name. Or maybe he recognized the address. Whatever, he spent an entire morning tagging along, just for a shot at the judge, alone.

Nick came back into the house to see old Judge Prewitt with a pen in his mottled, shaking hand, about to sign an inch-thick sheaf of papers. And scumbag watching over him, greed and anticipation on his plump, vicious face.

Five minutes later, the fuckhead was scurrying out the door, red faced and empty-handed.

So Nick was in a piss-poor mood by the time he made it out of town to the surveillance van. Not to mention that he was already missing Charity, which was a first. Iceman never missed anyone, ever.

Di Stefano opened the back door of the van and beckoned him in. The instant Nick stepped in, he was assailed by the smell of male sweat, dirty laundry, stale pizza, and farts. One deep breath and he was choking.

Three days in Charity's company and already he was spoiled.

"Jesus." He batted the air in front of him. "What the *hell* do you guys eat all day, beans? It's enough to make a man pass out. We don't need weapons. We should get Worontzoff's goons out here and gas 'em."

Alexei was, as usual, sitting on a chair, hunched forward, those huge, heavy earphones on his head. He lifted a hand in greeting, then bent his head again in concentration.

"Wow, listen to the gentleman here. *Lah-di-da*. Excuuuuuse us." Di Stefano rolled his eyes. "Not all of us are playing the part of billionaire businessmen, Iceman. Some of us are actually working. We've been here all weekend, haven't left the van once. So get off my case."

"Don't give me that shit. I've been on the clock, too. All weekend."

"Oh yeah?" Di Stefano gave him a sideways glance. "I'll just bet. I saw the photos. Real hardship duty. So, tell me," he said casually, picking up his can of diet Coke, "she's such a pretty little thing. How is she in the sack? I'll bet—"

Di Stefano didn't get a chance to say anything else because he was slammed up against the van's bulkhead with Nick's arm across his windpipe, pressing hard, the can of Coke rolling, forgotten, on the floor of the van.

"Jesus, Iceman!" Alexei scrambled to Nick's side and starting pulling uselessly at his arm. "Let go, you'll kill him. Let go, man! What the fuck are you thinking?"

He wasn't thinking. Nick didn't have any thoughts in his head at all, only a bright red storm of rage, drowning out everything else.

Di Stefano was turning purple, arms flailing, trying to club Nick on the side of the head, trying to kick him away. Di Stefano had been trained in self-defense—he was a cop, after all—but he had nothing like Nick's training. Nick had spent ten years being trained by the best to kill.

Ordinarily, Di Stefano would be dead. Nick knew precisely how to do it. Colonel Merle had spent a whole month on chokeholds and Nick was an expert. Smash the hyoid bone and in a second the adversary goes down like a felled bull.

But something was starting to penetrate, past the wall of staticky noise in his head. Alexei's voice. It was only the voice that stopped him. Alexei had no muscles at all, and though he was pulling at Nick's arm, he could just as well have been patting him.

Nick stared into Di Stefano's bulging eyes and loosened his hold. Half a second later, he stepped back, dropping his arm.

Di Stefano fell to his knees, head hanging, wheezing to get air into his suffering lungs. "You. Miserable. Fuck," he gasped, getting a word out every ten seconds. He rubbed his neck, red and raw looking.

Nick sat in one of the two chairs in the van, then bounced right back up again, as if the dingy off-white plastic chair had pneumatic springs. He couldn't sit, he was too wound up. Even his breathing was speeded up.

Jesus.

He was buzzing with nervous energy and had to force himself to stand still.

It wasn't like him. They called him Iceman not because he didn't have emotions. He had them, in spades. It's just that he'd honed his self-control since he was two years old and realized that fighting back against an eight-year-old was suicide. He could always put aside the inner man on the job.

Clocking Di Stefano was just insane. He could hardly believe he'd done it. He felt ashamed. Sort of. Except that if Di Stefano made another suggestive comment about Charity, he'd put him in a chokehold again, which probably meant that he wasn't *that* sorry.

Di Stefano was standing now, glaring at him, rubbing his neck angrily. "What the fuck was that about?"

Nick looked him straight in the eye. Di Stefano was a teammate. In the army, you defended your teammates with your life, whether you liked them or not. Nick liked Di Stefano, a lot. It's just that he had to learn what the new rule was.

"Here's the way it works. From this moment on, Charity Ames is eighty years old, with four chins and warts. You never mention sex and her name in the same sentence, ever again. She is officially sexless. I hope that's clear." He turned to Alexei. "That includes you."

Wide-eyed, Alexei mimed zipping his mouth shut. Nick speared Di Stefano with a hard gaze. "Clear?"

"Absolutely." Di Stefano shook his head, as if to clear it. "And I have a new rule, too. You ever pull that stunt again, and I'll take you down."

Nick bared his teeth. "You can try," he said softly.

Alexei stepped between them, hands up in a time-out gesture. "Hey guys, stop locking antlers. The smell of testosterone is overriding the farts. Let's just settle down—"

A faint buzz sounded from Alexei's headset and he dived for the console, switching on the sound from the speakers. It was the phone, ringing. Worontzoff picked up on the second ring.

"Hello." His voice was deep and calm.

"Hello, Vassily. How are you?" Charity. Charity was calling the motherfucker. Nick froze, every cell in his body dedicated to listening to the call.

"I am fine, my dear. Did you have an enjoyable weekend?"

"Yes." Nick could almost feel her blush through twenty
miles of wire. "Yes, I did, actually. Um . . . a very nice weekend. Vassily, I was wondering . . ."

"Yes, my dear?"

"You know your musical soirée on Thursday?"

"Ah, the soirée. Samuel Cha on the cello. It will be exquisite. We arranged the playlist just the other day. And I asked
him to include Elgar's Cello Concerto in E minor, because I
know it's your favorite."

"Oh, Vassily—" Charity's voice turned warm and affection-
ate. Nick clenched his fists. It was the tone she used when
she whispered in his ear while he was in her. "You remembered! I do so love that concerto, thank you. I'm going to love
hearing Mr. Cha play it."

"My pleasure, my dear. It will be very enjoyable listening
to it with you."

"Yes, indeed. Speaking of which, um, Vassily . . ."

"Yes, my dear?"

Listening hard, Nick could detect an oily undertone, as if
Worontzoff knew what was coming. Like a villain in a movie
inviting the heroine into his den. *Yesssss, my dear?*

"Um, I know that you don't like to invite more than thirty
people to your soirées, Vassily—"

"Quite right. Too many people ruin the acoustics of the
room. Chamber music was composed exactly for that—for
chambers. Most chamber music was written in the seven-
teenth and eighteenth centuries for a court. Never for gen-

eral consumption. With a royal family and perhaps some courtiers in attendance, no more."

"Well, I'm certainly not royalty. But what I wanted to ask you was, may I bring a friend along? He's a busy man and I don't even know if he'd be free, but if he is, could I invite him? I wanted to ask you first before broaching it to him."

"A friend? You want to bring a friend? To my soirée?"

Could Charity hear the dead, frozen tone in Worontzoff's voice? Nick could. He heard the instant morph from avuncular intellectual to dangerous mobster. Every hair on Nick's body stood on end and his pulse raced. This was one of the most dangerous men on the planet and Charity had just angered him.

Shit, tell him to forget about it. Say it was just a silly thought. Come on, Charity, let it go. I'll find another way to get into that damned house. Just stay out of this guy's way and out of the way of his anger.

He bit his back teeth, hard. Looked at professionally, this was a stroke of good luck, in a job that had all too few of them. This is what he'd been angling for all along. What he'd engineered the meet with Charity for. Ostensibly, what he'd been fucking her for.

It was the job. Just the job. Getting into Scumbag Central.

Di Stefano high-fived Alexei, who was grinning. *Mission accomplished.* An elaborate ploy had paid off and a federal agent was just about to be introduced into the home of a suspected criminal.

"Vassily?" Charity's soft voice came through the speakers. Hearing her voice made him ache, as if he'd taken a punch to the chest. Thank God she'd sensed something, though she misunderstood the reason. "Will this be a problem? Do you have too many guests coming? Because I could renounce my invitation, if you can't fit everyone in."

"No, no, my dear. Of course that won't be necessary. I wouldn't dream of not having you. Your enjoyment makes my evening. Your friend is very welcome, if he can make it. I trust he enjoys classical music?"

A startled silence. Nick realized that Charity had no idea whether he liked music or whether he was tone deaf. It simply hadn't come up. Actually not much beyond his dick had come up over the weekend.

"Y-yes. Yes of course he does."

She was such a lousy liar.

"Well, then, my dear," Vassily said smoothly, "of course he can come. Any musical friend of yours is a friend of mine."

Not in this lifetime, scumbag.

"Thank you, Vassily. I'll see you on Thursday."

"Yes, my dear. I'm looking forward to welcoming you." Delicate pause. "Welcome you both." Worontzoff waited until she hung up, then punched a button to close the connection.

Silence. Then an explosion of sound, a two-syllable word.

Nick looked over at Alexei. "What was that?"

"*Pizdets,*" Alexei said.

"Thank you, Alexei," Di Stefano said, rolling his eyes. "So what does it mean?"

Alexei's eyes gleamed. "Fuck."

Charity put the library phone down thoughtfully, wondering whether she'd done a good thing or a bad thing.

Vassily hadn't sounded pleased. At all. She knew his voices and this was his I Am Not Amused voice. He lived in a large home, a mansion, actually, and what he termed the Music Room was large. But he'd told her he didn't want more than thirty people and he'd probably already invited as many people as he felt the room could comfortably hold. His soirées were catered and the caterers had probably already been told the exact number, as well.

Vassily was a charming man. He had enriched her life in so many ways, she couldn't even begin to count them. However, Charity also recognized that the man had a dark side, a granite hardness to him that she sometimes saw people tripping over unexpectedly, like a rocky outcropping in a meadow. Part of that dark side was that he didn't like being crossed, in any way.

She respected that, always. She'd inherited from her mother an ability to read people and from her father an ability to avoid antagonizing the difficult. Charity knew exactly when to keep her mouth shut, and she did.

With Vassily it was easier than with most people she dealt with and who tried her patience, like the mayor or old Mrs. Lawrence. However difficult he became, he had earned every wrinkle in his character, and he was entitled to that dark side of his.

Vassily never spoke of it, but his body spoke eloquently. His grotesquely scarred and shattered hands, with all the fingernails missing. A thin, deep scar running from his temple to his jawline, just missing his eye. An inability to lift his right arm higher than his chest. A limp that was exacerbated in the winter when it was damp. And when was it not damp in Vermont in winter?

Vassily was endlessly fascinating to everyone—he was, after all, one of the world's greatest writers. A man who would be lionized in any of the world's great cities, even though he had chosen, inexplicably, to bury himself in a small provincial town in Vermont.

No one could give him back his lost years and his ruined health, however. No matter how famous and rich he became, he had been through hell.

So Charity forgave Vassily everything—his moodiness, his harsh, granite core, his dark side. She had no right to judge him, and she didn't.

Maybe she shouldn't have asked if Nick could come with her. It appeared that it was a breach of Vassily etiquette. It's just that with each passing day, she was more and more certain that Nick would soon move on. How many business opportunities could there be, after all, in the Green Mountain State, for an investor? Smart as he was, he was surely running them all down to the ground. And once he'd finished, what was there to keep him here?

Charity had no illusions about the two of them, as a couple. There was nothing here to tie Nick down. He had money, looks, health. A bachelor pad in Manhattan. Potent male charm. Charisma. He was a superb lover.

The world was his oyster.

There was no reason whatsoever for him to stick here with a small-town librarian who led a quiet life and was responsible for two elderly, frail relatives who tethered her as much as—perhaps more than—two small children would have.

Charity's life was circumscribed, hemmed in on all sides. His was not. It was wide open.

So, he'd be going soon. He might even be gone by Thursday, and maybe she'd just humiliated herself in vain, asking Vassily for this favor for a man who wouldn't even be here.

It was just that the thought of an evening without Nick, even one of Vassily's musical soirées, which she ordinarily loved, was painful in the extreme. Which meant, of course, that she was in for a great deal of pain in the very near future.

Thirteen

She was thinking about him—mooning over him, really—
when all of a sudden, like magic, there he was.

Nick. *Her* Nick. Such a delicious thought, however much
she chided herself for it.

Her Nick.

He wasn't hers, or if he was, it was just temporary, but still.
It sounded so nice.

It had been a very slow day at the library. The snow had
stopped around noon but the sullen pewter sky promised
more, once the temperature dropped at nightfall. The few
people venturing out of their warm houses and offices
did so for reasons more pressing than to return a library
book.

Coming in this morning had almost been a shock after the
intense weekend of sex and intimacy with Nick, the two of

them cocooned in her house, closed off from the outside world.

The weekend had changed her, inside and out. She felt like a completely different woman. She even moved like a different woman, a woman who'd had more sex in the past forty-eight hours than in the past eight years.

Everything about her felt different. Every time she moved, she felt her body. And she actually *felt* her vagina. It was a little bit of soreness, yes—he was big, after all—but more than anything else, it was an intense awareness of the area between her thighs. Just amazing. It was a part of her anatomy she never, ever thought about, neatly tucked away up inside her body. Oh, she had the odd tingle reading a hot romance or watching her favorite actors. George Clooney would do it every time.

But this was completely different. She *felt* it. All of it, deep inside her body and when she moved, it was as if she could still feel Nick, hard and hot inside her.

Her breasts felt heavy and supersensitive. She had on a lace bra she'd worn at least fifty times before without even thinking about it. Today, she could feel the pattern of the lace against her breasts, and her nipples rubbed against the bra. Nick sucked her nipples often and they'd become supersensitized, too.

But it wasn't just a question of her erogenous zones, though of course they'd been revved up beyond anything she'd ever experienced. No, it was odd bits of her body coming to life that surprised her.

Her ankles. There, neat and tidy at the end of her legs. She never thought about them, ever. And yet last night, Nick had kissed them over and over again, saying he'd never seen a prettier pair and ever since then, she caught herself looking down at her ankles and smiling.

Her neck. Wow. That had turned out to be one of her top erogenous zones. Who knew? Nick had somehow known. Every time he put his lips to that one particular spot under her ear, she broke out in goose bumps.

She was thinking about that, about the lazy way he'd licked her neck this morning, while his thumb rubbed over her nipple, when she saw Nick, appearing suddenly out of the icy mist.

She was staring dreamily out the big library window, thinking of him and for a moment, it was almost like a scene out of a movie.

The big, handsome man, black haired and blue eyed, tall and strong, striding out from the mist. He walked like a gunslinger, loose and lanky, big heavy coat swirling around his legs, looking right and then left, checking out the situation. He was always intensely aware of his surroundings, more like a sentry or a soldier than a businessman.

Watching him appear out of the mist, for a second she thought *What a looker.* And then, in an intense burst of pride, she thought *That looker's mine. For the time being, ladies, hands off because that one's mine.*

As he crossed the street, Nick looked up and met her gaze and Charity's breath froze in her chest.

Time slowed, stilled. Her heartbeat thickened, sounded loud in her ears. She watched him, utterly unable to move, as he crossed the street. Long-legged strides, hands deep in his overcoat, hatless. He walked directly under the streetlamp and his hair shone blue-black in the feeble light.

Each stride was met with an equal *thump* in her chest as he came closer, closer, never taking his gaze from hers through the big plate-glass window of the library.

As Charity watched him watching her, her body automatically readied itself for him. Her skin felt feverish, prickly. Her blood pulsed thickly through her veins, in time with his strides. The muscles in her groin tightened, the muscles in her belly clenched. Her breasts felt hot and swollen, pushing against her bra. She could feel the inner muscles of her sheath softening, growing moist.

Did he know what was happening to her body?

Nick looked grim, jaw muscles clenching, eyes never leaving hers. His eyes were glowing, a mystical cobalt blue that penetrated deep inside her skull.

For a second he disappeared and then he was at the door, pulling it open to let a gust of cold air enter. She welcomed the burst of cold air moving over her skin, cooling it, because when he walked through the door, she felt a blast of internal heat so intense it was like walking in front of a furnace.

Nick didn't break his stride and he didn't greet her. He took in the empty library in a glance then took her elbow in his hand, propelling her toward the back.

His grip didn't hurt but it was unbreakable. Charity found herself scrambling to keep up with him.

They were at the back before she could gather her wits about her.

"Nick? What are you—ah . . ."

What he was doing became clear as he herded her into the supply room and closed the door. There was only a dim 20-watt lightbulb high up in the ceiling but it was certainly enough to see his expression by.

Her heart rate kicked up.

Nick advanced slowly and she backed away. Not out of fear but out of excitement at the heat in his eyes. She stopped when her back hit the wall and, a second later, Nick's hands slapped against the wall on either side of her head.

His head moved down as her eyelids drifted closed. Her head fell back, tipped against the wall. She expected one of his bone-melting kisses, but he stopped just before fitting his mouth to hers. She could feel his hot breath washing over her face.

"Hello, gorgeous," he whispered.

Charity smiled without opening her eyes. "Hello," she whispered back.

"Did you miss me?"

Every cell in her body had missed him. "You have no idea."

Nick leaned in, pressing his entire body against hers. "Oh yeah," he said softly. "I have an idea."

His freezing overcoat was a shock against Charity's bare overheated skin. Her shins, wrists, cheeks. Nick leaned even more heavily against her, shuffling his feet between hers, so she was forced to widen her stance.

He gathered her skirt in his big, cold hands and started pulling it up, bare knuckles icy against her thighs. Charity clutched the lapels of his overcoat for balance.

She didn't open her eyes. She couldn't. Everything in her was concentrated inward, on all the sensations evoked by his heavy, strong, cold body.

The heat burning her up inside and the contrasting chill against her skin. The soft cashmere of the coat contrasting with the roughness of his hands.

Her skirt started hiking up and she could feel the cold of his clothes against her thighs.

He was pressing against her so hard now that she could feel his erection through the layers of clothes, hers and his. He was huge.

She gave a half laugh. "You were thinking about this."

He nuzzled her neck. "Oh yeah," he breathed.

Charity shifted a little, brushing her mound against the erection, feeling it grow even longer, thicker. Oh God, this was so exciting!

"You were—" She took a deep breath as he nipped at the skin behind her ear. "You were thinking about this in the *snow?*"

His nose was in her hair, mouth against her ear. Charity could actually feel his breath break when he discovered she was wearing thigh-highs. His hand froze as his penis leaped against her.

She'd put them on this morning, knowing she'd be cold when she left the library, but also knowing it would excite him when they got home.

It never ever occurred to her that he'd discover them in the *library!*

"God." His hands found the bare skin between the tops of the stockings and her panties. They were warmer now. Not even a Vermont winter could keep Nick cold for long. "You wore these to drive me crazy, didn't you?"

"*Mmm.*" Actually, yes.

His hand cupped her, middle finger pressing lightly, the silk a thin layer against her opening and she shuddered, the movement evoking another surge from him against her.

"For the record, it's working."

He kept his hand there, warm now, hot even. Just the pressure of his hand against her made her thighs clench.

He was kissing her now, slow, deep kisses, licking her tongue, her teeth in slow movements, echoed by his hand against her, stroking slowly.

She felt him everywhere, pressing against her, smelling of snow and pine and Nick. Then the smell of sex bloomed in the room after he unzipped his pants, the sound soft in the dusty room, as his penis sprang out.

Charity wanted to open her eyes and see him. She loved the sight of it—a hard column with thick veins in an unruly nest of curly black hair. But her eyes wouldn't open, not while he kissed her so deeply.

Nick pried her right hand away from his coat and curled it around him. She couldn't see him but boy, she could feel him. Everything about him tightened when she touched him. His penis became, impossibly, even longer and thicker. His heart beat hard and fast, and she could feel the heartbeat, right there in her hand. Her thumb covered the huge, rounded head and he wept for her, too.

Such power, she had.

Then Nick tugged sharply, tearing her panties right off, and his finger slid inside her and she gasped, legs trembling. Oh God, he had power, too.

His finger stretched her, mimicking the movements of his tongue in her mouth and she whimpered.

The smell of sex was suddenly stronger in the air–her arousal and his. He'd touched her for only a minute, but she was soft and wet. His finger penetrated with ease. She'd been thinking about him all day. And all day her body had been primed for this.

Nick withdrew his finger, running the tip around her opening, preparing her.

"You've been thinking about me, too, honey." Another slow penetration, withdrawal. She ached with emptiness when his hand pulled away altogether. "Haven't you?"

He was asking her something. She had no idea what. But with Nick touching her like this, there was only one possible answer.

"Yes."

He shuddered. She felt it all through her own body.

A ripping, crinkling sound and he had protection on. His kisses were wilder now, so deep she almost couldn't breathe, and had to breathe through him. His own breaths heated her cheek and she could feel his wide chest rising and falling at a faster rhythm.

"Lift your leg," he whispered, running his hand down the back of her thigh. Charity obeyed, as he helped her curl her leg around his, opening herself completely to him.

He had to bend his knees slightly to fit himself to her opening, swirling himself around her, trying to go slow.

She could feel his tight control in his hands, slow and trembling, in the drop of sweat running down his temple, in his harsh breathing. He pressed a little inside her and she clenched around him.

"Jesus," he breathed. Another drop of sweat fell. "It has to be hard and fast, honey, because I'm about ready to blow. I really have been thinking about this all day. Had a woody, too. Really uncomfortable, let me tell you."

Charity let out a burst of laughter, charmed at the thought of him negotiating business deals with an erection. Her laughter was cut short when he entered her completely in one hard thrust.

Charity's eyes opened wide, staring into his, an inch away. His eyes were narrowed, staring at her intently. A muscle twitched in his jaw.

"Fuck. Sorry." He took a second to catch his breath. "Did I hurt you? Honey?" He frowned when she didn't answer. "Charity answer me. Did I hurt you?"

She could barely hear him, his voice distant, as if he were a thousand miles away, instead of pressing against her, up *in* her. She was totally caught up with what was happening inside her, tightly wound, everything in her circling inward, hardly able to breathe. All the nerve endings between her thighs were on fire as she clenched and clenched again around the huge, hard rod inside her.

He pressed a little harder and the tension broke. The world spun away, everything inside her got tighter and tighter until, with a little cry, she began coming in long hard pulls, as if her body were trying to entice him even more deeply inside her.

"*Shit!*" Nick's entire body jerked in surprise and he started moving in her, short, hard jabs, completely unlike the easy, long rhythms of his normal lovemaking.

Both his hands were cupped around her bottom, holding her up to him as his tight, hard strokes banged her against the wall. He swelled inside her, his movements becoming irregular, almost frantic and then he started coming, too, teeth and jaws tightly clenched against a moan, a lock of raven-black hair falling over his damp forehead, tapping against his skin with each hard movement.

Charity softened, her contractions slowing down, her muscles turning lax. The only thing holding her up was his chest pressed against hers, his hands on her buttocks, and his penis inside her. Her arms dropped. She didn't even have the energy to hold on to him.

There was a faint noise, a clattering sound, which she couldn't decipher. It was only when she felt cold air against the sole of her foot that she realized she'd lost a shoe.

It was the only place she was cold. Every other part of her was steaming hot, particularly where he was still inside her. He had softened a little after his climax, but not much. He was still hard inside her and it felt like flameless fire.

"My God," he muttered. "That was—" He blew out a breath. "Well."

"Absolutely," she whispered. She couldn't have said it better herself.

They rested against each other. If it hadn't been for the wall, they would have both fallen to the floor. Nick rested his cheek against the top of her head and her lips curled in a smile.

Impossibly, his penis twitched and her vagina spasmed around him.

"No," she said. "Can't."

"Me, either." Nick let out a gusty sigh against her hair, ruffling a curl. "Like to, but can't." He shifted slightly. "As a matter of fact, I'd better do something before the rubber leaks." He straightened slightly, starting to pull out.

"Charity? *Charity?* Where are you?"

Charity froze and looked up, appalled, into Nick's amused gaze.

"Charity?" The tone was peremptory, her name pronounced in short, staccato syllables. Cha-ri-ty. A long stress on the last syllable. *Cha-ri-teee!* Only one person spoke her name like that. Mrs. Lambert, the former chief librarian.

Oh God, she couldn't even pretend not to be here. The door was unlocked and her coat was hung on the coat rack. Mrs. Lambert knew this place like the back of her hand—she'd worked here for forty years.

The supply room would be the first place she'd check. And there was no place at all in the room to hide a six-foot-two handsome devil of a man.

Charity pushed at Nick. "Let me go!" she hissed.

With a little sigh, he pulled out of her and stepped back, penis bobbling at half-mast. Charity looked at it, then at him, and with another sigh, he tucked himself away in his pants and zipped up, wincing, the zipper loud in the silence.

"Charity! Where are you, girl?"

Mrs. Lambert's sensible boots made a clomping sound on the library's ancient hardwood floor. Charity could follow every step she was making. She was checking the periodicals room, the reading room. A discreet knock on the lavatory door.

There was only one place left to check.

"Wipe that grin off your face," she said in a fierce whisper, hopping over to her missing shoe, straightening her skirt, combing her hair out with her fingers. Nick obediently assumed a serious expression, biting his lips not to smile. His eyes were full of amusement, though.

It was quite all right for him to be amused. He'd be leaving soon. Charity was going to spend the rest of her life here, and Mrs. Lambert was the biggest gossip in town.

Charity even had a morals clause in her contract, which had amused her when she'd signed it, the idea of infringing the morals clause of her employment contract as remote as the thought of flying to Pluto.

Nick cleared his throat and she leaped to cover his mouth with her hand. His eyes gleamed at her. The devil.

"Not a word," she said fiercely. "Not one word!"

When she dropped her hand, he mimed zipping his mouth. His smiling mouth, the scoundrel.

"Charity, my dear. Where on earth are you?" The boots clumped closer.

Charity checked her skirt, smoothed it out, fanned herself quickly in an attempt to cool down and winced at the thought of her kiss-swollen lips, and of being naked under the skirt. She was sure the smell of hot sex surrounded her like a cloud.

Well, there was nothing for it but to brazen it through. She lifted her head and took in a deep breath.

Showtime, she thought and opened the door, closing it quickly behind her.

"Why Mrs. Lambert," she said. "What a pleasant surprise. What can I do for you?"

Fourteen

The instant Nick walked up the granite steps and walked through the huge door of Worontzoff's crib—*palace* would be a better word—every hair on his body stood on end.

There was no visible reason for it. No reason at all why his blood was running cold. No reason for the adrenalin dump.

Everyone streaming up the steps and into the house was elegant and wealthy. Solid citizens. Culture mavens.

The buzz of well-bred voices echoed around the huge foyer, mixed with the murmur of well-trained servants taking coats, offering drinks, pointing toward a big reception hall.

Nick recognized the governor of Vermont, two senators from big states, a high-tech tycoon, and a famous movie director. Everyone else looked like they were famous. Average age fifty, average income several million dollars per annum on up.

This was it.

He was in the belly of the beast.

This was when Nick shone. He was at his best in extremis, close to the heart of the danger. He'd been here before, often. It was the whole point of being undercover, to get close to the unprotected center, as an insider.

It was when that internal mechanism he'd been born with revved up, the one that gave him the moniker Iceman. It was like a sixth gear and once it kicked in, his thoughts, sight, and hearing were enhanced. He was preternaturally aware of his surroundings, his entire body turned into a quick-response machine. He could be cool and calm on the outside while on the inside, his head was working its way through the complex geometry of betrayal.

While all the smug, self-satisfied elegant folk were eating Worontzoff's hors d'oeuvres and drinking his French champagne, congratulating themselves on being invited into the great man's home, Nick took stock.

Ninety-five percent of the people here were as clueless as lambs right up to the moment of slaughter. They had no idea what they'd walked into.

They thought they were among their own kind. They weren't. They were with monsters.

It was amazing to him. How people could be around predators and not *feel* that they were different.

One elderly gent with an ebony cane topped by a silver orb took a drink off a tray offered by one of Worontzoff's minions. He didn't notice the barbed-wire tattoo visible under the snowy white cuff or the slight bulge under the left armpit of the man holding the tray. No doubt the goon had a backup in an ankle holster and a knife in a hip sheath. Not to mention a garrote in the fancy cummerbund.

He was an operator, no doubt about that. Steel gray crew cut, knife scar along the jawline, in his fifties and fitter than any twenty-year-old could ever hope to be.

And Clueless Geezer happily lifting a drink from the tray Crew Cut held, unaware that with one word from Worontzoff, Crew Cut would rip his throat out. Jesus.

Nick knew, though. He'd been around people like Crew Cut all his life and every sense he had was on high alert.

So he walked around with a hand to Charity's back, not as a gentleman would, to guide her gently and stake his claim, but because he was ready at any moment to shove her to the ground and pull out his Glock at the first sign of danger.

"Charity! My dear, so good to see you." Nick stiffened as Worontzoff pulled himself away from a little gaggle of politicians, rich men, and journalists across the room to limp slowly toward Charity.

Nick could see the men and women Worontzoff had been talking to craning their necks to see who could possibly be more important than they were.

Nick had watched Worontzoff through his spotting scope and had studied hundreds of photographs. The photographs didn't do Worontzoff justice.

He wasn't tall—Nick was a full head taller—but he had an animal, magnetic presence that turned heads and stopped conversations. If you didn't look at his hands, he could even be considered a handsome man, with a leonine head of graying blond hair, light blue eyes, and high Slav cheekbones.

He made a beeline for Charity in his odd gait, ignoring everyone who tried to engage his attention as he crossed the huge room.

Charity was pink with pleasure, since she was so obviously the center of the Great Man's attention. There was a little buzz of *Who is she?* and then Worontzoff was right in front of her, bending to give her a little buss on the cheek.

Nick's jaws clenched but there was nothing he could do about it without looking like a boor. It was a fatherly kiss, though there was absolutely nothing fatherly about Worontzoff's face when he straightened.

"My dear, you're looking positively radiant! More beautiful than ever. What have you been doing?"

The tone was coy, but the glance he shot Nick was sharp as a saber. He knew perfectly well what she'd been doing and why she was glowing.

Charity held on to Nick's arm. "Vassily, I'd like to introduce you to my friend, Nicholas Ames."

Worontzoff smiled right into Nick's eyes. They were clear as glass and just as cold. "Well, Mr. Ames, it is indeed a pleasure to meet you. Any friend of Charity's is a friend of mine, as the saying goes. You will forgive me if I don't shake hands with you." He held up one shattered hand, mottled red and crisscrossed with scars. "I had . . . a little run-in once with a prison guard."

Don't worry, you fuckhead. I wouldn't shake hands with you, not even with a gun to my head, Nick thought.

Whoa.

This was bad. Being undercover means believing. You have to believe your cover story with every fiber of your being. You eat, drink, and sleep your cover story. You never, ever break cover, *especially* in your head.

Nicholas Ames, New York businessman, would be absolutely delighted to meet a famous man, someone he'd never meet ordinarily. Stockbrokers lived off contacts and this was a good one. If nothing else, Nicholas Ames could dine out on having met a contender for the Nobel.

Nick had to get back into character *now* or he would endanger not only himself but Charity.

He breathed like when he sniped. Long, calm breaths, guaranteed to drop his heart rate ten beats per breath and assumed an expression so bland it was as if he were alone in the room.

He nodded at Worontzoff's hands. "No problem, sir. I'm very pleased to meet you. Charity's told me so much about you."

Worontzoff turned to Charity. "Have you now, my dear?" He placed his claw of a hand on her forearm.

Nick had goose bumps so thick the hairs on his forearm brushed against his shirtsleeve at the expression on Worontzoff's face when he looked at Charity.

Nick's instinct—hot, immediate, primordial—was to attract attention away from Charity, the way a mother bear lures a hunter away from the den where the cubs are sleeping. *Look away from her, fuckhead! Look at me instead!*

"Yeah." Nick raised his voice a little, enough to carry. Enough to make Worontzoff instinctively look at him. "She said you were like a father to her. It's really nice of you to let me tag along tonight, though to tell you the truth, I don't know much about classical music. I'll let Charity tell me what's going on."

He grinned, clueless businessman mainly interested in the woman whose waist he clasped. Tightly.

"Yes, indeed." Worontzoff's gaze fixed on Nick's hand at Charity's waist, then rose to his face. He nodded gravely. It wouldn't have been out of place at an imperial court. "Well, all that remains is for me to wish you a pleasant evening, then. I hope you enjoy the music, Mr. Ames. Charity."

He walked away, the emperor who'd summoned them to his court.

The plan had been for Nick to wander the house. The palatial mansion was too old for its blueprints to be on record. They had a general idea of the layout, but Nick's task was to explore as much as he could.

A tuxedo ruled out a pen camera. He had a camera built-in to his wristwatch. They'd download the images in the van while Nick drew the floor plan of what he'd managed to see. Maps were his specialty.

So now what he needed to do was wander, but at the same time he was reluctant to leave Charity. He found a big group of boring-looking men and a few women discussing presidential politics and left her with them.

"Bathroom break," he whispered into her ear. "Be right back. Don't move."

She smiled up at him. *Okay*, she mouthed.

Nick checked each guy in the circle in turn, looking them in the eyes, sending the subliminal message—*Watch out for her*—and made for the back of the room.

He was good at scouting terrain. Their big break in the Gonzalez case had come when he broke into Guillermo's office at midnight for the tenth time and hit the jackpot. Ten bills of lading where almost a ton of cocaine was going to be traded for ten thousand military-issue rifles, which the same night were going into the hands of Somali rebels, with a neat 100 percent markup.

The bills of lading told them what, where, and when and the Unit's elite team had observed the first deal, confiscating the cocaine the next day, and had taken down the terrorists involved in the second deal.

Two for one. Head office had been ecstatic.

But making like a ghost through Guillermo's household had been easy. The tone of an enterprise is set at the top. Guillermo had been almost totally without self-control and the nights he wasn't shit-faced on tequila, he was stoned on his own product. The guards were the same.

Getting past them had been a piece of cake.

That was a 180 degrees from here, where the guards weren't half stoned. They were sober and vigilant and everywhere.

Nick had barely crossed the threshold of the room when a servant came up. "May I help you, sir?" he asked in accented English.

Nick rocked back on his heels and put his hands in his pockets, jiggling some change. Making sure his watch face was exposed and focused on the man.

"Yeah." He looked around admiringly. "Huge house. Beautiful, too. Lots of artwork." He grinned foolishly and leaned forward, as if imparting a secret. "Looking for the bathroom, you know. Can you tell me where to find one?"

There. He had the guy on video now, full face. If the goon was wanted anywhere in the free world, the face would be matched up to a name.

The man inclined his head gravely. "Down the corridor, last door on the right, sir."

"Great," Nick said cheerfully. He could turn the corner, see what other rooms there were. He stepped forward and found himself staring into the man's eyes, steely dark gray. Unblinking. Unyielding.

He'd just turned himself into a brick wall and Nick couldn't get through without exposing himself.

"Allow me to show you the way, sir." The man turned without waiting for an answer and walked ahead.

O-kay. That's the way they were playing it. Nobody was to be left alone to wander the house. Not even for a second.

It might just be to guard against theft. God knows there was enough to steal. The place made Judge Prewitt's house look like a Brazilian favela.

Spotlit antique vases on stands, paper-thin silk Persian rugs, silk tapestries, the odd Monet and Picasso . . . very civilized, indeed. The abode of a man of discernment and learning. The kind of house money alone couldn't buy

The whole place gave Nick the heebie-jeebies, a sense of discomfort so great that for a second there, he thought he'd throw up.

Each item he saw was paid for in untold blood and suffering. Every stick of furniture, the walls full of books and paintings, everything there was the fruit of crime, bought with some victim's body. Nick felt exactly as he'd felt in Guillermo's house—as if he were walking over human bones.

Without lifting his head, out of his peripheral vision he saw tiny security cameras embedded in the ceiling moldings every five feet. In the bathroom, forcing himself to squeeze a few drops of piss out of his dick, he saw another.

There was no question of going roaming and no question of planting bugs. He was going to get a glimpse of a big receiving room, the bathroom, and, presumably, the room where the music was going to be played. And that was it.

When Nick emerged from the bathroom, the guy didn't even pretend he wasn't waiting for him. Wordlessly, he followed Nick back into the room still buzzing with upper-class ladies and gentlemen getting a high on proximity to literary greatness and champagne.

Veuve Cliquot, no less.

Nick couldn't indulge in even half a glass. Not for security reasons—actually, not drinking a drop in an assembly like this one drew more attention and would compromise the mission more than getting shit-faced—but because the acid roiling in his stomach wouldn't let him drink a drop of the bubbly. He'd just throw it up, and wouldn't that be great for an undercover agent?

Nick barely recognized his own body. Danger didn't freak him out, didn't make him sweat or fill his stomach up with acid. Danger focused him, made him bright and hard, cool and controlled. Iceman.

Not now. He had a bad case of the jitters, for the first time in his life. The signals he was getting from the outside world— the armed guards everywhere, the cameras—weren't doing it. Those signals just confirmed he was dealing with criminals. What was messing with him so badly was intangible, a constant buzzing vibe he found it impossible to ignore, and it had to do with Charity's presence here.

Worontzoff had used the time in which he was outside the room to herd Charity away from the other guests and into a secluded corner. Nick saw them immediately, the instant he crossed the threshold, his eyes turned like a magnet to her.

Charity standing close to the wall with Worontzoff, his back to the crowd, cutting her off from everyone. Charity wasn't reading it that way at all. She was smiling up at him, talking animatedly, that lovely face pink with excitement.

Nothing in her body language even remotely communicated distress, though she was standing a hand's span from a monster. She hadn't learned to recognize what he was because monsters hadn't been a part of her life. She thought Worontzoff was human.

She sure as hell wouldn't smile up at him if she knew half the things he was capable of.

Then the fucker reached out an arm and put it around Charity's shoulders and her smile widened. Worontzoff bent down to whisper in her ear and Charity's bright laugh rose clearly in the air, audible all the way across the room.

Every cell in Nick's body screamed and jangled. He had to actually stop and take a breath, because what he wanted to do was to rush forward, break Worontzoff's arm, throw Charity over his shoulder, and get out of there, just as fast as was humanly possible.

His entire system buzzed with the need to *get Charity out*. Hand reaching for a gun that he couldn't use, adrenaline flooding his body with no outlet possible.

Usually, his hunches were fairly subtle—a vague feeling that he should *zig* instead of *zag*. But there was nothing subtle about this. This was full out red alert, the siren in the submarine booming remorselessly just before the incoming torpedo hits.

Part of it was jealousy, of course. Two hours ago, he'd painted kisses across Charity's shoulders, right where Worontzoff had his arm. That pretty breast pressing against the jacket of Worontzoff's tux—he'd kissed it and suckled it so often he felt like he owned it.

So, yeah. He was jealous. Jealousy wasn't anything he'd ever felt before, so it took him a second to recognize it.

He hated another man's hands on her, another man making her laugh, another man inside her space.

But it was more than jealousy. There was terror bubbling right underneath, sharp and electric. Worontzoff was obsessed with her, with the woman who could have been his Katya reborn.

But it was make-believe. Charity only looked like Katya. She was another woman entirely and when Worontzoff finally figured that out—that his Katya was forever dead and Charity could never take her place—God only knew what kind of revenge he would take.

Worontzoff moved. Nick's whole system jolted, another layer of sweaty fear added to the mix. Worontzoff had shifted so he could come closer to Charity, in profile to Nick. Who could now clearly see what had been hidden before.

A hard-on. The fucker had a *hard-on*. It was lightly hidden by his jacket but it was unmistakable. Thank God Charity didn't notice anything, smiling upward into Worontzoff's face, chattering away. Knowing her, she was talking about a good book she'd read, the upcoming concert, her garden. She was clueless.

Clueless people ended up dead around monsters, and they died badly. Charity's pretty head was filled with literature and music, love for her aunt and uncle, and kindness toward her friends. She had no idea what the outside world was like. She had no idea that the man she was probably discussing concerto movements with could have her strung up on a meat hook, as one of the women who'd testified against Worontzoff's proxy in Belgrade, Milic, had been.

Nick was the one who'd lifted the woman off the hook and down to the floor. The man who ran that prostitution ring answered directly to Worontzoff.

When Worontzoff's madness ebbed, when he finally realized that Charity really and truly wasn't his Katya come back to life, but a nice little American librarian, his revenge would be swift and terrifying.

Nick's feverish imagination could conjure up any number

of horrifying scenarios. Someone might lift Charity's body off a butcher's hook one day.

The thought drove him crazy wild, made his whole system buzz with terror, made his heart thud.

He wouldn't be there to protect her. One way or another, he'd be gone soon, leaving Charity staked out like a lamb for the wolves. There would be nothing between her and some of the most ruthless men on earth.

Nick's fists clenched and for a second, he forgot to hold his wristwatch in a position to record his surroundings. He watched Charity and willed her to leave. To just turn her back on this monster and walk away.

He could protect her now. Break cover, then put her in protective custody until they'd put the scumbags away. Even if that meant ripping her from her life forever, it was worth it. Once the image of Charity's broken, lifeless body bloomed in his mind like a poisonous flower, he couldn't get rid of it.

Leave him, Nick told her from across the room, sending her screaming mental vibes. *Get out of here. Run for your life.*

As if sensing danger, Worontzoff's back stiffened and he turned his head swiftly. Too fast for Nick to look away, or wipe the expression of hatred from his face. Their gazes met, and locked.

Nick could feel the cold blast from across the room and his stomach clenched as Worontzoff turned back to Charity and, smiling, held out his arm. From the next room came the sounds of musicians tuning their instruments. Worontzoff gave a look to one of his thugs dressed as a servant and a brass bell was rung.

Worontzoff raised his voice. "Ladies and gentlemen, the concert begins in five minutes. Take your seats, please."

With one last, murderous glance at Nick, he waited until she laid her pretty hand on his arm, and then escorted Charity into the music room.

Teeth grinding, sweaty hands shaking, Nick followed.

The concert had been exquisite. Cha had outdone himself, his bow weaving magic in the room. As always with great art, the world had fallen away. He felt as if there were just the two of them, Vassily and Katya, listening to great music, just like in the old days.

He was in his sitting room. Though the big hearth was ablaze, the fire was barely able to leaven his perennial chill. Vassily lifted his glass of vodka and sipped, letting the memory of the music go through him, tapping out the rhythm on the heavy silk brocade of the arm of the sofa.

Ah, money and power. There was nothing like it. It could buy everything, including bringing Katya back from the grave.

Vassily took his stylus and lightly pressed a button on the table next to him. As always, it only took a moment.

There was a soft knock on the door and at Vassily's command, Ilya walked in.

"Come in, my friend," Vassily urged. "Pour yourself a drink."

Ilya did, refreshed his own, then sat down on the armchair next to the sofa.

He had changed out of his livery and was dressed casually. He gulped the vodka down in one swallow and poured another large measure. Vassily knew what a solace alcohol was for his friend and employee and never begrudged him his release. Ilya had a lot to forget. They both did.

Vassily knew Ilya understood him, through and through.

"What did you find out tonight?"

Ilya answered promptly. "Nicholas Ames. Thirty-four years old. Retired from an American corporation, Orion Investments. Drives a Lexus with a New York State license plate. Property in Manhattan, a condo on Lexington Avenue. Value a little over two million dollars. No criminal record. That's all I have for now."

It was enough. Bravo, Ilya.

"I need wetwork done," Vassily said. Wetwork. *Mokrie dela.* Murder. The KGB's specialty. "But not by one of ours."

Ilya nodded.

"Someone untraceable to us. Someone efficient, who can make it look like an accident. And I want it done tomorrow."

Ilya looked at him. "I know someone in Brooklyn who can help us, Vor."

"Use a cutout," Vassily said sharply. "Nothing must ever be traced back to here. Is that understood?"

Ilya nodded. "I understand, Vor. This man I am thinking of is not one of ours. He is a free agent. Nothing will ever be traced back to us. "

"Make sure you get the best. Take what you need from the vault. Give the cutout ten percent of the final amount. Keep everything clean." Behind a false wall in the basement of the mansion was a bank vault with twenty million U.S. dollars in cash, another several million dollars' worth of foreign currencies, and the other intangibles of the trade, useful for barter—drugs, diamonds, ingots.

Vassily imagined that a job like this, using a top pro who had to make it look like an accident, would cost at least two hundred thousand dollars, plus twenty thousand for the cutout. Over and above that, he would make sure Ilya was sufficiently recompensed with a bonus, that went without saying.

Nothing. It was nothing. It was what his enterprises in the Caribbean earned in a morning. More than worth it for Katya.

Katya.

Vassily stared into the fire, his heart beating hard and fast. He wasn't going to make the same mistake twice. This time he'd marry her. He hadn't done it before, more fool him. He'd thought they had all the time in the world. He and Katya had been golden. Their future held only glory and fame in the new Russia.

Instead, the past had clawed them back, drawing them down into a pit full of vipers and monsters. He hadn't had time to marry Katya, but this time he would.

This time he'd get it right.

This time, he wouldn't lose her.

This time, Katya would be his. Forever.

Fifteen

"So, what are we doing here, Nick? And why couldn't I go to work today?"

Charity looked worriedly over at her lover. He had white stripes of tension around his mouth, jaw muscles clenched, big hands clutching the wheel so tightly the knuckles were white. He was looking grim and tense, as if privy to very bad news, though she couldn't imagine what.

Just looking at him made her tense, too.

Nick had been enigmatic and distant all morning, yet feverish with some secret plan. Mysterious and rushed. He'd insisted that she put on her prettiest dress and call in sick, which she'd refused. Nick pressed, and normally Charity would have given in, but she drew the line at pretending to be sick. It was dishonest. She was a lousy liar, even if she wanted to lie, which she didn't. The words would have choked in her mouth.

However, she did have tons of time off coming, so she finally caved in to Nick and phoned Mrs. Lambert to ask whether she could replace her for the day .

They were parked near Adams Square, in the courthouse parking lot, waiting for . . . something. Charity had no idea what and no idea why.

Nick's lovemaking last night had been . . . intense. Wild, actually. He'd pushed her into new territory, a place where she had hardly recognized herself. If she shifted in the car seat, she could still feel him inside her. It seemed as if he'd touched every inch of her body last night. She could still see his beautiful face, a lock of black hair falling over his forehead, gorgeous blue eyes staring into hers. His gaze never wavered from hers as he pumped in and out of her, claiming her in every way there was.

Charity had felt turned inside out, so strongly attuned to him that she knew what he wanted from her before he asked. They'd moved almost as one together, all night. A new creature, a fusion of two bodies. She'd fallen asleep in his arms only in the early morning and had been appalled when she'd woken up at nine. The library opened at nine thirty.

Before she could jump out of bed, Nick had tightened his arms around her, rolling her over and entering her in one smooth movement. They'd made love so much during the night that she was still wet. Pinning her down with his weight, Nick refused to move until she promised she'd skip work today and come with him for a surprise. No amount of wriggling budged him. It was so frustrating, she finally agreed and with a hot gleam in his eye, his hips finally started moving. He laughed when she came immediately.

But laughing Nick was gone and grim Nick had taken his place. He had been completely silent on the drive into town and now he simply sat there in the driver's seat, holding on to the steering wheel as if to a lifeline and staring silently out the window.

What could he possibly be looking at? The sky was pewter gray, so overcast it looked more like evening than late morning, bestowing a dull cast on everything. To the left, lost in the fog, was the Parker's Ridge equivalent of Fifth Avenue—Revere Street, three blocks of old-fashioned shops, with nary a boutique or a chain in sight. To the right was Kingsbury Square, the snow making the rhododendrons look like huge puffs of pink-white cotton. Ahead was the gray cement wall of the new courthouse, a 1960s monstrosity everyone hated.

Should she tell Nick the story of spearheading the campaign to have it torn down? He usually loved her Parker's Ridge stories, as if she were an anthropologist telling exotic tales of life in a tribe in a faraway country.

No, maybe right now he wasn't in the mood for Parker's Ridge stories. Not with his jaw muscles jumping so hard it was a miracle he didn't crack a tooth.

One of the many things that had happened last night, and that had changed her forever, was that Charity had completed the process of becoming attuned to Nick and his moods. The intense sex, the blinding pleasure, his body in hers for hours, had transformed her. It was as if she were made of iron filings and he was the magnet. She was sensitive to every breath he took, every move he made.

Right now she could tell he was in the grip of some strong emotion. The very air molecules in the car were buzzing with it. Nick was radiating something and she couldn't quite pinpoint it. Anger? No, that wasn't it. Sadness? Not quite. Whatever it was, it disturbed him deeply.

His hands unclenched and fisted once more around the wheel, as if he were bracing himself against something.

She repeated her question. "What's so important I couldn't go in to work this morning? And it better be good because I've never missed a day of work in my life."

His jaw muscles worked heavily as he turned to her, face serious.

"Charity, I—" He stopped. It was the first time she'd ever seen him at a loss. So odd, her graceful, articulate Nick, searching for words.

And then it hit her, a sledgehammer blow to her heart, followed by an icy chill that left her shaking.

Oh my God! Of course. Foolish, foolish Charity. How on earth could she have missed the signs? It would have been immediately clear to any woman with a little more experience than she had in beginning and ending affairs. She was going to pay a very heavy price for being so out of the dating scene.

He's leaving, she thought, and her heart gave another sharp blow in her chest. *He's leaving today and he doesn't know how to tell me. He'll be gone by nightfall.*

Nick was a gentleman. No wonder he hadn't wanted her to go into work. He hadn't wanted to say his good-byes on the library steps. Perhaps he wanted to take her out to lunch, break the news to her gently, and now he was finding it difficult. Probably more difficult than he'd bargained for.

Just as she was finding it difficult to take in a breath. Something big and heavy was pressing in on her chest. She had to choke back the grief rising in her throat.

She'd known all along he'd leave. It was inevitable, the way of the world. She'd even steeled herself to be stoic when the time came. It's just that she never thought the time would be quite so . . . soon.

Today was Friday. A week ago, he'd shown up in her life and they'd been practically living together ever since. The incredibly intense sex had hurried things along in her heart, but racing alongside the blinding physical pleasure had been all the small things that had made her fall in love with him.

A kind of steadiness, a—a manly kind of inner calm that she'd associated only with her father and her uncle, two men of a different era, never with a virile, sexy, relatively young man. A man with a strong internal compass, with no need to impress and, by the same token, no need to put others down. A careless kindness, which he wouldn't even recognize as such, but she did. He had an old-fashioned male courtliness that delighted her.

And the biggie—the way he'd completely come through for her with Aunt Vera. If she lived to be a hundred she would never forget the sight of him coming out of the swirling snow with her aunt in his arms, and the tender way he handled Uncle Franklin, quietly ensuring that the house would be alarmed without alarming her uncle. Few men would have been capable of that.

In her experience, modern men didn't do things like that. They stepped away from responsibility, not toward.

Then, of course, his looks. An entirely male beauty she'd never had the pleasure of encountering before. You had to put that on the scale, too. She was as susceptible to eye candy as the next woman. The incredible pleasure of touching him, all over. Running her hand along that perfect cheekbone, tracing the beautiful line of his mouth, the strong line of his jaw. Those had been moments of perfection, forever embedded in her heart, which would fade away only when she closed her eyes for the last time.

Maybe she had known it wouldn't—*couldn't*—last, but though the knowledge had been right there in the back of her mind all along, like low dark clouds on the horizon, it had been oh-so-easy to forget it. Forget that this was a passing thing.

It wasn't a passing thing for her. She'd fallen hard and fast and deep. And this was It.

It had taken her twenty-eight years to find love, and she couldn't even begin to imagine lightning striking twice. It wouldn't come again in her lifetime.

The Prewitt curse. In the three hundred years of Prewitt history she was aware of, there'd never been a divorce, never been a second marriage. Prewitts were like wolves. Or pigeons. Or voles. They mated once, and for life. This was good, unless you were twenty-one and widowed and spent the next seventy years mourning your husband, as her great-great grandmother had done.

Nick would go back to his Manhattan life, which was no doubt exciting, fast-paced, full of fascinating people and things, and she would stay here, tending Uncle Franklin and Aunt Vera and the library, growing older year by year, with only her memories of this remarkable week to sustain her.

Inside, she felt as gray and bleak as the weather outside. But she was a Prewitt. And, if nothing else, Prewitts had pride. Whatever else Nick had given her, he hadn't given her promises and she had no right to expect them. She would meet the end of this affair with dignity. There would be plenty of time later to cry.

The rest of her life, in fact.

And so, when she turned to him, it was with a bland smile completely hiding her shattered heart.

"Whatever's bothering you, Nick, you can tell me." She even managed a smile. "I'm a big girl. I can take it."

He paled. The ruddy, healthy color in his cheeks went. Oh God. This was going to be bad. He knew exactly how much he was going to hurt her, and it hurt him.

Though her stomach clenched in despair, she sketched a smile. Dignity. It was going to be the only thing left to her. She wrapped herself in it, forcing her hands not to tremble, forcing herself to look him straight in the eyes, forcing herself to breathe around the boulder in her chest.

He took in a sharp deep breath and she barely stopped herself from flinching when he opened his mouth.

"Charity . . . I have something to say to you."

She nodded her head gravely. "Yes, Nick?"

"Charity, will you—"

He was going to ask a favor before leaving? Well, whatever it was he wanted, there was only one possible answer. *Yes*. He'd barged into her life, seduced her, and was now leaving, but she wouldn't change a second of the past week. She'd lived more intensely, felt more deeply in the past seven days than in her entire life. He'd given her love. Even if only for a week, it was more than many people had. Anything in her power she had to give him was his for the asking.

He turned his head and looked her straight in the eyes, the muscles in his jaw working. There was a buzzing energy around him she couldn't understand, but it was jarring, completely foreign to his calm nature.

Another sharp breath and it came out in a rush. "Charity Prewitt, will you marry me?"

* * *

It was the only thing Nick could think of, to keep her safe. Or as safe as he could manage.

His entry into Worontzoff's lair had changed things, had somehow disturbed a pool that was deeper than he thought, with monsters residing on the bottom. He'd been expecting to enter, carry out a recon, then exit. Nothing he hadn't done hundreds of times before. It was, after all, what he did.

But something was deeply wrong and he didn't know exactly what. All he knew was that it involved Charity and that it scared the shit out of him, a man who didn't scare easily.

He didn't mind the feeling of danger encroaching. He'd chosen a risky path in life and this subliminal awareness, the kick to his senses, had saved his life more times than he could count. It was a tool he used, often and well, and he kept it shiny and well honed.

So the hot boiling feeling of things bubbling beneath the surface was fine. Worontzoff and his minions were dangerous men, and he was as ready as he could possibly be to deal with them, on 24/7 alert. He had the tools, the skills, the training and the will to strike back. What he was absolutely unequipped to deal with was a threat to Charity.

Worontzoff's look, his possessive arm around Charity, the cold glance he'd given Nick, that fucking woody—it was clear that, in Worontzoff's head, Charity was his. The fuckhead had actually convinced himself that Charity was Katya come to life. That Nick's presence had made Worontzoff come out in the open and stake his claim made it even creepier. Nick's presence had brought something to a head. Something cold and evil, which would roll right over Charity and leave her crushed and broken.

Last night he'd made love to her as if he could tuck her body into his, make her part of his flesh. As if all he had to do was fuck her hard enough, and she'd be safe for all time. But of course, he couldn't, and morning came, bringing with it not only a clear-eyed analysis of the situation but this buzzing, itching, nagging feeling in his bones that something was going to come down soon. That someone was about to die.

There'd been a sickness in Worontzoff's house, for all the elegant people, fine works of art, exquisite music. None of it, none of the beauty and culture mattered. It didn't mean shit with the cold hand of death closing its gelid fist around it.

Since before he could talk, Nick could recognize evil, and it had been strong in that house.

He'd felt his death, or at least the possibility of his death. It wasn't the first time he'd felt it, but it was definitely the strongest death vibe he'd ever had.

The vague feeling he would die young sharpened, came into focus.

For the first time in his life, Nick was afraid to die. Terrified, even. If he went, Charity would be alone. He'd spent enough time with her to know that she was not protected in any meaningful way. Christ, even her house was unprotected. There was absolutely nothing around Charity, nothing to shield her from the evil of the world. From Worontzoff or his minions, when he turned on her, as he inevitably would.

Her family was an elderly, very frail couple who relied on her to help them. She wasn't equipped in any way to save herself, if he wasn't around. She didn't have the mental tools to sense danger and defend herself.

Charity was light itself—goodness and grace, the very qualities which were the first to go when evil stepped out from the shadows. Bad guys focused in like a laser beam on people like Charity, wanting to wipe them from the face of the earth. Because they could, because the Charities of this world represented something they could never have and never control.

Charity could never be bought, never be forced. She'd die first and that was what had Nick terrified.

This buzz of imminent danger Nick was feeling was making him nauseous. He'd sweated the problem all morning.

For the time being, he was at her side. As long as he was alive, no one was going to touch her. But suppose he wasn't alive? How the fuck could he keep Charity safe even if he bought it? How could he protect her, even from beyond the grave? It roiled around in his head, a dilemma with sharp edges that sliced, drew blood.

Though last night he'd fucked her frantically, for hours, when he finally quit because she was exhausted, he still couldn't sleep. Couldn't even come near it.

The early morning hours had been spent on his back, staring wide-eyed at the shadows in the ceiling, Charity snuggled up close to his side, head on his shoulder. He couldn't hear her breathing and would have panicked if he hadn't felt her narrow rib cage slowly rising and falling.

Such a thin line between life and death. He'd seen countless men and some women cross it. In battle, the line was crossed in a microsecond. You were there one moment, a fully alive, thinking human being, and the next you were meat.

Charity was crossing a minefield, with no one to look out for her. She could cross that line between life and death in a heartbeat.

Nick couldn't stand even the thought of it. His head churned uselessly throughout the night, as he ran through improbable scenarios in his mind.

And then, as the sky turned from black to slate then pewter, a solution hit him. There was a way to keep her safe, even if he was snuffed. One thing he could do that would protect her no matter what happened to him.

Marry her.

Or rather, Nicholas Ames would marry her. Didn't make any difference that Nicholas Ames didn't exist. The important thing was that a member of the Unit, a federal agent, had married her.

It was against every rule that existed, even illegal, since he'd be using fake ID. It was unheard of, in the Unit, and in every law enforcement agency in existence. Undercover agents seduced, lied, cheated, and killed. But they didn't marry, not while undercover.

The shit would hit the fan back in D.C. If he lived, they'd throw the book at him, his teammates would chew his ass out good, he'd probably have to retire in disgrace, but by God . . . it would work. Oh yeah.

If he got whacked, the Unit and all its resources, his teammates, even his boss would provide a shield for Charity, protect her. The Unit took care of its own. By marrying her, he would make Charity one of theirs. As soon as he announced the marriage, he'd make sure they understood that.

Charity was staring at him, light gray eyes wide.

"I—" She cleared her throat. "I beg your pardon? What did you say?"

Her astonishment brought a smile to his face, a lightness he hadn't felt all morning. The way ahead was full of darkness and traps, but there might be a path through it, if he could just feel his way.

Nick took her left hand and slowly removed the supple kid glove. Her skin was soft, warm. He brought her hand up to his mouth and kissed her fingers, watching her eyes, choosing his words carefully.

"I know this sounds crazy, honey. We've only known each other a week. But it's been a . . . very intense week. I know that I've never felt this way before about any other woman, and that's not going to change. In my job, I'm forced to make fast decisions and so far, they've all been good ones. This one is a good one and time won't change it in any way. I don't want to wait. I love you and I want to spend the rest of my life with you."

What was left of it, anyway.

Nick watched her carefully. Her hand had gone slack in his, then had tightened. What was she thinking?

"Marriage," she whispered, eyes searching his.

It sounded crazy to him, too. But he had to convince her. Now that he'd come up with his plan, he couldn't wait to put it into effect.

He nodded. "Marriage. Now."

Her hand jerked in his. "Now? You mean—*right now?*" She looked at the gray courthouse wall. "Just . . . walk in and get married?"

"Yes. Right now." He wished it were already done. He kissed her hand again. "I'm not certain, but I might have to go away on business next week, and I might stay away . . . awhile." This time next week, he might be dead. "I want to know when I leave that you're mine. Forever." And alive, he added silently. "I'm thirty-four and I know myself. I know what I feel and I know this is serious. This is it." He paused. "At least for me it is. I'm hoping you feel the same."

"Yes, I do," she said simply, and his heart soared. His lovely Charity. How typical of her. No coyness, no dancing around, no games. "Yes, I feel the same. That it's serious, and true, and deep."

"Exactly." Inside, he exulted. This was going to work! He

couldn't think about when he'd leave. Right now, he was concentrated on getting her into the Unit's protective embrace. "Now, you know and I know that we could have a long engagement. We could date for another six months, a year, and nothing would change except we'd be a year older. I'd still feel the same and I hope you would, too."

She nodded, eyes unwavering on his.

"My job as a stockbroker is basically to understand not so much what to do but when to do it. I have an instinct for good timing. And my instinct says that this is the right thing to do. Right now."

"Nick," she said quietly, looking troubled, slowly sliding her hand from his. "You must understand, I can't move to Manhattan, much as I'd like to. It would be exciting, and I can't hide from you that I love the idea, but I have responsibilities here. I'm sorry. I don't know if you can accept that."

His heart squeezed and for a second he lost his voice.

She loved him. He knew that, or else he'd never have had this crazy idea, never could have hoped to make it work. It was there in the way she looked at him, touched him, fucked him. No—made love with him.

It spoke to her nature that she'd be willing to give up marriage to the man she loved for her elderly aunt and uncle.

"I don't have to live in New York," he said gently. "They have these fantastic inventions called the Internet and e-mail. I can do most of my business from here. What little I can't do over the Net, I can take care of on short trips."

With each word, he saw joy blossom more brightly on her face, artless and devastating, because he knew what he'd be leaving behind after he was gone. He was going to break her heart.

But—however miserable she'd be when he disappeared,

however devastated and grief-stricken, she'd be alive, and that was what mattered. Nobody dies of a broken heart. They do die of a meat hook through the heart.

Nick was a hard man. Hard men made hard choices. And he'd made his.

"Come with me," he murmured, lifting a hand to tuck a curl behind her ear. He gestured out the windshield at the big door set in the gray wall in front of them. "In there. We can be married in an hour. And since we're doing this the unconventional way, afterward we can go shopping for rings. Soon, maybe next week or when the weather clears up, we can have a little reception for your folks and friends. I was thinking at Da Emilio's. You'd like that, wouldn't you?"

She nodded, smiling. "Yes, I'd like that."

"As long as they let me pay," he added.

He stroked her face, the skin so soft. Warm. Alive. "I need to take care of something this afternoon, but I'll be back by five, six at the latest." A quick kiss. "And we'll have our wedding night tonight." He stirred, just thinking of it.

It came to him with a quick punch to his stomach that tonight he could be making love to his wife. Words he never thought he'd ever say. Not even in his head.

Even if the marriage lasted only a week or two, and he disappeared forever afterward, he'd have had that. More than he ever thought he'd have.

Nick nodded at the big steel doors leading into the courthouse. "What do you say, darling? Shall we get married?"

She didn't say anything, just looked at him. Charity had an open face and Nick could always tell what she was thinking. All her emotions were up front and visible. Except now, when he couldn't read her at all.

Charity said nothing. And it suddenly occurred to him that she hadn't said yes yet.

Sweat gathered along his spine, under his arms. Fuck. It had never even occurred to him that she might say no. If she refused, what the hell was he going to do?

The only other option would be to take her into protective custody. Essentially jail her. And he'd do it, by God. Cuff her if he had to. Drag her into custody kicking and screaming and keep her there until this whole sorry mess was settled.

"So?" he growled.

Nick could feel his muscles tensing. The low, insistent noise of imminent danger in the back of his head dialed up a couple of notches. If she said no, he was taking her in, right now. To hell with Worontzoff. They could get Worontzoff on their own. Nick would go crazy worrying about her, compromise the mission, so the only way he could function was to restrain her and drive her immediately into Birmingham.

They'd put her in a safe house, under guard 24/7. Safe houses were miserably dingy at best, and most were downright seedy. He'd been in more than one with cockroaches. And anyone under guard in a safe house subsisted off stale pizza and beer. Standing guard in a safe house was the most boring security work imaginable and the only way men could stand it was to let themselves go. Inside a day, any safe house in the world looked and smelled like Animal House and the men on guard lost about twenty points off their IQ. Lighting farts was a big diversion on guard duty.

She'd hate it—used to pretty surroundings and perfumed rooms and cut flowers in vases and fresh fruit and vegetables. She'd hate being in a safe house, with no privacy, none of her things around her, guarded over by loutish, uncaring men.

"So," he said again. He tried to keep his voice soft. Nicholas Ames, asking a woman he'd fallen in love with to marry him. Not Nick Ireland, willing to abduct her if she said no. "What's your answer?"

Charity suddenly smiled, eyes shining. "Yes," she said softly. "Oh yes!"

Sixteen

It went smoothly. And fast.

Nobody else wanted to get married on this dark, icy winter day, so after filling out forms and producing IDs, the clerk ushered them immediately into a large room with a podium at the other end.

The room was filled with remnants of weddings past. Big vases of wilted flowers flanked the podium and formed a little honor brigade on either side of the aisle. White satin bows hung from the windows and the smell of scented candles still lingered in little pockets of fragrance. The empty chairs were like ghosts in the room.

A smiling woman and a gray-haired man stood at the podium, watching benevolently as Nick and Charity walked up the aisle, hand in hand.

Half an hour later, they walked out, man and wife.

Or rather, Nicholas Ames walked out a married man. Nick Ireland was still . . . what? Single? Legally, yeah, he was single. He didn't *feel* single any more, though, not with a beaming Charity on his arm, responding happily to her new name, Mrs. Ames.

Like pulling the petals off a daisy. Married. Not married. Married. Not married . . .

It was a farce, of course. The whole marriage thing. He was a nonexistent man taking vows to be faithful until death. Ridiculous. He didn't even believe in marriage. Nothing in his lifetime had ever led him to think that marriage was anything but a legal way to scratch an itch. Stupid, expensive way, too, when there were so many other ways to get laid.

Most of the men in Delta Force were divorced. Several times over, too, which just proved that the smartest men in the world could be led around by their dicks. For a while, at least.

And in the Unit—few of them even managed girlfriends, let alone wives. A long-term commitment was twenty minutes. Roll on, roll off, good-bye. It wasn't a lifestyle conducive to relationships. That wasn't anything that bothered him, until now. Marriage was for civilians.

And yet—and yet.

There'd been a moment there, when the gray-haired man read aloud some bible thing about cleaving unto each other, then made them repeat vows to look after each other in sickness and in health, then quietly pronounced them man and wife. When Charity lifted her radiant face for his kiss. When a goddamned shaft of sunlight unexpectedly broke through the slate gray sky to fucking shine at their feet like some fucking sign from heaven.

Then, right then, the whole thing felt . . . real. For an instant, he could believe he really was Nicholas Ames, businessman, marrying a wonderful woman, till death do us part. They'd live in that beautiful house which they'd fill up with kids.

Take a week's vacation in Aruba each winter. Plant roses and establish a wine cellar and buy a goddamned dog.

It was like a fork in the road and he could see far down where that road would take him. He'd become a family man, pillar of the community. Mow the lawn on Saturdays, coach Little League. Father, husband, neighbor . . .

Nah.

Nick wasn't born for that life. What the fuck did he know about families? Dick is what he knew. His mother had abandoned him at an orphanage; she probably didn't even know who his father was. He had tainted, renegade blood in him. And his upbringing, well . . . Charity could never know what his childhood had been like. What he'd done, what he'd seen. She'd recoil in disgust. Any woman would. And what he was would come out, sooner or later. No one can stay undercover for a lifetime. So a real marriage wasn't in the cards, ever.

But still, for just a minute there . . .

Afterward, he took her to a jewelry store. *The* jewelry store, the only one in Parker's Ridge. This was one thing that was on him. He wouldn't make Uncle Sam pay for this. But what the fuck, he had a million dollars now, didn't he? He could afford a pair of rings.

The store didn't have a big selection and he was just about to settle for a plain regular wedding band size extra large and a band and a diamond for Charity, when he saw them.

A pair of claddagh rings, set in a velvet box under glass. A large, broad band of gold with four claddaghs etched on the ring for him, and the symbol itself as a gold ring for Charity.

The claddagh, the Celtic symbol of true love.

It was the only thing he had of his mother.

On the twenty-first of December, 1976, the night watchman of the orphanage heard a bell ring. It rang only a few times a year and it was the sensor of the only baby hatch in America at that time. Now there were 150 of them, most of them funded by Jake.

The hatch was a warmed baby bed, and it was why Nick had survived that night, the coldest night of the winter of 1975. He had been placed in a cheap plastic basin, wrapped in a blanket stolen from the downtown homeless shelter. The doctors wrote down that, in their estimation, he was three or four days old and that he'd been breast-fed sporadically. The only object in the basin was a small, cheap trinket, sold by the millions in Ireland. A claddagh medallion.

Nick had that medallion in his pocket.

"Honey," he said, "come here."

Charity put down the ring she'd been looking at and walked over to him.

Nick picked up the smaller ring, meant for a woman's hand. He placed it in the palm of her hand. "Do you know what this is?"

Charity picked it up, turning it around. Two stylized hands clasping a heart topped by a crown. "No, but it's very pretty. An unusual design, though." She looked up with a frown. "What is it?"

"A claddagh. It's an ancient Celtic symbol. Look, see the hands holding the heart?"

Charity nodded. "And what's that on top?"

"A crown." Nick smiled mysteriously. "There's a story behind it. You'll love it."

The jeweler had discreetly retreated to the other side of the room to give them privacy. A wind-borne burst of sleet rapped against the big picture window, rattling it. If it rattled, it meant it was a thin pane of glass loose in the casement.

Jesus, Nick thought. The geezer didn't even have bullet-resistant windows. A small fortune in gold and diamonds and any dirtbag could smash his fist through the window and grab a handful. What was *wrong* with these people?

Without thinking about it, he angled his body so that he was between the front window and Charity.

He placed the two rings on his open palm and held them out to her and told her the story of the claddagh. One of the stories. There were dozens. He chose the one he thought Charity'd like best.

"Many, many years ago, in Galway, Ireland, a man named Richard Joyce left his true love to go to the West Indies to seek his fortune. He promised her he'd come back to her a rich man and marry her. But on the way he was kidnapped by pirates and taken to Algiers, where he became a slave to the most famous goldsmith in the Mediterranean. Joyce was an enterprising young man and the goldsmith trained him well. He became a master goldsmith.

"One day the British king demanded the release of all British prisoners held in Algiers. The goldsmith offered Joyce half his fortune and his daughter in marriage if he would only stay. But Joyce wanted to go home and marry his true love, and he did. While still a slave, he'd forged a ring to symbolize his love and upon his return, he gave it to his sweetheart, who'd waited faithfully for him all those years."

Charity was listening intently to him, face rapt. "When the ring is put on the right hand, it means that person's heart is open. When it's on the left hand ring finger with the heart facing outward, it means the person is engaged. When it's on the left hand ring finger with the heart pointing towards the body, it means that person is married to their true love."

Nick picked up the smaller ring and gently slid it onto her left ring finger, heart facing the body.

A perfect fit. He curled his fist around hers.

"When Joyce gave it to his wife, he said, 'With these hands I give you my heart and I crown it with my love.'" He smiled down at her. "And that's what it means to me, too."

"Nick," she whispered. Her eyes were shiny, white throat moving as she swallowed.

"No crying," Nick said, alarmed. Jesus, that was the last thing he needed, a bawling female. No tears, she couldn't cry, no way. His own throat felt tight and hot. She'd set him off and he never *ever* cried. Never. Iceman.

"Here," he said swiftly and held out the man's ring. "Put it on my finger."

She slid it on and they both looked down at his hand. It was a little tight, but that could be taken care of. Or not. He wasn't going to wear it for very long, anyway. Another week, two, max.

The thought dimmed some of the joy and he pushed it out of his head. Concentrate on the moment. And this moment was a fine one, one he'd remember for a long, long time. Charity, looking up at him as if he'd invented sunshine and found the cure for cancer, the old geezer smiling at them both as if they were his beloved grandkids.

Oodles of love and warmth floating around. Nick was surprised they weren't melting snow at a hundred paces.

Okay. Enough of this. There was stuff to do, pronto.

He had to break the news to his teammates camped out in an uncomfortable van that he'd married their prime contact.

Nick knew he was going to take a lot of flak for it, he'd be yelled at and threatened, he might even be demoted, and his boss would have a coronary, but in the end, they'd agree to protect Charity as long as necessary and that was what counted. A team of good guys would have her back.

Let them scream. He was tough. He could take it. What he couldn't take was the idea of Charity alone and in danger. He'd just brought the talents of a lot of very tough guys and an entire government agency over to her side.

He paid for the rings in cash and bundled Charity back into the car. She kept her left glove off, holding her hand up and admiring the ring. It *was* pretty.

He flexed his own left hand. The broad band felt heavy and cumbersome on his hand. He didn't like male jewelry and never imagined he'd ever wear any, let alone a wedding band. It felt weird, awkward, alien.

Even driving at his poky Nicholas Ames speed, it wasn't that far to Charity's house. In ten minutes they were there. Nick parked on the curb and kept the engine running.

He lifted Charity's chin with a forefinger and bent down to her. Her mouth opened immediately, tongue touching his with an electric stroke that went all the way to his balls.

Nose against her cheek, he drew in a sharp breath, scented with shampoo and cream and her perfume. He didn't know what it was, but it was worth every penny she paid for it. It was sheer dynamite. Though it was light and springlike, it went straight to his dick, in a pure Pavlovian reaction. It was automatic. Smell Charity's perfume, get a woody.

Charity murmured into his mouth, a soft groan and cupped his face with her ungloved hand. This was supposed to be a little peck—*bye honey, be good, I'll be back soon*—but Charity's mouth was a little honey trap, warm and wet and welcoming, almost as exciting as her little cunt.

He hadn't gone down on her yet. Chicks loved it. He could take it or leave it, but he'd long ago figured out it was a fast, easy way to make the woman wet and soft enough to take him fully. So it was basically a little speed bump on the way to what he considered real sex.

Suddenly, holding Charity's head still, tongue in her mouth, he had a sharp, sudden hunger to kiss her pussy. Exactly as he was doing with her mouth. Not as a prelude but as the main course. She was so soft down there, even her pubic hair. He flashed on the two of them in her warm bed on this freezing winter night, Charity spread-eagled on the flowered sheets, with his head between her thighs, tongue in her cunt like it was in her mouth right now.

He could see it. Charity's slim, lithe form stretched out, sharp hip bones bracketing her concave belly, pale breasts trembling with every breath, heartbeat visible in her left breast.

He loved it when she came, loved the feeling of the sharp contractions of her cunt around his cock. Jesus, how much better would it be to *taste* her climax, feel her coming against his mouth?

Just the thought of it brought him fully erect, when he had nowhere to go with his hard-on. *Ouch.*

He broke away from her, breathing hard, and curled his fingers resolutely around the steering wheel.

Her mouth was wet, a little swollen, the way her cunt probably was. . . .

Think of something else.

Nick flashed on telling Di Stefano and his boss about marrying Charity. Their reaction, the reaction back in D.C. It was like dipping his dick in a glass of ice water.

He smiled at her, at her confused look and nodded toward the house. "Go in now honey, or I'll never get these things done. I'll be back around five or six and we'll spend the entire night . . . celebrating."

She turned pink and Nick laughed and reached across to open her door. "Hold that thought."

Charity turned and smiled at him. "You betcha," she said softly and got out. Nick watched until she was in the house and the living rooms lights went on, then pulled out.

He called Di Stefano and was relieved when he got a busy signal. Bumped over to voice mail, he left a brief message that he was on his way.

Then he called Jake on his cell. "Hey big guy," Jake answered. "Or should I say rich guy?"

"That's funny, coming from you. You have more money than God." He heard Jake chuckle complacently, because he did. "You could buy me out with what you spend for breakfast."

"Maybe. But I think I'm going to set another goal for you. How about another million by this time next year? I've been crunching numbers and reading some interesting stuff on Moldovan bonds. And there's this new Brazilian company making hybrid cars. I'm going to make you so much money, you'll figure it's ridiculous keeping that job of yours and you'll quit and do something that won't get you killed."

Perfect opening. "Hey Jake, about that getting killed stuff . . ."

"What?" Jake's voice rose with tension, all humor gone. "What? Are you in trouble? Goddamn you, Nick, how many times have I told you—"

"Can it, Jake," Nick said wearily. Jesus, what had he got married for, when Jake did the nagging wife thing so well? "I'm not in danger." Yet. "What I am is married. I think."

"You *think*? Jesus, Nick, you *think* you're married? That's like being a little bit pregnant. What the hell's going on?"

The promise of that slate gray sky was kept. Snow started

falling in earnest, thick white sheets dropping out of the sky, reducing visibility to just a couple of feet beyond his front fender. Even he had to pay some attention here. He put his cell on the dashboard and switched to speakerphone.

"Listen, I don't have time to explain. I want to change my will. I'm going to disinherit you. You okay with that?"

His first day in the army, when he had exactly $10.75 to his name, when asked about next of kin and asked to make out a will, he'd put down Jake as his next of kin and beneficiary. Over the years, as he renewed his will, that hadn't changed. Jake had power of attorney over his affairs and was his heir.

If Jake didn't inherit all Nick's worldly possessions, even if they topped an unlikely million bucks, it wouldn't make any difference at all to Jake. What was a million bucks to him? Walking around money, that's what it was.

"Hell." It wasn't the thought of losing Nick's money that made Jake's voice so somber. "You're in trouble, Nick. I can feel it. Something really bad is coming down and you're right in the middle. Oh my God. Oh shit. Oh *fuck*. I just flashed on your funeral. Fuck this, fuck whatever you're doing. Wherever you are, *get out now*!"

Jake's voice rose with anxiety.

A trickle of sweat ran down Nick's back. Jake's hunches were good, almost as good as his. Jake was a genius at crunching numbers, but his incredible success was also due to the way he could sniff trouble coming and could slalom his way out of it, fast. As the *Wall Street Journal* said, "Jacob Weiss's hedge fund, JLW, has demonstrated a sixth sense for emerging markets and, in today's volatile world, an even more useful sense for tanking markets. JLW has the golden touch—it knows, to the day, when to abandon ship."

When Jake talked, markets listened. More to the point,

when Jake talked, *Nick* listened. Ordinarily, when Jake said jump, Nick answered how high? He couldn't bail now, though. There was no way out now but straight through the heart of trouble.

Nick didn't even try to snow Jake. He was too smart to swallow false reassurances. "Whatever's coming down, Jake, I'll deal. You know me. I'm harder to kill than a cockroach. But there's a new element now. A . . . a woman. I . . . married her." The words were hard to get out. They sounded surreal and false. He was married. He wasn't married.

Yes, he was. No, he wasn't.

This was messing with his head.

Concentrate.

It didn't make a lick of difference if he was married or not. What was important was to settle his affairs right now so he could face the showdown that was coming with a clear head.

"Yeah? About time." Jake's nanny gene rose to the fore. He'd been nagging Nick to get married for almost ten years now. "About time you tied the knot, you idiot. I don't know what you were waiting for, hell to freeze over? So tell me that means you're going to settle down, find yourself a job that won't get you killed—"

It was Jake's favorite rant and Nick was tempted to zone out and let him get it off his chest for the billionth time. But he wanted to drive as fast as he could to the van and the weather was worsening with every passing minute. The snow had let up a little, but the temperature was dropping and ice was building up. He needed to pay attention to the road. These conditions tried even his driving skills.

"Can it." Nick fought the wheel as a sharp, strong blast of wind rocked the vehicle. "Listen, I'm tight for time, so

I can't explain the whole situation. Believe me when I say it's . . . complex. All you need to know is that one Nicholas Ames—that would be me—married one Charity Prewitt a couple of hours ago." He gave Charity's full name—which turned out to be Charity Prudence Prewitt. He had smiled at that and the smile had earned him a poke in the ribs from her sharp little elbow. He gave Jake DOB, SSN, and address. "If something happens to me, you'll know." Jake was the only person on the government "To Be Notified in Case of Death" form. "Can I change my will on the phone? Right now? I want her to be my sole beneficiary. Sorry, Jake. When I kick the bucket, Marja's going to have to do without her fiftieth fur coat."

"She'll live," was Jake's wry reply.

"Okay—so now I really need to know whether I can legally do this over the phone. This is a formal request to you. You have power of attorney. I want to change my will and make Charity P. Prewitt my sole beneficiary. Is that possible right now?"

Clacking in the background. Nick waited patiently, wrestling the wheel, trying to concentrate on the road.

"Done. Let me read it out to you."

Jake read out the new will, which was identical to the old one except for the date, the name of the beneficiary, and an addendum to the effect that Jacob Weiss, who had power of attorney over Nick Ireland's affairs, recognized Ireland's voice and was willing to swear an oath in court to that effect. "I'll get that notarized, just to be on the safe side. Soon."

"Now," Nick said.

Silence. Jake processed that. "Okay, I'm leaving the office right now. There's a very grateful notary on Lexington who bought himself a vacation home in Tuscany with what JLW earned him, so he owes me. I'll get this notarized within the hour, Nick. That's a promise."

Nick knew it was as good as done.

"Thanks, buddy." Nick felt an overwhelming sense of relief, as if a granite block he didn't know was on his back had been lifted. "I owe you. Big time."

"Pay me back by staying alive."

"Do my best and thanks."

Nick hit the Off button and devoted all his attention to the road. Though it was early in the afternoon, the sky was almost black. The few cars he passed on the road all had their headlights on and were driving at twenty miles an hour, feeling their way over the roads rather than driving their way along.

The surveillance van was only twenty-five miles away, but there was a dangerous patch of road that wound in hairpin turns up a steep hill. It would be hairy with ice on the road. He wanted to get there, fight with Di Stefano and Alexei and get back before sundown.

Most of his head was taken up with negotiating the turns, but what remained of his hard disk was focused on Charity, and on what he was going to do to her when he finally got back to her.

Tonight was going to be probably the closest he would ever come to having a wedding night, and he was going to make the most of it. He had no intention of sleeping tonight. They were going to fuck all night long, punctuated only by food and wine and maybe the odd shower or two.

Nick was shaken out of those pleasant thoughts by a sharp jolt. Instantly back in combat mode, he checked the rearview mirror and saw high headlights coming closer, close enough to ram him again.

It was only now that he realized his subconscious had noticed the black SUV all along. He'd simply put it down to some nervous driver following another driver on a night of bad visibility.

It wasn't that, it was a tail. Shame on him for taking so long to pick up on it.

Nobody tailed him for long. He was hypervigilant in and out of a car. That this guy had been able to follow him just went to show how much Nick's head was up his ass. Or up his dick.

God, if he did get offed, he'd fucking deserve it.

Thoughts of Charity and everything else fled from his head when the bastard behind him bumped his rear fender again.

Nick pulled away fast. The SUV had tinted windows. All he could make out behind the windshield was a male figure, tall and broad shouldered, wearing a watch cap. Mud had been smeared on the plate. There was nothing to call in.

Nick bared his teeth when the guy behind him bumped the Lexus again, only this time harder.

Fucker was making a bad mistake. Nick was a good shot, but there were better shots around. He was a good man in a fight, but he had never won any martial arts awards. He'd been a damned good soldier and was shaping up to be a fine law enforcement officer, but he wasn't the best there was.

But by God, no one could beat him in a car. No one. If Watch Cap wanted to kill him while Nick had a steering wheel in his hands, he had the wrong guy.

The guy behind him bumped the Lexus again, only this time harder, maintaining contact while swerving hard to the left. He was angling to drive Nick across the next lane and off the road. This stretch of winding road had a thin guardrail against a sheer drop of four hundred feet. The guardrail wouldn't hold against a big heavy car like the Lexus crashing into it.

Another jolt, harder this time, just as they were coming up to a curve. The SUV driver messing with his head. *I'm coming after you.*

Did the guy know this road? Nick did, intimately. Besides strong driving skills, he had a natural compass in his head. He never got lost, ever. All he had to do was drive a road once to find it again and if he drove it a couple of times, it was as if he'd been driving it all his life. He'd been driving this road to the surveillance van several times a day for the past ten days. He could do it blindfolded.

With a little luck, the scumbag behind him had been called in from outside. By Worontzoff, no doubt about that. Whether he'd made Nick for a cop or he was just crazy jealous of Charity, it didn't take much detecting to realize that Worontzoff had put out a contract on him.

Nick didn't think Worontzoff would send one of his goons out on local wetwork. That would be fouling his nest in case something went wrong. Mobsters like Worontzoff were executives. They thought along cool, rational lines and the cool, rational thing to do would be to bring in hired muscle with a cut-out for deniability.

But even if this shit head trying to ram him off the road had been born and bred here, he'd just signed his death warrant.

Okay, Mr. Hired Gun, Nick thought grimly. *Let's see how good you are.*

They were coming up on the first leg of a big, sharp S curve. At the next jolt, Nick applied the brakes, hard, as if panicked. As if he were someone who has just now realized that the taps from behind weren't minor accidents and that the other driver was trying to drive him off the road. The first thing a civilian would do is freak and then brake. Nick could almost feel the smile of satisfaction behind the dark windshield.

Enjoy that feeling while you can, fuckhead. You've got about five minutes left to live.

The SUV rammed his back fender again, violently, and this time stayed in contact with the Lexus. Then the driver gunned his engine as Nick braked harder. The Lexus had excellent brakes, Nick was almost completely stopped. The only thing propelling him forward now was the SUV. Even above the wind, he could hear the SUV's engines whining as it took the burden of driving two heavy vehicles uphill in the snow.

Nick waited until the road started its first curve, long enough for the driver to have gotten used to the feel of strain in his vehicle. Long enough to make him complacent.

Just after the SUV shifted gears to start the steep, climbing curve, Nick gunned his engine, shooting forward, the Lexus taking him from almost zero to sixty in a couple of seconds. He rounded the curve, losing the SUV, and then took the other curve as fast as he dared. He'd effectively disappeared from sight.

As soon as he rounded the second curve, he made a bootlegger's turn, big hood pointed back from where he'd come. He pulled over to the extreme left-hand side of the road and waited, engine running.

Sure enough, a minute later, the SUV appeared, headlights on bright, cutting through the darkness. He saw Nick too late and stood on his brakes. He didn't have Nick's experience driving in extreme weather and he lost control of the heavy vehicle. The SUV spun almost 180 degrees on the ice, and Nick rammed into it hard.

He used the momentum of his own heavy vehicle to keep the SUV pinned in, then suddenly swerved left, hard, straight into the SUV, ramming it against the cliff.

The impact could be heard over the wind as the SUV's front fender ran into the cliff. The airbag inside deployed. Nick could see the driver slumped over the airbag. An airbag deploys at two hundred miles an hour in the first fractions of a second. As a distraction, it wasn't as good as a flash-bang, but it would have to do. The guy would be disoriented for at least two minutes and that's all the time Nick would need.

Inside twenty seconds, he was out of the Lexus and had picked the SUV's lock. The airbag was slowly deflating and the man was moaning, moving slowly, still in shock. His eyes sharpened with panic when he saw Nick and he fumbled for the Sig Sauer P210 in the passenger seat. Expensive gun. Nothing but the best for Worontzoff's goons.

But the airbag impeded his movements. He never had a chance.

There was a quick way to do this. Nick placed the flat of his hand against the man's right temple, his other hand on the left side of his neck and in one quick motion, broke his neck.

He pulled out his Maglite and looked around the vehicle, checking registration papers.

The SUV was a rental. The name on the rental contract was Stephen Anderson, no doubt a false name. The inside of the vehicle was clean, almost sterile. He checked the ash-trays, under the seats, inside the side pockets. Nothing. No cigarette butts, no food packages, no marked maps. No clues, no prints, since the guy was wearing gloves and probably no DNA.

Nick frisked him, fast. No ID, no labels on his clothes. He

was more or less Nick's height, more or less Nick's weight. Perfect. This would work.

Nick ran back to his car, popped open the trunk, and got out his suitcase and emergency kit hidden under the spare tire. He always kept a jerry can of gas and got that out, too.

Go, go, go!

Even in this weather, someone might come up along this road any moment. Bending down in the SUV, he pulled the man up in a fireman's lift, carried him over to the Lexus, and put him behind the wheel. His neck was broken, but that would be attributed to the fall of the vehicle from over four hundred feet. The clothes would burn up and with any luck the skin of his fingers would, too. Together with the skin all over. A suspicious coroner might want to match dental records but there weren't any for Nicholas Ames and who was going to demand it, anyway? There would be a six-foot-two male charred body in Nicholas Ames's car and Nick Ireland would drop out of sight.

Nick placed his non-Unit-issued cell phone in the guy's pocket, on the off chance the SIM card would survive the fire. No one would be contacting Nicholas Ames ever again, anyway.

Working fast, Nick grabbed the jerry can, poured some gas into the driver's footwell, and in the trunk, close to the gas tank. He checked the level. Thank God it was full. He figured there were over eighteen gallons of fuel in that sucker. Basically a rolling bomb.

Buckling the seat belt over the guy slumped in the driver's seat, Nick checked everything and was about ready to drive the SUV over the cliff when he stopped and picked up the dead man's left hand and removed the glove. He worked the claddagh ring off his finger and put it on the dead man's left hand ring finger. It had been tight on him but fit this fucker perfectly.

Time was tight, but he took a moment to look down at his wedding ring on the man's hand.

Always knew I wasn't made for marriage, he thought.

Reaching in and igniting the Lexus's engine, he put it in gear, placed the dead man's foot on the gas pedal, and pressed down on his knee. The Lexus rolled forward. Perfect. In the last possible second before the car drove off the cliff, Nick threw an open match into the footwell, slammed the door closed, and ran back to the other side of the road.

The Lexus caught fire in midair. Nick watched the fiery ball in its long descent down into the valley below, lighting up the dark afternoon sky.

It took several seconds for the Lexus to hit the bottom. When it did, it exploded, the sound echoing through the valley.

Someone was going to come check out that explosion soon. Nick had to get out of here, fast.

Nicholas Ames, stockbroker, was gone now, forever.

He strapped on his shoulder rig, tossed the guy's Sig Sauer into the glove compartment, threw his suitcase and emergency kit into the back of the now-battered SUV, and pulled out, heading for the van.

Not only was he now going to have to tell Di Stefano, Alexei, and the boss that he was married. He was also going to have to break the news that he was dead.

Seventeen

Charity raised her left hand and admired her wedding ring for the bazillionth time. The first thing she'd done when she got home was to switch on her computer and research claddagh rings on the Internet. She was a librarian, after all. Getting information was her specialty. Inside an hour, she knew everything there was to know about the claddagh symbol.

The story Nick had told her was there, together with others, each more charming and more romantic than the last. It was the perfect wedding ring.

It was the perfect wedding.

Over the years, Charity had been to a lot of weddings—of high school friends and college chums and colleagues. It seemed everyone was gripped with wedding fever. Not marriage fever—a lot of the marriages were already over—

but some insane compulsion to turn the wedding ceremony into a ridiculously expensive and overblown spectacle.

She'd accompanied friends to fittings of $50,000 gowns they'd never wear again and helped choose $10,000 brides-maid's outfits. Agonized with them over outrageously ex-travagant floral arrangements and debated the virtues of ten tiers of vanilla meringue buttercream cake as opposed to eight tiers of chocolate truffle ganache. With the solid-gold monogram cake topper.

Leafing madly through bridal magazines as thick as *War and Peace*.

And the orchestra and the favors and the wedding meal menu—one friend had had over twenty-two courses—and the going-away outfit. With the special lingerie and the stockings and the shoes. Oh, and the beautician and the hair-dresser on call . . . the details were never ending.

During the course of the average planning sessions, her friends would fight with their mothers, their fiancées, the bridesmaids, then make up in tears. Some lost ten pounds. Some gained twenty from anxiety. She'd laughed and planned with them and let them vent their nerves and all the time thought how foolish all this fluffy fuss was for an event that was supposed to be the most solemn event of one's life. A private act of love between two people. An avowal of lifelong fidelity.

The end of one life as a single and the beginning of another as a couple. Except for parenthood, the most sacred bond of all.

Her marriage today was one she'd never have dared planned on her own—one lived in society after all—but it had been perfect for her. Especially after Nick had said that they would have a reception at Da Emilio's afterward. Her aunt and uncle were too wrapped up in their problems to feel left out. Her friends would be happy with the party later. The wedding itself—that had been between just her and her husband-to-be. Husband, now.

Perfect.

She so wanted the rest of the day—and night—to be as perfect as the ceremony itself. Nick said he wouldn't be back until after five or six, so that should give her plenty of time to prepare things.

Bless Mrs. Marino, her aunt and uncle's housekeeper, who was on a crusade to fatten her up. Charity didn't have to make a mess or smell up the house cooking a wedding feast. It was as if Mrs. Marino had known and had cooked a feast just for her.

In the freezer was exquisite finger food, platters of lasagna, veal in Marsala sauce, gratinéed vegetables, and even a wedding cake in the form of the best tiramisú this side of Rome. She had smoked salmon and caviar in the fridge and two bottles of superb Chilean champagne in the cellar, courtesy of Mr. Hernandez, owner of the only landscape gardening business in Parker's Ridge, whose son she'd coached in English.

They could have their honeymoon right here. A week in the house without ever coming up for air.

And . . . she had the perfect outfit. A heavy silk peach-colored low-cut full-length nightgown with matching negligee, still in its wrapping paper. She'd never worn it. It had been the fruit of a hunting trip in Filene's Basement while visiting a friend in Boston. She'd been looking for serviceable work sweaters and had stopped, awestruck, when she'd seen the beautiful outfit.

Mary, her friend, had urged her to buy it. Even discounted

from $700 to $300 it was outrageously expensive, and for what? There wasn't a man in her life at the time and hadn't been for years. Who would she wear it for?

She'd been about to say no when Mary had taken her hand and curled it around the bias-cut skirt. The silk felt like cool water beneath her fingers. It felt sexy and classy, like an artifact from another life. One more exciting than hers.

When she tried it on, it was as if it had been tailor-made for her. So she'd caved in and bought it, feeling guilty, and placed it in the bottom of her dresser drawer, thinking she'd never wear it.

And now she was wearing it for her wedding night! The thought was so enticing she shivered.

She set the table carefully, bringing out the heavy white Flanders tablecloth, Grandmother Prentiss's Limoges service, and her parent's Waterford crystal glasses. The family silver. The big, heavy silver candelabra family legend had it that her great-grandmother had used to break the skull of an intruder during the Depression.

She filled the candelabra with candles and then continued around the room. She loved candles and had them in every shape and size, most vanilla-scented. She covered the sideboard, the mantelpiece, and the coffee table with candles and stood back, pleased.

Around five, she'd switch off all the lights and light the candles. Nick would come back to a candlelit home. It would be so beautiful.

In the bedroom, she placed candles on her dresser, nightstand, and the windowsills. The small cozy room looked like a bower, ready for a night of love. Between husband and wife.

What a delicious thought.

She changed the sheets on the bed, choosing her finest set—300-thread count flowered Egyptian cotton sheets, thick, starched and smelling of lavender.

Charity pulled out the nightgown and negligee. They were as gorgeous as in her memory. She fingered the heavy, beautiful silk, imagining Nick's face when he saw her in it. No princess on earth would have a finer outfit for her wedding night.

Everything was more or less ready, except for herself.

She ran a rose-scented bubble bath, a little too hot, piled her hair on top of her head with two picks and eased into the water with a contented sigh. The hot water sank deep fingers of heat into her, loosened her muscles. Charity tipped her head back against the rim of the bathtub and closed her eyes, inhaling the scented steam and thinking of nothing at all, completely happy.

When she opened her eyes, the bubbles had dissipated and she could see herself in the water. She took in a deep breath and watched her breasts rise. Her breasts. Nick had made love to her breasts so intently, so single-mindedly, you'd think they were a source of pleasure for him, too. If she concentrated, she could feel his mouth right now, tugging gently at her nipple.

At the thought, she could actually see her nipples swell and turn deep pink.

Every inch of her skin was sensitized by Nick. She tried to think of a part of her body he hadn't touched, but couldn't, unless you count internal organs. Toes, the backs of her knees, elbows, belly button, the skin behind her ears. Memories, images flooded her mind and she felt a now-familiar tingle between her thighs. That tingle would be connected to thoughts of Nick until the end of time.

Her body. It amazed her that it could harbor these sensations. Where had her body *been* all these years? With hind-sight, she realized that all her life, she'd essentially thought of her body as a carrying case for her head. It required rest, good nutrition, and regular exercise, but that was about it.

Who knew that there was this amazing world inside her, a world of unimagined pleasure? And it was Nick's for the asking.

She had so many images in her head. Nick's face as he thrust in and out of her slowly. He'd sometimes push himself up on his arms, biceps bulging, big veins standing out, and look down between them. She'd look too, watching as his big penis pulled slowly out, wet with her juices, thick and ropy. She could feel him every inch of the way, leaving emptiness when he withdrew. He'd pull out until they could see the big plum-colored head which turned a deep red while they were making love and wait until her eyes met his and she whimpered. Then and only then would he push back into her.

Once, Charity had curled her nails into his hard buttocks and lifted herself in frustration because he was taking it so *slowly*.

Her nails didn't even dent his skin. No matter how hard she dug into him, she knew she wasn't hurting him, couldn't hurt him. He was amazingly hard, all over. He said he took martial arts lessons to destress and they had created a re-markable male body.

The lips of her vagina were clasped around the big head but the rest of her was so empty. . . .

Enough Nick, she'd whispered and the small half smile he'd worn disappeared. His eyes turned a deep hot blue and he'd whispered back *yes, enough*, and had slammed into her so hard it took her breath away. He'd begun making love in earnest, hard, long, deep strokes that made her old bed creak, so fast she thought she'd burn up with the friction. . . .

With a cry, Charity climaxed in the water—hard, fast contractions that went on and on, almost as long as they did while Nick was making love to her.

She lost herself, as she always did, heat flowing throughout her body, a small sun of it concentrated between her thighs. When she came to, she unclenched her fists and relaxed her muscles again. She had a deep flush on her chest, down to her breasts. The effect of the hot water but also the climax.

Amazing.

It wasn't the first time she'd climaxed on her own, of course. After all, she hadn't had a lover for many years. But it was certainly the first time she'd climaxed without touching herself. And it wasn't her usual tight, almost painful self-induced orgasm that was over almost before it began and left her feeling depleted, restless, and lonely. No, it was one of those majestic, pulsing orgasms that left her feeling like the queen of the world. A very relaxed queen of the world.

Amazing. Nick was with her even when he wasn't. He was in her heart, now, never to depart.

On that happy thought, her happy body climbed out of the bathtub and she began preparations worthy of a geisha. Scented moisturizer everywhere, rubbed in deeply until her very cells were fragrant. Pedicure, manicure, masque.

She pinned her hair up again, more carefully this time, letting a few tendrils fall artfully on her shoulders and began making up. Light makeup because the instant Nick began kissing her, it would all disappear immediately. No mascara. Who wanted to be the Raccoon Bride?

She slid the nightgown over her head with all the care and

solemnity of a medieval knight donning armor, then slid her arms into the negligee.

She had a pair of mules, a gift from a friend, and wondered whether it would be overkill, then decided that overkill was just fine for a wedding night. Her first and only wedding night. This night would never come again. Any extravagance was justified.

She twirled in front of the mirror, delighted with what she saw. She was flushed pink, eyes bright. For tonight, she was beautiful, as all brides must be on their wedding day.

It was five and completely dark by the time she finished her preparations. The table was set, the dishes ready to be nuked, and she set about the house slowly, ceremoniously lighting all the candles in her bedroom and in the living room.

She made a little wish with each candle. For so many things. For a long, happy life with Nick. For healthy children and the grace and wisdom to teach them to grow up to be honorable human beings. For the courage to face life's vicissitudes. And at the last candle, she wished for serenity for Aunt Vera.

There. Everything was perfect. The house glowed. She glowed. Now all she had to do was wait. It was so hard to be patient, though. She'd sit down, then jump back up as if the chair had lifted up to eject her.

After an hour of pacing, she finally sat down with a glass of white wine to calm her nerves. She sipped slowly, enjoying the cool fruity liquid as it slid down her throat. A second glass would be welcome, but she didn't want Nick to come home to a soused bride.

Another hour went by. The fire in the hearth needed feeding. She knelt to put twigs and a small log in the embers, and heard a car on her street.

Heart pounding, she jumped up and rushed to the door but the car passed on by. It wasn't Nick. Disappointment pounded through her body.

Her heart had started pounding at the thought of Nick coming up the walk and she had to wait for it to slow down. It was so *hard* to be patient! So hard to be alone.

Wow.

She had to sit down for that thought. Not being able to entertain herself, being dependent on someone else for her emotional equilibrium, was entirely new. An only child, she was accustomed from birth to being on her own. Solitude had never weighed on her. If anything, she enjoyed being on her own, never thinking of it as loneliness.

If Charity had had to describe herself to someone who didn't know her, one of the first attributes she'd mention would be her emotional and intellectual self-sufficiency.

One week of Nick and that was all blown out of the water. New lover, new life, new her.

She gave a brief glance at her bookshelves, completely indifferent to what was on them. There were two new books by favorite authors, but she couldn't bring herself to feel any spark of excitement. There were CDs galore along one wall but the thought of listening to anything alone, without being in Nick's arms, was almost painful to contemplate.

No books, no music, no movies could begin to compare with Nick. In a week, he'd become her touchstone. Her reason for living. It was a scary and exhilarating thought. Scary because she realized she was now dependent on someone else. Exhilarating because Nick loved her and she'd never be alone again.

Another car drove past slowly, but it wasn't Nick.

She wore no watch—who wanted a watch on her wedding night?—but the grandfather clock against the wall ticked away the minutes as she watched the hands make their rounds. Eight o'clock. Nine o'clock.

Clearly, the business deal or whatever it was, was taking longer than usual. Should she phone?

Start as you mean to go on. Charity had no intention of being a clinging, cloying wife, so she decided against it.

Ten o'clock. This was . . . odd. Nick was a courteous man. He knew perfectly well she was waiting for him, had been for five hours. It seemed impossible that he wouldn't let her know he'd be late. Even if he was immersed in business, a quick phone call wouldn't be out of place. Or he could have someone call her, a secretary or something.

Eleven o'clock. Charity finally broke down and called his cell phone, but only got a recorded message that the party she was dialing couldn't be reached and to try again later.

Many of the candles were guttering, some had died. She'd overdone it. The fragrance of all those scented candles vied with the sharp scents of food and made her slightly nauseous. Something roiled in her stomach and she felt bile and the white wine start to come up. By a miracle she avoided vomiting but it was touch and go.

That would teach her to drink wine on an empty stomach.

By midnight she was pacing in a tight circle, thoughts racing, fists clenching and unclenching. She'd just picked up the phone to start calling local hospitals when the front doorbell rang.

It couldn't be Nick. He had the key. Peeking through the living room curtains she saw a police car parked at the curb, lights flashing. She rushed to the door and found a highway patrolman on her porch. Not too tall, dark hair cut military-short. He looked about twelve and was nervously holding a big Smoky hat, twisting it in his hands.

"Ms. Charity Prewitt?"

"Yes?" Her hand went to her throat. Charity stared at him, wide-eyed. "Actually, Mrs. Nicholas Ames. What is it officer?"

He swallowed. "I'm sorry to have to inform you, ma'am, that there's been accident."

She could barely take in his words. "An . . . accident?"

He blinked and gulped. "Yes, ma'am. A Lexus drove off the cliff this afternoon, broke right through the guardrail. On Hillside Drive. The vehicle was . . . destroyed. We found the engine block number and the car was registered to a Mr. Nicholas Ames. Our computer system tells us you'd married Mr. Ames this morning. Is that correct?"

Charity stared at him, his words barely making sense. "I'm sorry?"

Ill at ease, the officer looked down at a notepad in his hand. "Did you marry a Mr. Nicholas Ames this morning, ma'am?"

"Yes, I—" Her throat was scratchy. She tried to swallow but her mouth had gone dry. This couldn't be happening. Nick was smart and strong. Surely he got out of the car before— "Yes, we married this morning. Is—is my husband, is he—?" The words wouldn't come. Her throat simply closed up tight and all Charity could do was stare at him.

For an answer, the officer dug into his jacket pocket and held something out to her in the palm of his hand. Her knees buckled and she had to cling to the door-jamb for support.

"I'm really sorry to have to give you bad news, ma'am," the officer said sorrowfully. "This was found in the car. There was nothing else left that could give us an identity. Do you recognize it?"

On his rough palm, the claddagh ring gleamed in the bright light of the porch lamp.

Eighteen

I buried my husband today.

Charity Prewitt Ames hugged her cold knees with her cold arms and shivered.

Husband. He'd been her husband for what? Five hours? Maybe six?

It wasn't very long to be a bride. And now her husband was in the stone-cold ground and Charity wished she could follow him.

The phone rang. And rang and rang. Charity Prewitt Ames couldn't pick up. She hadn't answered the phone since the funeral. She didn't want condolences, she didn't want any gentle inquiries into how she was feeling. Everyone wanted to know if she needed something.

Why yes, yes she did need something, thank you.

Her huband back, alive.

Condolences were words. Mere words. They wouldn't bring her husband back. Short of Nick back, there wasn't anything anyone could give her that would make any difference whatsoever.

Uncle Franklin and Aunt Vera, bless them, stayed away because she told them she wanted to be alone. She loved them, but she couldn't face them right now. Even knowing that Aunt Vera was probably hallucinating, out of control, and Uncle Franklin was dealing with it alone, she simply couldn't face her aunt's needs right now.

She couldn't face anything right now. The only thing she could do was curl up on the couch in an aching ball of grief and sorrow. There was nothing in her to give to anyone.

Everything in her was crushed, broken. She could almost feel her rib cage caving in, sucked in by the collapse of her heart. Every cell in her body was rejecting the idea of Nick in the stony, frozen ground. A collection of charred bones in the place of her handsome, vital husband. She'd spent the past three days vomiting the notion out of her body. But however much she emptied her stomach, the reality didn't change

The phone rang again. She counted ten rings before whoever it was hung up again without leaving a message. The cordless was nearby—all she had to do was stretch out her hand and grasp the cold plastic, punch the button to turn it on.

She'd listen to some tinny voice, tuning in and out. She'd absorb only the odd word or two. *Terrible. Shocked.* All the usual words. *Sorry* would definitely be in there.

There were proper answers to give. Little murmurs to say that she was bearing up, grief passes with time, thank you for calling.

The few times she'd answered the phone before the funeral, though, the words wouldn't—*couldn't* come out. They simply remained in her throat, like hot little knives, slicing her to bits.

The phone rang again.

Her hand stayed where it was.

The house was cold. She hated the cold. In winter, her heating bills were atrocious because she liked her house toasty warm. The fire was lit almost every evening, well into spring.

But now it was cold. She hadn't had the energy to turn the heat on or light the fire after the funeral. She hadn't had the energy to do anything but collapse on the couch in a miserable huddle.

The last time she'd sat on this couch, she'd been in Nick's arms.

The cruelty of losing someone so suddenly, particularly a man as vital as Nick, was that it was impossible to take in the fact that he was dead. Not long ago, she'd been lying along her couch, Nick on top of her, kissing her neck, her breasts.

She grabbed one of the big couch pillows and buried her face in it.

It still smelled like him, like Nick. She could smell wood smoke from the blazing fire he'd built, his shampoo and soap and something that was simply . . . him.

If she closed her eyes, she could almost imagine him back, the man who'd become her lover and then, crazily, her husband in the short space of a week.

Her husband.

Now gone.

Midnight, November 28
Sixty miles south of St. John, New Brunswick,
  Canada

The Vor had said the ocean journey would take about a week and he'd been right. Of course.

Arkady was a scientist. The rigor of science, the fact that the laws governing this world were knowable through reason, had kept him from going insane in the Gulag. But if the Vor woke up one day and said that the sun was going to rise in the west, why then Arkady would get up in the morning and look to the west for the sun.

He was up on the deck, his first taste of fresh air in a week. They'd called him an hour ago, as he knew they would. A quiet knock on the steel bulkhead to let him know they were approaching their destination.

Now they were approaching land. The coastline was dark, visible only because it was darker than the surrounding ocean reflecting the light of the crescent moon. This part of the coast was as deserted as Siberia. No one to see them come, no one to see them go.

Arkady breathed deeply. The air smelled of nothing but pine trees for a thousand miles, with no hint of industry. Man's hand here was light. Just as it was in Siberia. The earth would be better off if mankind were to simply disappear.

Arkady believed that with all that remained of his soul.

The captain was good at his job. The ship had doused its lights, but he put into a narrow inlet as if driving into a parking lot. Arkady looked overboard and was surprised to see a long jetty. There were no other boats, nothing else at all, actually, just this lone, long jetty stretching out to sea.

Waiting on the shore was a truck. Anonymous, a little battered and mud spattered. The license plates were smeared with mud. Arkady had no doubt that the heart of the truck, its engine, was top of the line.

He climbed down the ladder and waited quietly as two crew members brought up the container and offloaded it to a four-wheel hand truck. They worked smoothly and quickly, maneuvering in the darkness as if it were noon.

Arkady watched as they placed the container in a special compartment in the back of the truck. Until they opened the partition, there had been no sign of the secret compartment. Suspicious border guards would have to actually measure the inside and outside dimensions to discover it. Arkady had never been to North America, but he understood that, however heightened security might be at airports, road border controls between the United States and Canada were light.

There was barely enough space for a comfortable chair and six liters of mineral water. Arkady wouldn't be as comfortable as he'd been up until now, but it would only be for a little while. And he'd survived worse, much worse.

They would get through. The Vor had thought of everything.

For a second, in the freezing midnight Canadian cold, on a clear night, with the Milky Way a cloudy rope across the sky, Arkady felt at one with the universe.

Arkady had one last phone call to make. The truck driver told him that though there was light snow in Vermont, the roads were clear. They should be in Parker's Ridge tomorrow in the late afternoon, in about eighteen hours. He hauled out his last untraceable cell phone, the red one.

As always, Arkady thrilled to hear the Vor's voice when he answered.

"Our good luck with the weather is holding." He looked up at the inky winter sky. "Brilliant sunshine, warm winds. Weather forecasts say that the weather will hold for about eighteen hours."

"Excellent news, my friend. See you soon, then."

The red cell phone met the same end as the others. The SIM card was buried underneath a juniper bush, the rest of the phone crushed beneath his boot heel and tossed into the Atlantic.

Arkady watched as the ripples the plastic made edged their way outward, then subsided gently.

The last stage of a chain of events that would change the world.

The captain and his crew had already boarded the ship, which was turning to head back out to sea. The captain and his crew had been efficient carriers. Arkady would report this back to the Vor. There would be many other trips. The captain would retire a very rich man.

Arkady was left with the truck driver. He awaited his orders.

"We depart now," Arkady said quietly in English, and he nodded.

With one last look at the night sky, Arkady climbed into the secret compartment and waited to be sealed up with his lethal cargo.

November 29
Harlan's Motel, thirty miles from Parker's Ridge

Finally, morning came. The dull gray sunlight seeping through the cracked blinds of the motel room didn't flatter the room any. It highlighted the stains and worn patches in the carpet, the cracks in the plasterboard walls, the thin film of dust everywhere.

It was a miserable little motel room, the most anonymous, cheap one he could find. Though Nicholas Ames's photo had been briefly on the news all day four days ago, the man who checked into Harlan's Motel looked nothing like the sleek businessman on the TV screens with his barbered face, styled hair, eight-hundred-dollar suits, and cashmere overcoats.

Nick Ireland hadn't shaved or showered or combed his hair for days. So when a tall man in black jeans, black turtleneck sweater, and cheap black parka, tousle-haired and with black stubble on his face, checked into the motel, the pimply teenager manning the desk barely put down his skin magazine to look at him.

Nick registered as Barney Rubble.

That was a provocation, just as remaining within a thirty-mile radius of Parker's Ridge was a provocation. He'd promised he'd drive back to D.C. yesterday. Today the boss was waiting to debrief him.

If his partners knew he was still here, they'd probably shoot him. If his boss back in Washington knew, he'd fire him.

Yesterday, he'd been ready to go back. Some stupid sentimental thing, some strange compulsion, had led him to stay on for the funeral, and Di Stefano had chewed his ass out for it.

He'd seen the funeral, seen Charity one last time, had climbed down from the mountainside and gotten into his SUV. Well, the hit man's SUV, slated for forensics once Nick hit D.C.

And Nick had had every intention of heading out.

It was 4:00 p.m. by the time the funeral was over. He

shouldn't have gone at all, because he had over a ten-hour drive to get home. Or eight if he wanted to drive his frustration off.

Either way, he had a long night of driving in front of him.

And yet he got as far as the turnoff that would take him straight down into Burlington, and then pulled off the road and sat in the SUV, engine idling, for a quarter of an hour. The very few vehicles out on this gelid day, with its promise of more snow toward evening, hissed by. No one paid him any attention whatsoever, which was as it should be.

He was dead, after all.

He sat and sat, knowing that each minute spent here just made his long trip even longer. Knowing that he was forfeiting even a short nap before having to haul his sorry ass down to headquarters to be debriefed.

And though his foot was on the accelerator and his hand on the gearshift and all it would take was about four pounds of pressure from his foot to shoot on to the road to Burlington, he couldn't do it. He spent a fucking hour at that fucking intersection until finally, angry and frustrated, he turned the SUV around and drove to the most anonymous motel he could find, where he could be miserable for only forty-five dollars a night.

In his Delta days, Nick had lived rough. He'd once spent seventy days in Afghanistan sleeping on the ground and crapping in a pit he'd dug himself. This room was somehow worse.

He'd tried to ignore the pubes in the shower stall and the faint smell of sewer coming from the drain. He'd started drying himself with the thin towel then stopped when he saw brown streaks.

Still damp, he'd padded back into the room and sat down, naked and damp, on the side of the bed.

Jesus only knew how many traveling salesmen had jerked off on the bedspread. He needed something to sterilize the germs. Luckily he'd stopped off at a 7-Eleven to buy it. A bottle of whiskey, five bucks, pure rotgut. Just what he needed tonight.

He uncapped the bottle and looked for a glass. The one he found was stained and chipped. With a shrug, he simply tipped the bottle up and took a big slug. It burned all the way down, so he took another.

Bad shit was coming down. Nick was the world's greatest expert on bad shit. He had a sixth sense for it, and right now his Bad-Shit-O-Meter was way, way over into the red zone. And Charity was right in the middle of it, whatever was going to happen.

He took another swig, a long one this time.

Charity, in danger. The thought made his skin crawl, burned his throat, squeezed his chest until he thought he'd choke.

Nick tipped the bottle up, chugged. But there wasn't enough whiskey in the world to drown out the image of Charity hurt, wounded or—*God!*—dead.

Charity, with her pale, delicate skin. She'd once told him that her family had lived in Parker's Ridge for over two hundred years. Nick believed it, absolutely. It would take at least two hundred years of breeding to get that perfect skin—smooth as porcelain, except no porcelain on earth had that pearly sheen. Every time he touched her, he was scared shitless he'd bruise her. After a while, after he touched her gingerly, she'd laugh and put his hand on her breast. Or pull it down between her legs.

Nick lay back on the filthy bedspread, naked, half drunk from the bad whiskey and the good memories.

Charity was soft all over, but she was softest between her legs, with the sweetest little cunt he'd ever fucked.

Nick groaned, looked down at himself through slitted eyes. He was hard as a pike, with nowhere to go with it.

This was new for him. He rarely beat the meat. He didn't have to. When he was on a mission he was too busy trying to save his ass to think about sex. And when he wasn't on a mission, well, half the world was female, after all, most with all the right plumbing. Lop off the under eighteens and over fifties, then lop off the dogs and you were still left with a world full of women to fuck.

Right now, for instance, he could be in bed with the waitress in the dingy diner where he'd eaten a cheeseburger. Or the checkout girl where he'd bought the whiskey.

He could have more or less any woman he wanted. He could dress and drive down to the tavern he'd seen five miles down the road. Half an hour after walking through the doors, he'd have company for the night, guaranteed.

He didn't want anyone else, though. Just Charity.

His hand dropped down, fisted around his cock.

He sucked in his breath between his teeth and thought of her. He gave an experimental pull with his fist, then opened his hand immediately. His hand was calloused, rough. The exact opposite of the softness of Charity. His cock refused his hand, simply rebelled. He didn't even try another stroke, just let himself go and lay on his back, naked, hard, and aching.

He didn't want to be here, in this musty room smelling of hundreds of traveling salesmen jacking off and two bit whores selling twenty-five-dollar blow jobs.

He knew where he wanted to be. With Charity. In her lovely little house that smelled of lavender and lemon polish and the scented candles she continually lit.

He wanted—so fiercely he thought his heart would beat its way out of his chest—to turn the clock back.

He lay on the bed until gray light started to fill the room, then got up and dressed. He'd worn the same clothes for three days running now. They were rumpled and smelled of sweat.

He walked down the stairs to the lobby. Basic tradecraft: take the stairs if you're undercover. Fewer people will see you and you won't be trapped.

He'd paid the night before in cash, so he could walk right out without being stopped. He waited until the guy behind the desk was busy checking in a family of five, then slipped out the front door.

It was a cold day—gray and sleety. The cheap nylon parka he had on barely mitigated the cold. He felt chilled down to his bones and not just because of the weather.

When he was behind the wheel, Nick started the engine and drove to the feed road into the interstate where he'd been yesterday, braked, and idled.

If he turned left, he'd start the journey back to D.C., where he was already in a world of trouble for not showing up. Right was back to Parker's Ridge. It would be crazy to go back to Parker's Ridge, of course. If anyone recognized him, he'd blow the mission. Instant FUBAR.

Nick sat in the car, watching the exhaust rise like smoke in the rearview mirror. Even wasting this much time was criminal, a career buster.

Fuck it.

He gunned the engine and headed right, straight for Parker's Ridge.

Nineteen

Charity lifted her head when she heard a car drive up the street outside her house, the sudden movement making her nauseous. She swallowed the tickle of bile, knowing from experience that bile was the only thing she *could* throw up. The only things she'd been able to choke down—half a dozen crackers, a glass of milk, half a peach—had come right back up again.

That she couldn't eat didn't surprise her. She could barely breathe. Sleep was almost a forgotten concept, which was for the best. When she did manage to nod off, she would wake up immediately in a cold sweat. Her dreams were filled with images of flaming cars flying off a mountain, explosions, and charred bones. Her nightmares were incredibly vivid, down to the smell, which would remain a part of her forever.

Charity had insisted on going to the coroner's office to

identify Nick. The sheriff and the coroner both had told her that visual identification was impossible and so she was exonerated from viewing the body. What remained of the body.

Something, some Prewitt concept of honor, made her insist on seeing the remains, overriding the sheriff's and coroner's wishes. At one level, she wished with all her heart that she'd listened to them. Nick's charred remains had been enough to make even the coroner wince.

What had been laid out on the autopsy table bore no relationship to a human being—it was simply a collection of blackened bones, some cracked open to the marrow, laid out in a terrible facsimile of a human shape.

Blackened skull on top, the flesh burned away, baring Nick's mouth of perfect teeth in a macabre grin. The coroner had arranged all the bones in the anatomically correct positions, except for the right tibia, which had never been recovered. It left a blank spot in the sooty sketch of what had once been a human being.

The sheriff clutched her elbow, hard, in case she fainted.

Prewitts were made of sterner stuff than that, though. She didn't faint and she didn't break down. Whatever she felt was to be saved for the privacy of her own home. As she gazed at Nick's remains, she could feel her own face, stiff and expressionless.

She'd stepped forward, away from the sheriff's hand, and approached the table.

The sheriff had said that it wasn't necessary to view the body, but it *was* necessary.

She had to stand witness for Nick, let him leave this life under a loving gaze. She was his family. He had no parents and no siblings, just like her. They were each other's family and this was the last thing she could do for him.

Fate had stopped her from bearing witness for her parents. She never saw them again after the night of the fire, not their bodies, not their coffins. She didn't attend their funeral. By the time she woke up from her coma, her parents had been in the ground for two weeks.

So she was determined that she would stand by Nick in the only way she could. If his spirit lingered anywhere near his broken, burned body, he would know that she stood steadfast by his side, no matter the cost to her.

She didn't regret it, not once, though what she'd seen would, she knew, forever color her nightmares.

And until the end of time, on her deathbed, she would smell that terrible stench of charred bones and burnt flesh.

Her stomach quivered again and she swallowed heavily.

The car rolled slowly to a stop outside her house. She had visitors. Her heart beat slow and heavy in her chest.

Whoever was coming, they were not welcome.

In a token attempt at trying to stem her bottomless, dark grief, she'd switched on the living room lights. Unfortunately, they were visible from the street. She couldn't even pretend nobody was home, as she had done for the past three days.

Her living room window framed the big black limo parked at the curb. She could see everything perfectly.

The driver, dressed in elegant black livery, came around the car and opened a backseat door, extending a hand to the man who emerged. The man's deeply lined face was sharply handsome. An expensive Borsalino covered his longish, graying blond hair. He was dressed for the cold—a heavy midnight blue overcoat and thick leather gloves covering what she knew were scarred hands. One hand was clutching an ebony walking stick with a polished ivory knob.

He was making his limping way slowly up her walkway, leaning heavily on the arm of his driver, who held Vassily's arm with one hand and a big black box with another.

Vassily.

He'd come out in the freezing cold, just for her.

Charity winced. Vassily coming out on a cold day was a big deal. A very big deal. He made no secret of the fact that he hated the cold, venturing out only when necessary in winter. Watching him make his slow, laborious way to her, it was painfully clear that this cost him sacrifice.

It was a magnificent gesture. Charity knew she should be grateful, even flattered. This was something Vassily would do for very few people in the world. Maybe she was the only person he'd do this for. But though she was touched, she was in no condition to receive him.

She wanted to be left alone and not have to gather her scattered, grieving self together enough to make conversation. There was no conversation in her, not enough energy left in her to deal with anyone.

But this had to be done. Vassily was an old man. Well, if not old, much older than she. He was a great man who had suffered great tragedy, and he was making an effort to come to offer her comfort in the hour of her own tragedy.

On any possible scale of suffering, Vassily's suffering far, far exceeded hers. He'd been to hell and back, and for five long years. He'd not only lost loved ones, he'd been injured, tortured, forced to work in mines in subzero temperatures, whipped and beaten.

No, her suffering was a paltry thing in comparison. Shame made her stiffen her spine. Somehow, she had to claw her way up out of the slippery, gory, deep, dark well of mourning she'd fallen into. For the next half hour or hour, or however long Vassily chose to stay, she had to somehow take her suffering and compress it, tuck it away somewhere, just long enough so she could function while he was here.

Afterward, when he'd gone, when she was alone, she could let the grief unravel and swell to monstrous proportions again, until it occupied every cell of her body and mind, as it had for the past three days.

But for now, whatever it took, she had to cling to control.

Vassily's slow walk up to her front porch allowed her to rush into the bathroom and dash some cold water on her face, pull a comb through her tangled hair. She looked up into the mirror above the sink and shuddered, hardly recognizing herself.

Her eyes were red rimmed and swollen, testimony to her sleepless nights and the endless tears. Dark bruises shadowed her eyes. She'd lost weight, in just these three days. Her cheekbones were sharper, the line of her jaw more pronounced. Her skin was paper white, bloodless. She looked caved in, beaten. She looked ready for the grave herself.

The grave . . . in a flash she was at the cemetery again. The dark gouge in the earth yawned at her feet, the heavy mahogany coffin's gleaming brass handles starkly contrasting with the frozen black earth. The smell of unearthed sod rose in her nostrils, churning her stomach. The smell of death and . . .

She froze on the threshold of her bedroom.

Oh my God.

There was another smell in the room, lingering in the air. Musky, faintly citrusy. Familiar, unmistakable.

Impossible.

Nick's smell.

How could—

The front doorbell rang and her head whipped around, making her faintly nauseous again.

Every hair on her body rose because together with his scent, she somehow felt . . . *Nick*. Felt his presence, felt his aura. Nick's aura was strong. He was a force of nature. Whenever she'd been near him, it was as if the molecules in the air speeded up. He cast an energy field around him. He punched a six-foot-two Nick-shaped hole in the universe.

The bell rang again, longer this time.

Charity should be rushing to the door, opening it, and welcoming Vassily into her home. It was beyond discourteous letting an elderly man wait outside in the freezing cold. But Charity was frozen herself, with horror.

She was drenched in Nick's scent, drowning in his aura and it terrified her.

Oh God, this was infinitely worse than smelling charred bones, horrible as that was. The moments by Nick's poor, ravaged body had been traumatic, the memory seared into her very being. No wonder, in her grief, that she could revisit them. She knew she'd revisit the images until the end of time, in her nightmares.

Still, smelling Nick's death, however awful, was normal.

But smelling and sensing Nick—the live, vital, sexy Nick, not the sad charred sticks that were all that was left of his mortal body—in her bathroom and bedroom took horror to a new level. This wasn't a memory, something real, something she could hold on to, however horrible. No, this was her mind playing tricks on her. This was insanity.

That slippery hold she had on reality was starting to fray.

She looked down at herself. Her forearms were covered in goose bumps.

The bell rang again, two long rings.

The idea of feeling Nick in empty rooms for the rest of her life was terrifying. Her stomach rejected the very notion.

She bolted for the toilet where she miserably retched the few remaining molecules of milk left. Her stomach spasmed and spasmed again, bringing up only green bile, until she didn't have the strength to stand and sank down to her knees.

She rested like that, feverish cheek against the cold porcelain bowl, for a full minute. Vassily was waiting outside, but she simply didn't have the strength to get up.

Another ring, this time with impatience behind it. Vassily would be feeling the cold. His leg ached when the weather was damp and cold, like today. She simply couldn't make him wait any longer.

Using the toilet for leverage, she stood slowly, straightening and waiting a second to see if her stomach had settled. It had.

She rinsed her mouth out with water to rid herself of the terrible taste.

Gritting her teeth, Charity forced her feet to move, using sheer willpower to make it to the door. One foot after another. Left, right, left, right. Spooked, trembling.

Fuck, that was close!

Nick's heart was still pounding as he crouched in the space between the garage and the house. His thermal imager had shown that she was in the living room, so he'd taken the chance to seed the back of her house with bugs. In her purse, in the vase on the sideboard, in the pockets of her jackets. He was fast and he was quiet, but she'd almost caught him.

Checking in with the head office this morning had driven

his anxiety levels off the charts. After giving him a scolding Nick barely listened to, the boss provided an update.

Chatter in Sandland was off the charts, spiking yesterday, about an upcoming meeting with "the Russian." They'd intercepted a call between Hassad al-Banna and Abu Rhabi, who were a little less circumspect with their cell phones than Worontzoff was.

There was going to be a meeting, soon. And something else was going to happen, soon. And it was going to be big. The details weren't there but it was enough to make the office crap its collective pants.

That was the only reason Nick hadn't been sent to Alaska or North Dakota to check on terrorist ties there. And since he'd flat-out refused to come back to D.C., he was allowed to continue with the mission. Under strictest orders to stay in the surveillance van and not even crack the door open for a piss.

But Charity's house was a magnet, he simply couldn't stay away. He'd get on the road to drive to the surveillance van, then find himself driving back in. It was as if Hit Man's SUV was sensitive to some kind of force field around Parker's Ridge.

The operator who could never get lost now found himself lost beyond saving, unable to leave.

Being here, now, outside Charity's house, was breaking every single rule in the book, and about a dozen beyond that.

He wasn't going to be recognized. Dressed in black from head to foot, with thin black shooting gloves and a black Nomex balaclava, nobody could possibly recognize him even if they saw him, which they wouldn't.

He had his head against the downstairs bathroom wall.

Through the siding, he could hear her vomiting, then quietly crying. He heard it twice—through the wall and over the mikes he'd scattered through the bedroom.

Her misery came through, loud and clear.

Nick reached out a hand and lay it against the cedar siding. Not a foot from his hand, he knew, was Charity. He'd give his left nut to be able to hold her, ease the tears, though they were for him.

His hand curled into a fist and he beat it, gently, against the wall, body tense with frustration, while Charity whimpered.

A big black limo with smoked windows had come to a rolling stop in front of the house and Nick crouched even farther, watching through the alleyway between the house and the garage. A big rhododendron bush hid him from sight.

He came to high alert when an ivory-tipped black cane came into view, followed by an elegantly shod foot. The man's uniformed driver held a back door open for him. The driver was carrying a big black box with one arm and supporting the man with the other.

Several minutes later, Nick heard the doorbell chime through his headset. In the bathroom, silence, then the sound of running water.

Vassily Worontzoff, world-famous writer, international crime syndicate boss, had come calling, to console Nick's widow.

Twenty

Charity opened the door just as Vassily was lifting his gloved hand to ring again.

"My dear," he said warmly, looking her up and down. He walked in, taking off his hat and pulling off his gloves. "I've been worried about you. On the table by the window, Ivan," he said without looking around.

The driver deposited the big black box on the table and quietly left. A minute later, the powerful engine of the limo fired up and the big car drove away.

Vassily waited until they heard the car depart, then stepped forward and enveloped her in his arms. Her own arms came up automatically.

He was the first person she'd touched since . . . since Nick. She hadn't wanted to be hugged by anyone at the funeral and had avoided even those pointless air kisses. Even Uncle Franklin had seemed to understand that she couldn't be touched, otherwise she'd fly into a million pieces. And Aunt Vera—the poor darling had been barely aware of what was going on.

So no one had hugged her and no one had held her and she realized now, right now, how much she desperately needed both. These past days had been spent on another planet, far from humankind. A big, dark, airless planet with heavy gravity and no life. Vassily's tight embrace bumped her back to Earth, among her own kind.

He was a man who'd known great sorrow. He held her as if he wanted to absorb some of her own.

"My *dushecka*," he murmured, head bent over hers.

His heavy overcoat was warm from the car, as was the pocket created by his shoulder and neck. He gently pushed her head down more tightly onto his shoulder, her cheek nestling against the soft cashmere of his overcoat, her nose against the warm skin of his neck.

"Cry, *dushka*," he commanded softly. "It's best. Get it out."

Her heart was drumming, so quickly she thought it might just beat its way outside her chest. A high keening sound rose in the room and it took her a second to realize it came from her. Her lips tightened against the sound, but it wouldn't be contained. She took one big gulping sob of a breath, another and then it was meltdown. Utter and total meltdown.

How could she have any tears left? Surely she'd cried them all, buckets, lakes, oceans of tears.

Charity cried as if she'd never cried before—a deep upwelling of despair. She was racked with sobbing, shaking, and shivering, tears spurting from her eyes. She was trembling so hard she'd have fallen to the ground if he hadn't been holding her up.

Vassily held her tightly, letting the crying jag take its course, letting the hot, poisonous ball of grief work its way through her system, the sounds she was making raw and ugly in the quiet house.

She cried until her throat ached, until her lungs hurt, until she felt her bones would shatter from the trembling, holding on to the lapels of Vassily's coat, drenching his shoulder.

The hot ball of fiery grief had moved on, at least for the moment, leaving Charity clinging to Vassily, weak-kneed and dazed.

"Come, my dear. Let's sit down." It was the first time he'd spoken since the crying jag had begun. She was infinitely grateful that he hadn't spoken platitudes while she'd been crying her heart out.

But then that wasn't Vassily's style. He wouldn't reassure her that things would get better. This was a man who understood tragedy down to the depths of his soul.

Vassily walked her to the sofa, sat her down, unbuttoned with difficulty his overcoat, and sat down next to her. Again, he put his arm around her and kissed her gently on her forehead, and again on her cheek. His lips were warm and dry.

Some time later, when the wildest stages of grief were passed—however impossible it was to think of that time— Charity knew that she would cherish the memory of his gestures of affection.

He rarely touched anyone. He always seemed to her to be so self-contained, not ever needing human warmth. Content with his music and reading and whatever it is he did all day in that enormous, beautiful mansion. Certainly, she'd never seen him with a female companion and, at many of his musical soirées, she had somehow ended up doing the honors of the house.

Suddenly, Charity wondered whether Vassily had a love life.

It had never even occurred to her that he might. Perhaps because she'd been blinded by his fame or had been unable to look beyond the scars to the man underneath. He wasn't even *that* old. Though the years in the prison camp had aged him terribly, Vassily was only fifty-four. Young for a man. Especially for a rich and famous one.

Did he have a secret lover he didn't want to share with the world? Perhaps a Russian émigrée, a woman of letters that he saw discreetly from time to time? Someone he could speak to in his native tongue? That would be best. She hoped he didn't have a series of paid liaisons—dry, heartless, mercenary affairs, swift and cold. How awful.

A large linen handkerchief had appeared in his hand and he wiped her eyes carefully, then he held the handkerchief politely against her nose while she honked into it. She must look awful—red-eyed, red-nosed, gaunt, dazed.

He was speaking as he wiped her face. "The very best remedy for situations such as these is chai and vodka. An age-old cure for the Russian soul and perhaps even the American soul, who knows?"

He stood and walked over to the box his driver had carried in, bringing out objects. A big silver thermos, a brightly colored ceramic teapot, a silver flask, a jar of something that looked like jam, and two glasses with silver handles.

His movements were awkward and slow, but he was in no hurry. She marveled at how well he had learned to deal with the disability of his hands.

"I wanted to bring you a samovar, my dear." His voice was calm as he worked. "I have a perfect one for you. Solid sterling, late nineteenth century. They say it was used by Tolstoy himself, though there is no documentation. I didn't bring it this time, but I will. It will be my gift to you."

Charity sat passively, tears drying on her face, watching Vassily. She loved listening to him, to his low calm voice with its faint trace of a Russian accent. His English was careful, precise. She'd heard that he spoke perfect French and German, as well.

Vassily opened a big thermos bottle with a special loop that allowed his shattered hands to unscrew the top. He shook dark loose tea leaves from a special paper packet into the teapot and poured boiling water from the thermos over it.

Instantly, the room was filled with the scent of fragrant tea steeping.

"In Russia, we often use several teapots at once, stacked one above the other. Like samovars, they keep the tea warm for a very long time. But the tea becomes very strong." He slanted her a glance. Charity knew he was seeing a pale, shaky woman, barely able to stand upright. "Perhaps too strong for you, right now." He took out the two glasses with silver holders. They had an elegant look, with some intricate design etched into the glass. "Believe it or not, these *podstakanniki*, these tea glasses, once belonged to Czar Nicholas. They are part of a set he had commissioned for himself and his wife. I find it amusing to drink out of the czar's glasses and reflect upon destiny."

A faint smile creased his thin lips as he spooned what looked like a red berry jam into the glasses. "Russians rarely sugar their tea. They use either honey or berry jam. This was made by my housekeeper. Vermont jam, to go with Russian tea." He slanted her a cool glance. "A fusion of our two worlds, my dear."

Charity sat up straight, trying to stiffen her spine, drying her eyes with the heels of her hands, depleted and wishing she were alone.

How awful, how ungrateful to wish Vassily were gone, when he was being so kind. All winter, Charity had cherished every moment she'd spent with the great man, afterward reliving their conversations over and over again in her head.

She dutifully read every book he ever recommended to her or even mentioned. She bought the CD of every piece of music ever played at his musical soirées. She'd read everything he'd ever written, time and again. She'd steeped herself in Russian literature and the tragic history of the Gulag.

Vassily had appeared in their remote little hamlet like a shooting star, sending sparklers of heat and light into her life, illuminating all the dark corners of their provincial corner of the world. No one knew why he'd chosen Parker's Ridge. Charity herself had no idea, nor had Vassily ever spoken of it. He'd just appeared one day, having purchased by means of an intermediary the old McMurton mansion.

By the same token, Vassily could suddenly decide to pull up stakes and move to a more accessible and sophisticated part of the world at any moment, once he got bored with Parker's Ridge's limited offerings. So Charity knew that her time with Vassily was of necessity limited. He was being very kind to her. She must put her grief aside and be polite back.

But oh, how she longed for her solitude right now. To be alone with her grief, not have to struggle for composure or make polite conversation.

He poured a clear liquid into their tea glasses. A generous portion each. Charity could smell the alcohol from across the room and her empty stomach clenched tightly in protest. "Vodka," he murmured, the word pure Russian. *Vuodkya*. "Sometimes a man's only solace. A true friend that never betrays you."

"Vassily," she murmured. "Not quite so much in my tea, please." Like many Russians, Vassily drank on an industrial scale. However much he imbibed, though, she'd never seen him drunk.

"My dear," he replied, his voice amused. "Just the merest few drops. Normally, I drink tea that is one-third vodka. We call it 'sailor's tea' and it has gotten me through many a dark night. Here." He held out one beautiful glass by its silver handle. "And I don't want to hear any nonsense about not being able to drink it. You need warm liquids, alcohol, and some food. In that order. My cook prepared you some dishes and you'll find them at the bottom of the box. They're still warm. I want you to promise me you'll eat them."

The idea of food made her whole body seize up, squeezing her insides upward. She was motionless for a moment, willing her stomach to make the journey back down her throat.

"Charity, my dear, come." Vassily sat down next to her, close enough for his arms and thighs to press against hers. He tapped her glass, which she still hadn't touched. "Step number one. Drink your tea." A finger under her glass, lifting. She had to bring the glass to her mouth or risk spilling it all over her lap. "That's it," Vassily crooned. "Very good."

Charity drank half of it, slowly, trying to ignore the strong smells carried up by the steam. The hot liquid and alcohol burned their way down to her stomach.

Vassily had already emptied his glass and poured himself straight vodka now. "I listened to Vivaldi's Opus 11 last night, all the way through. So touching, so heartfelt. I was thinking that perhaps I would choose that for another one of my soirées. Perhaps I could call in the De Clercq Quartet. I met their manager in Paris, a highly intelligent and cosmopolitan man. He said the quartet would be in the New England area before Christmas, so they might be free for an evening. I imagine you'd enjoy that."

"I imagine I would," she murmured. He lifted his hand to tuck a curl behind her ear and she cringed inwardly. She hadn't combed her hair this morning. Hadn't even thought of it.

"Excellent. If it pleases you, I'll speak with their manager tomorrow. I'll make it worth their while."

This was amazing. The De Clercq Quartet was world famous. They commanded top prices and could fill concert halls. Vassily had casually said he would hire them for a concert for only thirty people, just to please her.

"Finish your tea now, my dear." She did, hoping her stomach would behave. He was watching her closely, with almost a feverish look in his eyes.

She sat still, consulting her insides, hoping she could keep everything down.

She could. Actually, it was the first time she felt warm since the terrible news. She'd forgotten about even the concept of warmth.

Vassily laid a hand on her knee and tightened his poor, scarred fingers. He was hurting her, just a little, his grip was so tight. But Charity didn't have the nerve to say anything. It wasn't his fault—he couldn't gauge the strength of his grasp. God only knew how much feeling he had left in his hands.

Charity looked up and met Vassily's eyes. Such a clear, pale blue, like a chilly spring sky. He was watching her unblinkingly, intently. "Well?" he asked again. "Feeling better?"

She drummed up a smile. She actually had to remind herself how to do it. *Lift muscles around edges of mouth, show teeth.*

She had another quick consult with her stomach. Yes, everything was going to remain safely inside her and not decorate Vassily's coat, at least not any time soon. So she wasn't going to humiliate herself. Not in the next ten minutes, anyway. Upchucking all over one of the world's greatest writers was not something she wanted to do.

She was terribly flattered that he'd made the effort. He hadn't shown up for the funeral, but she hadn't expected him to. She knew how much he detested being out in the cold.

Indeed, his presence here was a sign of his affection for her. She was flattered, she really was.

But she really, *really* wanted to be alone.

Another forced smile. "Yes, I am, Vassily. I am feeling much, much better. I, um, I hadn't thought to make tea for myself and it was very kind of you to come all the way over here for me. I promise I'll drink it all, don't worry. And I'll eat what you brought me."

Maybe. If her stomach behaved.

Charity made to rise, but his hand on her knee stopped her. Vassily's grip was *really* strong. He was pressing down on her knee, in an unspoken command to be still.

He was still watching her intently, pale gaze fixed on her face. His eyes were ice blue but they looked almost hot. Vassily had a strong personality. It was a little unsettling to be studied so carefully.

"I have—a business meeting this evening. Some partners are coming to . . . seal a business deal a long time in the making. It's something I've worked hard on for a long time and I want to celebrate the occasion. I would very much like it if you would have dinner with me tonight."

Charity simply stared at him.

"I will have my driver pick you up here at about 6:00 p.m. It will give you a few hours to rest and freshen up."

She could hardly believe her ears. He wanted her to *celebrate* something with him? How on earth could she go to his house when she didn't feel up to walking out to her mailbox?

Celebration? Would they have to dine with his business partners?

Oh God, facing people, making conversation, choking down food. There was no way on earth she could do that. Her stomach clenched just at the thought.

He lifted his hand, fingered a lock of her hair, expression dreamy. "You really must dye your hair, my dear. You would look so beautiful with your hair blonder. White blond. And cut it." He indicated her jawline with a gnarled finger. "To here. So beautiful . . ."

"*What?*" The word came out on an expulsion of breath. "My *hair*? You want me to bleach my hair and cut it?"

"Yes. Immediately." There was something about his pale gaze, dreamy yet unwavering, as if he were seeing something that was not quite there. Seeing into her but also somehow past her. "Pale, pale blond. And the cut—a 'bob,' I think it is called. So lovely. You would be so lovely." He overarticulated the word *bob*, lips pursing, making it sound at once ridiculous and impossibly exotic.

"Vassily, I'm—I'm flattered that you want my company tonight. Don't think that I'm not, but . . ."

"But?" His eyes were glittering, thin nostrils tightly pinched.

She opened her hands. "I buried my husband yesterday, Vassily. I don't feel up to dinner out." Or dinner in, if it came to that. "I simply don't. How on earth can you expect me to dine out so soon after Nick died?"

Vassily didn't react, his pale gaze calm and direct.

"You must," he said simply, as if it were self-evident. As if there was no questioning the fact that she would.

Vassily's personality was so strong, it was as if he had a force field around him that created its own reality, a reality where she automatically did his bidding.

"You must dine with me tonight, there is no other way. It is time. I need you to be with me." He touched her cheek with the back of his hand, his touch cold, the scars thick and ropy. "You will come with me, Ka—Charity. You must. I will not take no for an answer."

Something had flared up within him, some primal force of nature that he must have kept banked and only unleashed when he needed it. Now he wasn't just a strong-willed man. Now he was almost superhuman.

She knew his history, but for the first time, she *felt* it. Felt the inner force of a man the Soviet Gulag, the entire resources of a powerful country founded on immense cruelty, had been unable to break. A man who'd withstood torture, beatings, privations unimaginable to her soft Western imagination. Nothing had ever broken him. Not the worst life could throw at him. Starvation and hard labor in subzero temperatures that would have killed a lesser man. Broken bones and betrayal. They had left their scars but they hadn't crushed him. He'd come out stronger than before.

In a very real sense, Charity knew, Vassily was almost like another race of man. Stronger, brighter, tougher. A literary genius, a man of great vision. The kind of man who came along once in a generation. Shakespeare. Dante. Tolstoy. Humanity existed in order to produce men like this. They were rare and they were precious.

He picked up her hand and rubbed her knuckles with the pad of his thumb. "Please," he said softly, his voice shaking. "Please dine with me tonight. I need you. You cannot begin to imagine how much I need you."

She'd never heard that tone of voice from him, ever. Vassily's normal speaking voice was precise and cool, strong and deliberate. He had a natural arrogance that precluded pleading.

Her heart shied away at the thought, becoming a cold little fist in her chest. She'd give anything not to do this, but life sometimes simply tossed these challenges at you, like dice at your feet.

Either you picked them up or you didn't. Either you dealt the hand life threw your way or you didn't.

Charity liked to think that she'd met every challenge so far, no matter how difficult. She remembered that her father, who had volunteered for Vietnam right out of high school and who had never talked about his two tours of duty, always said *do the hard thing.*

She prepared herself to do the hard thing.

She tried another smile, had no idea how successful it was. Stomach churning, hoping she could keep the tea down, she gave the only possible answer to his plea.

"Yes, of course, Vassily. I would be honored to dine with you tonight."

Nick snatched his cell phone out of his pocket the instant it vibrated and crouch-walked to the back of the garage, where no one in the house could possibly hear him. He didn't check caller ID. He knew who was calling.

He pulled at his earbud, where he'd been following what Worontzoff and Charity were saying.

"You fucking well better not be where I think you are," Di Stefano's furious voice lashed out at him.

Nick clenched his jaw and hunkered down, his back to the

garage wall. He waited a couple of beats so he could get his voice under control. "Bingo."

"Listen, fuckhead. I don't know what the hell you think you're doing, but you are compromising the mission. That's nothing new. You've been compromising the mission for days, but this is beyond your normal craziness. Fall back. Now."

"No can do. Listen to me," he whispered urgently. "Woront-zoff's here."

"What?"

"You heard me. Here at Charity's house. Right now. He's been here for over half an hour. I, um, bugged the house here and before you blow up, you better thank me for it, because something is happening late this afternoon and he wants to celebrate it with Charity over dinner at his place."

The thought drove him insane. He could conjure up with preternatural clarity Worontzoff's expression the other night in his mansion, touching Charity and getting a hard-on. He could also conjure up, no prob, Worontzoff's reaction when Charity refused him.

Worontzoff was a king in his world. Kings were used to being obeyed. Kings punished people who didn't obey them.

"I'm going to tell her," Nick said suddenly. It was the only thing he could think of to rescue her. Let it all come out. Once she knew the truth, no way would she hare off to his mansion. "Tell her who he is and that she can't go to his house. He'll have her killed." The blood in his veins ran cold as he conjured up possible Worontzoff reactions. If he could have a proxy hang a prostitute up on a meat hook, what he would do to Charity didn't bear thinking of. In his crazy mind, she was his long-lost love. Once Charity rebuffed him, his revenge would be swift and insanely cruel.

Of course, Nick would have to break cover twice to warn her off—he'd have to reveal his real identity and reveal the nature of the mission.

Men had died rather than break cover on a mission. Keeping the code was the closest thing to a religion Nick had. What Nick was doing was off the charts. He knew it, but was helpless to stop himself.

Big bad Iceman, so out of control he couldn't travel more than thirty miles from this spot.

It was like being on a runaway train, headed for the gorge with the bridge out. He was known for his icy self-control, but right now, someone else in his head was handling the controls and levers in the engine room. "As soon as that fucker leaves, I'm going in."

Di Stefano's sharp indrawn breath sounded loud over the cell phone. "No way," he growled. "You most definitely are not. Are you crazy? What the hell has happened to you? You're going to toss this mission right down the toilet. As soon as Worontzoff figures out she knows something, it'll all come crashing down."

His voice sounded tinny, far away. Certainly too far away to change Nick's mind. Yap, yap, yap. Nothing Di Stefano could say would affect his decision. The second he'd made it, it felt right. He had to go in and convince Charity not to go to out tonight.

He could see it clearly—the divide, the fork in the road. He did one thing and this happened. Another and that happened.

He'd walk into Charity's house right now, take her into protective custody, tuck her away in a safe house until they got the job done. Once Worontzoff was put away, he'd go back for her.

Oh yeah. She'd be pissed at being lied to, but bottom line—she'd have a pulse.

So that was Option One.

Option Two.

He did nothing—simply crouched out here behind Charity's garage, listening to her cry and throw up, then listen to her get ready to go out and hook up with a known mobster. Worontzoff would make his play, thinking to get his Katya back in his bed and discover that Charity wasn't his long-lost love and had no intention of warming his bed.

Nick had no problems whatsoever envisioning identifying Charity's body on some slab in the local morgue. He'd done it often enough and he knew that Russians could get real creative with women and a knife.

Every cell in his body was screaming for Option One, the clearest hunch he'd ever had in his life.

Unless, of course, Nick Ireland's famous hunch machine was completely broken, crushed and charred just like the bones in the coffin with his name on it, six feet underground.

Nick hunkered down, watching Charity's road. As soon as he saw Worontzoff's limo and driver appear and Worontzoff depart, he'd make his move.

It was the smart thing to do, the only thing to do.

And if it also meant that he'd see Charity again, hold her in his arms again, well, hey . . . a twofer.

Whatever went down, though, one thing was sure. Charity was not going out tonight to a murderer's house. To prevent it, he'd die. And he'd certainly kill.

Twenty-one

"Excellent," Vassily said, pale eyes glittering. "I knew I could count on you, dushka. It is meant, my dear. Never tamper with fate; you will only get hurt. It is one of life's harshest lessons."

He put his arm around her and squeezed her shoulders. His voice was louder than usual and his arm around her was so tight it almost hurt. There was something odd about him, something almost feverish, so unlike the normal, coolly rational Vassily Charity knew. She wondered if he were ill, coming down with flu.

He was holding her so tightly his fingers bit into her shoulder. Charity breathed deeply, thinking perhaps that would discreetly dislodge his hand, but it didn't work. It only made his grip more painful.

There was the strangest vibe coming from Vassily—it was as if he were . . . excited. Or worked up, or overwrought. It felt as if he were losing his grip on himself. His breathing was speeded up. She could feel his rib cage rising and falling against her side, so quickly he was almost panting. He looked agitated, restless, and fitful.

If she'd felt any better, she would have inquired after his health. He was a friend, more or less the same age her father would have been if he'd lived. Certainly her elder.

It would be the polite thing to do, after all, for polite Charity Prewitt. You could always count on her to do the right thing.

Not right now, though. She wasn't going to do the polite thing, be the nice little girl who'd been well brought up in a nice family. The fact was, she was barely holding it together— utterly depleted, rendered down to bedrock herself, clinging to the shreds of her self-control by her fingernails. She could barely stand upright. The last thing she needed was to deal with Vassily's agitation.

What had possessed her to accept his invitation? Where would she find the strength to go out, when all she craved was solitude and the dark?

And it was entirely possible she was coming down with the flu herself. She'd thrown up three or four times between yesterday morning and this morning.

Right now, there was nothing left in her to give to Vassily, sick or not. She was down to scorched earth.

"Vassily—" Charity tried to gently pull away from him, but found to her astonishment that it was almost impossible. He'd put his other hand back on her knee so that she was effectively pinned down. Or at least that was what it felt like.

He wasn't doing it on purpose, she was sure. How could he know he was hurting her? But he could certainly know he was crowding her.

She stood. It was the only thing she could think of to break Vassily's grip and start getting him out of the house. She craved solitude the way an alcoholic craves a drink, an addict a fix.

Deeply, desperately. Like she would die if she couldn't get it right *now*.

Vassily stood, too. Charity didn't see him do anything, he certainly didn't pull out a cell phone or make a gesture, but the instant he stood, she saw his limousine pull up out front, long and sleek and black. The driver stopped precisely at the point where the passenger door met her walkway.

Vassily walked slowly to the front door, helped along by his cane, elegant, controlled, limping. Charity accompanied him, hoping her legs would hold out at least until she could close the door behind him. She was close to total collapse.

Vassily turned to her, pale blue eyes staring intently into hers.

"Ivan will pick you up at six, my dear. Until then—" He reached out a scarred finger and caressed her cheek. It took all her self-control not to jerk away. He dropped his hand and pulled on gloves, looking around for his hat. Charity picked it up and brought it to him. The felt wool was thick, of excellent quality. He donned his hat, never taking his eyes from her.

"I will see you tonight, dushka." His gloved hand picked up hers and he bowed over it. "À bientôt, cherie."

Charity withdrew her hand and reached around him to turn the doorknob, something he would find difficult to do. "Good-bye, Vassily."

He moved excruciatingly slowly. Out of politeness, Charity stood behind him in the open doorway, freezing. The gelid morning air sent painful frozen fingers of ice deep into her bones. She tucked her hands into her armpits in a vain attempt to keep some warmth in her system.

Very little light penetrated the slate gray cloud cover. It

was almost too cold for snow. A few tiny frozen flakes tried to settle on the ground, but the wind whipped them into a frenzy before they could. Charity felt the *ping* of sleet needles against her cheek as she waited impatiently for Vassily to leave.

Finally, he was over the threshold, walking haltingly toward Ivan waiting at the top of the steps, his arm out. As soon as Vassily was safely in the care of his chauffeur, she scrambled to shut the door behind him, trying not to slam it in her haste to have him out of the house. Once she heard the snick of the latch, she sagged against the door, eyes closed. Panting, exhausted.

Alone again. Thank God.

After a while, she heard the *whump!* of an expensive car door closing and the deep purr of a powerful engine. She watched through the living room window as the limo pulled away. The windows of the limo were tinted but she thought she saw Vassily's pale face pressed against the glass. Looking at her.

Oh God. What had she done?

Charity pulled the living room curtains closed—she'd had enough of the outside world—put the tea glasses, tea pot, and jam onto a tray and carried it into the kitchen. She was feeling so weak the tray shook in her hands, the tea glasses rattling. That moment standing in the open doorway had sucked what little warmth she'd had right out of her, together with what little strength she'd been clinging to.

She stopped and leaned against the sink, arms around her midriff. Such a bone-deep chill, as if her insides held a core of ice. She felt completely ground down, reduced to bone held together by skin. Not too far from the grave herself.

The trembling grew stronger. Bile rose in her throat again. Tears leaked out of her eyes. She didn't know whether to try to make it to the bathroom to throw up or simply collapse to the floor and throw up there.

With difficulty, she swallowed back the bile trickling up her gullet, then waited while her stomach settled. She locked her knees.

No vomiting, she told herself sternly. No collapsing to the floor. *There will be no one to pick you up if you do.*

It felt as if there couldn't possibly be enough heat in the world to warm her up. The only thing that could make her warm again was Nick, and he was in a coffin in the stony cold ground.

Oh, how he had warmed her! She hadn't felt cold once in the week they'd been together. Sleeping naked in the dead of winter hadn't been a problem with Nick in bed with her. He was a furnace. A constant source of spine-melting heat.

Had been. Now what was left of him was frozen bones.

She would never be warm again, for the rest of her life.

Oh God, how she missed him! A sob wanted to rise from her chest but she repressed it, clapping her hand over her mouth. Her throat shook. A wild keening sound escaped from behind her hand.

She couldn't cry again. Crying required an energy she simply didn't have. The tears would be wrung from some irretrievably shattered place inside her and she would never be whole again.

She pressed her hand so hard against her mouth she could feel her lips pressing against her teeth and waited. Waited for the upwelling of grief to subside, like the lash of a scorpion's tail. All she needed was for it to go down a little, just a little, just enough for her to make her wobbly way back to the bedroom and collapse onto the bed.

She hugged herself even more tightly, in a vain attempt to give herself the warmth Nick had so easily given her.

This sharp, lancing pain had to stop at some point. Didn't it? Didn't all the books say grieving eventually abates?

It was all she had to cling to, that some day this wracking pain would lessen, even if it would never go away. She was like someone who had been grievously wounded in battle. The surgeons and nurses could give her blood transfusions and stitch her up, but deep inside her, the tissues were rent, and the wound would never completely heal.

Surely the craziness would stop some day. It would have to, wouldn't it? Prewitts were long-lived. She could easily live to ninety. Her skin crawled at the thought of another sixty-two years of this madness.

Over the past three days, she'd felt Nick's presence a hundred times a day. He was around the corner, behind that door, he'd just left the room. And each time her heart would soar and then crash and burn when he wasn't there.

He wasn't there. He would never be there again.

So why was her body tormenting her so? Wasn't it bad enough that her husband was gone, without having these flashes of his presence?

Like . . . now.

Every hair on Charity's body rose as she walked slowly toward her bedroom. Her feet dragged, her heart thudded. A big boulder of terror pressed down on her, cutting off her breath. Spots formed in front of her eyes, like a big buzzing cloud of gnats.

For she could feel Nick, feel his presence. She could *smell* him. He was here, in this house, right now. Thinking that was craziness, she knew it, but she couldn't stop herself.

This was an entirely new level of slick horror added to the grief, the terror that she was losing her mind.

With each step toward the bedroom, she could feel his

presence more strongly. It was insane. Her mind was telling her she was crazy but every sense was on alert, sending frantic signals to her brain. *He's here he's here he's here!* Like the beat of a jungle drum.

In the week they'd been together, her entire body had become a tuning fork, attuned to Nick's body. He was here, she could feel it. No amount of reasoning could convince her he wasn't.

This was beyond horrible.

She'd observed firsthand Aunt Vera's slow, awful slide into dementia and it was the most terrifying, horrific, heartbreaking thing she'd ever seen. Aunt Vera, too, saw long-lost loved ones in the shadows in the corners.

Terrified, Charity reached out a shaking hand and pressed it flat against her bedroom door. There was nothing behind that door but an unmade bed and tear-sodden handkerchiefs strewn about the floor. She knew that. She *knew* that. But on an entirely different level, her body knew something else.

She stood for long moments with her trembling hand on her door, afraid to open it because behind it would be nothing but proof that she was losing her mind.

Chilled, sick, trembling, she finally gave a little push. The door slowly yawned open, the sound loud in the still of the house. The room behind was shrouded in shadows. She hadn't bothered to open her bedroom shutters.

Nick's presence was very strong.

Charity was rooted to the spot, utterly unable to enter her own bedroom. Her perfectly ordinary bedroom had suddenly become a place of monsters, waiting to eat her alive. A black pit with her sanity on the bottom, forever lost to her.

The door opening had created currents of air that brought Nick's scent, Nick's presence even more strongly to her.

There was a slight noise inside her bedroom.

She couldn't stand this, simply couldn't. There was nothing left in her that could withstand this kind of madness. She tried to lift her foot, tried to chide herself into walking into her own bedroom, but she couldn't. Her feet were anchored to the floor, as if mired in quicksand. She couldn't move. She couldn't breathe.

The shadows in the room swirled, or maybe it was her vision blacking out. Her legs were trembling now, barely able to hold her up.

The shadows shifted and shifted again.

The sound of a boot heel striking her hardwood floor. The darkness coalesced, gained an outline.

A tall, broad-shouldered figure dressed in black stepped forward. A deep voice said, "I won't let you go to Worontzoff's house, Charity."

Nick. Back from the dead.

Her eyes rolled to the back of her head.

Fuck!

Nick leaped forward to catch Charity before she collapsed onto the floor, cursing himself as he did. He hadn't war gamed it. He hadn't run it through his head in any way, which is what he always did, no matter what the move. This time, for the first time in his life, he just barreled ahead without any thought for consequences.

Otherwise he might have thought about the shock to Charity's system at seeing her dead husband alive once more.

Nick eased Charity down, icy dread flooding his system. People died of shock, he knew that. Fuck, fuck, *fuck!*

Charity's face was bone white, almost waxen. Her system was sending as much blood as possible away from the periphery toward the heart, as always happened in moments of great stress. Some shocks are so great blood circulation slows and eventually stops.

In Bosnia, ten days into his first assignment, Nick had seen a mother keel over dead from shock upon viewing the remains of her daughter's body after Serb soldiers had finished with her. There hadn't been much left.

Shock kills.

He took Charity's ice-cold slender hands between his, trying to warm them up. Her hands were completely still. She wasn't moving at all, not even her chest.

In a sudden panic, he put a hand under her sweatshirt, feeling for her heartbeat. She wasn't wearing a bra and Nick was half ashamed of the surge of desire as he felt her soft breast under his hands. He loved her breasts.

A Delta teammate, Kit Sanderson, once said he worshiped at the Church of Big Tits and without thinking about it too much, Nick had, too.

The first time he'd touched her there, cupped her in his hand, feeling the velvety pink nipple harden to a point, he'd become an instant convert to the Church of Small Tits, this classy little Greek temple, where they played Bach on an organ, so unlike the other church—loud with raucous country music.

He laid two fingers over her left breast. Ah, there it was—fast and thready, but a definite beat. He rocked back on his heels, still crouching beside her.

Jesus, what now? He'd had basic medic training. If she were

bleeding from a bullet wound, he'd know precisely what to do. If she had a broken bone he could probably set it, if she needed stitches he could do that, too. But this was beyond him.

"Charity," he said softly, then louder. *"Charity!"*

Christ, she was barely breathing. Her nostrils were pinched and white, her muscles completely lax.

This wasn't good. She was run down anyway. Her cheekbones were sharper, that sharp little chin more pointed, collarbones more prominent. She'd lost weight and she hadn't had that much weight to lose in the first place.

Damn, he should have played this differently, but how? How do you tell a grieving widow—*Whoops! Husband not dead, after all! Big mistake; sorry about that. Hey, shit happens.*

Nope. There was no way he could have revealed himself without shocking her in a big way. And no way he could keep her from going to Worontzoff's tonight without revealing himself. What was he supposed to do—send her e-mails from beyond the grave? Leave her messages written in lipstick on her bathroom mirror?

No, this had to be done in person.

The story of his life—only one possible hard road to take, dead ahead, with narrow walls and no side streets. The only way out was straight through. No alternatives, no detours.

Charity moaned and he watched her face carefully as a little color crept back in. Thank God she wasn't paper white anymore. She was coming round.

He'd have poured her a finger of whiskey and forced her to drink it, but that fuck Worontzoff had already made her drink vodka. With nothing in her stomach, that much alcohol would knock her right back out. And besides, he didn't want to leave her side.

She moaned again, her hand flexing inside his. He lifted her torso up, keeping his arm around her back for support.

Unexpectedly, her eyes opened. No coming-around process, no fluttering of eyelids, so he'd have a chance to prepare. Just those beautiful light-gray eyes, closed one second, wide open the next.

She looked frightened, lost.

"Nick?" she whispered. She lifted her hand, tentatively. It trembled. She moved it slowly toward his face, as if she were pushing her hand against a waterfall. Slowly, slowly closer.

Finally, she touched his face, gingerly. As if touching him might burn her. Cheekbone, temple, jaw. Reassuring herself by touch that he was here, alive. As if the evidence of her eyes and ears weren't enough. A little line appeared between her ash-brown eyebrows. "Is it you? How can it be you?"

Nick slid his other arm around her knees and rose with her in his arms, frowning at how slight she felt.

This next part was going to be . . . tricky. Before he even got to the part where he convinced her not to go out tonight, which was like climbing Everest, he had to hack his way through thorny woods, ford raging rivers, cross blazing deserts.

Worse. He had to tell her that every word he'd ever spoken to her was a lie.

So he knew he was in for an uphill battle and the best way to deal with that was to tell her the truth—or as much of truth as he could—while touching her.

His words had been lies, but his body hadn't lied. Not once. Every time he touched her, every time he slid into that lovely, warm, welcoming body, his body's delight was genuine. No lies there.

Touch is a powerful tranquilizer, soothing animals and

soon-to-be furious women. He was going to need every advantage he could get.

He sat them down in the corner of the couch, Charity's back against his right side, her legs stretched out. Her eyes never left his. One shaking hand was on his shoulder, kneading his shoulder muscle.

"You're alive," she whispered finally. It wasn't a question.

Nick nodded, watching her face. "Yes, sweetheart, I'm alive."

She blinked and shuddered. "I'm going crazy, like Aunt Vera. You can't be alive. I buried you. I'm hallucinating."

"No, you're not hallucinating. You're touching me," Nick said. He bent to kiss her cheek. "You can feel me. I'd pinch you to make you believe, but I don't want to. I don't want to hurt you in any way."

It was exactly the wrong thing to say. She drew in a deep breath and sat up straight in his lap.

Ouch. Right over his hard-on.

Yep. Unbelievably, with all this heavy stuff coming down, danger on the horizon, Apaches outside the gate, he'd got himself a woody.

Her eyes widened. She felt it. For a moment, it was as if everything in the world stopped. They even stopped breathing. There wasn't a sound in the house or from the street outside. Utter silence reigned as he watched her struggle with the concept of a dead man having a hard-on for her.

This could go either way. Sex between them had been more than good, from the first quick kiss in his car on the way to Da Emilio's to the last time they had made love on Friday morning. Her body was attuned to his. Though she was small, she had been requiring less and less foreplay for him to fit. Sometimes all it took was a kiss, a touch, and she was ready, wet and swollen and hot. As if simply being near him was foreplay for her.

So he had to watch her eyes very carefully, and if she softened, it was entirely possible that he'd start kissing her and one thing would lead to another, maybe right here on this pretty little couch—it wouldn't be the first time, either—and he'd say *I'm sorry I deceived you*, and she'd be looking up at him after coming, all rosy and dewy, and say *I forgive you, Nick* and he'd say *good and by the way, don't even think of going to that fuckhead Worontzoff's tonight* and she'd go *whatever you say, Nick* and that would be that.

Charity reared her head back and narrowed her eyes. "Don't. Don't even think of going there."

Then again, maybe not.

"No," he said. Damn, it would have made things easier, cut through a lot of the crap.

"Who—who did I bury?" Charity whispered.

Nick shrugged. "I don't know."

Her mouth tightened and she tried to get out of his arms. No way. She was staying right where she was, with him touching her. He tightened his hold.

"I'm sorry, honey. That's the honest truth. I don't know who he was. But he was trying to kill me and I do know who sent him."

She was barely listening, watching his eyes carefully, as if trying to identify him. She licked dry lips. "Where have you been these past days?

"Here," he said bluntly. "Mainly outside your house. I slept in a motel about twenty miles from here."

"*Here?*" she whispered. Her eyes left his face to wander around the living room, as if seeing her house for the first time. Her gaze locked back onto his face.

"You were outside the house while I was crying my eyes out? *Grieving* for you? So hard I thought my heart would stop?" She straightened suddenly in his lap and he winced. "You came into the house, didn't you? You were here. It was real."

Charity wrenched herself out of his lap and stood, trembling. He'd opened his arms to let her go. Her movements were so violent he'd hurt her if he tried to keep his hold on her.

She was shaking, arms wound tightly around her midriff, gemstone eyes bright in her white face. "I thought I was losing my mind. I felt your presence all the time. I smelled you. I'd walk into a room and expect to find you. I thought I was going crazy." She glared at him narrow-eyed. "Is this some kind of game for you? Pre—pretending to be dead, letting me think I b—buried you, then coming around later? Is this your idea of a *joke*? Because if it is, I'm not laughing."

Nick stood. He moved slowly because she looked like she would bolt—or shatter—at any untoward movement.

"No joke," he said softly. "No game. And if I could have avoided this, I would have, believe me. It's just that—"

Charity went even whiter. "Avoided this?" She brought a shaking hand to her mouth. "You wanted to *avoid* me? You wanted to just leave me hanging, thinking my husband was dead?" She swallowed heavily. "You're not Nick," she whispered, shaking. "You can't be. He would never do this to me. He'd never leave me mourning him. Who *are* you?"

"No!" God, this was going badly. "I didn't mean I was avoiding you, it's just that—"

But Nick was talking to empty air. With a moan muffled by the hand she clapped to her mouth, Charity bolted for the bathroom, making it barely in time. She slid to the porcelain bowl, slammed both hands on the tiled wall behind the toilet and bowed her head. Nothing came out but tea and vodka. She coughed and retched alcohol-scented brown liquid, eyes streaming.

Nick was right behind her. He ran a small hand towel under the sink faucet and wrung it out. He wrapped one arm around her from behind and gently wiped her face. She was gasping, shaking, sweating, coughing. Her stomach muscles clenched hard under his hand as another bout of retching seized her.

They were dry heaves now, but no less wrenching for the fact that there was nothing left in her stomach to come up. She made little moves to dislodge Nick's arm, but he wasn't having it. She needed his support. She was running on fumes and he was sure she'd fall to the ground without his arm around her.

When a few minutes went by with no more spasms, she finally stepped away, trying to escape his arm. Nick didn't budge. He rinsed the towel out again, turned her toward him, and wiped her face and neck.

Charity stood meekly, head bowed, eyes closed. He'd seen ice with more color than her face.

She looked so miserable his heart squeezed in his chest.

"This is ridiculous," he said. "You belong in bed. We can talk about things later, but right now you need to be lying down." Frowning, he lifted the back of his hand to her brow. She was cool. Still— "You're probably coming down with something, you're so run down. We'll be lucky if it's just the flu. This is bronchitis or pneumonia weather. I think I'm going to take you to the hospital."

Good idea. The hell with opsec. He'd drive Charity to the hospital in the next town over, stay in the background. Make sure she checked in, make sure she was all right while Di Stefano and Alexei kept watch over Worontzoff.

"No." She made an effort and stood up straight, moving away from him. "I'm not sick. I'm grieving." She glared at him.

"I didn't know grieving made you throw up a thousand times a day. That's a new one."

"I haven't been throwing up a thousand times a day! That's ridiculous. Just in the mor—"

She stopped suddenly, eyes wide. Nick froze, too. They looked at each other. There was utter silence in the pretty little bathroom as Nick searched her eyes for the truth he suddenly felt in every cell in his body.

"Go ahead, finish that sentence. You only throw up in the mornings. You know what that means, don't you? It means you're pregnant."

"No," Charity whispered. Her hand went immediately to her belly, as if trying to feel what was there through muscle and skin. Nick knew what was there. A baby. *His* baby. He would bet his new million dollars on it. "No. No way. I can't be pregnant." She looked appalled at the thought.

Nick frowned. "You certainly can be pregnant. God knows we fucked enough, and once without a rubber is all it takes. Ask any teenaged girl."

Charity flinched. "This is—this is ridiculous. I can't possibly know anything for sure. Not now, not yet. I'd need tests, blood tests, urine tests, whatever, it takes weeks to be sure. . ." Her voice tapered off as she stared wide-eyed at Nick. Both of them were absolutely certain, he knew it, but Charity was having problems coping with it.

Nick was a soldier, Charity wasn't. All his life he'd never flinched from reality. He saw what was, not what he wanted, always, and he saw it immediately. He never needed time to adapt. Christ, if you need time to adapt to new situations, stay away from battlefields.

Taking time to process things is a very good way to get killed.

Charity came from a gentler background, where bad news came rarely and there was time to acclimate. She was still processing the idea while Nick was already planning ahead.

A baby. A *baby*! Jesus. He'd never wanted marriage and he'd always rejected even the thought of kids. What the fuck did he know about families, about raising kids? He'd grown up in an orphanage and brutal foster homes, not exactly role models of domesticity.

Of course, Jake had grown up the same way and he was the best husband and father on earth. But that was Jake. Nick was Nick. All it took was a hint from the woman du jour of wedding bells or even jewelry and Nick was in the next state. It wasn't anything he wanted, or anything he ever expected to want.

Which is why the jolt of desire he felt nearly knocked him to his knees. Desire for Charity, but also desire for their child. It was a totally new emotion, but he processed it instantly as it settled inside him. There was no doubt it was real. He recognized it instantly, as if it had been there all along, patiently waiting for him to acknowledge it.

That angry buzzing that had filled his head and clouded his mind was gone. His mind was completely clear, and he knew exactly what he wanted.

He wanted Charity and this child he'd made with her. He wanted it ferociously, more than he'd wanted to become a Delta operator all those years ago.

In a flash, his life turned around 180 degrees.

He wanted it all. A real marriage and fatherhood. He wanted to live with this beautiful woman in this beautiful house in this beautiful little town. He wanted to raise their son or daughter in a loving home, protected and cared for. And he wanted more kids. Why the hell not? Why stop at one?

Of course, between now and that future there were a few hurdles to overcome and one of them was staring at him right now, white-faced and shell-shocked.

Nick took her hands in his. They were ice-cold. He brought them to his lips and kissed them. Charity drew in a deep breath and snatched her hands away from his. He let her do it. Right now was not the time to force her in any way.

Like a child, Charity hid her hands behind her back. She looked up at him, searching his eyes, trying to read him.

Nick knew exactly how to deflect curiosity and hide whatever he wanted to hide. It was one of his gifts, together with stillness and emotional detachment. It was what made him such a good undercover cop. He knew how to keep people out. But now he needed to switch gears, fast.

He deliberately drew down the shield he'd had all his life around his mind and heart and let her in.

Charity shook her head slowly. "Who *are* you? I think I'm going crazy. I fall in love with a man in the space of a week, then I marry him and become a widow on the same day. And now my husband comes back from the dead. It's too much to take in." She swallowed heavily. "I need the truth. Tell me what's going on, Nick. Or is Nick even your real name?"

"Yeah, my name's Nick. I'll tell you everything, but first you're going to clean up and then you're going to sit down before you fall down."

He held her hair back with one hand while she splashed

cold water on her face. He put a toothbrush and a tube of toothpaste on the sink shelf and looked at her pointedly. She brushed her teeth, then rinsed her mouth with mouthwash. He put a comb in her hand and she combed her hair. Nick knew that these small grooming motions made her feel better, more in control.

A little color was returning to her face, but her hands were still shaking. He turned her toward him. "Okay now. We'll have our talk, but not in here. It's too important a conversation to have in a bathroom, so we'll go to the living room. You're going to walk to the couch or I'm going to carry you. Your choice, but you have to take it now."

Charity blinked. He knew how to put command in his voice. She obeyed instinctively. She made for one of the armchairs, but he steered her to the couch and sat down next to her. She drew back, alarmed.

She wanted to avoid him. Tough shit. He was here and he was staying. He reached over for her hand. She gave a little halfhearted tug to try to get her hand back, but his grip was firm. He didn't want to hurt her, but he wasn't letting her go. He needed to be touching her for this part.

She turned to him. "Okay," she said quietly, hand still in his. "This is what I know about you. Your name is Nicholas Ames, you're thirty-four years old, you are—were—a stockbroker in New York. You made some money and this year you retired from the office you'd worked in for twelve years. You want to open a business of your own. Your father was a banker, your mother was a lawyer. So tell me—how much of that is true?"

Nick was so goddamned proud of her. Any other woman would be screaming by now, but not Charity.

Her words echoed in his head. *How much of that is true?* "Basically none of it," he confessed.

She lost what little color she'd acquired. Her hand slipped out of his to cover her mouth. "Oh my God," she breathed. "You're already married. That's what this is about."

"No!" He grabbed her hand back. "God no, I'm not married. Never have been, either. Or rather, yes, I *am* married. To you."

"No, you're not. My husband's dead," she whispered. "I buried him."

"No, honey, you buried someone else. Someone who tried to kill me. I have no idea what his name was because he had no ID on him."

Charity blinked back tears. "He might not have had ID, but he did have your wedding ring."

"Yes, he did." Nick looked her straight in the face. "And putting that ring on his finger was one of the hardest things I've ever had to do. But it had to be done. It identified the body as me, didn't it?"

"Yes," she whispered, her face drawn. "When the police officer gave me that ring, I thought my heart would stop."

Nick bent forward slowly until his lips touched her hair. She held herself stiffly but she didn't draw back. One small victory. "I know," he said against her hair, his breath moving a silken strand.

He'd almost forgotten the smell of her. A mix of shampoo, some springlike scent, and her skin. He breathed it in and somehow it calmed him. He'd been running on adrenaline since he'd driven the man off the cliff, wound tighter than a drum, feeling as if someone had ripped a huge, gaping hole in his chest.

Touching Charity, breathing her in, calmed him down, cooled something inflamed in him. He'd been like some wounded creature in the forest, blasted by a hunter, stumbling around blindly, in pain, losing blood. Charity healed him, made him whole.

"Start with your name. I need to know your name." Her head tilted as she studied him.

"Nick. Nick Ireland. But that's not my family name. I have no idea what my real name is. I was left in the baby hatch of an orphanage in upstate New York. There was a note pinned to the blanket saying that the baby's name was Nick. Later that day, a girl called, asking if I'd been found. She was crying. The secretary of the orphanage said she had an Irish accent, so they called me Ireland. No one has any idea who she was."

Nick watched Charity's eyes. He'd never told this story to a woman, ever. He was really good at making up fake legends. It never even occurred to him to tell the truth. He didn't want to see pity or horror.

He wasn't seeing them now.

Charity was listening quietly, watching him, face somber. "Go on," she said.

"I was in the military for ten years. Army." He didn't say which part of the army. Actually, he *couldn't*. Delta operators' jackets were kept confidential for twenty years. "I was wounded on a mission and had to resign my commission. I've been working for the government for the past couple of years, on a special task force investigating international organized crime collaborating with terrorists. There's more and more of that, and we're there to stop it."

He watched her process the information. He was sure she was filing away every piece of data he was giving her, putting it all together. He kept forgetting how smart Charity was. It was easy to forget, at times. She was so pretty, so gentle you could easily overlook the fact that she was as sharp as a tack.

"The army," Charity mused. "So, I guess you didn't fall on your aunt's shower curtain rod, did you?"

"No, I didn't." There was utter quiet in the room as she absorbed this news.

Charity was losing that shell-shocked look. She had no expression at all, like a porcelain doll. He didn't like it, because more bad news was coming, as inevitable as a wave rolling in to shore.

"So—if your job is as an undercover cop—that *is* basically what you said, isn't it?"

Nick nodded.

"So, what are you here for? Parker's Ridge is a quiet little New England town. What could you possibly be looking for here?"

This was it. Nick had to walk carefully here, over hot coals. Barefoot.

He tightened his grip on her hand. "We're here because of Vassily Worontzoff. He's the head of one of the most powerful Russian mobs and there's a lot of chatter that he's about to get in touch with an al Qaeda cell. And that is highly classified information, Charity. I don't have to tell you that it goes no farther than this room."

She was staring at him. She gave a half laugh. "You're investigating *Vassily*? Are you crazy? He's a writer, what does he have to do with—wait a minute." Nick could almost see the cogs in her head, spinning so hard they generated steam as she put the pieces together. "If you're after Vassily—which is crazy—then that means that you were after *me*. Everyone knows I'm his best friend here." Charity pulled her hand away and suddenly stood up. "Oh my God." She put her hands on her head and spun around, as if finding it hard to be in the same place with what she was saying. "You came to me for information. I was—I was your *mission*. Oh God, oh God. You were sent here to seduce me. Like Mata Hari, only a male. I can't believe this. I was your job." Her voice was rising in agitation.

Nick opened his mouth, then shut it as a car braked sharply in front of her house and a man emerged fast, coming at a run toward the front door. A second later, the bell rang.

Well, this was getting interesting.

It was Di Stefano, and judging by the look on his face, he was furious. At Nick.

Here to join the rapidly growing I Hate Nick Club.

Twenty-two

The one good thing about being angry—really, truly angry, as she never had been in her life—was that it settled her stomach and warmed her up.

Charity's head was reeling at seeing Nick, alive and well, and here in her house.

The man before her was Nick, but not Nick. *Her* Nick was a reassuring sort of man, exuding a kind of bland calmness. *This* Nick was like a dangerous animal, a panther or a lion. Instead of elegant business clothes, he was dressed all in black from head to toe, like a ninja. Jeans, sweatshirt, light parka. Instead of shiny, elegant shoes, he had well-worn black boots on, the kind of footwear meant for serious business and not for show.

He held himself differently, too, with a coiled energy just waiting to spring. Instead of the affable half smile that was his default expression, he looked grim, mouth tight, jaws clenched.

It didn't surprise her that this new Nick said he'd been

in the army and was now a law enforcement officer. Then again, he could actually be a criminal—right now she was reserving judgment on anything he told her. One thing was for sure—he looked dangerous, every inch of him.

And, unfortunately, incredibly sexy.

This was not a good thing. She didn't want to notice that at all. The doorbell rang a second before Nick yanked it open. There was a tall blond-haired man on her porch, as grim-faced as Nick.

"I knew it," he began furiously. "What the *fuck* are you doing here?"

Nick was unfazed by his anger. His shoulders stiffened and he stepped forward and got right into the man's face. "We've had this conversation already and watch your mouth, you fuckhead, there's a lady here."

The man's mouth closed with a snap as he looked past Nick's broad shoulder and saw her. "Ma'am," he said warily.

Charity nodded. She had no idea what to say.

He sighed and dug into his jeans pocket, coming out with a leather wallet he flipped open. There was a brass badge on the bottom and photo ID on the top. He held it out at chest height and walked into the room, stopping a foot from her.

Charity stepped forward and examined the brass badge. It had an intricate design with symbols she didn't understand. *Department of Homeland Security* was etched along the bottom. The ID had a photograph of the man in front of her, obviously taken in happier times, since he was faintly smiling, totally unlike the grim expression he wore. Above the photograph was his name: Special Agent John Di Stefano.

She looked up at him. He wasn't quite as tall as Nick, but he was still much taller than she was. "Special Agent Di Stefano," she murmured.

There was sudden silence in the room, as if no one knew where to go from here. They all waited for someone to take the lead.

"Show her yours, Nick."

Charity's eyes widened and she almost said, *I've already seen his,* but she bit her lips before the words could tumble out, pure hysteria bubbling in her throat.

Nick took out the exact same kind of leather wallet, with the exact same kind of brass badge with the symbols and *Department of Homeland Security* written on it. The photo ID was the same, with a grim-looking photograph and Special Agent Nick Ireland above it. He snapped it shut and tucked it into the back pocket of his jeans.

With a hostile glance at Nick, Di Stefano cupped her elbow and started steering her toward the couch. She didn't have the strength to resist.

He sat her down on the couch and took an armchair, shooting another hostile glare at Nick when he sat right next to her.

Di Stefano leaned forward in the classic male position, legs apart, hands dangling over knees. He stared straight into her eyes and said, "You haven't seen me. I don't exist. This meeting never happened. That has to be said and understood right up front, ma'am." Another dirty look at Nick. "I'm sorry it's come to this, though. You shouldn't know about us at all."

Nick placed his arm along the back of the couch, angling to hold her against him. She leaned forward, away from his grasp.

"Special Agent Di Stefano," she said clearly, turning her head away from Nick. "I imagine you are referring to the fact that apparently you are both here on a confidential mission. I assure you that I have no intention whatsoever of divulging information that might be harmful to my country. However, if your mission here is to spy on Vassily Worontzoff, then I think you are wasting your resources and our country's resources. The man is a great writer and nothing more."

Nick threw some objects on the coffee table between her and Di Stefano, stopping Charity just as she was getting heated up in her defense of Vassily.

She looked at them. A box of medicine, what looked like a steel bolt, and a CD.

"What are these?"

Nick's jaw muscles rippled. "My own little Worontzoff kit. Pick them up." Charity just looked at him. He waved a long finger at the little pile. "Go ahead. Pick them up."

She did so, gingerly, wondering if maybe they hid something. But no. They were perfectly normal objects. A box of medicine by a big international pharmaceutical company with a vial for IV administration inside, a bolt, and a CD with no markings. When she finished studying them, she put them back quietly and waited.

Nick picked the box up again and put it back in her hand. "This is a breakthrough drug, used in the treatment of some advanced cancers, especially effective in pediatric medicine. Look at the price."

She turned it over and searched for the price on the bottom flap. Her eyes widened.

Nick nodded curtly. "That drug is worth eight hundred euros, more than one thousand dollars at the current exchange rate. It's experimental, and expensive. Or would be, if it were genuine. What you're holding is about ten cents' worth of printed cardboard, glass for the vial, and tap water. Worontzoff's business partners slipped these packages into shipments to hospitals. Not a bad business at all. One thousand dollars for ten cents' worth of product. We're talking a markup of nearly a million percent. Most profitable business on earth. Nothing else comes even close. In comparison, dealing in cocaine and heroin is for chumps. The only downside is that some poor kid dying of leukemia will get a shot of tap water in his veins instead of a drug that could save his life."

Shocked, Charity turned to Di Stefano. He nodded. "Yeah. New spin on the drug trade."

"And this?" Nick continued, handing the bolt to her. "A very expensive component of the latest generation of wide-bodied airliners, made of a titanium alloy and machined to within a tolerance of a few microns. They cost seven hundred and fifty dollars each because of the rigorous testing each bolt goes through. Except that this one is made of cheap nickel. It'll start splitting at about the tenth takeoff. For a while there, until they figure out what's going on, it'll be raining planes."

Charity dropped the bolt as if it had suddenly become red-hot.

"And this?" Nick held the CD up. "I saved this for last. On this CD are the access codes for about twenty percent of our nuclear arsenal. We intercepted it on its way from Worontzoff to the Iranian minister of defense and replaced it with fake codes. Cost—something in the range of ten million dollars. It will take the Iranians some time to figure out they've been ripped off, and when they do, it is my earnest hope that they will whack Worontzoff for us, so we won't have to go to the expense of bringing him to trial." He clenched his jaws so hard the skin over his temples moved. "And right now? Right now, good old Worontzoff, man of letters, is going to meet tonight with one of the world's top terrorists and it is very likely that scumbag one will have something nuclear to sell to scumbag two."

Charity swallowed. Her throat had tightened so much it was hard to get the words out. "That's his business meeting?" she whispered. "With a terrorist?"

"Not just *a* terrorist," Di Stefano said. "*The* terrorist. A guy we've been after for years."

"So you see, Charity," Nick said heatedly, "there is no way on this earth that you can go to Worontzoff's house tonight. As a matter of fact, we're going to take you into protective custody as of right now, until this whole thing is over." He slanted a hard glance at his partner. "That right, Di Stefano?"

"Yes. It wouldn't be a good idea for you to be there, Miss Prewitt. Some bad things are going to happen and it's best you be far away."

"But—I still don't understand what Vassily is doing *here*. In Parker's Ridge. It's certainly not a crime center. It's not a center of anything. It's a remote little town in northern Vermont. What could he possibly want here?"

"You," Di Stefano said bluntly.

Charity jolted. *"Me?"*

Nick tossed something else on the table—a photograph of a woman. "Last item in my Worontzoff kit."

Charity turned it around and gasped.

The photograph was a color close-up of a woman done by a professional photographer. At the bottom of the photograph were Cyrillic letters, perhaps the photographer's name. The woman had dangling earrings and was made up in a way that was slightly old-fashioned. She had pale blond hair cut in a bob. Charity scanned the familiar features, heart pounding.

She made a little sound of shock. The woman could have been her twin.

"Yeah," Nick said. "She's a dead ringer for you."

Charity couldn't take her eyes off the portrait. She picked it up, drinking it in with her eyes. It was like looking at herself in the mirror, wearing a wig. She touched the hair in the photo. A pale blond, several shades lighter than her own.

"He—he wanted me to bleach my hair. Light blond. And cut it. In a bob. Like this." She ran the tip of her finger along the line of the woman's hair, cut at the earlobe.

Di Stefano winced. "He's wanting to turn you into her in every way. To make you exactly like her. Physically at least. Wasn't there some creepy Hitchcock film about something like that?"

"What was her name?" Charity whispered, without looking away from the portrait. So many things were becoming clear to her. The way Vassily sought her out. The way he looked at her, seeing her but not seeing her. He wasn't seeing her at all. He was seeing his long-dead love.

"Katya." Nick's voice was harsh. "Her name was Katya Artamova. She was a poetess and the love of his life. She was arrested together with him. They were both sent to Kolyma. She lasted about a week."

"Katya," Charity murmured, touching the face that could have been her own. Poor Katya. Poor Vassily.

Vassily had not only lost his love in the prison camp. He'd lost his soul.

Charity turned to the table and touched the objects, one by one. She was cursed with a vivid imagination. It took very little to imagine a child dying of leukemia, desperately hoping that the tap water in his IV was going to save him. Or to imagine one of the planes going down. She'd read that the newest generation of planes could carry from four to seven hundred passengers. Thousands of dead, charred bodies. Or—God!—nuclear secrets in the hands of an Iranian minister who hated America.

She looked up. "How are you going to follow the meeting tonight?"

Di Stefano and Nick looked at each other. Finally, Nick gave a what-the-hell shrug. "We've got a special device aimed at his study window that lets us listen in on conversations."

"Is it the same kind of device that let you listen in on my conversation with Vassily just now?" she asked sharply.

Nick looked embarrassed. "Ah, no. Those are just old-fashioned bugs I planted. What we have aimed at Worontzoff's study window is a laser-driven remote listening device, controlled from a surveillance van about a mile out."

Charity frowned. "Just the study? What happens if they talk business in the living room, or the conservatory or the winter garden? Vassily's house is huge. If you're just listening in on one window in one room, what are you going to do if they hold their talks elsewhere?"

Di Stefano heaved a huge sigh. "Good question. With no good answer. All we have is the one laser device, so we're just going to have to hope that they meet in the study. And that they meet soon. Because of course there's the problem that—" He stopped suddenly and looked uncomfortable.

"What?" Charity asked. "The problem what?"

Nick slanted Di Stefano a hard glance, a warning. Di Stefano bit his lip.

"What?" Charity asked, her voice sharp. "What problem?"

"Well, the thing is, we can't use the laser much after last light. Just like we can't use it in a heavy snowstorm. The laser beam becomes visible. It's like a huge neon sign—we're listening to you."

"So what happens if they meet after dark? Vassily invited me over for dinner, presumably after the talks or negotiations or whatever are over. Or what happens if it starts snowing, just like the weather forecast says. What's Plan B?"

Silence. Di Stefano looked embarrassed and Nick looked grim, jaw muscles jumping.

Finally, Di Stefano spoke. "There really isn't a Plan B. We'll try to get photographs of who goes in and out. Use thermal imaging to count warm bodies." He shrugged. "We'll do our best with what we have."

"There's another way," she said softly. "To get more information."

"Yeah?" Di Stefano raised his eyebrows. "Which is?"

"Wire me," she said simply.

Nick exploded. "No!" He jumped up from the sofa and ran a hand through his hair. "Not just no, but *fuck* no. Are you crazy? Hassan al-Banna and Vassily Worontzoff in the same fucking room and you walk into it? Together with God knows how many of their goons? There's no way in hell you're going anywhere near that place." He whirled. "Goddamn it, Di Stefano, you tell her."

But Di Stefano was looking at her thoughtfully.

"It could work," Charity said, ignoring Nick.

"It could," Di Stefano replied.

"No! Jesus, you can't send a civilian into that! There's no precedent, no protocol. We can't do that!"

Di Stefano swiveled his head to stare at Nick. "Seems to me that you're the first one here to have thrown precedent and protocol out the window, Nick. We're just picking up the pieces here."

"Well, I don't want to pick up *her* pieces," Nick snarled. "Did enough of that in Bosnia. This is not an option, so you can just forget it."

Charity stood, too. Nick had an unfair advantage with his height. It was bad enough while standing, with her on the sofa and him upright and quivering with indignation. It was positively lopsided with both of them standing, an angry Nick looming over her.

"I'm not too sure that is a decision for you to make, Nick," she said softly. She was speaking to him, but looking at Di Stefano.

What they'd said about Vassily had sickened her. Was that where he had got all his money? Not from his books but from essentially killing kids and abetting terrorists?

Charity didn't really think of herself as a brave woman. She didn't go in for martial arts, she didn't rock climb or go parachuting. She was a very staid librarian who thought a new Nora Roberts book was a real thrill.

By the same token, though, she had a strong sense of honor and of patriotism. It turned out that the man she admired so much, Vassily Worontzoff, was a dangerous man, a man to be stopped.

In some small portion of her heart, she understood well that it was Kolyma that had changed him. He wasn't responsible for the horrors that had been inflicted on him, that had cost him his health, his love, and, in a real sense, his sanity. But he was responsible for what he became.

She recognized that she was faced with another one of those moments where you show what you are made of. And she was made of steel. Life had handed her the possibility of stopping something horrendous and she wasn't going to walk away.

"Do you have the necessary equipment?" she asked Di Stefano softly.

"Yeah, I've got a body wire in the car and a button camera. All you'd have to do is just spend some time there. We'd need everyone's voice on tape and clear visuals of everyone's face, which we won't get with long-range cameras. This would be invaluable, Ms., ah Mrs.—"

Di Stefano stopped, not knowing what to call her. Fair enough, she didn't know what to call herself, either.

"Charity will do."

You could actually hear Nick's teeth grinding.

"This is *not* going to happen!" Nick's voice rose to a shout. "Goddamn it, this is insane! Have you forgotten who we're dealing with? These aren't white-collar criminals; they're some of the most deadly men on the planet."

"And yet, by your own reckoning, Nick, one of them loves me. Vassily won't hurt me. I know that," she said.

"You can't know anything of the sort, goddamn it!" His breath huffed out like that of an enraged bull. "Shit, am I the only one with any sense in this room? Di Stefano, you didn't do service in Bosnia, but I did. I know what these people can do, especially to women."

"But he loves her. And no one is going to suspect Charity of anything. She's there because he invited her. She's going to go in, get a few visuals, then pretend to have a headache. In and out, in half an hour. What can happen in half an hour? And we might just catch a big break."

"It doesn't take half an hour to die," Nick grated. "It takes a second. She's not doing this, and that's final. I'm team leader and that's my order."

"Sorry." Di Stefano bared his teeth. "You're not team leader any more, Nick, I am. The boss thought your behavior was too erratic, so he relieved you of your command. Effective half an hour ago. As a matter of fact, you're not even on the team at all, anymore. Though I'll let you stay in the van, as a courtesy, and seeing as how you have . . . an emotional investment in the outcome. So I want you to go out and get the kit to wire Charity up." The two men stared at each other. "Now," Di Stefano added softly. "That's a direct order."

Nick's breathing was loud in the room. With a vicious *"Fuck!"* he turned and walked out the front door, slamming it violently behind him.

Di Stefano winced and sighed. He looked at the floor for a second, then looked up. "I know what you're thinking. You're mad at him. I'm mad at him. Our partner, Alexei, is mad at him. Our boss is mad at him, together with the whole head office. Everyone's mad at Nick."

"He lied to me," Charity replied steadily. "From the first moment."

"Yeah." Di Stefano nodded sharply. "He did, that's his job. He's one of the best undercover cops I've ever seen and being able to lie is a big part of that. It's for the job, though, he's not a habitual liar in real life, though God knows, he doesn't have too much of that. If anything, Iceman is too straight. That's what we call him, Iceman. Because he's always cool and in control." He shook his head. "You blew that right out of the water. I've never seen him like this before." He grimaced. "Though it pains me to say anything in his favor, what he did, when he married you, it was way off the charts. He threw his entire career down the drain for you. If they let him stay in the service after this, he'll end up cleaning toilets, without the benefit of a brush. And he knew that when he did it. But it was worth it to him, to keep you safe. He told us in no uncertain terms that if he was killed, we

were to look after you, his widow. He did it to protect you."
He shook his head. "Hard as it is to imagine it of Iceman, he
loves you. I know you're feeling lied to and betrayed, but he
did it to protect you in the only way he knew how."

Charity's throat shook. She couldn't get any words out at
all. She took a breath, two, three, but nothing came out.

"And hard as it is to say this, I think you might want to cut
him some slack."

Di Stefano had taken her righteous anger and twisted it
around. She was furious, and she had every right to be.
Nick had lied to her right from the start, and continued to
do so.

And yet, and yet. He was doing what he thought right.
And Charity knew, deep down, where there were no lies,
only truths, that Nick's lovemaking had been real. That there
were real feelings there.

She had no idea what to do with that information,
though.

Nick burst back into the room, carrying a black suitcase,
grim faced and tense. A gust of cold air came in with him
and she shivered. Not just at the cold air.

All Charity could do was look at him. So different from the
Nick she'd married. He had a dangerous edge to him, sharp
as a knife. The features of his face, familiar as her own, were
somehow different. As if a layer had been stripped away,
leaving only skin and bone and truth.

Truth. The Nick before her was the real one—hard and
grim and focused. Not a soft businessman at all, but a man
built for power and speed. A man who faced danger on a
daily basis. Who'd undoubtedly killed and who looked perfectly capable of killing again.

He set the briefcase down on the coffee table, unsnapped

the locks, and lifted the lid. Inside were gadgets embedded in foam rubber.

He lifted two out, one a long wire with doodads at each end and the other a small, complicated electronic thingie. As with all things electronic, their outsides gave no indication to what their insides did.

"Okay." Nick straightened and speared each of them with a hard glare. Then his attention focused intently on his partner. "This is the way it's going to work. The only way it's going to work, or I'm pulling the plug right now. This is not optional. First off, we're going to need backup."

"Done," Di Stefano snapped. "I'm calling in our Boston SWAT team. They'll be here by around four. I hope to God we don't need to use them, that we can get her in and out smooth and easy, intercept Hammad after he drives away, but they'll be there. In case."

"Two." Nick's gaze was unwavering. "You and I are going to be right outside the house all the time Charity's in there. I don't care what it takes. If we have to take down guards, that's what we'll do. She's not going in unless I'm two seconds away from breaching the front door to get to her."

"Uh . . ." Di Stefano shifted uneasily. "I don't know—"

"That's nonnegotiable," Nick snapped.

Di Stefano was silent for a long moment, working his way through Nick's ultimatum. "Okay," he sighed.

"And three," Nick continued. "She stays in the house twenty minutes, tops. Whatever she gets, she gets, but twenty minutes after she walks in through the front door, she's going to develop a major headache and she's heading right back out."

"But—"

"That's nonnegotiable, too. Otherwise we're not doing this. And it goes against every instinct I have, as it is."

"Okay. Okay." Di Stefano shot his arm out and checked the time. "We'd better start getting her ready."

Nick stepped in front of Charity. "I'll do it. You get out of here and wait for me at the van. I'll be there in about an hour."

Silence. Di Stefano breathed in and out, then finally spoke. "I can count on that? That you'll get out of here? Because you look an awful lot like you're about to go cowboy again on me, Iceman. More than you already have, and I can't accept that. I'm going to need your word that you're going to leave here and let her get to Worontzoff's house on her own."

"A driver will be coming for me," Charity offered. She didn't quite understand the tension humming between the two of them, but it was palpable.

Nick's jaw muscles jumped. "Precisely," he said to her, while staring at Di Stefano. "You're going to be alone in a car with one of Worontzoff's goons for—what? Fifteen, twenty minutes? A lot of things can happen in that time. Lots of bad things."

Charity's heart jumped. "I—I don't think Vassily would hurt me."

Nick turned to her, jaw muscles jumping. "Vassily wouldn't hurt Katya Artsemova, no. He loved her. But Katya Artsemova has been dead for over fifteen years. He thinks he loves you because you look so much like her, but you're *not* her. When the craziness in his head dies down and he realizes that, who knows what the fuck he'll do?"

"You come back to the van, Iceman," Di Stefano said, his voice cold and steady. "You will not compromise this part of the mission before it's begun, I hope that's clear."

"Or what?" Nick asked, swiveling back to him.

"Or I'll fucking cuff you, that's what."

Nick bared his teeth. "You can fucking try. And you watch your fucking language. There's a lady here."

"Shit." Di Stefano's teeth clicked together in exasperation. "I don't want to get into a pissing contest with you. I want your word that you'll wire her up and get out."

Nick touched her hand. "Charity? This is up to you. Do you still want to do this? Because I'm dead set against it. We're listening in on Worontzoff's study and we'll keep the beam on until the last possible minute. We've tapped his phones. We're going to photograph everyone coming in and going out. Maybe we can put a snake mike in. We don't need you to do this."

Di Stefano opened his mouth, then closed it, clearly not wanting to influence her. Because, of course, they did need her.

Vassily's mansion was huge. Most of the times she'd been to see him, he was in his living room, which had the largest hearth in the house, not his study. It was entirely possible that he would be meeting with his people there instead of the study. It was entirely possible they would meet after five, which is when the sun went down. They needed eyes and ears and it looked like she was it.

Charity didn't in any way underestimate the danger, though she was also certain that Vassily wouldn't hurt her. Nonetheless, she was walking into a room full of criminals, with no training to deal with violence should it erupt. On the other hand, she knew, beyond a shadow of a doubt, that Nick would be as close to her as he could get.

She didn't have to do this, and yet—she did. Charity trusted her moral compass and her needle was pointing at true north right now. She was in a position to help her country and she was taking it. How could she refuse? The deep calm of knowing she was doing the right thing came over her.

Even her nausea had abated and she felt well, for the first time in days. Of course, she'd been grieving over Nick's death, and seeing him in front of her, looking strong and vital and angry, completely wiped her grief away.

The front door closed quietly and Nick rounded on her. His hand shot out, curling around her neck. He bent until his forehead touched hers, eyes a fiery, deep blue. "I don't want you to do this," he whispered.

Charity stepped back, but he just followed her. A couple more steps and her back was against the wall, Nick's long, lean body pressing in against her.

"I know," she answered. "But I have to." She took a deep breath and asked the question that was haunting her. "After—afterward." She swallowed. There was no moisture left in her mouth, her lungs felt empty. It was hard to speak. "Afterward, will I see you again?"

It was painful to humiliate herself like this, but her need to know overrode her embarrassment. If he said no, he was leaving as soon as his job here was over, she'd crumple to the ground.

Her knees stiffed, her spine stacked back up. No, no she wouldn't. Prewitts didn't fall to the ground. They took what life dealt them, and did the best they could.

It was as if he hadn't heard her. "You are staying twenty minutes, not a second more. The instant you step outside of Worontzoff's house, I will be at your side and I'm not leaving you, ever again."

A low growling noise came from Nick's throat, the noise a dying, wounded animal would make. He bent down to her, eyes blazing, mouth open. Her own mouth opened, instinctively, helplessly, for his kiss. But he stopped a breath away from her lips, eyes burning into hers. He was panting, his breath hot on her cheek. A trickle of sweat fell down his temple to plop on her neck.

It was impossible to think of anyone calling him Iceman. He looked like he was ready to explode into a fireball.

"I came back from the fucking dead for you, Charity, so no, I'm not going anywhere. I'm going to live with you here or in another house; I don't care. I'll do something—maybe I'll run for sheriff. I don't care about that, either, as long as I'm with you and we can raise our child together. Is that clear?"

She could almost feel the waves of his strong male will beating against her. There was no way she could resist him even if she wanted to. But she didn't. Living with him for the rest of her life, raising their child together, sounded like heaven.

"Yes, very clear," she whispered.

He brought his mouth down to hers again, stopping at the last second, then pulling back. His eyes dropped to her mouth, then rose again.

"I can't kiss you," he said starkly. Deep grooves bracketed that beautiful mouth. "I can't send you in there with your mouth swollen with kisses. We can't make love, either, though I'm about ready to burst out of my skin." He angled his lower body to rest against hers and she could feel his erection against her stomach, hot and hard. "I can't. I can't guarantee I won't leave any signs on you. But when this is over I'm taking you to bed and I'm going to fuck you breathless."

"Okay," she whispered, watching his eyes.

As if it pained him, he let go of her neck, one finger at a time, and stepped back. It was like a force field suddenly switching off, or the planet's gravity disappearing. She stumbled, in free fall.

Nick's arms were around her in an instant, pulling her against him again.

She wriggled a little because her back was pressed against the wall and he was pressed hard against her. She felt his penis ripple as he drew in a sharp breath.

"Jesus," he muttered. He stepped away reluctantly. One step, two. He turned to the briefcase and came back with the electronic doodads in his hands, wires dangling.

He reached his hand out and he slowly unzipped her track suit jacket, then stepped back, pulling in a deep breath, eyes closed.

She stood there, feeling the cold in a little strip along her chest where the jacket was open.

Nick opened his eyes again, face stark. He put his hands on her chest, watching her carefully, then slowly opened his hands. Up over the balls of her shoulders, sweeping the jacket down. His jaw muscles were jumping, his forehead beaded with sweat. He looked down at her for several long moments.

Charity stood straight, arms at her side, not knowing what to do. She'd been naked with Nick so many times and so joyfully. But that had been Nick Ames. She still didn't know how to react to Nick Ireland.

He lowered his head until his forehead rested on her shoulder. She could feel the dampness and heat of his skin against hers. They stood there, unmoving, for five minutes, ten.

Charity couldn't think with Nick so close to her, pressed up against her. He seemed to suck up all her emotions and thoughts. Mind utterly blank, her body took over. As if she had no volition of her own, her hands rose hesitantly, up the outside of his black parka, to finally hold him in an embrace. His whole body shook, a long tremble that seemed to rise from his black boots and encompass his tall, strong body.

One big hand moved from her back to cup her breast. Such a familiar feeling, Nick's hand on her breast. In an instant, all the feelings that had been kept at bay, somehow remote from her, flooded her in a wild rush. Arousal, anger, fierce joy, agonizing pain.

He thumbed her nipple and the pleasure was electric, bolting through her system like lightning.

His head pulled up and back as he watched his hand on her breast. "Do they feel different?" he asked, his voice hoarse.

"A little," she whispered.

His hand moved from her breast, down to cover her belly. It rested there, warm and large. Right over where their child was growing.

Finally, Nick moved, pulling away to get the electronic paraphernalia.

The body wire was complicated to strap on, and required several pieces of tape. Nick worked slowly and carefully, face intent. He was sweating so hard a bead dropped down his temple.

He disappeared into her bedroom and came back with a black cardigan and dressed her, slowly, carefully. A tiny video camera took the place of one of the buttons.

"I'll be watching you," Nick said. "Watching everything."

She nodded.

He ran her through the precautions. Her head swam with frequencies and audio cones and battery life, though he made her promise again, looking him straight in the eyes, that at minute twenty after entering Vassily's house, she'd plead a headache and come home.

Finally, it was done.

Nick wrapped her in his arms and they stood there, both shaking, his head buried in her shoulder. She felt moisture on the bare skin of her shoulder. She pulled back, surprised.

Tears, not sweat.

She reached up to run her hands through his blue-black hair. Nick. Her husband. Who'd lied to her, who wasn't what he said he was. But she loved him all the same, with everything in her.

A deep shudder rippled through his long body, then he straightened. He looked at her, not even trying to hide the tears streaking his cheeks.

"I'll be close by," he said starkly.

She nodded.

"Say as little as possible, get in, get out."

She nodded again.

They looked at each other in the silence of the room. Nick was panting, as if he'd run a race. His fists clenched tightly, then opened.

"Go get dressed," he said, "before I change my mind."

Twenty-three

"My dear Arkady," Vassily said, coming toward him. "My dear, dear friend." They embraced, kissing each other's cheeks.

"Vor." Arkady's voice was thick. He coughed to hide his emotion. He hadn't seen his Vor in four years.

"Come my friend, you must sit down. You must be weary after such a long journey." Vassily indicated a comfortable leather armchair next to what was obviously his desk and brought Arkady a glass of vodka himself, a sign of respect.

The Vor sat next to him, placing his shattered hand on Arkady's arm. "You have done well, my friend. There will be many such trips, if you are willing to take them—" He paused while Arkady nodded.

No question. If the Vor needed him, he was at his service.

"Good." The Vor nodded. "We will make much money and when we have finished, I will send you to look after my interests in Europe. Would you like to settle in Switzerland? France?"

"Italy," Arkady breathed and the Vor nodded again.

"Italy it shall be. There will be work for you there. Our empire is growing. You will be my viceroy."

Arkady bowed his head. "It would be a privilege, Vor," he murmured.

The two men turned their heads at the sharp knock on the door. A man stuck his head in. A former zek. Arkady could tell. "He's coming, Vor. We just got word. He'll be here in less than an hour, in a three-car caravan."

"He comes in alone," Vassily said sharply. "Or not at all. Tell him I will be without bodyguards myself. There will only be the engineer in the room."

The man looked uneasy. "Vor," he said. "Is that wise? These are dangerous men."

"Yes, they are. But we have something they badly want. And we have more coming. They won't harm me." He flicked his hand. "Now go and be prepared to greet him when he arrives."

The man hesitated briefly, then bowed his head and withdrew. The heavy door made a soft *whump* as it closed.

Vassily gave a wintry smile. "This business will be over soon. Come, let us retire to the living room where we have tea waiting for us. And when this is over, there is someone I must introduce to you. You will be astonished, my friend."

Outside Worontzoff's mansion

Those were the last words they heard before Alexei pulled the plug. Nick knew Alexei had to—if you looked carefully, you could see the laser beam as a faint line in the gathering darkness—but he had to stop himself from banging a fist against the wall in frustration.

He and Di Stefano were hunkered down behind a bush, to one side of the study windows, unable to see into the room. Essentially blind and now that Alexei had cut them off, deaf, too.

They were clad head to toe in a special uniform and balaclava made of Nomex that repelled thermal imaging.

Worontzoff's security was shot to shit tonight, all his guards milling about, offloading the truck that had driven in a quarter of an hour before. He and Di Stefano had been careful and they were good. They'd had zero trouble infiltrating.

Nick knew that the SWAT team was deployed, ready. They'd spent the past hour getting into position. He couldn't see them, but he knew they were there. The comms system clicked steadily every quarter of an hour, ticking off men in position.

He'd been expecting a knock-down drag-out fight from Di Stefano about being down here where the action was and not up in the van, watching Alexei pace in frustration. But Di Stefano clearly realized Nick wouldn't let anything get in the way between him and Charity while she was in Worontzoff's house. Di Stefano had simply told Nick to suit up and that was that.

Di Stefano pulled out a small LCD monitor, holding it so that no one could detect its faint glow. It was a little miracle of technology, programmed for thermal imaging and able to tune into the frequency of Charity's microcamera.

He studied it carefully and signaled to Nick that everyone had left the room. To Nick's surprise, he drew out a tiny drill and proceeded to drill a hole through the wall, at the level of the baseboard inside the house. It was high speed and utterly silent. As soon as the drill perforated the inside wall, Di Stefano threaded a combo microphone–fish-eye lens snake into the hole.

Di Stefano fiddled with the tiny handheld computer, and suddenly Nick had sound and could see inside the room. It was at foot level, but the camera had a good range. He knew it was a little miracle of optics.

Great, now they had eyes and ears in the room and could see and hear what Charity was seeing and hearing. Better than he'd hoped.

There was no one in the study, but there was music in the background. One of those sad Russian songs that had driven him crazy when he was on listening duty.

The comm system was piping sound to everyone on the loop, including Alexei. If Russian was spoken, Alexei would give a simultaneous interpretation.

Everything was good to go. Now all they could do was wait.

Nick was usually good at waiting. Stillness and darkness were his friends. Right now, though, his insides were racing at a thousand miles an hour. He gripped his MP5 tightly, glad for the gloves because his hands were sweating.

Two clicks from the SWAT team members. Nothing happening.

Iceman hunkered down to wait. There was nothing else to do.

Nick had carefully picked her clothes. The black cardigan was loose and didn't show the tiny mike taped between her breasts or the battery pack taped to the small of her back. Even she had difficulty in seeing the microcamera, it was so well camouflaged. He'd also picked slate gray lightweight wool pants and comfortable boots. He hadn't said it, but clearly he'd chosen her clothes not only to hide the camera and mike, but also for comfort if she had to move fast.

Nick had filled her head with instructions, but she hadn't absorbed much beyond not turning her back, not letting material rub against the mike and not scratching herself.

She jolted at the sound of the front doorbell. Vassily's driver, come to pick her up.

She looked at herself in the mirror. She was about to betray Vassily, something that she would have thought herself incapable of. She thought of the fake medicine, the counterfeit bolts, and what Nick had told her about the human trafficking Vassily's organization engaged in.

And then she thought of Nick.

Two men. She'd loved both of them, in her way, and she never really knew either of them.

The doorbell rang again and she picked up her coat. Taking a deep breath, she walked to the door.

Showtime.

Al-Banna was late. But Vassily had learned patience at a hard school. The hardest. He wasn't worried. Al-Banna would come. He was too invested not to. Vassily had something al-Banna wanted very, very badly, with more on the way.

In the meantime, Vassily chatted amiably with his old friend, Arkady, over tea and vodka. They didn't reminisce about days gone by, as old friends usually did. The past was much too painful. No, music and books wove their usual magic.

Finally, Ilya stood in the doorway. "He's coming, Vor," he said quietly. "He'll be here in fifteen minutes."

"Did you tell him to come alone?" Vassily asked sharply.

"Yes. He wasn't happy about it, but he's coming alone. Only the driver and him."

Vassily didn't care whether he was happy or not. All he cared about was that a new and safe route had been found and that al-Banna would be bringing ten million dollars.

And that afterward, he would be celebrating with Katya. Together. At long, long last.

Five clicks. The prearranged signal that someone was coming. A sentry was posted two miles up the road, well camouflaged, with powerful binoculars.

"Al-Banna," Di Stefano mouthed. Nick nodded.

Word must have been given to Worontzoff, too. On the screen, Nick could see him and the Russian who'd brought the container and who was called Arkady enter the study.

They were speaking softly, calmly.

"They're talking about books," Alexei's voice sounded clear as a bell in his ears. "Nothing important. Worontzoff just made a joke about Arabs being late. Used a term for Arab that is very politically incorrect."

It was almost completely dark, which helped their concealment. The floodlights were on a timer, which hadn't been changed since summer. They would be turned on in an hour. In an hour and a half, Charity would be safely out of the way and everyone in the mansion would be in restraints. Or dead. Nick didn't much care either way, as long as Charity was safe.

Nick and Di Stefano held their position, barely breathing. Every once in a while Alexei would give them the gist of the conversation going on in the study.

With a loud clanking sound, the big front gates started

opening, exactly in time for a black Mercedes with tinted windows to pass through them and drive up to the front steps without slowing down. An act of pure arrogance.

Two men got out, the driver and a passenger. Nick stared hard at the man who emerged from the passenger side. He'd studied the fucker's file until it was burned into his brain.

He looked older than the pictures in the file, thinner. There'd been some plastic surgery done. The nose was narrower, cheekbones higher. His hair was pewter gray instead of midnight black.

But Nick would recognize him anywhere.

Hassad al-Banna, the man who'd masterminded the attack against the USS *Cole*, once Osama bin Laden's right-hand man, now setting up a terror franchise all his own.

Di Stefano clicked once on his lip mike. Nick could almost feel the tension of the invisible team.

He watched al-Banna climb the big granite stairs, the driver right behind him, carrying a large suitcase. Big, beefy guy. Clearly a bodyguard doubling as driver.

A few minutes later, they were walking into the study and Nick and Di Stefano bent over the small screen, watching as if lives depended on it. Which they did.

Vassily got up to greet the Arab. Luckily, there would be no niceties, no pretending at social politeness. This was a business transaction between two men and two organizations that wanted nothing to do with each other, besides exchanging money for a commodity.

This suited him. The quicker this was over with, the faster he could be with Katya. He felt her presence very strongly, even if she hadn't arrived yet.

There was power in this room, great power. In the hidden history of the world, what happened tonight in this small town in northern Vermont would change the course of human affairs. Vassily felt that fate had deemed that he should live, though he should have died a thousand times over in Kolyma. A powerful force had led him to this point, and to his reclaiming of his lost love.

From this day forward, there would be no more pretense. He and Katya would be reunited and rich and powerful. No one would ever—could ever—harm them, ever again.

Nick and Di Stefano watched it all on the small screen. Worontzoff limping across the study to greet al-Banna, whose bodyguard was wheeling in a large suitcase. Worontzoff stopped right in front of him and gave a brief nod.

Nobody offered to shake hands.

Al-Banna was followed by his bodyguard. The man was carrying. The bulge under his left armpit was clear. Nick could only imagine that Worontzoff's bodyguard, Ilya, was also carrying. It was entirely possible that if Worontzoff had tried to have al-Banna disarmed, a firefight would break out. Both Ilya and the bodyguard looked tough and proficient.

Mutual assured destruction. It worked. For fifty years it kept the United States and the Soviet Union from bombing each other into oblivion.

There were five men in the room. Worontzoff, al-Banna, his bodyguard, Arkady, and Ilya.

"I don't think we need to waste time," Worontzoff said and Hammad nodded. "You go first."

Hammad looked at his bodyguard. The big man lifted the huge suitcase onto Worontzoff's desk and opened it. It was filled with bricks of dollars. Everyone in the room froze.

Hell, even Nick and Di Stefano froze.

The camera was at floor level, but the suitcase was so packed with money, it overflowed. The big bodyguard picked up one banded brick and rifled through it. Nick could clearly see Benjamin Franklin's likeness. One-hundred-dollar-bill denominations. Nick tried to think how much money could possibly be contained in that big suitcase. Millions and millions.

"Ten million dollars," al-Banna said, his voice tinny in Nick's earbud. Well, that answered that question. "What does it buy me?"

Worontzoff nodded and the man called Arkady walked over to a large container. It had a complicated closure system, but finally he opened it and lifted the lid.

He stepped back and gestured with his arm at the contents. "A canister with one hundred kilos of cesium 137. Given the temperature, it is currently in a liquid state. There is enough cesium in this canister for one large dirty bomb or several smaller ones. You can irradiate central Manhattan, say the Wall Street district, or several military bases, as you please. We have more than one hundred other canisters, ready for shipment."

A wintry smile creased al-Banna lips. "Excellent."

Nick and Di Stefano exchanged grim, startled looks. This was way worse than Nick's worst imaginings. Thank God they were here and were going to stop the transaction. The mere idea that one hundred canisters of cesium 137 were back in Russia, waiting for shipment to terrorists, was terrifying.

They weren't going to take down a transaction, they were taking down a network. Ordinarily, this would have filled Nick with satisfaction, but his whole head was taken up with worry about Charity. There wasn't room for satisfaction, only room for terror that she'd be hurt.

The gate clanged open again and one of Worontzoff's cars, a Mercedes, drove through. Nick whipped around, watching the car as it drove in. He could barely make out a small, pale figure in the back.

Jesus. Charity.

He broke out in goose bumps, angry that they'd had this half-assed idea of wiring her up and sending her into the lion's den, scared shitless that something bad would go down.

The big black car disappeared from sight, but he could envision her getting out and walking up the big stone stairs.

A few minutes later, Nick heard a soft knock on the study door. They watched on the monitor as a servant spoke softly to Worontzoff, who said something back.

Nick's blood ran cold when he heard Alexei's translation in his headset.

"Bring her in here."

It was strange walking into Vassily's home, now that she understood who he really was. She'd been here often, mainly to his soirées, when the big beautiful mansion was filled with people. A few times for tea, with just the two of them, but what seemed like an army of servants hovering in the background.

Now, the big building seemed dark and deserted, a place of danger, not delight.

All winter, she'd loved visiting Vassily. Each time she entered the mansion, it was with a little frisson of excitement, not the shudder of fear and horror pervading her body right now.

Now she knew what he was and what he saw in her. All those long, soulful conversations, the heartfelt talks about books and music—it had all been false. Vassily hadn't been conversing with *her*, Charity, but with his long-lost love.

And now that she understood where the money came from, the sumptuousness of Vassily's home made her queasy. Perhaps it was because she was so depleted, had been through such wringing emotions over the past couple of days, but it seemed to her that Vassily's home gave off evil vibrations.

She'd never come alone after dark before, without it being a social event. The other times, the mansion and the grounds had been lit up like a Christmas tree, with servants everywhere. Now the mansion was dark, the only outside lights over the porch, leaving the big lawn and the grounds in darkness.

The big black car slid to a stop at the big stairs leading up to the porch. The driver got out and opened the back door. He hadn't said a word coming here and he didn't say a word now. He simply held the door open, staring into the far distance.

With each step up the big staircase, the sense of dread increased. She could feel her heartbeat, slow, thudding. It took an effort to move her feet, which felt as heavy as lead. The very air felt dead.

The temptation to look around, to see whether Nick and John Di Stefano were around, was almost irresistible. It would make her feel so much better walking into the dark, forbidding mansion to know that two federal agents were close by, one of them Nick. Whatever would happen to them once this was over, Charity didn't doubt for a second that Nick would defend her with everything he had.

She also knew that there was a SWAT team somewhere out there, in hiding.

They were good at their job, because she had no sense of protectors being out there at all. She felt alone and small and defenseless, climbing those stairs, palms slick with sweat.

Before she could even ring the chime, the big front door opened. There was almost total darkness beyond, unlike all the other times she'd walked through this door, lit to day-light brightness by the huge chandelier in the foyer.

It wasn't on now. The only light came from a few lamps on in the big living room at the other end of the foyer, where she and Vassily had spent hours chatting. Her heart squeezed in pain at the thought.

She automatically headed for the living room, when the servant who'd opened the door touched her arm briefly.

"This way, ma'am," he said, and indicated the study door.

Charity frowned. She'd never been in Vassily's study. Why did he want her in there now? She approached the study door slowly, heart pounding. The microphone felt like a hun-dred pound weight between her breasts and she was certain the microcamera was as visible as a red flare.

The servant opened the door and Charity walked in slowly, feeling as if she were going to the guillotine. She wished she'd worn her black turtleneck sweater because she was ab-solutely certain her trip-hammering heartbeat was visible in her neck.

There was utter silence in the room, five male faces turned to her. Her boot heels sounded loud in the hush of the room.

Vassily's study was much larger than she'd imagined, almost the size of a ballroom. This being Vassily, it was lined with books, floor to ceiling and, being Vassily, he'd probably read them all. As usual, a fire burned in a hearth even larger than the one in the living room. The huge room was luxurious beyond anything she'd ever seen, with priceless Persian rugs on the flagstone floor, an enormous mahogany desk polished to a high sheen, large pieces of antique furniture barely visible in the gloom. Crystal and brass and silk.

All the light was concentrated around the desk. And on that desk was an open suitcase. It took her a second to recognize what was in the suitcase, it seemed so outlandish.

Money. Money was in the suitcase, brick after brick, tightly packed, overflowing. It must have been millions of dollars. More money than she would ever imagine could be in one place at one time.

Startled, Charity's gaze flew to Vassily's. He was watching her carefully, that burning light in his eyes. Charity had no idea how to react. Clearly, Vassily wanted her to see all this money, but why?

It was dangerous, to him and to her.

If she'd harbored the slightest little doubt that Vassily was a criminal, this suitcase shattered that doubt. No one but a criminal could possibly need to handle so much cash.

Vassily was watching her feverishly, expectantly. He knew she'd seen the money. What was she supposed to say? Charity felt the danger in the room, so acutely she felt faint.

She looked around at the other four men. Vassily might look at her with affection—at least until he finally realized that she wasn't Katya—but the other male faces were watching her with hostility.

Particularly one man, dark with silver-gray hair and harsh-set features. When she met his gaze, her heart jolted at the black, fathomless hatred she read there. It came off him in sickening, dark waves.

The terrorist. Oh God.

Nick had said that the mike wouldn't pick up her heartbeat, but it seemed impossible to her that it wasn't. Her heart was trying to beat its way out of her chest.

"My dearest Katya," Vassily said softly. He was standing to one side of the desk, leaning on his cane and staring at her, as if the open suitcase packed with money weren't there. "Come to me, my dushka. Give me a kiss and then go wait for me outside. We have much to discuss."

Charity was rooted to the spot, throat too tight for words. There was something terrible in the air, some evil presence just ready to reach out with claws and rake her. The very molecules in the air were screaming *danger.* Her skin prickled with it.

Vassily wasn't moving. He simply watched her with glittering eyes. "Come, my dear," he said again, and held out his arms, elegant black cane dangling from one ruined hand.

She had to do this. Simply had to. And then she was going to plead a headache and never come back here again.

She wasn't built for undercover work. It felt like her entire body was signaling that she was lying as she slowly walked forward, knowing that Vassily was going to embrace her, knowing that she couldn't flinch, knowing that she would.

The dark man watched her progress with ice-cold eyes, then turned to Vassily. "Is this necessary?" His voice was harsh, guttural, with a strong Middle Eastern accent. "She is an outsider. She has no business being here."

Vassily didn't answer. He didn't even look at the man. He simply watched as Charity approached, arms wide to receive her. Vassily murmured something in Russian, which she didn't understand, but she saw two of the men in the room open their eyes wide in surprise.

The dark man made a sound of disgust, swivelling his head to follow her.

"Katya," Vassily murmured. Her skin broke out in goose bumps. He was all worked up, eyes shiny, red spots on his cheeks, hands trembling. The cane swayed with his excitement.

The dark man slapped his hand down on the desk in frustration, and she jumped. He was watching her with such hatred she was frightened he'd attack her as she walked by him. If she could, she'd have skirted him, but she couldn't. He was right in her path

Charity actually heard his teeth grind as she drew even with his chair.

A sudden keening whine started, so loud it hurt her ears, a huge whistling noise that seemed to rise up out of the ground. Everyone froze, except the dark man, the terrorist.

"Spy!" he screamed, jumping up, pulling out a gun. "She's a spy! She dies!"

"Katya!" Vassily shouted, throwing himself at her. There was the sound of a shot, and she slammed against the wall, her back erupting in pain. Another shot and then all sounds were drowned in the huge explosion that knocked her off her feet and blinded and deafened her.

Christ.

Nick watched, sweating, as Charity entered Worontzoff's study. This wasn't in the program. She was supposed to stay far away from everyone except Worontzoff and plead a blinding headache as soon as possible.

Walking into a room with Worontzoff, al-Banna, his bodyguard, and a man who'd smuggled in radioactive material wasn't what they'd bargained for.

His eyes were glued to the screen, jaws clenched so tightly his temples hurt. Charity was completely alone in a room full of criminals and terrorists. Not just Charity. Charity and his child.

Nick could barely breathe as she entered the room.

Worontzoff, the fuckhead, looked at her as if she had become his personal possession. Al-Banna was coldly furious.

He saw her realize what the open suitcase held and watched her swallow heavily. Charity was no fool, thank God. She knew the danger she was in. He trusted her to remain alert.

"Prepare for dynamic entry," he said quietly into his mike. Clicks sounded in response. Nick knew the men were moving, though he couldn't see them and he couldn't hear them.

He slanted a hard glance at Di Stefano, ready to take him down if he objected. But Di Stefano was readying his breaching weapon, ready to blow the French windows open if necessary.

It was going to be a fucking miracle if she got out of there alive. Nick started pulling material out of his rucksack. Flashbangs, extra magazines.

They were taking everyone down, no question. That canister was not leaving the building, unless it was in the hands of Homeland Security biohazard experts. Only the takedown had to happen after Charity left. Just the thought of her caught in a crossfire made him nearly insane with fear.

This was a clusterfuck just waiting to happen.

Sweating heavily, he stared at the screen, willing everyone on the screen to simply tell her to go away. She'd go into another room, wait, plead a headache, and would be driven home. Once he'd ascertained she was home safely, *then* they'd go in.

Not going to happen.

Nick's blood ran cold at Worontzoff's expression. He was getting off on Charity understanding what was going on, totally gone in some alternate universe with his dead love, Katya, dead all those years ago and now come back to life.

"Come, dushka," he said, and held out his arms.

Nick could practically feel Charity's hesitation and fear. *Don't do it.* He sent the thought to her, though he understood she had to. Right now, her life rested on a knife's edge. It depended on keeping Worontzoff's illusion that she was Katya alive.

She moved forward slowly toward him. Nick had to fight tunnel vision, that anomaly of battle where you could only see what was right in front of you. It was dangerous, in battle and now. He had to be aware of everything, all senses fired for signs of imminent danger. He deliberately spread his senses wider and caught al-Banna's expression.

Every hair on his body stood on end. Al-Banna watched Charity with cold hatred. He would look for an excuse to bring her down. She was an extraneous presence, one unplanned for. A danger to him.

Nick gripped the stock of his gun more tightly.

Charity passed al-Banna and suddenly a piercing whistle sounded incredibly loud in his headset, so loud he could also hear it through the walls of the mansion.

Busted! A countersurveillance device! Al-Banna had hidden a countersurveillance device on his person and knew that Charity was wired.

A gunshot sounded. Two.

"Go, go, go!" Nick shouted into the headset, moving fast. The preternatural calm of battle took over now, time stretched, and he was able to calculate every move.

Di Stefano's breaching weapon blew open the doors and he lobbed in an M84 flashbang. He and Di Stefano flattened themselves against the wall. He signaled with his hands to Di Stefano. *Me left, you right.*

Di Stefano nodded.

A blinding and deafening blast exploded in the room: 8 million candela, 180 decibels. Guaranteed to stun anyone within a twenty-foot radius. Everyone in the room would be blinded for at least five seconds until the photosensitive cells in the retina could return to normal, and the fluid in the semicircular canals of the ear would be so disturbed, it would be as if everyone in the room had received a round-house punch.

He was protected from the worst of the blast by the mansion's wall, but he'd trained over and over again to withstand the shock. A second after the flashbang had gone off, he was in through the door, tracking left, knowing Di Stefano was tracking right. Between them, they covered almost 180 degrees.

He moved fast, disarming the two stunned men, slapping PlastiCuffs on them. Al-Banna was down, blood pooling under his back, Di Stefano putting a pack over his chest wound.

Nick scanned the room, then scanned again. Where was Charity? Where the fuck *was* she?

He heard a soft cry, whirled, and his heart stopped. Simply stopped.

Charity was lying on her back against the wall behind the desk as if a giant fist had carelessly punched her there. Half of her was covered by Worontzoff, and all of her was covered with blood.

* * *

Someone was crying, a sound of raw animal pain that dug deep into the bone, that hurt the heart. Charity was aware of it, but only dimly. Her head swam and every inch of her hurt. Where was she? She looked around without moving her head, though she still had huge spots in front of her eyes from the massive explosion that had gone off in the room.

Other men began shouting, men dressed in black with black helmets, looking like insectoid aliens, holding huge guns. They came into the room in a controlled rush. "Clear!" one shouted and the echoes came from inside the room and out.

"Clear!"

"Clear!"

"Clear!"

It was hard to breathe. Something was wrong with her chest, she couldn't expand her lungs. She looked down at herself and saw Vassily, still and unmoving, on top of her. One of the men in the room, the one who looked like a scientist, was draped over Vassily, screaming like a wounded animal. Raging in a foreign language. Russian?

She couldn't breathe with two men weighing down her chest. She couldn't breathe, she couldn't see, she couldn't hear.

It made no sense. None of it made sense. She couldn't gather her thoughts, they kept scattering. Her ears rang and spots moved in front of her eyes.

She moved her hand slightly and felt something wet and viscous on the floor. With enormous effort, she lifted her hand and brought it close to her face.

It was dark red.

Blood.

"Charity!" Nick, on his knees beside her, sliding a little in the blood on the floor. "Oh my God, you're wounded! Where were you shot, love? Where does it hurt?" He looked up at all the men in black milling around. "Medic!" he screamed. "Medic, over here!"

Frantic hands felt her all over, starting from her head, down her torso, down her legs.

"Not—" Charity wheezed, trying to pull air into her lungs. Vassily and the man over him, still screaming, were so heavy. "Not wounded," she managed to get out finally, lungs heaving for air. "Not . . . me."

It had to be Vassily, had to. Charity found it almost impossible to think, but she could feel. Her entire back was wet with blood. With the amount of blood on the floor, the wound must be grave. Though she hurt everywhere, she knew she didn't have a mortal wound.

Another pair of hands. Not Nick's. One of the men in black.

"Step away, sir, so I can examine her."

Nick was holding her hand, slippery with blood.

"Sir? I can't examine her if you don't move."

Charity could feel Nick's reluctance as he let go of her hand and stood up. He looked around and beckoned to one of the men in uniform.

"Get rid of that," he said coldly, indicating the howling man. The man had pulled Vassily off her—she could finally *breathe*—and had scooted up against the wall with Vassily's limp form cradled in his arms, rocking back and forth. He bent over Vassily, his cries painful to hear, a long lament in Russian.

The medic gave her a quick, thorough check and pronounced her essentially unharmed.

Thanks to Vassily.

Some of the shock of the explosion was dissipating, the memories of the moments before the explosion returning. The high whine, the terrorist brandishing a gun, aiming it at her. Vassily's cry, launching himself at her.

The bullet had caught him, not her.

Vassily had saved her life. Charity looked down at his dead body, held tightly by the Russian who was now covered with Vassily's blood.

Vassily was a criminal, a renegade.

He'd saved her life.

The huge room was lit up now, people milling about purposefully. The big suitcase full of cash had been closed up, and a number of men were examining a big metal container.

She swayed.

"Fuck this," Nick growled, and swung her up in his arms. He marched over to where Di Stefano was conferring with a knot of men. "You guys can clean up, I'm taking her home."

Di Stefano opened his mouth, looked at Nick, then closed it again. "Yeah, okay, get outta here."

Nick stopped on the porch and Charity breathed in deeply. It felt like days had gone by since she'd walked up these stairs.

Nick looked down at her, grim, jaw muscles moving as he clenched his teeth. "This is the way it's going to be," he announced. "I'm taking you home and to bed and we're not coming up for air until a week has gone by or my hands stop shaking, whichever comes first. Then we're going to city hall and we're getting married all over again, only this time legally. I'll be damned if my son grows up a bastard."

He said all this belligerently, as if expecting her to argue. But as always with Nick, only one answer was possible. "Yes, Nick."

Epilogue

Jacob Franklin Ireland was in a big hurry.

Charity Ireland moaned and Sheriff Nick Ireland stepped on the gas. He had to clutch the steering wheel hard because his palms were wet with anxious sweat.

They were in the middle of a raging summer storm, the rain coming down so hard the windshield wipers were almost useless. It didn't make any difference. Nick knew the way to the hospital, though this was more like piloting a boat than driving a car.

Charity gave another little moan, biting her lips.

He was driving as fast as he could without risking an accident, to the very edges of his driving ability.

"Hang on, honey," he said, keeping his voice soft and reassuring when he was sick with anxiety and fear. He glanced quickly over to where Charity was slumped in the passenger seat, panting between contractions.

Suddenly, he saw her belly ripple. God!

She gave another little cry and he pressed on the accelerator. Any faster in this wet weather and the car would be a hovercraft. Charity's forehead was beaded with sweat, though not as much as his.

"Nick," she moaned.

"It's okay, honey," he said, trying not to let his panic show in his voice. *It's okay?* What the fuck did he know? All the prenatal lessons had left him so queasy hardly anything penetrated. Any time he opened one of those birth and baby books Charity consumed by the ton, he never got beyond chapter one before breaking out in a cold sweat.

He turned the corner and knew that now it was just a straight run, directly into the hospital's emergency area, and risked upping the speed a little, hoping no other cars were crazy enough to come out in a storm that was dumping a year's worth of rain in one afternoon.

A few minutes later, he was carrying Charity in through the hospital doors, shouting for nurses, doctors, anyone. Charity's face was drawn in agony and he tried to remember why anyone ever had kids.

Nurses came, brisk and efficient and calm, rolling Charity onto a gurney. A nurse palpated her distended belly, lifted her skirt, cut away Charity's panties and jolted.

"The baby's crowning!" she said. Even if Nick didn't know what that meant, he could see it. Between Charity's legs he could see a rounded thatch of black hair.

His son.

Nick held Charity's hand, shouting, "Breathe! Breathe!" like an idiot.

While he stayed by Charity's head, a gaggle of medical personnel gathered around the foot of the gurney, calmly doing things Nick didn't want to see. Charity was squeezing his hand so hard it almost hurt. He hated to see her suffering, hated it.

Then, suddenly, it was all over. Charity let out a huge cry, astonishingly loud for so small a woman, a bundle of something red slid into the attending doctor's hands, and the nurses and doctors started snipping and suturing.

A loud wail started, and Nick looked over, heart pounding.

His son. That funny creature that looked like a skinned rabbit was his son.

Charity laughed and he looked at her in astonishment.

"That was funny?" he asked.

She smiled that slight witchy smile that drove him nuts. "Not funny," she said softly. "Wonderful."

Someone touched his elbow. "Sheriff," one of the nurses said. "Here's your son." She placed Jake in his arms.

Nick looked down at his son's face, features a tiny replica of his own. The fury of coming into this world was already gone. His small face was calm, a little pucker between two tiny eyebrows showing that he was puzzled at this new world.

Nick brushed Jake's cheek with his forefinger, amazed that anything human could be so soft.

Suddenly, Jake's eyes opened wide—they were a bright, brilliant blue—and to his dying day, Nick would swear that his son smiled at him. A tiny hand clutched his finger. His son, holding onto his hand.

His son. Jesus. His *son*.

For the second time in his life, Iceman burst into tears.

LISA MARIE RICE is eternally thirty years old and will never age. She is tall and willowy and beautiful. Men drop at her feet like ripe pears. She has won every major book prize in the world. She is a black belt with advanced degrees in archaeology, nuclear physics, and Tibetan literature. She is a concert pianist. Did I mention the Nobel?

Of course, Lisa Marie Rice is a virtual woman and exists only at the keyboard when writing erotic romance. She disappears when the monitor winks off.

Lisa Marie Rice